*FOR SOME IT WAS THE
FIRST STOP ON THE ROAD
TO STARDOM—FOR
OTHERS, THE END
OF THE LINE.*

Southern California. A glittering playground for big-time directors, high-powered agents, and jaded celebrities . . . where ambition fires the dreams and booze fuels the bodies . . . where there's a pill to calm you down, pep you up, turn you on—or wipe you out forever . . . where sex is a smorgasbord and everyone's starved.

It drew them like a magnet . . . the stunning women willing to trade passion for a part. Their soft-skinned bodies were the stuff of hard-core movies. And if movies meant money, they would act out their most secret fantasies. But where would they be when the last reel was run . . . when the last frame was shot?

Novels by Herbert Kastle

ONE THING ON MY MIND
KOPTIC SUMMER
BACHELOR SUMMER
CAMERA
COUNTDOWN TO MURDER
THE WORLD THEY WANTED
THE REASSEMBLED MAN
HOT PROWL
THE MOVIE MAKER
MIAMI GOLDEN BOY
MILLIONAIRES
ELLIE
CROSS-COUNTRY
EDWARD BERNER IS ALIVE AGAIN!
THE GANG
DEATH SQUAD
LADIES OF THE VALLEY

Ladies of the Valley

Herbert Kastle

WILDSIDE PRESS

For Maria

"I'll come no more behind your scenes, David;
for the silk stockings and white bosoms of your
actresses excite my amorous propensities."
BOSWELL'S LIFE OF DR. JOHNSON

BOOK ONE

One

Monday, May 2

It was the first rain in weeks, maybe months, he couldn't remember. To celebrate the back-east feeling it gave him, Don Baylis got in his car and drove down the canyon to Sunset and west toward Beverly Hills. He'd decided to visit Fred and his great porno film collection and listen to more of his talk of "making a fucking fortune" on the last of Don's novels.

He hit the brakes as traffic in front of him suddenly slowed, backing up two blocks from San Vicente. He had no trouble stopping in time, but he was still shaken.

Traffic moved again, and he moved his Mercedes sports coupe with it. After five years in Los Angeles, he drove slowly, as if on ice instead of moderate rain, in common with most Angelinos. Except, of course, for the crazies who cut in and out and pressed and strived as if in Grand Prix competition. One almost put him on the sidewalk near the Whiskey. He smiled to himself, alive and well, telling himself he was no longer willing to rage and shout and, occasionally, fight. But he felt a murderous edge to his smile. And dreamed a murderous dream of having a silencer for the automatic in his glove compartment and being alone late at night with this particular crazy, a shaggy youth in a van—weren't they all?—and putting two bullets into his briefly turned, aggressively sullen face.

He took a deep breath as tightness invaded his chest. He breathed through his nostrils and followed the breath in his mind's eye—in the nostrils, out the nostrils—this according to his nonreligious, non-mantra-chanting meditation process.

Still, he remained under stress, watching the van cause horn-blasting and fist-shaking. Bad for a man to feel such stress, especially a man just five months removed from what Dr. Goodsand referred to as a "severe myocardial infarction," which sounded rather like gastritis but was in fact the deadly heart attack.

Then he lost sight of the van in the twilight of grayish-black clouds and steadily falling rain, in the crawling jam of traffic, because unlike New Yorkers Southern Californians didn't know from rain, from wet roads. And after the last few years of drought, they drove into each other even more than usual. And usual was a world's record.

Always a pleasure to enter Beverly Hills. Especially when rain hit the palms, the shrubs, the flowers planted by seasons, the manicured lawns. But rain or not, drought or not, the sprinklers worked and so did the Japanese and Mexican gardeners. And Beverly Hills in the flats between Sunset and Santa Monica smelled sweet, peaceful, pleasant.

It was money, certainly, but money didn't always smell so good. Take Manhattan, the expensive East Side areas. Not at all peaceful and pleasant any more.

Take Rome. Take Berlin. Take Beirut and Rio and Jo'burg. Take anywhere in the world where money was running scared.

That's why the Italians and all the rest were settling in Los Angeles. No kidnapings, no terrorist bombings and class struggle, no civil wars, no riots. Some race conflict, certainly, but that was so standard in

American cities it almost passed unnoticed. And it never reached L.A.'s fine white areas . . . in one of which Don Baylis had settled five years and four months ago, when he'd come to Los Angeles for a brief stay and never returned home.

He turned down Bedford, driving south. He was aware of the figure in the red slicker even before he'd straightened the SL's wheels. She was almost at the end of the long, downward-sloping palm-lined street.

He didn't really believe the jolt of recognition, the quick pleasure followed by slow pain. Because what the hell was she doing here, where Fred lived, when she'd never met Fred, he'd seen to that. He didn't trust her with anyone, not to say Freddy. His friend. His womanizing friend. Who knew *about* Cecily as Cecily knew about him.

He was almost on her now as she ran across the street, matching red hat pulled low against the drive of rain. He tapped his horn. She didn't look up, and he was by and at the corner when she reached the old green Jaguar sedan.

He U-turned and came back up the street, heart hammering dangerously. But he couldn't be bothered with doctor's orders. He looked across from the Jag at Fred's marvelous brick castle with the great tennis court behind and the pool and jacuzzi and other cunt bait.

And Don Baylis's cunt had gone for the bait. And for the man full of penis pride; his "nine-inch beauty," as he called it. God, nine inches! In *his* Cecily?

A joke, the nine inches. And it was something innocent, her being on this street.

He pressed down on the horn, stopping beside the Jag. He saw her head turn behind the rain-spattered glass. And saw her big smile; her happy-to-see-you-my-love smile. And he knew she'd have a perfect explanation.

She got out of her car and into his. She kissed him, her lovely face red-lipped and radiant, pushing the hat off her head and into the back of the car without caring, shaking out her dark, almost black hair, laughing and saying, "Wherever I go I meet my Donny. It's fate. It's got to be. We're meant for each other." And laughing, opened the coat in the warmth of the Mercedes, like peeling the skin off some lush, bursting-with-sweetness fruit. Her breasts, of course. But the belly and the thighs pushing against the cling of silklike tan cloth; the long legs gleaming in pantyhose casing; the perfumed smell with the other smell underneath . . .

He kissed her, purposely harder than she liked. She smiled still, and pulled down the visor for the mirror. She worked on her lips with tissue and lipstick. He suggested they eat. She checked her watch, then nodded. "I'll skip Mr. Hornstein's cattle call."

"Fritz Hornstein?"

She said yes and did he know him.

"Only by reputation. He does that TV cop show 'Big and Little,' right? He casts small parts on his office desk, right?"

"Who in this town doesn't?" she murmured.

He pushed laughter. "If you take that attitude, why not hit the party scene, get the rep, do it for walk-ons? You'll have fun."

She looked at him. They'd agreed he wouldn't discuss her career. *Career!* God, the tricks men pulled in Hollywood!

He made another U. He asked if Nate & Al's was okay with her. "I'm dying for at least the *smell* of good pastrami."

He used the lot across Beverly from the sporty delicatessen. She got out first, and he quickly checked himself in the rearview mirror. His mustache was almost solidly gray. Hadn't been that way before

Thanksgiving. Maybe Grecian Formula . . .

She called to him. "You don't have to look. You're beautiful."

"One of us is," he said, and got out ánd took her delicate hand. The hand that did so many wild, erotic things to him. The hand that would kill him yet, she'd joked.

A young man in Dernier Cri denims held the restaurant door for them, and turned to check out Cecily's ass. Even behind the pink slicker, it pushed, it shouted for attention.

Breathe in the nostrils, out the nostrils.

They sat in a booth. He had a roast beef sandwich on whole wheat, no seasoning, and a Quinidine tablet with his tea. She had corned beef on onion roll with mustard and sauerkraut, seven-layer cake, and milk. She leaned back and looked around the square room. "Always full."

He asked what she'd been doing at Fred Gower's.

She never blinked. She smiled happily. "Can't tell you, bun. It's a surprise." That hand played with his. "You're a god-damned bull for your age."

He knew then what her story would be. His fiftieth birthday was next Friday, the 6th of May. She would speak to Gower . . .

He stood up. "Got to call Fred and ask him not to bother. I'm not really well enough for surprise parties."

She was looking at him, her face smiling but her eyes . . . he imagined he could read good-bye there.

"I never said you were getting a party, bun." Very cool voice now. "And if you want to call my surprise off, shouldn't you tell *me?* I'm the one who would arrange things for you."

He sat down. He was beaten. Unless he was willing to catch her in a lie, and lose her. "On second thought," he said, "go ahead with your plans. I guess I'd enjoy it."

The radiant smile returned, along with the hand. "Got an hour for Cecily?" The fingers circled his wrist, stroked his wrist.

He wanted her. But as always before in his life, his spotted history, when a woman lied to him and beat him, he began to hate her. Especially since the heart attack and his loss of confidence, loss of macho.

But there was no loss of desire, and when she left his home she was smiling mistily and he was eased, drained . . . and able to face his desk and a task he'd been putting off for months: Answering Mel's February 10th letter, which was two pages, typed, single-spaced, ending on the back of the second page with the usual, "Let me hear from you, Donald."

And with a far from usual P.S.:

Don't take umbrage, but from my position as resident father-figure, I feel that your last two letters hide far more than they reveal. As when you experienced that long period of writer's block shortly after arriving in L.A. Now, as then, you appear to be trying to entertain rather than inform your old friend. I'm worried, Donald, because you seem even more evasive now, even more frantic to tell stories about everyone but yourself. *Cut the bull! Tell poppa!* And a little more promptly than is your recent wont. One letter every two or three months is slow even for us, not so? I await your confession, whatever it is, hoping for something on the order of entry into a girl-swapping or orgying cult.

Mel was sixty-four to Don's fifty. He'd been Don's boss at Benton & Bowles, Advertising. At one time they'd lunched twice a week; then, after Don began writing full-time, they saw each other twice a month; now they exchanged letters every two months, maybe.

He re-read his friend's letter, and asked himself: "Why not tell him about it?"

He hadn't actually told the full story of his heart attack to anyone. He'd given wise-guy accounts of it to his children, not wishing to frighten them . . . and himself. Cecily had seen the hospital end of it—as much as she could see almost any week on TV, either fiction or documentary.

But that wasn't *his* heart attack, was it? Saying he'd been "in a tense career situation and it brought on pain and then I found myself down and almost out"—as he'd put it to Freddy—didn't touch upon the true events.

Could he describe it?

He put paper in the typewriter and quickly began to write:

Dear Mel:

Sorry to hear about straining the thigh muscle in your right leg. Painful, yes, but as you yourself point out, it could be worse. A heart attack, for example, which is what happened to me on November 24th. (We'll skip my reasons for trying to hide this from your astute, between-the-lines eye; at least until I can articulate those reasons.)

It happened while I was involved in a telephone argument over contracts for the movie version of *Galt's Island*, which I was (and once again am) co-producing with Frederick Gower, whom I've mentioned in previous letters. My nerves hadn't been all that stable because I was putting together notes for the start of a new book, and you remember how sweet my personality becomes at such times. I was actually screaming at the man, since that appeared to be the only way to get him to accept the fact that I wouldn't allow him to delete a paragraph, protecting my right to half the total percentages we as co-producers would get.

There I was, standing at my desk, shouting: "Fifty percent! Halfies, got it? Or no deal!" when a steel band suddenly popped into place around my chest and began *squeezing*. Inexorably, Melvin. Increasingly more painful by the split second. No time for bad moves, wrong decisions.

Now here's one for your file of anecdotes in defense of the years we spent in advertising: I'd seen a Heart Association commercial a few nights before with Pearl Bailey not only urging people to donate money, but telling them how easy it is to die of a coronary if you refuse to admit you're having one. She was especially effective featuring herself as an example, citing all the excuses she and others have used—particularly stomach ache. And I was standing there, telling myself I had the granddaddy of upset stomachs, hanging up on Gower with a muttered, "Gotta go." (By the way, he still doesn't know I had my seizure while talking with *him*. I figure it's a low blow to say such a thing, especially since I later won my argument by simply sending him the contract to be signed or rejected, and he signed.)

Now get this. I'm standing there, thinking, "God, what a stupid thing I did, eating cold leftover spaghetti for breakfast," giving myself excuses to avoid facing the possibility of the dread heart attack, just as Pearl had warned against. Then I stumbled toward the bedroom, doubled over, to lie down and wait for it to pass. Where I'd probably have died if not for the recollection of Pearl's voice begging me not to be a fool, to admit what was happening.

Panic came to my assistance, turned me around, and sent me running—well, I think I was running—next door to my neighbor. He conducts a mail-order business from his sublevel office floor, and was home as usual. He was also upstairs, having a sandwich, which was a break since he answered the door almost immediately. I fell past him and into his living room; rather down on his living-room carpet.

The pain was by this time beyond measurement by any of my standards. I'd entered a different world, where polite behavior didn't exist. Where I, in fact, didn't exist as the man we've both known. I was a dying organism, who knew it, and managed to say (as Chris, the neighbor, later told me): "Heart attack!" Chris didn't waste time. He called the police, the fire department, and the paramedics, in reverse order. He knew the police would most likely come first, followed by the fire truck with its resuscitation equipment, and finally the ambulance with everything I'd need . . . but ambulances often come too late.

That's just the way it happened. The police arrived ready to give me mouth-to-mouth, but I was still breathing, still conscious, rolling around in agony, refusing to lie quietly and on my back as per instructions, the fetal position the only one I would assume. Which was when another lucky break took place: A doctor was driving by the house (on a motorcycle, no less, but that's L.A.), and stopped to see why the cops. He got me on my back, and the fire department truck arrived, and he fed me oxygen from the tanks they carry.

The pain by this time was almost impossible. I felt that an explosion had to take place, a blowing apart of my chest. But about then my awareness began to fade. The doctor meantime was shooting adrenalin into my left arm . . . and the ambulance with the paramedics arrived.

A short conference, and the doctor shot morphine into my right arm, placed a nitroglycerin tablet under my tongue, and withdrew as the paramedics used their walkie-talkie equipment to contact the Cardiac Central Unit at UCLA. The morphine worked quickly; the pain decreased; my awareness faded even more. But I was still seeing a little, hearing a little.

One of the two paramedics examined me and the other transmitted what vital signs I was showing. I remember hearing a cop laugh as something came over the radio from UCLA. It was: "Okay. Less conversation and more transportation."

That laugh stuck in my mind, Mel. The first laugh of that dance of death, if you'll forgive a touch of the purple. Something else stuck in my mind. I must have looked well out of it by then, unconscious, though my eyes were slitted open according to Chris. Because the doctor said to one of the cops: "I doubt he'll make it."

It made me angry as hell. The anger kept me from losing consciousness as I was placed on a stretcher. I said—actually, I didn't, but I thought I said—"You stupid, bearded freak!" to the doctor, who was a young hippie type. "I'll outlive you and any little freaks you whelp!" I was cursing him, calling him every vile name I could think of, as they carried me out to the ambulance. Afterward, my neighbor told me that the cop said, "Doc, I think he heard you," and the doctor said, "Then he'll have something to live for."

Chris went to my house; the door was wide open. He got my private telephone book and called my children in New York and Cecily in North Hollywood. Cecily got to the hospital perhaps twenty minutes after I did, while I was still in Emergency. I remember seeing her walk in, and the shock on her face, and the way she covered it and approached where I lay on a table, smiling and shaking her head and making jokes about my going to any lengths to avoid eating her Thanksgiving turkey.

The kids flew out that night; I saw them early the 25th, while in Intensive Care. Cecily came every morning, staying almost all day. She got the kids settled in at my place and brought them over at least once a day, but didn't let them stay too long, as it depressed both me and them. After the third day, I felt a change, a small knitting together of ruined parts, a first gathering of strength. I was out of Intensive Care in five days, and out of the hospital in eighteen. There was one small setback, twelve days after I returned home. Irregular heartbeat, called "arrhythmia," became severe during the night, and before I could reach my doctor I'd grown weak, sick, felt myself deteriorating by the minute. Once again I went to my neighbor for help, and he broke speed records getting me to the Emergency Room. When my doctor finally arrived, he termed my condition "heart failure" and too advanced to respond to medication like Quinidine. I was asked to sign a release for electro-cardiac-conversion treatment, which means applying one hell of a jolt of electricity to the heart.

Have to admit I was terrified, much more so than during the actual heart attack, when I had no time to make decisions. But it was over in a moment. I jumped a good foot into the air, it seems to me, just like the intro to the old "Marcus Welby" TV show, and my heart converted to a normal beat. With minor variations, it has stayed that way.

Since then, my recovery has been steady. Of course, I take much medication. I exercise only mildly, walking instead of jogging, and I no longer play tennis. My diet is what you would expect—without salt, fats, or stimulants. And, in great part, without taste. But sex is as good as it ever was, and I look forward to other things, if not everything, returning to what they were before.

So forgive my bland letters; I needed time to get
to this revelation. Anyway, I hope your leg grows
well in time for summer walks through those
lovely Connecticut woods. I also hope to see you
in the fall, when I might risk a flight to New
York. Next spring for sure.   ·

Regards to Lainie.

He read through the letter quickly, sighing as he realized how bare a description it was, how devoid of the
other reality; the reality of *feeling*. Of nights in that
hospital that were long as weeks to him. Of days at
home that first month, full of the sound of his pulse,
of his heart; an exaggerated, drumlike sound that kept
him constantly fearful. Of the poisonous effects of
Quinidine, before he developed a partial immunity—
cramps and diarrhea and vomiting. Of weakness that
made it an agonizing effort to walk two blocks on Cecily's arm; *heavily* on Cecily's arm. Of lungs filling
with water as his heart failed to do its job, causing
nighttime panic and early morning visits to the doctor.
Of despair at so simple a task as driving the Mercedes
to the supermarket and buying a few groceries. Of self-
hatred and a growing sense of impending doom—despite
a corresponding growth of strength. Of the retention of
that sense of doom.

He folded the paper and sealed it into an envelope.
No point in communicating such horrors. No point
subjecting friends, children, lovers to personal anguish. It would be an act of cruelty, of self-pity. And
there were worse illnesses, worse deaths.

The searing torment of cancer, for one. At least if he
went, it would be reasonably quick.

Which was a good enough note on which to take a
nap!

Johnny played with Klaus and they moved their
pieces over the war game's board and watched TV at

the same time. They were in the study, on the floor, and he sat so he could see the driveway through the side window. So that when the Jag's green nose turned into view, he could run out and shout: "Hey, big momma!" Because he was a North Hollywood baby and cool as they came at twelve years of age.

He tried not to listen for the phone. At least half the time she didn't make it home; called and asked how school had been and said what to take from the fridge and that she'd see him before bedtime. She *always* made it by bedtime . . . unless she'd lined up a sitter. And if it was Mary from down the street, it was okey-doke with Boy Wonder!

Klaus caught him cheating; made him move his piece back one space and into a mine field the way the dice read. He called Klaus a stupid Kraut. Just like on "Hogan's Heroes" re-runs, but Klaus surprised him by getting real mad. Only Mexes and blacks and Jews were supposed to get mad at things like that, weren't they? He got scared as Klaus, smaller and lighter than he, knocked over the board and swung wildly. Johnny scrambled backward and to his feet and ran out the door to the pool. Klaus yelled something: ". . . mother says . . . and that's *your* mother . . ."

Johnny stood in the rain, looking through the open door to the study. Klaus was going into the kitchen. Johnny followed cautiously, refusing to admit he'd heard anything more from Klaus. Like *tramp*. What did that mean anyway, coming from an eleven-year-old Kraut? What did it mean coming from any of the trash on this street, as mom said, which they'd leave soon as she got her shot. Then they'd move to a mansion in Beverly Hills. They could do it now, if she wanted to marry any of the men in love with her; rich guys, but she didn't care for any of them. Still, she might do it for Johnny, so next year he could go to Beverly Hills High . . .

He suddenly began to run, crying, shouting, "Dirty

Kraut like in the war when we killed all you dirty . . ."
and half-swallowed the last word because mom would
smack real hard for that word . . . *"fucks!"* Klaus
was going out the front door and Johnny ran for
him, that *tramp* clawing into his mind no matter
how hard he pushed it back, and he cried because
someone—dad?—had called her that and hit her and
called her the other word. He hadn't found out what
the other word meant until much later, but he'd remembered it. *Whore.*

He caught Klaus on the lawn and shoved him.
Klaus fell. He kicked at him, at his head, like he'd
seen on "Starsky and Hutch," waiting for the thunk
and the soft cry, but he missed. Klaus got up and made
fists. He had real big hands, and Johnny began to get
scared again. He swung wildly, and caught Klaus on
the side of the neck. Klaus said, "Bastard!" and ran.

Johnny went back into the house, throwing
punches, delighted with his performance, preparing
the story he'd tell mom about how he beat up a kid in
school who'd tried to shake him down for money.
Like that movie on the pay channel with the actor
from "McHale's Navy," Borgnine.

No, that was a bike they stole from McHale's kid.
But niggers, bullies, he'd tell her, and she'd be proud.
No use bringing in Klaus because then she'd ask questions and when she asked questions she dug out everything and she'd get real mad and real sad. He'd never
tell her that tramp business.

He heard the Jag before he saw it. He began to run
out, but it was raining and she might yell. And the
game was all over the study floor and she'd yell about
that if her day had been bad.

But if she'd got a part, they'd eat someplace nice,
maybe over the hill in the city on Restaurant Row.
Like Lawry's or that place the musician had taken
them where the captain from "Gilligan's Island" came
over to talk to them and autographed a menu for

Johnny. Then maybe they'd go shopping, his favorite thing, and he'd get some new clothes and she'd get some new clothes and the old credit card would get a workout.

He stuffed everything back in the box, and even though the cover didn't fit right it looked okay. He was done before she came in and the only thing she had to say was: "Shut the TV, will you?"

He said, "Wasn't really watching," and shut it and ran to her. Her face got smily and she was beautiful and she bent and they hugged. She kissed him up real good, and he said, "Red momma rides again!" because she was wearing the red slicker. She had a yellow one too.

She laughed. He hugged her harder, closing his eyes, happy for the first time since leaving home this morning. "What about the cattle call?" he asked when she let go.

She made a face. "Didn't bother, man. Had lunch at Nate & Al's. Lots of celebrities. We'll have to go there one Sunday afternoon and let you get autographs."

"Who'd you go with?" Because sometimes she dated actors; once the dude who played the young partner in that show about lawyers who ran around beating up on bad guys. He forgot the name because it was off now and no re-runs and he forgot the actor because it was three years ago, maybe more, when he was a baby and didn't know anything. Now he knew everything, even sex.

"A friend," she muttered, walking to the kitchen . . . so he knew it was someone who didn't know about him. She didn't tell everyone about Boy Wonder. An actress had to be young and having a twelve-year-old kid, almost a grown-up kid, made some fools think she was old. She'd been married at sixteen and had him right away and that only made her twenty-eight. Except she was older than that; she was thirty-one, thirty-two, or so dad said, making her red in the face and mad. Maybe dad was lying. If she wanted to be twenty-eight, why couldn't she? It didn't hurt anyone.

He followed her to the kitchen. She had the slicker off and was taking stuff from the fridge. "Can't we eat out?" he asked.

"Don't you *ever* want a home-cooked meal?"

"Nothing big. Sambo's or Norm's or MacDonald's."

"You keep eating burgers and fries and you'll never play football."

"I'll have eggs," he said, seeing the way she looked at the groceries, knowing she was weakening. Because they loved eating out and didn't care where or what. "No dishes," he added slyly.

"No cooking," she said smiling.

"And a good time was had by all!" he shouted, running for his bedroom.

"Wear a hat," she called.

He hated hats, except yachting caps. He found his admiral's cap with all the braid and his blue windbreaker and ran back to the kitchen. She looked him over. "Not warm enough," she said, but it was okay because she was turning to the door.

At the restaurant, a fool with a bushy mustache sitting at the counter kept turning his head to look at their table. Johnny was used to it, proud, kind of, and sometimes mom liked it, but only in expensive places.

Johnny said, "The eyes have it," jerking his head at the mustache.

She didn't even look up from her plate. "Poverty, man. Who'd eat here if they had two dollars?"

"Yeah, who, like us."

"But we're slumming, Boy Wonder. We're just killing time until I get my shot. You know that."

He said he did, and leaned back and made the biggest belch he could.

"Small time," she said, and looked at the counter and waited for the mustache to turn his head again;

then gave him one of her special belches. It sounded like thunder!

A lot of heads turned, and she patted her lips with her napkin like Lady Something on "Upstairs-Downstairs," and he couldn't hold in the laughter.

He was still laughing when they went out past the counter and she gave the mustache a little good-bye burp.

He bounced around in the front seat of the Jag, until she snapped: "Sit still, *fool!*"

He quieted instantly. He'd lost her attention and she'd been thinking bad thoughts and her face wasn't smily anymore. He knew how fast her mood could change; knew how hard she could hit; knew just what to do. Which was absolutely nothing.

Later she said: "Did you finish your homework?"

"Didn't have any," he lied.

"You sure about that?"

He cringed a little inside, but kept his cool and nodded. He could do it later tonight. At the worst, he'd get up a half-hour early tomorrow morning.

"Maybe we'll drive into the Basin, to Wilshire, and look in the stores."

"Okay," he said, quiet on the outside but jumping on the inside.

"Don't expect us to buy anything. Your father is two months behind on your support."

He nodded . . . but he kept jumping inside. She always said that, or something like it. And they always gave the old credit card a workout.

"I'm getting sick of North Hollywood," she said. "I'm thinking if something doesn't happen soon in my career, I might get married again. How'd you like a rich stepfather?"

"Do I know him?"

"You *will*, long before I make such a move. You'll have a say in it. I wouldn't marry anyone you didn't like."

She was glancing at him. He nodded, and didn't want to think about it. He liked it just this way, the two of them, even if it meant no mansion in Beverly Hills. He liked the visits with dad, the camping trips with dad and his girlfriend, but he liked coming home even more.

"Does the idea of my marrying again bother you?" she asked.

"Why should it? You'll always be my mom."

"Right. And Andy will always be your dad. You'd just gain a smart, rich, gentle man for a friend. I'd make sure he was all of that."

They were on Sunset, and he pointed at a John Denver poster. They talked about music. About movies. She said she'd take him for lunch at the Universal commissary next time she visited a producer friend of hers.

"Hey, cool!" he said, jumping around on the seat.

She didn't yell at him. It was a great night! Until a load of Mexes in a big, beat-up Mercury pulled alongside at a light, on mom's side. One made that sucking sound they made with their lips, like calling a dog, and another in back said, "Ai, grande chi-chis!" which Johnny knew from the workers on his father's farm meant big tits. Then the driver leaned across and said, "Maybe you get rid of your small boyfriend, eh, baby?" and they all laughed.

"You ugly brassero fool," she said coldly.

"What?" the driver yelled, and one in back began opening the door.

She leaned on her horn and gave one of her special stage screams.

Man, they took off with that heap shaking and belching blue smoke.

She smiled at Johnny. "Easy," she said.

He nodded, looking out the window, hating them and feeling sick.

"Don't be upset, Boy Wonder." Her hand stroked his cheek. "They're trash."

He said he wasn't upset and kept his face turned to the window.

Later, she bought him dark green corduroy pants with bell bottoms and a wild shirt. She bought herself a pair of brown boots and a suede skirt. He forgot about the brassero fools and Klaus and that she might get married.

Back in the car, he told her the story about beating up the bully in school, and made him a Mex. She said, "Way to go, Boy Wonder!" then grew worried he might have been hurt.

He shrugged and said, "Little ache in the gut," and enjoyed her concern. At home, he took a hot bath like she asked and got cookies and kisses.

His dreams weren't good. It was that way most of the time. The ground kept falling away. Nothing was what it seemed. Monsters lay hidden everywhere. Gangs chased him. Until he screamed, raising his arm, striking them all with something . . . something like a bomb, a ray gun, lightning. Killing and silencing the whole world. *A hundred-million-dollar man!*

Afterwards, he met his mother and they walked, holding hands.

And that too wasn't what it seemed.

And the gangs returned.

And he was afraid for himself, but most of all for his mother.

Whose clothing fell away. Who walked naked, as he'd watched her in her bedroom when she didn't know he was awake and watching. Whom he loved beyond her knowing. Loved so much it shamed him.

Then she changed to Mary, the babysitter, and shame turned to lust.

Fred didn't get Cecily in until almost nine. "That *was* Don who hit on you outside my place, wasn't it?"

"Yes."

"Yes?" he shouted into the phone. "I've got a deal going with him! I stand to lose a couple hundred thousand! Cut the shorthand and tell me what happened!"

She hung up on him. He couldn't believe it. He dialed, raging, and had to dial all over again. He calmed himself, because the broad was nuts, hanging up like that. She answered. He said: "Take it easy. I'm sorry. Just want to know the facts, ma'am."

"I've got delicate eardrums."

"Delicate everything," he said, chuckling, ready to bring her around. The way he'd brought her around to his bed.

"Sweet," she said, and her voice wasn't. "You want to know if Don knows what I was doing on Bedford? He does."

Fred groaned. "Jesus Christ, why'd you ever come around here?"

"You asked me, remember? About a hundred times in the past two years. So I finally decided to find out if the nine inches was fact or fancy. And there it was, a fancy nine-plus. Curiosity satisfied, private parts sore, I said good-bye, and I meant it. This first meeting was also the last, Mr. Gower. Just you remember our deal when it comes time for casting and Don puts me up for that second lead."

"I said I'd help. But there won't *be* a picture if he knows what you and I . . ."

"He knows, yes. He doesn't know he knows. And he won't push it."

"But how'll he act with me?"

"Time'll tell. And time'll make it like it was before. Just go ahead and package that movie. I'll do what I can to make Donny happy . . . and that's quite a bit."

He began warming to the toughness of her, the casual sexuality of her—like a man, this Cecily Warren, in her tasting of partners. "Why does it have to be our last meeting? Why not an X-rated motel the next time, with no chance of being seen together? With waterbeds and porno movies?"

She said nothing, and he dropped his voice. "I enjoyed you mightily, baby. I think you managed to get off a few times, maybe three. Now I want my cock up your ass. Your big, gorgeous . . ."

She hung up again.

He shrugged and walked out of the bedroom. He had all the women he needed, though Cecily was one hell of a body, one hell of a lay. No wonder Don held onto her. More than three years. As for why Cecily held onto Don, that was in the realm of love or finances or other games Freddy Gower didn't play. His women came to him for kicks. And they didn't stay, even if they wanted to. A month or two, maybe three in a rare case, and the kiss-off. A quick turnover was one of the joys of his life.

But he hadn't counted on Cecily walking away *this* quickly. He hadn't gotten her on film yet.

He went down the stairs, shouting for Bub, his cook, his valet, his bodyguard, his X-rated cameraman, his occasional sidekick in an orgy for three, his one and only friend.

The husky, well-built black man came out of the kitchen, running a hand over his short-cropped hair. He might have been fifty-four or -five; Fred couldn't tell and Bub wouldn't. He was, for certain, older than Fred's forty-eight, a head shorter than Fred's six feet, and a hell of a lot smarter than Fred in the ways of the Strip, the street, the slightly under world he inhabited in order to satisfy both their needs. Like for a joint at least once a day, a snort a few times a month, some Angel Dust and Q's for difficult situations, and plenty of wild nude-club and massage-parlor hookers to add variety to Fred's diet of actresses.

And for the occasional boy they enjoyed on holidays like Christmas, Easter, Ramadan . . . one of Bub's jokes.

"Dinner ready?" Fred asked.

Bub nodded, the expression on his not-too-black face blandly guarded. As always. Even in sex, Fred had yet to see him completely lose the blandness, the guardedness. But that was when white-man, boss-man Freddy Gower was around.

It bothered him to think Bub might relax with blacks. Fred himself was never completely at ease with anyone but Bub. "Hog jowls and grits?" he asked.

The rare, illuminating smile flashed. "Ribs and beans; we rich folk," Bub nigger-talked.

Fred followed him to the kitchen. The table was set and he took his usual seat facing the counter TV. It was tuned to a basketball game. He drank down his vegetable juice cocktail, which Bub made fresh in the blender, and exclaimed, "Hey!" at a smooth layup.

Bub watched as he worked at the cooking island in the center of the big kitchen. "And a white man, too. Rare seeing a white man score in pro basketball."

"More truth than humor there, baby."

Bub served him. It was a meat-heavy stew and Hungarian spaetel, soft noodles with gravy. One taste and he was relaxed and happy.

"Coors or steam beer?" Bub asked.

"We got any stout left?"

Bub brought him a Guinness, then filled his own plate, poured himself some wine, and joined Fred at the table. "You seeing that Cecily chick again?" he asked.

"Got the hots for her?"

"I wouldn't mind. But that's not why I asked. You got business with her main man, haven't you?"

"No sweat. It's all under control."

"Don's a good dude, a straight dude. He's had years with that chick. He could pull a loser."

A loser in Bub's patois was an act of violence.

"She's cut me off." Fred drank stout, watching the tube. "But I'd like her on film."

"If she's ended it, you're gonna have to use magic, and that's never too safe." Magic was trickery and drugs. "What if she runs to Don?"

"She won't. I'll make sure she really digs it. Stop worrying."

"If I stopped worrying, you'd be dead."

"Then *thanks* for worrying."

"Well, good jobs are hard to find. And I've got almost eight years sunk in this one. That's what you call longevity."

After the meal, they shared a joint while they talked about chicks, basketball, and then about poker. Which meant the battle was joined.

Fred went to the card room off the patio to set things up. They played dealer's choice. For five-dollar chips. Which could lead to tears.

Bub was slightly ahead in their year-long contest. Maybe a grand. Fred was determined to win that back. It was a matter of pride.

At midnight, Bub said he'd had enough. Fred had won twenty dollars, and made careful note of the amount in their log, a double-entry ledger.

"Going to bed?" Fred asked.

"Going out."

Fred looked up, surprised.

"Hey, boss-man, you had your poontang today. I haven't."

"Be careful," Fred said, and Bub answered, "Always."

In his bedroom, Fred went to the projector which rested on a fold-out wall shelf facing the white-painted door. Beside it stood an antique sea chest which held his pornography. He unlocked it to reveal stacked booklets, photos, and reels of film; then opened a separate side compartment that held far less—his very private collection. There were a few blowups of Fred with various women, but mostly boxed reels of film marked by white strips of tape on which were written the names of women.

He selected one, mounted the reel on the projector, and sat down on the half-couch facing the door.

He watched himself with the beautiful blond starlet; watched himself get head, get pussy, get off. And smiled, thinking how fear of this film falling into her agent-lover's hands had brought her back a dozen times.

After showering, he composed himself for sleep. But found himself thinking of Cecily Warren.

He wondered if Don really could pull a loser over her. Wouldn't be fists, not after that heart attack, though he was still a feisty bastard. Which meant it would be worse: a weapon.

He tried to end that train of thought. With his life-style, he faced the possibility of irate husbands, lovers, brothers, parents, each and every day. Take Joan White, dancer-singer-actress, and now getting guest shots everywhere from "Dinah!" to Johnny Carson, because he'd maneuvered her into solos on two selective TV specials in payment for a few trouble-free months of kinky sex. He should have waited until the few months were *over!*

She'd assured him there was no man in her life at the time. And, in a way, she hadn't lied. It was a goddamn *woman*, a tough-as-nails dyke, with a stiletto yet, who had tried to kill him at the door of his own house. Bub had heard him yell, and put the powerful dancing instructor down with a solar plexus blow; then whispered something in her ear that brought her back to sane and sent her stumbling to her car.

There was the time he'd had to jump from a second-floor window, breaking his right ankle, and crawl nude to a cab stand two interminably long streets away. Lucky it was four A.M. and no one around.

That crazy Wop singer was supposed to be working in Vegas, not shooting the lock off his wife's door.

There was the time he'd had to stay under a shower forty-five minutes, the water turning cold toward the end because of an over-worked hot-water heater, while the girl he'd been balling tried to convince her crazy ex-husband it was a *woman* friend bathing in the locked bathroom. The ex-husband, a Marine major, beat on the door and eventually broke it open. Fred used an inspired falsetto to scream, "Get that man out! Eunice, call the police! Help!" and hoped the nut wouldn't make out the lack of certain physical properties through the showerstall's frosted glass.

His thoughts turned to another soldier in the field, another man facing the squares, the nuts, idiots who would kill for what was the most available product in all the world—a woman's body. Bub was out there tonight, screwing some nude dancer, some massage-parlor girl, some hooker on his string of dozens who owed him favors. And when you grabbed *that* stuff for free, you really faced hard-ass antagonists—the people who lived off them.

Still, he wished he'd asked to come along.

But tomorrow was a big day and he had to be clear-headed and ready to bargain. He was meeting with Coleman Berry and the Italian speculator to talk financing of *Galt's Island*. They'd read Don's novel, and his own twenty-page film treatment, and he could tell they liked one, the other, or both.

Money (whoever put it up) could get better than fifty percent of profits these days. It was his job to keep that percentage as low as possible, so that he and Don could get a few more points of their own—hopefully seven to ten each, depending upon what had to be given to the lead actors. These were impossibly high percentages when a major studio was Money, but Coleman and his partners generally went for a cheapie budget of a million to a million five, handing out pieces of action to stars and directors, settling for comparatively small profits, doing three such films per year, and thereby coming out with a healthy buck. So low points—like one and a half—which might be valuable in a studio production, were practically meaningless here.

If he'd been able to sell the property to a major studio, or to a major star who would in turn put together a deal with a major studio, he and Don could have forgotten percentages completely and walked away with immediate profits—quick sale and settlement of their ownership. And he'd have begun working on a new project; probably another of Don's novels: that fantasy about the man who returns to his slum childhood, a forty-year-old in a fourteen-year-old's body.

Which got him to thinking about boys, sexually. The younger, the better. Dangerous, yes, when dealing with juveniles, but the thrill was worth the risk. Like the last one Bub had dug up: swish little fifteen-year old from Glendale. Pink-white candy. Already well into the gay scene, but still innocent in appearance. Already a male hooker, but when he'd knelt between Bub's thighs and turned his freckled ass up for Fred . . .

Say he got a truly innocent boy. A child, just into erections, who didn't know what it was all about. A twelve-year-old; even younger. Jesus, what a thrill to seduce such a boy, jack him off, suck him, bring him to ecstasy for the first time in his life!

It was one of those nights. He got up and took a pill. Even so, it was half an hour before he lost the fantasies and fell asleep.

Burleigh "Bub" Kane turned off the old Caddy's windshield wipers as the rain ended. The farmers sure could have used another few days of downpour; so could the reservoirs. But that's not the way it had been lately. Water rationing up north, and talk of it for L.A. Jesus, how he hated the idea of *policing*, any kind of policing! Scared him; hit him where he lived.

Freddy also scared him lately. Appetites getting out of hand. Those boys meant too much to him. And pushing a dangerous make with a friend's heavy steady. He shook his head, muttering, "Bells tolling, baby. Time to jump ship."

Which was why he was driving west on Santa Monica, going all the way to the shore and the Good Time, a nude club. At fifty-eight he was anxious for the security that a hundred grand or more in the mattress represented.

For a while, Freddy had represented security. But he was going to blow things; Bub felt it in his bones; Freddy was *too* hot to trot.

So Bub was driving to the shore, and not to make out with sweet Melissa of the red hair—head and crotch. He was meeting with two gentlemen who were interested in what he knew about the gentry in Beverly Hills, Bel Air, and the better canyons like Benedict and Sunset Plaza, down low where the mansions were. A deal might be made, with Bub supplying addresses, information on what to search for during a robbery, and what sort of security to expect, this information gained while serving as free-lance bartender at parties thrown by Freddy's friends.

His cut would be fifty percent. What he hadn't figured out yet was how to *insure* his payoff. He wouldn't deal until he knew he could collect. Otherwise, the two heist artists would do the job and disappear. As they said in the trade, Bub couldn't go to court over the loss. What he needed was a hostage.

It was dark in the Good Time, except for a lighted square of stage, and pretty nearly empty this bad-weather night. And who should be going into her ground work—doing an energetic humping routine on a fake white fur rug—but Melissa. Bub wished he were sitting at his usual up-front table, instead of back

here in a booth with the two heist artists, hiding his
sour expression in the darkness.

The one called Albert had hands like black hams
with black bananas for fingers. His partner—white
and with the late-show-movie name of Brains—was
older, a little smaller, but still one hard-looking customer.

Their drinks came. The recorded rock music
changed. Melissa rolled over, got to her knees, gave
them a back view. Brains said, "So who is your hostage?"

"Let's see those pictures you showed me last night,"
Bub said, tensing to leap away in case Albert reacted
badly.

"What?" Albert said, turning his big head.

"Your kids. The two boys."

"You talking about a ten-year-old and a twelve." Albert's voice was rumbling dangerously. "You talking
about *children*. And they living with my wife in San
Diego." He paused. "Whyn't you take *her?"*

"She's far away for a loving wife. Who knows if she
means shit to you. And who knows if you wouldn't
pay not to get her back alive."

Brains laughed, but very quietly, because the big
head was turning to him. "C'mon, Albert, it's the only
guarantee Bub's gonna buy."

"Not *my* kids," Albert said, and finished his Scotch
and water. "Where's that saggy-tit waitress?"

"One kid," Bub said. "I don't care which. Just until
you come up with my share of the take. I'll babysit . . ."

Albert interrupted with a string of obscenities.

Bub said: "Man, you're just too worried. If you
mean to take me, I can understand. Otherwise, you got
no worries."

Brains said: "He's right, Albert."

"No," Albert said, and rose. Both Brains and Bub
slid away to allow him exit. "I'm going to the john.
Order me a double."

After he was gone, Brains said: "What would guarantee *me?*"

"You wouldn't want to be responsible for anything happening to Albert's son, would you?"

"And if we're caught? And if we name you?"

"Who's gonna love ya, baby?" Bub cracked. "Who's gonna get the lawyer and try to make bail? I'd be all you'd have. I'd work hard for you, to save myself the trouble of saying you're both liars. And with *my* friends, you'd never make it stick anyway. But like I say, to save myself the trouble . . ."

"Okay. When Albert has a chance to think it through, he'll agree. When he comes back from the john, fill us in on the plan."

Bub smiled.

"We gotta have some trust here, man!"

"Trust, sure, after I get the kid."

"I thought we'd bring the kid the night of the game. And pick him up right after, when we make the turnover."

"Fine. Then the night of the game I fill you in. And I want those pictures in Albert's wallet right now, so he can't snatch a ringer off the street."

"Wait, damn it! The pictures, sure. But we gotta run through everything at least three four days before the game!"

"Then that's when you bring the kid." He looked across the room, and stood up as Albert reached them. "Can I see those pictures, Albert?"

Brains said: "It's important. And they're just pieces of paper."

Albert took out his wallet. Brains reached over and removed the pictures from a plastic sheath. Albert began to protest. Brains said: "Maybe a million!"

"Yeah, *maybe!* Give 'em back!"

"And a sure piece of ass," Bub said.

Albert glanced at the stage.

"It'll be one of the dancers."

"No sister," Albert muttered.

Bub took the pictures from Brains, and began walking. He heard the two quarreling behind him but never glanced back. He was at the stage, smiling at a new dancer, a tall, fleshy brunette with silicone-steady boobs, when the hand came down on his shoulder. He sighed and turned, but it was Brains.

"I'll have him convinced by morning. Give me a phone number. That P.O. box's too slow now that we're gonna roll."

"We got time."

"A girl's number. A friend's. Someone you trust who can get word to you quick."

"We got time," Bub repeated, and walked off. There wasn't anyone in the world he trusted with his freedom, his life.

At the little desk in front he talked to Gary, the buck-toothed manager who was a stomper-gay and could handle the tons of wild cunt passing through this club. He gave him two fifties and explained what his companions needed.

He drove to the Strip and the Montezuma Massage. Ada, the Jap chick, was napping in one of the four curtained booths. No one was around to see him go in and wake her, so no hassle about payment.

She gave him a lovely fifteen minutes of head, and he came with his fingers digging into the cleft of her ass. By then she was turned on, blew him back up, and they did a straight number on the table, she coming off, he faking it.

Once was enough for Bub Kane, unless he had all night in which to party.

On the way home, he thought of Albert and Brains. In his room off the kitchen, he examined the pictures of Albert's sons. He allowed every possible disaster to run through his mind, and ended convinced he was in control all the way.

Before he fell asleep, he'd totalled up a million-dollar take in four houses. He had three more in mind . . . but if they could score just those four, he'd be able to fence out his share of jewels, coin and stamp collections, and portable objets d'art at over a quarter million. And that didn't include wall-safe cash, which could be considerable.

But a hundred-thousand tax-free old-age pension for sure.

If Albert and Brains could follow simple directions.

Cecily watched the Carson show; then worked over her savings and checking accounts. Not much left in savings, and checking would be empty by week's end. But she'd be seeing Sr. Resordo, so no pushing of panic buttons. He paid beautifully for the privilege, and was educated, successful, wealthy, gentlemanly— the qualities Cecily admired in men, the qualities she judged them by, not their race, their color. She enjoyed her doctor twice a year, on his examining table after her free check-ups . . . free because the lovely black man enjoyed her just as much. That many Hispanics and blacks in this town were poor and coarse and dangerous, were trash, was beside the point. So were many Anglos. She only hoped Johnny understood . . .

But of course he didn't, couldn't since she'd never found the way to explain. He *saw* all the trash that hit on her, that she rejected violently. He couldn't see her "acceptance" of Resordo or Dr. Moore. She was afraid that unless someone who knew how to educate and handle a child took over soon, Johnny would turn out to be trash himself.

That was why she hadn't taken money from the man she saw most often. She asked nothing from Don but love . . . though he knew how much a shot at a major part in a major flick would mean to her, and all on his own had offered it.

She asked nothing but love . . . yet didn't fool herself that she wouldn't count on Don if Resordo disappeared and the bills came due and it was desperation time.

She asked nothing of him because she wanted theirs to be one relationship based on pure feeling, as much as that was possible in this hard-ass, macho world that men had created in Hollywood, USA. She hoped that when the time came, that feeling would also include her son.

When Don had asked why she didn't rent out her two-bedroom-and-pool ranch and move in with him, she'd told him she wanted her independence . . . "until I get married again, which won't be for some time yet." Her independence included hiding the facts of the man who helped pay the bills and her son.

She had to reveal Johnny soon. She had to take the chance Don would forgive her her fear of having love-at-first-sight go sour.

So many men didn't want a child around when they could find pretty women without children, and Hollywood was full of such young, childless women. So many men would write off a long-term relationship because of a child. And Don had a family back east: a son and daughter who visited, whose feelings he considered, who might get nervous at the thought of his taking on a new family and apply pressure.

Why the hell *should* he want to involve himself in a father role, especially with so complicated a boy as Johnny, so fucked-up a kid, she knew, since she herself had done most of the fucking up? The blond who'd preceded her with Don, Fanny, was still around, still sending him birthday cards and get-well cards, still sending signals she'd be willing to break her current liaison and come back home. And the blond had no son, no daughter, nothing but her twenty-six-year-old ass to move into Don's place.

She looked at the phone, suddenly frightened, wanting to speak to her man, wanting to tell him everything right now—about other men and Johnny and that she was almost ready to go the love and marriage and true-to-you-alone route.

Almost. Because another fear set in immediately. She'd gone half-crazy as a teen-aged wife and, later, mother, subordinating her ego to a macho male's, trying to forget her own ambitions as he talked end-lessly of grapes and alfalfa and irrigation and called actresses "whores" and mocked her requests for dramatic lessons.

She took a long, hot tub. Stepping out, she looked at herself in the steamy mirror, at the shimmery reflection of head, breasts, crotch, and thighs. And looking couldn't help remember how Fred Gower had worshiped her body, had ravaged her body; and realized there was something more to him for her than a chance to strengthen her shot at Don's movie. And was excited enough to wish Jorge Resordo didn't choose such late hours. But then again, a married man had to be careful.

She was in the bedroom, picking out a nightgown, when she remembered she'd made Donny believe she and Fred were throwing him a surprise birthday party.

Which meant she'd have to speak to Fred, see him again, in order to arrange something. And the turn-on wasn't worked out of her system. If he pressed the right buttons . . .

She got into bed. She wasn't married, yet, though Don had finally begun hinting at the subject. She was still free. Whatever developed, she wouldn't feel guilty.

She turned off the lamp. In the room across the hall, Johnny made crying sounds. Poor kid had bad dreams. She sat up, listening, intending to go to him if he continued the sounds. But he was quiet and she went to sleep.

Gray light was in the window when she awoke to a touch on the face. She reached up to take Jorge's hand . . . but it wasn't his hand. He crouched over her, naked, his drooping penis rubbing her cheek. His voice, in slightly accented English, murmured: "Beautiful lady, open your mouth."

It was five A.M., and Jorge Resordo had come to pay his respects. She received the well-preserved Mexican businessman of seventy-one, the man whose appetite for her was youthful enough once a week, in the way he'd requested. She tightened her lips as he moved in and out of her mouth, sucking strongly. When he lay down beside her, she enfolded him with arms and legs, kept his penis rigid with her stroking hand, enjoyed the empassioned caresses to her buttocks, the repeated licks and kisses to her nipples. Finally, he was ready to enter her. She mounted him, to save his strength, and rode him first slowly, then more and more quickly, watching his face in the faint light, listening to his breathing, growing excited in direct proportion to his excitement.

At his climax, she squatted hard, moaning as her own explosion approached, bending to kiss his open mouth, humping again, and attaining release.

They washed with the master bathroom door closed. He had her envelope ready—cash, as she preferred, because it was almost deadline-time at the bank. Three hundred, every week, for once a week. And she liked the small, neat man so very much! She enjoyed *his* enjoyment of her so very much! She wondered how she'd be able to give him up when—if—she married Don.

He dressed, held her close, whispered: "I love you, querida, do you know that?"

She said, "Of course," a little insulted.

"But I myself didn't know it at first. Almost six years, Cecily." He kissed her neck, fondled her bare breast. "It was *this,* I thought that was the only thing between us." He grasped her big, firm buttock. "Esta!" he said hoarsely, smiling, making her smile with him. "Yet there grew another feeling."

She nodded, turning him to the door, anxious to reduce the chance that Johnny would awake and see him. Johnny never said anything, but after all this time she was sure he knew *someone* came to call. "I understand all that, Jorge. Do you think it's just money with me?"

"If I stopped paying you?"

"I'd stop seeing you." She rubbed playfully against him. "But I'd miss you."

"Ah, if only the years would drop away."

"From me or you?"

He laughed. She said, *"Shush,"* and moved him through the hall and kitchen and out the door. He went to his car, turning to look and wave at her. How very sweet a man he was! And how well dressed, with that lovely tan suit and the old-fashioned fedora hat. If only she could teach Don to care about clothes. Jeans and sweatshirts were what he liked.

Oh well, writers were accepted that way at the studios.

She put the envelope under her pillow and closed her eyes. She smiled, thinking of her Donny, and stopped smiling, wondering about his health, and smiled again, thinking now she'd *really* throw him a party. It was Monday and she had until his birthday, Friday. The invitations would be by phone.

She wet her lips, wondering what might happen with Fred Gower at their next meeting. Hung, the bastard. Cruel, the mother. Built and strong and violent . . . and exciting.

She turned on her side. She'd gone along with Donny and Sr. Resordo for a long time and no quick makes for a long time, and it was good for a woman to play the man's game every so often, added joy to life.

Her body was satisfied with this day's lovemaking. Her mind was titillated by the possibilities this week held for lovemaking. The bills would be paid and there'd be a party and she'd get her shot at a strong movie role. She was in full charge of her life.

In her dreams, Johnny followed her around. She told him he should do his homework, he should stop watching TV so much, he should stop lying and cheating so much. He said: "Why, big momma? I'm just like you." She grew enraged. She chased him, slapped him about the face and head, sent him stumbling away. Later, she was in bed with Sr. Resordo and heard Johnny approaching. She tried to tell Resordo to take his penis out of her mouth, but she couldn't speak, couldn't move. Johnny walked in, and his face went white with shock. He began to weep, pointing, saying he loved her, begging her to stop. Resordo came, and when she looked up it wasn't Resordo, it was Johnny coming in her mouth.

She awoke, twitching, choking, wailing. She sat up, hands over her face. "Dear Lord Jesus! Am I like pop to dream such things? Am I crazy like Teresa?"

Two

Tuesday, May 3

He was so many different kinds of people, he thought. Don Baylis, fifty, was also Donald Bayalichofsky, child and teenager. Don Baylis, bachelor, was also husband and father for seventeen years, until six years ago. The retired, moneyed novelist was also the reluctant ad man, editor, and way back in Brooklyn, teacher of high school English.

It was seven-thirty. He was shaving; after having showered. Before then he'd taken a Lanoxin tablet, the first of nine pills he took each day. Before that he'd lain awake, determinedly trying to sleep.

So many mornings like this, simply because the doctor said he should get between eight and ten hours of sleep . . . and he'd never managed more than six since puberty. Lying awake, thinking of Cecily, of how he'd like to have her beside him, to nestle up to, to make love to, to stop him from thinking as much as he did while trying to sleep.

He knew what she was. Men were staples of her diet. No sweet Miss Innocence dreaming of kinder and kuchen was Miss Cecily Warren. Maybe even part hooker . . .

But he dug her, perhaps in part *because* of the way she used men; so different from the girl he'd married, from the Brooklyn Jewish girls of his youth. He dug her for what she was . . . or he had, when he'd been fully competitive with other men. Now he feared her free ways, tormented himself with the possibility she'd fucked Freddy.

With no more tennis, jogging, handball, with no more occasional lost weekends with other women, and especially with no more writing—the lifelong thrust which had filled half his waking hours—what else *was* there to think of but Cecily? She was the one remaining proof that he was still a man, still able to make waves in a man's world. He planned to ask her to marry him; but first she had to bring her son out of hiding, without Don's having to reveal he knew about the boy and had spoken to him twice outside her North Hollywood home.

He also knew about the sister in a mental hospital. He knew where the ex-husband lived, and the mother. He marveled at Cecily's thinking he would be naïve enough not to wonder at her lack of availability, her many excuses, her secretiveness.

Finally, he knew about the old man who'd been calling on her once a week for at least five years, generally very early on a Tuesday. Knew all this by means of a private investigations firm.

The old man accounted for where Cecily got enough money to make ends meet, since her occasional modeling, singing, and acting jobs didn't total more than fifteen hundred to two thousand a year. And she was bitter about her ex-husband's unwillingness to pay what she called enough alimony, but which obviously included child support.

It failed to bother Don. The old man was established, he had tenure, longevity over Don't three years and two months. He also had love for Cecily, because anyone as wealthy as the investigator said Jorge Re-

sordo was, taking a full floor in a Wilshire high-rise
office building for his import-export firm, could get
ass easily enough. A five-year-or-longer relationship
meant love. Love of a sort on her part, too.

But the investigator had also come up with a then-
current three-night stand with a young photographer
who'd helped Cecily make up a new composite. And a
two-week idyll with a freaky rock musician. And from
this Don was able to assume that she reached out every
so often for a man who took her fancy.

If he married her, that would have to end.

If he married her! *If* he could trust her after catching
her coming out of Fred's house! *If* she wasn't an out-
and-out whore!

He left the bathroom and walked quickly through
the bedroom, testing himself, wanting to see if today
would be a good day, a day free of chest pain, of debil-
itatingly irregular heartbeat. Most days were good
now, but for a while . . .

He walked even faster along the corridor connecting
the two sets of rooms.

The cliffside house was one of those Southern California marvels, built in a canyon just minutes from
the action and traffic of the Sunset Strip, cantilevered
out over space, giving a jet's-eye view of the city and,
on smog-free days, of the Pacific beyond. There were
two bedrooms and two baths on one side of a U-
shaped sundeck, a living room, dining room, and
kitchen on the other. A wrought-iron spiral staircase
ran down from a corner of the sundeck to a recent
addition: a combination study-bedroom-playroom, the
viewside floor-to-ceiling glass, because this spreadout,
white-washed, sun-washed city deserved to be looked
at.

Breakfast was skim-milk cottage cheese, a slice of
whole wheat toast, and Postum coffee substitute. He
didn't mind the solid food. What he minded was the
loss of strong black coffee, with an occasional shot of

brandy, and a cigarette. God, he's trade all the Postum, salad, and broiled fish on earth for one unfiltered Camel!

Mrs. Clark arrived at eight. He'd forgotten today was cleaning day. She was a nice black lady, about his age, and before November 24 he'd enjoyed talking to her. But now . . . now she had cleaning to do and he had nothing to do and she made him feel the way his mother had—useless, guilty, irritable.

He fled downstairs to read. At ten, the sun burned the smog away, and he put aside his book and went to the stairs. Time for his daily walk. He'd be back long before Cecily's expected arrival at two.

The phone rang. It was Fred Gower.

"Hey, Don, so you blew our surprise! Now we'll just have to make it a plain old birthday party. Or would you prefer costume?"

He sat down, feeling slightly ill, remembering he hadn't taken his morning Quinidine and Inderal. "Whatever you say, Freddy."

"Your gal and I will talk it over. Meanwhile, there's big business today, or have you forgotten?"

"The meeting with Coleman Berry and Don Corleone."

"You keep calling him that and I'll do it at the meeting. I'm sure they're going to make some sort of offer. Hopefully, the whole budget. At worst, fifty thousand for development . . . which means for a scriptwriter and assorted odds and ends, mainly a few great nights out for the two producers, thee and me."

Don chuckled. It wasn't easy. He didn't feel ready for Fred yet. Maybe tomorrow.

"Everything all right, buddy?"

Don said: "Fine."

"Haven't changed your mind about skipping the scriptwriting chores, have you? Because I'll insist on you as the writer, if that's what you want. And you'll bet as big a buck as I can manage."

"It's not that, Freddy. Just feeling lousy this morning." He disliked himself for using *that* as an excuse. "Talk to you later."

"Hey, take care, man. We got lots of deals to put together."

Don sat a while after hanging up, losing the sick feeling, thinking that he couldn't be sure about Fred and Cecily.

"Hi, bun. Good news and bad news. First the bad. Won't be able to make lunch. Now the good. Got a call on the service from my agent. Thought he was dead, but he finally got me an audition. New TV series: 'Seven Stunning Spies.' Said the producer picked me from file photographs. Said I fit one of the types to a T! Could be a break, bunny. Something like 'Charley's Angels,' but ninety minutes and with seven leads instead of three. Not all are featured in each show . . ."

He said, "Sounds good, sweetheart," when it sounded like most of the parts she pursued—pure shit. "For what network are they doing the pilot?"

"Well . . . no network. The producer told my agent the show was pre-sold to independents—like 'Mary Hartman' was."

"Oh," he said, keeping the irritation from his voice.

"And no pilot," she said tersely. "We're supposed to shoot thirteen shows. But first there's a promotion tour . . ."

He laughed. It had nothing to do with humor. "No pilot? Right into thirteen shows—ninety-minute shows—which means a production budget of about five million dollars? And no network to pick up the tab? And a promotion tour before anything's on film? You know what you are? You're one of seven stunning *stupes!* You're going to be farmed out for fucking!"

"For Christ sake! Let me go on my first interview! I know it sounds like a scam, but the producer is Blake

Margolin, who did that big spy series a few seasons ago."

"What spy series?"

"Damm it, I don't know! But my agent wouldn't send me out unless there was at least a *chance*."

"What agent?"

"I'm going to hang up in a minute! If it was up to you I'd spend my life playing housewife and never stick my head out the door! If it was up to you I'd be like that wife you dumped, and in no time you'd dump me too! If it was up to you . . ."

He said: "I'm sorry. I can't seem to remember your agents, new or old." And then couldn't help adding, "Because they're all such marginal characters." And again said, "Sorry. I know I promised never to interfere."

She was breathing hard, perhaps crying.

"I worry about you, Cecily. This business has a few good people, and a ton of scum. You yourself told me about the girl who thought she'd landed a part in a foreign production, was given passage to Uruguay, and then had to fuck the so-called producer and three of his friends for a month to get passage back home."

She said, "Yeah," thickly. "My agent's Carl Jugland. And don't say it—*no one* knows of him. But he seems so straight, never made a pass." She sighed. "You've heard it all before."

He had indeed. "See you tonight. We'll talk then."

"I'm not sure about tonight, honey bun. Please don't be mad. I've got to see Freddy about that not-such-a-surprise party . . . hey, that's a good name for it!" She bounced back so quickly; was beginning to giggle. "You are invited to not-such-a-fucking-big-surprise-party for not-such-a-fucking-big-deal, Don Baylis."

He couldn't change gears, or moods, as quickly as she could. "Call me when you have a spare minute. I'd

call you, but there's no way since the service is always
on."

"Please, bun. No more scolding. I'll try for a better
agent. And maybe I'll come over later, after . . ." She
stopped.

He felt she'd been about to say, after Johnny's
asleep.

". . . after I rest up a bit. But don't count on it.
Tomorrow for sure."

He said, "Fine," and, "Good-bye."

"Wait, bun! Aren't you going to wish me luck with
Margolin?"

"Yes, you'll need it."

"I mean, that he turns out to be straight and that
the show is really on and that I get a part."

"That's wishing for miracles."

"I know. But anyway."

"I wish you luck."

"Thank you. Now wish me a miracle."

He smiled a little.

"And give me a kiss."

He popped his lips into the mouthpiece.

"Call that a kiss?" She gave him one of her great
effects; a wet, sucking sound that made him think of
more than kisses. "Now here's one for your mouth."

He was laughing, and aroused, when she hung up.

He sat a while, looking out the glass wall at the
view, then decided he wouldn't eat alone this afternoon. He'd try Barry Salvadore, an old friend from
New York who was finally into a TV production company of his own after years of apprenticeship with a
well-known partner.

He and Barry had worked on commercials back at
B&B thirteen years ago. And Barry had published two
well-constructed if not popular novels.

A literate man, Barry, as few out here were. A gentleman, as even fewer were. He wondered why they
weren't closer, why he seemed attracted to men like

Freddy since arriving in L.A. This town seemed to bring out the worst in him.

He made the call, and lunch was set for one-thirty. He went upstairs, swallowed his pills, then drove to Santa Monica, and took his walk along the beach. It was bright, sunny, not too windy for the shore. He remembered other beaches—taking the family to Sanibel; to Miami; to Jones Beach back when they'd lived in Queens. He remembered laughter . . .

He *heard* laughter, and looked up to see a young couple running toward him, the girl's face flushed, her mouth open and laughing, her boobs bouncing behind a sweatshirt. The boy said, "Hi," and Don nodded, dropping his eyes. Not from the boobs. From the running, the youth, the health . . . everything he'd lost.

Hell, they'd lose it too.

Everyone lost it.

He kicked at the sand, wanting to break into a run, wanting to play some ball, wanting to rip off his clothes and dive into the icy surf and see if it would all end in another chest explosion.

He actually came to a stop, fingering his windbreaker, looking at the water.

But he had a lunch date with Barry. Later, Fred would have news about the movie deal. Cecily might be over tonight; definitely tomorrow. He was going to a birthday party Friday, his own. And there'd be cards in the mail from the kids and from friends.

He resumed walking. Too busy to die this week. Maybe next.

The meeting was in Coleman Berry's office at Twentieth Century-Fox, off Pico Boulevard. A much smaller studio, of course, since they'd sold the back lot to the developers who'd created Century City. Walking from his car to the two-story building, Freddy remembered the old days when his PR operation had been blasting along, when he'd attended studio pre-

views not only in the large theater but in private
screening rooms. And dated stars and starlets by the
ton. And spent the bread faster than it came in; and it
came in at over a hundred grand a year, which was
real money in the fifties and sixties. It was real money
now, too, because he was no longer making it.

That studio bustle, that studio excitement, was missing. The place still had some nice street sets, some
good-looking chicks parading here and there, but in
the main it was Deadsville.

He climbed to the second floor. Coleman Berry and
Don Cice—he had to stop playing *Godfather* games
with the Italian!—were waiting in the large corner office. "Just twelve," Coleman said in his theatrical bass
voice. "Still a dependable man."

"You know it." He turned to the Italian, hoping for
a reintroduction. He'd only met him once, briefly, and
hadn't had occasion to use his name since.

Coleman lowered his tubby shape into a huge chair
behind an old desk, and didn't help at all. "You know
my partner."

Freddy said: "Nice to see you again." They shook
hands and the Italian sat down in another huge chair
beside the desk. A small straight-back was Freddy's.
He gave it an exaggerated once-over. "If I were sensitive . . ."

Coleman laughed, his belly shaking. "Forgot to get
you something comfortable."

Freddy sat down. Coleman moved Don's book into
the center of the desk. "We've read *Galt's Island*. I
liked it. Signore Pandaro more than liked it, and
picked up on an interesting point."

Freddy remembered the name was Umberto Pandaro. "My treatment digressed from the book only
when visually necessary," he said.

"The treatment, you'll forgive me, was garbage,"
Pandaro said quietly.

Freddy laughed, waving his hands. "No apologies necessary. As long as you like the basic story . . ."

"And the basic sex," Pandaro interrupted. "The story can be compressed, reduced, though the idea of a robbery, a caper you call it, will remain. The gambling resort will remain."

Coleman murmured: "The treatment wasn't that bad, but in terms of what Umberto has in mind . . . I think you should hear his concept, and tell us whether the author will go along with it."

"I can say right now Don Baylis will go along with anything I consider a major production."

"The degree of financing is not a problem," Pandaro said, strong, long body slouching in the chair. He had a rich Italian look: pale blue clothing, tanned skin, and youthful graying hair. He was totally at ease, the bastard, while Freddy was beginning to sweat. Something in Coleman's statement, in his eyes . . .

"Then what *is* a problem?" Freddy asked.

"Ah, not exactly a problem. More of a question of how the writer sees his work, his reputation, himself. From what you've told Signore Berry, this Donald Baylis has a literary reputation for some of his books, has been on the bestseller lists with some of his books."

"*Fanny Hill* was on the best-seller lists," Fred began, and saw the two men exchange a glance. And without a single word of explanation, knew it could be the biggest thing in his life!

"A porno version?" he asked, looking from one to the other.

"Not a good description. Would you call *Last Tango in Paris* pornography? Would a star of Brando's eminence be part of pornography? X-rated, yes . . ." The Italian came up in his chair. "And with some detail in the sex encounters."

Freddy looked at Coleman. Coleman cleared his throat. "Three million, with a possible expansion to four. A major studio version. A major male star. A mature female who really has it in the body department. The caper plot, fully developed, though the cast of characters must be trimmed. The rape scene, also detailed, so two of the supporting cast must also be willing to engage in lovemaking on camera. Four actors, one a luminary. If we can get names for the supporting players, fine, but not really important. The male star *is* important. And the author's written permission so that later there are no lawsuits. Understood?"

Freddy grinned. "It's inspired! A big movie, hardcore in spots, with a star participating. A big-budget caper, with an explicit rape scene involving two supporting actors. And Lord, *what* a rape, eh, boys?"

Pandaro murmured: "Very Italian in its revenge. I think it was there I decided it would be worth taking the risk . . ."

Freddy cut in, which he didn't usually do with Money. But he wanted them to think he was more worried about Don than he was. "About the author. He's not all that hungry. He has family, two children back east, and would feel embarrassed. He has a fiancée, a beautiful actress . . ."

"This is one starring role he won't push her into," the Italian said, and they all laughed.

But Fred wasn't sure what *Cecily* would have to say. They were willing to go with a newcomer for female lead, and this could be a very big flick indeed. There'd be a hell of a lot more straight acting than fucking involved. Maria Schneider had done well after *Tango*. And playing opposite someone in the class of a Paul Newman, Rob Dennings, Burt Reynolds, or any of the other ten or twelve stars who ruled the box office—someone who could be convinced that it was as smart a thing to do as what Brando had done in *Tango*—would be the making of her! The sex action itself would be the making of her! Most importantly, if she got to want the part badly enough, she could help push Don into line.

They discussed male leads. They narrowed on three names, careers that were beginning to falter. They admitted it would be tough . . . but Fred had a hunch about one of the names, a man Bub had fed girl after girl when Fred needed the actor-director's help, a man who had a streak of sexual exhibitionism just under the surface. He'd be able to indulge it in the name of revolutionary technique, of art, of business and money.

It would take more than up-front cash, of course. They all agreed on that, on having to offer a hefty percentage of profits. And as they talked, there was no doubt in any of their minds that there *would* be profits, big profits.

Fred then began a pitch to get Donald Baylis a good-sized piece of the action. It was important to him; his contract with Don stated that each of the two partners would receive exactly the same percentage of profits. Whatever he could get for Don, half would be *his*.

"You were right about the author, Signore Pandaro. He's the most difficult problem we have to face. Tougher than the star, since I believe I know who our star will be."

Pandaro was down low in his chair again, watching him.

Coleman lit a cigarette, took a deep drag, and spoke words and smoke. "You're old friends. Do a job on him, Freddy. We'll be willing to pay you two grand a week during production as working producer."

Fred hid his contempt. Did they think he was all that stupid? Twenty or thirty thousand to give up points worth *hundreds* of thousands? Maybe *millions?* "I'll try. But since his illness he's even less inclined to play games with his reputation. I'll have to present it to him for what it is: a possible breakthrough movie that will make him immensely popular, and richer than he's ever dreamed of."

"Not richer than he's ever dreamed of," the Italian said disapprovingly. "That is misleading."

"Maybe." He spoke quickly. "But ten percent of total gross profits for him. Five for me. In addition, he gets the five percent of budget I originally discussed with Coleman, on signing, this to put a hundred fifty thousand in his hands, the most powerful inducement to accept a contract I know of."

Pandaro sat bolt upright. "Ten percent? Outrageous! We're prepared to be generous—one and a half to each of you. That will amount to an enormous sum if all goes as we think it will. And your salary as associate producer—now that Coleman and I will be the producers—could be raised so that you would make . . ." he pursed his lips ". . . let us say seventy-five, eighty thousand."

"Generous," Fred said, with no inflection whatsoever.

The Italian bridled. "You must understand we have the star's percentage to negotiate. It could be as high as twenty-five percent!"

"Not if you let me handle it. And the man I have in mind will direct, too."

"There are our own profits to consider. Remember, we're putting up three, possibly four million dollars."

"I certainly won't forget your investment, signore. That's why, again, I ask you to let me handle the star. You won't have to give away nearly as many points as you think."

"An absolute limit of five percent between the two of you," Pandaro said, but he had come up two points and would come up more.

"I wouldn't be able to advise Baylis to accept on those terms."

Coleman said: "We'll reach an agreement, Freddy. The project is a strong one, and as reasonable men . . ."

And so it went as Fred inched toward the door, debating them all the way, feeling that the deal would be satisfactory.

If he and Don shared ten percent, it would be a *win!* And if the movie did what he felt certain it could do if produced properly, they'd have a breakthrough. Which in Hollywood parlance meant a box office giant: a *Godfather, Exorcist, Jaws, Star Wars.* Say half of those hundred million plus takes. Say a *third.* He and Don stood to make from a million and a half each, on up! And "on up" could top five million!

He headed for the phone booth on the ground floor, wanting to get right to work convincing Don.

A woman answered that Mr. Baylis was out.

He went to his car. And thought he should have claimed experience in producing porno films. And remembered that he had planned to produce his latest film tonight, with Cecily. She was coming over to make up the list for that party they had to throw for Don.

He shouldn't play further games with her.

But he had a memory flash of her body, of what she would look like on the big screen with an Adonis like Rob Dennings, and was desirous on the instant.

He knew he could get Dennings, especially if he offered him the hyphen role of actor-director. Get him for ten percent, despite Dennings still hanging up there in the top dozen male leads; despite his being a hell of a director, actually better than he was an actor. Because Fred knew what buttons to push, and knew how to handle the agent: half a million up front to placate Boyle, who like most actors' agents fucked up more deals than he put together.

Fred would feed Dennings the dream of Numero Uno fame, of the hottest career in film history, along with that barbed hook implicit in the movie itself: the all-time champion act of exhibitionism. And the star was perfect for it, having no children, no living family, nothing to inhibit his funkiness.

Driving out of the lot, Fred realized his hands were shaking.

Cecily knew it was bullshit the minute she entered Blake Margolin's office. It was the look of the man, the place, the smell of things. He reminded her of the manager of a hot-pillow motel (Special Rates For Half Days). And the address of Margolin Enterprises—a three-story walkup building on Ventura, top floor, no secretary, stroll in off the hall—fit too.

Yet she managed to subvert the knowledge. Because *how* could she know? Hadn't big productions come out of rat-trap offices before? And hadn't her agent sent her here?

The small, fortyish man with curly brown hair and dandruff on the shoulders of his blue suit was motioning at the door. "Please release the snap-lock, Miss Warren, so we won't be interrupted by the next interview*ee*." Proud of that last word, he was . . . but a nice voice; fuller, softer than his appearance led her to expect.

She hesitated an instant, then turned and released the lock. Logical enough what he'd said about being interrupted. And no way, she told herself, she couldn't handle him.

He was motioning her toward a green leatherette chair in front of his desk. Except for his own chair—a big, swivel job with a back that came up over the top of his head—a gray metal filing cabinet and two scenic prints were all the office held.

She walked to the chair. His eyes moved over her, but she was dressed conservatively enough in white cotton pants, pink man-type shirt with lacy white kerchief around the neck, and a good tan jacket matching her tan shoes. Of course, those pants were tight, and the shirt open at the top three buttons.

Before she could sit down, he held out his hand. He didn't rise, and she had to lean forward over the desk.

His eyes flickered to her cleavage, and he was sweating on his upper lip.

It went with the territory, and she murmured her nice-to-meet-you.

His hand was hot and damp. It held hers just a little longer than was necessary.

"Won't you sit down, my dear?"

"Thank you." She sat down, putting both feet primly on the floor and her black leather portfolio in her lap, because now his eyes seemed to be *jabbing* into her tight pants. She began opening the zippered case.

"I don't need to see your book, Miss Warren. I'm looking at the original. And *what* an original!" He chuckled.

"Mr. Margolin, my agent Carl Jugland raised . . ."

"I insist that my stars call me Blake."

She winced a little. "My agent raised some questions about how you were going into production without a pilot or a network."

"I don't think Carl raised those questions, Cecily. He understands the unorthodox way in which I work." He waved a hand around the office. "Low-budget surroundings. The expense of a pilot, the heavy-handed veto power of a network over my creative output, both eliminated—my own independent-station contacts taking their place. In other words, Carl trusts me and wouldn't question my methods."

"They're my own questions . . . Blake."

He beamed at her. "And I respect you for them; shows professional knowledgeability." He looked down at a sheet of paper and some photographs. "Your résumé, your composite, the body shots from Carl's files all prove you're right for the part of Marya in 'Seven Stunning Spies.'" He leaned back. "However, it's taken me two years to put this project together, and I've got to be careful about the talent. Looks aren't everything, right? I'll give you a script to study. On your next interview, you'll read for me."

She began to believe that at least *he* believed what he was saying. "About that promotion tour . . ."

". . . a build-up for print media and local television in various parts of the country. A few nightclubs. A few fairs and rodeos. Some society, art- and music-world parties. You and the other girls—I've got them under contract, all six of them—you'll meet the crème de la crème! You'll probably marry a millionaire before I can make you a star!" He stretched in his chair, laughing. "I know how you girls think, and I assure you no one's planning to sell you into white slavery." Again laughter, in which she joined. "Relax, Cecily, relax!"

Which was exactly what she was beginning to do. She put her zipper case on the floor and crossed her legs.

He was leaning far back in his chair now, still chuckling a little, and said: "Mind taking a walk around the office? First naturally. Then the way a sexy spy would. Just to please the camera rolling behind these wise old eyes."

She rose and walked to the door, crisply, a little in a hurry, as she usually walked. She turned, model fashion, posing in haute couture, then went toward him, and past him, giving it lots of hot, rolling her hips and sticking out her chest. She came back to his desk with more hot, leaned forward on both hands, and spoke in the high, breathless, Marilyn Monroe voice that always cracked up Donny. "Is that what you mean, Blake?"

He didn't laugh. "I'm convinced, dearest. Now come around here and look at the script."

So it would be a feel, a kiss, whatever his toll charge was. As they used to say at the Sunset Actors Lab, "A hand on the ass and a contract." It went with the territory. Too bad he wasn't a little more attractive.

She was coming around the right side of the desk, and he was opening a drawer, smiling—so fatherly, so helpful. She was beginning to like him because maybe, just maybe it was going to happen at long last here in this shabby office with this shabby little man—the break she'd dreamed of. And without Don's help, without anyone's help. So that she could come to the *Galt's Island* role with a major win . . .

She stopped dead. He was holding out a script. "Take it, my dear." His voice was sweet, sweet, and full of promise. And his fly was wide open and his cock stuck out, thick, red, angry-looking against the white of his underwear.

She said, "I'll come back when you're feeling better," and got her folder and went to the door. Where she fumbled with the lock before walking out.

She stopped at the Thrifty Drugs corner of Laurel, and called her agent. He asked, "Is the audition over?"

"You could say that. The bastard's a flasher. A sit-behind-the-desk flasher."

"That so?" Jugland said coolly, and chuckled. "You run into all kinds in this business. Well, better luck next time." He didn't ask for details.

"I'm going to report him to SAG," she said, to see what would happen.

"Yes, you could do that. But he'd deny everything, and you'd blow a day's scale."

"A day's scale?" She was burning now, but holding back to draw him out as much as possible. "For what?"

"For today. Just so you won't feel you've wasted your time." He paused. "He obviously doesn't have a project. At least that's my educated guess."

"And does he pay *you* scale?"

"I'm busy now, Cecily."

"I'll bet you are! Fixing up more *producers* with whatever suits their turn-ons!" Her voice shook with outrage. "Margolin is a creep, pure and simple. But

you . . . you're my agent! The one person I'm supposed to be able to trust!"

"Hey, don't give me any shocked-maiden routines.
You've seen and handled more cock behind desks and
on beds . . ."

"Even if that's true, you've still no right to pimp me
out! I'll go to the union!"

"You do that, baby. Margolin and I will stand together, and we'll see whose rep gets dragged through
the mud. We'll see whose son won't be able to show his
face at school."

She hung up, so mad she was crying.

On the freeway she let the Jag out, hitting eighty.
She made it to Las Virgenes in about half an hour,
and then to the narrow private road which dipped and
turned past clumps of trees and leveled out to reveal
the two-story, mansion-like building painted a soothing pastel green. To keep the nuts quiet, she supposed; though that and everything else had failed with
Teresa.

At three, she sat in the anteroom while the skinny
male receptionist called the doctor's office, looking
out at her through the glass panel, staring straight at
her boobs without seeming to know it.

"Your sister's available now," he finally said, and got
up and opened the metal door. "Have a nice visit." As
usual, he waited until she'd walked the length of the
fifty-foot hallway before returning to his office.

A female attendant opened the second door, which
was heavy wire mesh. After that, there was another
hall, this one lined by regular wooden doors. And the
rooms in this better-than-average asylum looked like
regular rooms, except they were really maximum security cells for violent patients, with barred windows,
special soft-plastic walls, and signs warning that no
sharp instruments or utensils were to be brought in.

"Hey," Teresa said, as Cecily stopped in the open
door. A nurse was inside with her, a big woman with

meaty arms sitting on a chair near the window. Teresa sat on the bed, hair messy, wearing the drab gray dress all the patients wore. She was two years older than Cecily and they'd once looked and lived much alike . . . except that Teresa hadn't been able to stand the memory of pop's visits to their bedroom that terribly long year she was fifteen; the year that ended with Teri threatening suicide.

"Hey," Cecily answered, and didn't move from the doorway. Teri insisted on her privacy. When she'd began to slip, she'd shown it by attacking anyone who entered any room she was in without first knocking or asking her permission, because pop had forced his way into the room they'd shared, breaking the lock when they'd tried to keep him out. And done what their mother still refused to admit he'd done, what no one had ever known he'd done, until Teresa fell apart and tried to kill her boyfriend, thinking it was pop, telling the police it was pop.

So it finally caught up with the old man. Pop shot himself, after Cecily confirmed Teresa's story. She hadn't wanted to—Christ, the shame!—but she couldn't let everyone in that lousy North Hollywood police station think Teresa was crazy for no reason at all. Even then, it was only because of an experimental team of social workers monitoring the San Fernando Valley police that Teresa got out of jail. She was transferred to Restwell for what the psychologist who headed the family sex team said was, "Hopefully, a short stay; perhaps a year." Since Teresa had put her boyfriend in the hospital with three knife thrusts to the stomach, that didn't sound too bad.

Except it didn't work out as the psychologist hoped. It didn't work out at all. Teresa had been going mad a long time, and when she slipped she slipped all the way. She got worse, not better. She'd been here four years now.

"Could we have some privacy?" Teresa asked the nurse.

The big woman looked at Cecily. Cecily was a little scared, but nodded. Teresa had put a fist into her mouth three years back. Luckily, it broke only the two rabbity uppers that she'd always wanted capped.

The nurse squeezed past where Cecily still stood in the doorway. She'd be waiting in the hall close by.

"C'mon in, babydoll," Teresa said, soon as the nurse was gone. "Close the door. My, you look nice. I was gonna wash my hair, use a little lemon rinse for blond effect." She shrugged, frowning. "They gave me some goddamn hassle or other, I don't know. Sometimes I think I should bust outa here and go home. I mean back to the farm with you and your hubby. You divorced yet, baby?"

Cecily stepped inside, leaving the door open a crack.

"Shut it, for Chrissake!" Teri snapped.

Cecily quickly complied. "Can I sit down?"

"Well, what the hell else you gonna do, stand there and pee?"

Cecily went to the chair the nurse had been using. Teri turned to face her, bringing her legs up on the bed. Such great legs, better than Cecily's. Such a great face, too, when it hadn't been twisted in rage so much of the time. Bitter lines now around the mouth. And deep ones in the forehead.

"Well," Teresa said, "what about the divorce?"

She asked that every so often. She'd liked living with Cecily, Johnny, and Andy that month she'd returned to the San Joaquin Valley from L.A. to rest up. She remembered what she liked.

"It's final," Cecily said.

"Oh, poor Johnny. Does he cry about it?"

"Not any more. He's a big boy."

"But a four- or five-year-old . . ."

A bad day with bad lapses of memory. More and more such days lately. Cecily hadn't brought Johnny here in two years. Didn't dare. It would shake up the kid. Shake up his aunt, too, if she frightened him and saw it.

Quite suddenly Teresa said: "Wait a minute. Who're you kidding? Johnny can't be four or five. Last time I saw him he must've been at least eight!" She leaped up, face suffused with rage.

Cecily tried to say, "*I* never said he was four or five," but Teresa was shouting now, drowning her out.

"His tenth birthday party, dammit! He brought me cake! And *that* was a hell of a long time ago! Why're you lying to me, you fucking tramp! Just because I'm in this stinking . . ."

The big nurse opened the door. Teresa wet her lips and sat down. "Okey-doke. Tranquil-time, Rose."

The big nurse said: "Leave the door open, Miss Bajorka."

Teresa waited until she was gone. By then her rage was gone, too. "They won't call me by my stage name. You remember it, don't you, sis?"

"Teri Barker. Great name for a movie marquee."

"Yours isn't bad either. One of the few good things about your marriage, right?"

"Right." Big sister was clearing up fast now. "Have you been sleeping well? Eating?"

Teri glanced at the open door. "The food here is killing me. Look at my stomach. Starches mostly, and they won't get me fresh fish or whole-grain rice." She put her head down. Her shoulders shook. When she looked up again, Cecily could see the teen-aged Teresa weeping after one of their father's visits. Huge round tears. Mouth clamped clown-tight with grief. Eyes glazed with pain, with rage.

"Oh, honey," Cecily whispered. "Don't."

"Help me," Teresa sobbed. "Get me outa here. Why hasn't Huey been to see me?" (That was the wounded boyfriend, long gone from the scene.) "Why haven't you brought Johnny? Where's mom? Did she kill herself like I dreamed it? Why don't you move closer to here so we can be like we used to?" She wept, glancing fearfully at the door, putting a hand over her mouth, shaking, suffering, tearing Cecily's heart out.

Against repeated instructions, against her own instincts for survival, Cecily went to the bed, sat down beside her sister, took her in her arms, rocked her, wept with her . . . and stayed tense, ready for flight.

"Tell you what's the worst," Teri finally said, drawing away and wiping her eyes and nose with her sleeve. "Not getting any. The old finger just doesn't do the job. It's been weeks now, maybe months."

It had been four years, unless the beanpole receptionist or another male attendant had sneaked in here. But it wasn't likely anyone would take a chance with Teresa Bajorka. She was bad news for sex partners.

Teresa was asking why Cecily didn't bring her a blind date so they could get it on the next visit.

"I don't think the doctor wants that, hon. I think it'd be better if you wait until you get your release."

"Bullshit!" The voice was suddenly raging again.

Cecily stood up. "Got to get home now. See you next week. Oh, forgot, I brought you some issues of *Variety* like you asked." She was backing toward the door. "Left them in the car. I'll give them to the nurse."

"Bullshit! Bullshit! I'll never get my release! I'm here for life because I killed mom and pop!"

"Mom's coming to visit as soon as I can drive her." (But mom refused to visit, saying her daughters had told "filthy lies" about their father. Mom lived with the hired hand and drank and straightened out only for Johnny's summer vacations.)

"You rotten liar! You want me in here so I can't compete for parts with you! I was always the most talented, the most beautiful, and you want me out of the way!"

The big nurse and a male attendant appeared in the

doorway. Teresa grew quiet and watchful. The male attendant began to move forward. The nurse said: "Matt . . ."

But it was too late. He'd come in without knocking or asking permission. Teresa launched herself at him, screaming.

Cecily flattened against the wall, shaking her head, moaning.

Teresa's nails gouged, raked, and before the attendant could grab her, he was bleeding from the left eye and cheek. The nurse rushed to help him, getting behind Teresa and pulling her head back by the hair with both hands.

"Please, please," Cecily whispered.

The three were struggling near the door, Teresa screaming endlessly. Another male attendant arrived, and they shoved Teresa face down on the bed, immobilizing her. The nurse disengaged, saying: "I'll get a hypodermic."

Cecily followed her into the hall. Her voice shook. "Be kind. She's been hurt so much already."

The nurse kept going. "We try to keep her off sedatives for your weekly visits. We're aware you're all she has. We want her to understand you're there, but this can't go on."

So Teresa would again become the dull-eyed zombie who rarely spoke. The tranquilizers and stronger medication would be used seven days a week instead of six.

Maybe that was best, she thought, driving away from the soft green mansion. Maybe best of all would be death for big sister.

The Warren chick showed at six. Bub served her and Fred cold ham, salad, and fresh melon slices in the dining room. Fred sent back the bottle of white wine, asking for iced tea instead, so Bub knew he was planning to slip her a Quaalude, which was dangerous as hell when mixed with alcohol. Q's—also called Lu-

lus, Ludes, Lullabys, Sopors, The Love Drug, and Free Pussy, on the street—did a job. It was a sedative hypnotic with strong barbiturate action that killed inhibitions, opening the subject to all sorts of suggestions. Like a cock in the mouth or up the ass.

Bub slipped the boss two joints while serving coffee in the living room. Maybe Freddy wouldn't need the Q, since they began laughing it up pretty good on the pot.

When Bub came to refill their coffee cups, they were using both phone lines, inviting friends to a birthday party for Don Baylis.

After an hour of phone calls, when Bub came in to empty the ashtrays and to check things out, Fred gave him the pill-gulping sign, and said: "The lady'll have some fresh coffee, Bub. To clear her head."

Bub thought it insane, what with that big porno flick hinging on what Don Baylis decided could or couldn't be done with his book. The chick was no dumb hayseed fresh out of backwater Kansas or North Dakota or wherever the dreamers came from to Hollywood. She was experienced and wise in the ways of the game. She'd know she'd been had; it took about eight hours to sleep off a Lulu, and the odds were strong she'd tried them on her own.

Bub knelt to the under-sink cupboard and the metal box held by a magnetic lid to a pipe behind the drain. Nothing that would fool a full-scale drug bust, but such busts rarely came down in Beverly Hills. This was good enough to keep the curious from getting anything on old Frederick Gower.

He pulled the box free and opened it to find the bottle of Robaxins, a mild muscle relaxant and sedative which, even with the pot, wouldn't do more than make the chick's arm, leg, stomach, and ass-hole muscles looser than normal. Without booze to complicate things, her mind wouldn't be too affected . . . which wasn't the case with Quaaludes.

He put the box back and stood up, looking at the pill in his hand. A fucking big tablet, maybe a half-inch in diameter, almost a quarter-inch thick. Q's were the exact same size and color, so he should be able to get away with a substitution. He'd done it before.

He heard Freddy coming, and tensed, If the boss-man examined the pill, really looked at it, he'd know he was being conned. For while Q's and Robaxins were identical on the scored side, on the other the Q's were marked RUREH and the Robaxins AHR.

Bub closed his hand over that upturned AHR as Freddy entered, sporting an uncharacteristic hard-on, which with *his* size pushed the hell out of his fly front. "Can you imagine?" he said, grinning. "Like a kid up on Mulholland!" And he grabbed himself.

Bub's eyebrows rose. The boss-man was really flipped over Cecily chick. Still, when Fred asked for the Q, he said: "It's a dumb play. This isn't the right chick to put on Lude; not Baylis's heavy steady."

"I'm going to make her a star. Why shouldn't she do anything I ask?"

"Right. So *ask*, like you did yesterday. Why use magic and risk problems?"

"Because she'll go a straight fuck, like yesterday. Maybe even cooler. Her turn-on's almost over and it might be the last trick and I want a lot more than straight fucking. I want to get head, go up her ass, and see you do the same! Then a session with the belt." He swallowed hard and held out his hand. "Plus film."

Bub bent to the under-sink cupboard and went through the motions of finding a Quaalude. He glanced up once to see Freddy smiling, touching him-self, looking out the window to the tennis court. When he straightened, he handed Freddy the pill and turned quickly to the electric percolator. He poured a steam-ing cup and turned again. Freddy was looking at the pill.

Bub held out the cup, planning to say he'd grabbed

the wrong bottle, but Fred dropped in the pill and stirred vigorously. He said no when Bub offered *him* a cup. "I'll have brandy from the sideboard," he said, and left.

And so once again, Bub realized, he the black man was the smarts for Freddy the white man, who couldn't control his sexuality. Quite a switch on the old stereotypes of black and white, and not the first time he'd made that switch.

The time Freddy threw an afternoon pool party for a small group and one of the men, divorced and on a Sunday visit with his son, brought the sixteen-year-old along. The kid was swish, and Freddy got drunk and tried to sixty-nine with him upstairs with the father wandering around the living and dining rooms. Bub sent the kid downstairs with a kick in the ass, and held Freddy on the bed, talking about what the father—a criminal lawyer with heavy connections—could do to him, until part of it seeped through.

And the time Freddy'd brought home a knockout redhead from Vegas, early twenties, and her name rang a bell, though she kept saying she was "just a college girl." She wouldn't play properly, so Freddy decided to go the magic route. It was hunch more than anything else that made Bub call a friend who was with the *Examiner* and ask what the name Angie Pennington meant. The friend identified her as the wife of a very jealous Southern governor who was suspected of doing away with a previous suitor, using a hit man on the Highway Patrol, no less. Bub had waited until Freddy had gone to the john, then told the knockout Freddy had the new, durable, Asian clap. Exit redhead.

Now, he heard laughter from the living room. He started for his own room to prepare the camera and wait for the signal buzzer, when Fred hit that fucking bell Bub hated—little tabletop ding-ding the boss used when he was impressing company.

He strode to the living room. Fred must've been trying to set her up for orgying, because he had her laid back on the couch with both her tits out, and they were *champions*. Bub watched Fred suck on one, and said: "You rang, sir?"

The chick's eyes flew open and she tried to stuff the boobs back into her dress. Freddy said: "Hey, baby, Bub's family. And he's also very good."

Cecily chick laughed a little and settled for keeping her hands over the champions. Her eyes were glazed from the pot and Robaxin; she accepted Fred's kiss, and his pulling her hands away. She was stoned solid; she was ready, but no slave as she'd have been on Q. Freddy wouldn't notice until she started saying no.

Fred raised his head. "Bub, my man, would you turn down the sheets, light the lamps, and retire so the master and his wench can get it on?"

Bub nodded and went upstairs. He got the room ready, which meant making sure the cluster of over-head lights was on. Not that he couldn't film with less light: the new infra-red-style loads didn't need much lighting. He then moved the paintings so that the view-slots were free. He could get side and foot-of-the-bed shots now, even if Cecily refused to continue when he entered the room. Some chicks froze when he came in, but most were either turned on by it, or tamed by magic.

He wet his lips as he came downstairs, hearing them laughing again, almost tasting those 38's. "Sorry, Mr Baylis," he muttered. "I wouldn't've, believe me."

He was in his room, loading the camera and smoking a roach, when he heard them start up the stairs. He settled back in his armchair, sucking reefer, and it wasn't long before the buzzer—its button positioned behind Fred's headboard—sounded behind his own.

Bub dragged twice more, dumped the roach, and took off his shoes. He unzipped his fly and pulled his semirigid penis through the opening. Then he picked up the camera and went through the kitchen to the stairs.

He slowed three steps from the second-floor landing, because sometimes Fred forgot to close the master bedroom door, and the chick might not be happy about a black servant with his dingle dangling holding a movie camera. One blond had grabbed a blanket and fled, hiding out by the pool, thinking it was rape-time. Took them an hour to find her, and another hour to reassure her, and by then the magic had worn off and she'd gone home.

This time the door was closed. Bub went into the adjoining guest room and left the lights off. The eight-inch slot glowed in the dark. He drew up the chair, sat down, and put eye and camera to the slot. Freddy was standing with Cecily chick, kissing her, holding her dress up, and massaging her thighs. At Bub's tap on the wall, Fred turned her around, ass to the camera, and pulled her red lace panties down.

"Action," Bub muttered, and concentrated on another epic. Damn, she was a lot of woman! He just had to squeeze his cock a little.

He had a fifty-foot cartridge, and when the warning light flickered red, he again tapped on the wall. Freddy had already done a missionary and was now eating the chick. He was too far gone to hear anything; the chick wouldn't have heard an atom bomb; and Bub was about to stop filming.

Couldn't be helped. He just hoped he didn't miss the chick's orgasm. Freddy treasured those.

He ran out of film and the chick was still grinding away into Freddy's mouth. Bub reached to the night table and the extra cartridges. He unloaded and loaded quickly, and twisted back to the slot. The chick was still moaning, grinding, and he figured he had time to use the hall slot.

He ran out on stockinged feet, moved the round mirror aside on its sliding clip, and focused the camera. Not too good an angle. Freddy hadn't turned her enough from a straight up-and-down bed position, which meant Bub was getting too much of Freddy's ass and not enough of his mouth and the chick's reaction.

So back to the guest room, where he used maybe twenty more feet before Cecily heaved up, clutched Freddy's head and socked her groin into his mouth. It was rough action. Freddy was trying to pull those hands away, when she went limp.

Bub stopped filming while they used the bathroom. When they came back, Freddy got her on her stomach and began kissing and stroking her big white ass. Bub started filming again. Freddy was keeping his right hand out of the action, holding it up and away from flesh and bedding, which meant he'd sneaked some lubricant onto it—a heavy, scented oil especially formulated for anal intercourse. Which also meant the chick might soon surprise him.

She was lying quietly, head turned away from the camera. Freddy lowered his right hand, inserting a lubricant-dripping finger into her rectum. She grunted, turned her head, murmured: "Hey, man, what . . . ?"

Freddy removed his finger, stroking off the rest of the lubricant on his penis. He spoke softly to what he thought was a Lulabyed chick. "Gonna fuck your beautiful ass, baby. Been dreaming of it. Just loosen up." He was raising her with a hand under her belly, was pushing his long tool between her cheeks, was groaning, "Oh baby, baby."

It looked like she was going to play, and Bub ran for the hall and a better angle. By the time he got there, the chick was rolling over, rubbing her eyes.

"No more, Freddy."

"Do as I say, Cecily." He was stroking her full thighs, hands shaking with excitement . . . and Bub had to steady his own hands on the camera. "You'll get the biggest kick out of it. Think, baby. Think of my cock going up your tight ass. Think of the lovely *ache*. Think of being tickled off." He lunged forward, laughing, pushing her down, turned her over. He began to pull her ass back up, saying, "You're gonna love it, sweetheart."

She tore free, half fell off the bed, pushed herself back on the carpet to the wall. "Stop calling me sweetheart! *Don* calls me that!"

Freddy stared at her. "You've either got the nervous system of a whale, or that Lude . . ." He shook his head. "C'mon! I want your ass!"

He was coming off the bed after her. She got up, backing away. "You're crazy! I'm getting dressed." But the pot and Robaxin regained hold; she staggered and didn't know where her clothes were.

Freddy decided to change tactics. "Bub, come in here!"

Bub sighed and stuffed his cock back in his pants because this was no longer turn-on time; it was black-mail time. Well, that worked, too, so he left the fly unzipped.

He came into the bedroom and began filming the naked chick as she stared at the camera.

"You get it from the start?" Fred asked.

Bub nodded, sorry for the chick. Her expression was really something.

"If you ever show Don, he'll kill the three of us, but you two first!"

"I wouldn't show it all, baby. Just some blowups of you with a cock in you . . . could be anybody's. But it won't come to that. Let's lie down and talk about it." Freddy reached for her arm.

She shook her head, but let him draw her back to the bed.

"Get on your knees, momma. It'll feel great, believe me. And afterward I'm going to reward you, I swear, with a part any actress would give her soul to get." He laughed, stoned pretty good himself on that fine mountain-grown marijuana and twenty-year-old brandy. "Bub, try filming the action while Cecily blows you."

The chick moved groggily, unwillingly, turning her ass up for his giant tool. She opened her mouth as Bub kneeled on the edge of the bed, maneuvering his open fly and partially erect penis in front of her. He felt her breath on his dick, stiffened immediately, and began filming as Freddy shoved.

The chick raised her head and groaned. "We're shit," she said, her voice full of pain. "But I'm the worst and I wish I were dead."

Bub got off the bed, put down the camera, and zippered his fly as he walked around to where he could grab Freddy. He dragged him off the chick and said: "Get dressed, Miss Warren."

Freddy tried to shove him away. "What the hell do you think you're doing? If you want to play fucking square, split! Just don't get between me and my pleasure!"

Bub still held him by both arms, looking into his face—a wild-eyed face, the dark pupils dilated by pot and alcohol. But the boss-man's penis was wilting. Bub murmured: "Millions, baby. You'll blow it."

"The hell I will! I'll *help* it!"

"No, man. When you make someone hate you, you blow it. Just look at her."

Freddy's voice suddenly turned childlike, querulous. "But I want her, Bub. Why should she hate . . . I really . . ." He shook Bub's hands off his arms, and turned to Cecily. She was covering herself with a blanket, looking at him, and the look wasn't good.

"But I want you. Maybe more than I ever . . ."

She shook her head violently.

Freddy took a deep breath. "Yeah," he said. He waved his hands a little, smiled a little. "Sorry, Cecily. Mixed angel dust in my joint. Never again."

Bub said, "Your clothes, Miss Warren," and pointed at the chair beside the dresser.

She went there. "Thanks, Bub. And what's that whispered business about *millions?*"

The bad scene was ended. She'd forget the arm-twisting, the rape-style push toward sodomy and orgy, because it hadn't come off.

She had her panties on, had just fastened her brassiere, was stepping into her shoes. And Jesus, if he ever got another chance at her . . .

She looked at him, and he dropped his eyes.

Freddy said: "Maybe the villain should leave the star-crossed lovers alone? Bub deserves it, after what he had to watch."

She said: "I agree. And with his cool, he can get it a dozen places a night."

Which was compliment and good-bye in one. Bub took himself, his camera, and his erection downstairs. He was surprised to see it was only nine-thirty.

He put on his shoes, went to the kitchen, and got the metal box from under the sink. He was out of rolled joints, and had just started to load a clay pipe when Freddy yelled for him.

"C'mon, Bub! We got business to discuss! We need your advice!"

Yeah, *free* advice. He lit the pipe, inhaled, and began walking. He liked old Freddy, wanted to help him in any way he could—but as an equal, not a servant.

Which made Albert and Brains and getting his own hundred grand plus more important than ever. If he lived with Freddy after that, it would be because he wanted to, not because he had to. If he cooked and served up meals and orgied with Freddy, it would be because it was a pleasure, not a duty. And it *was*, mostly . . .

He stopped thinking. He didn't believe in going over and over things. Like memories. Like childhood. Like Sylvia and Carter, who were his mother and father back in New Orleans, only Sylvia was dead. Carter still fucked the girls at seventy-seven or -eight, still plied his pimp's trade, still held Bub in contempt for thinking of women as human. "They's not *people,* Burleigh. Not your gramma, not your momma, not any of 'em. You keep 'em in line with your prick or your fist or your money, depending on if they work for you or they related to you."

He was in the living room. Cecily was on the couch, looking beat. Freddy was pacing up and down, a snifter full of brandy in his hand, and stopped to say: "I offered her the lead, and she thinks the whole thing's a gag!"

"So did I," Bub said, sitting down beside the chick, "the first I heard of it." He wiped the image of her animal self from his mind. He concentrated on the person behind the big gray eyes, whom Carter said didn't exist. It wasn't easy for Bub Kane. Because for him, as for Freddy, orgasm was what made life bearable; all the rest was side orders. "But he means it. It could be the making of your writer-man's fortune. Yours, too, if you do what you have to do in front of a camera . . . what you did upstairs."

She didn't seem the blushing type, but her face turned pink. "That's like *Deep Throat.*"

"No way!" Freddy said indignantly. "There are no stars in shit like that! No four-million budget! No bestselling novel, and top scriptwriter. No major studio. No solidly professional director, cameramen, technicians, and supporting cast. No national distribution and advertising. Much bigger than *Last Tango,* and you can't call that . . ."

"They never really *did* it in *Last Tango in Paris.*" She shook her head. "My God, doing it in front of the whole world! What about my son?"

"Don never mentioned a child."

"An inside joke," she muttered. "But . . . in front of my family. My mother. Donny."

"And when it's over, you'll be a star! An international celebrity! Because you'll play opposite some-

one like Newman, like Redford! Because this flick
should break a hundred million easy! Afterwards,
you'll get your pick of starring roles and never have
to show your ass again."

"Your boobs, maybe," Bub said, to break the shouting
match.

Cecily looked at him, and suddenly laughed. So did
Fred. Bub said: "If you don't take it, Miss Warren,
there're a thousand women in this town who will."

She nodded slowly. She asked if Fred had any spe-
cific male star in mind. Her eyes widened and she said,
"No!" when Freddy sprang Rob Dennings on her.
"Would he really?"

Freddy nodded.

"Could he really? I mean, he was in those Bible pictures when he was a baby." She covered her mouth.
"He must be sixty!"

Freddy spoke sharply: "Closer to fifty. And I can
tell you stories ... ."

She said, "Even if I wanted to," and she already did.
Bub saw the dream of sudden stardom shining from
her eyes, her entire face. "Don would never let me.
And he'll never let his book be filmed that way."

Freddy drank some more. "Yes, he will, if you make
it a condition of continuing to see him."

She waited.

"You tell him how much it means to you—the
whole bit about career and last chances and never having to do anything like it again. The truth, Cecily;
what you feel in your gut. He should come around.
But if he's still opposed, you say, 'I can't love a man
who stands in the way of what I want most out of life,'
and walk out. He'll give in."

"And if he doesn't?"

Freddy shrugged, and turned back to the sideboard
and more brandy.

Bub said: "You can always come back to him after a
week or two. Nothing's forever in Hollywood. Not

marriage. Not divorce. Certainly not walking out on a man."

She thought a moment. "But Don isn't from Hollywood; not even a little bit."

"Sure, sure," Freddy said impatiently. "Just give it a try. And I'll put a hundred fifty thousand in his hands and the dream of millions in his mind. He wants big money as much as anyone else."

She said, "I really don't think so," but then she asked when he was going to talk the project to Baylis.

"Tomorrow morning."

She rubbed her arms as if she were suddenly cold, and said she had to be going.

Fred fell into the big armchair, waving a hand, drinking. Bub showed her to the door.

Back in the living room, Bub said: "How about a snack?"

Freddy shook his head. "Gotta think," he muttered. "Goodnight."

Bub went to the kitchen and turned on the countertop Sony. He finished his pipe, but somehow didn't take off. He felt . . . rejected. Dumb, sure, but that's how it was tonight—the black boy banished to the servants' quarters.

Which only made him more determined than ever to pull off that big robbery, to get that big hunk of bread, to gain independence.

Malibu was a section of beach front and backup property seemingly like many others along America's vast coastline. Malibu was houses, the ones on the beach looking rather shabby from the outside, closed against the Pacific Coast Highway's heavy traffic by solid walls and thick front doors, wood and paint weathered within a year by sea wind and air. Malibu was far more impressive houses in the Colony, on the cliffs, back in the hills with ocean views.

Malibu was also a millionaire preserve, though it

didn't always look it, a place where one could own beach along the treasured California coastline. And Rob Dennings owned his piece of beach: joggers could go by near the surf and lovers could stroll along hand in hand, but no one could camp on his sand, his rise, the warm whiteness leading to what was the true front of his house, a deep redwood sundeck.

Not that he had ever chased anyone off the beach in his seven years' ownership. Not that there were more than a few a year to chase. Not that he didn't revel in the faces shocked by sudden recognition, the pointed fingers, the squeals and shouts of, "Hey, Rob!" when he was recognized sunning on his deck.

Rob Dennings was fifty-eight—fifty-six with the help of a long-ago doctored driver's license—and was in excellent shape, if he did say so himself, except for those goddamn bleeding hemorrhoids, and recent stomach cramps caused, the doctor said, by nerves.

He'd been a star since the DeMille-style epic, *Prophets*, in which he'd played Jeremiah, with the help of considerable makeup since he'd only been nineteen. He'd stalked his tall, blue-eyed, fair-haired, Anglo-profiled way through a half-dozen Biblical blockbusters, ignoring the reviewers' jibes about his "anti-Semitic looks" and his "acting ability, or lack of it," to quote that bastard in *The New York Times*. The public had adored him.

He'd been a matinee idol in the days when that meant two major films a year, and he'd made it early enough to carry over into today's industry, which had barely two, three major films a year for *all* the stars to compete for. The other pictures were dominated by the freak-rock stars, the kids, the TV-transfers, who worked for percentages and pieces of foreign countries and every conceivable thing but cash money.

And he was slipping in today's industry. The few big pictures were being packaged by independent producers with studio or private backing, and they considered him a bad risk because of the disappointing grosses on his last two features, both of which he had directed as well as starred in.

He walked from the living room and the gas-log fire out onto the deck, sighing, determined not to think of failure. The sky was alive with moon and stars. The sea rolled darkly, quietly. Tomorrow would be good beach weather, according to the newspaper. He would swim all morning, driving out the devils.

Joy-Joy, his latest companion, his Oriental belly dancer, called: "I'm knocking with five points, honey."

He didn't turn from the ocean. He didn't turn from what he couldn't reject tonight, from what had been growing increasingly clear: He was slipping badly.

It terrified him. He'd come up from nothing, and been a *god*. Jesus, these kids didn't understand what fame was, what high living was! He'd spent on four wives and every conceivable self-indulgence. And he was near-broke, except for the house (which would soon be worth a million) and a lousy eighty-grand savings account. Out of more than twenty million in earnings, much of it during low-income-tax years!

All this made Freddy Gower's call important when Freddy's calls had rarely been important before. He'd used Freddy as a promo man for a time. He'd considered a few of the scripts Freddy had been peddling the past three or four years, but never done one. He'd thought of Freddy as small time . . . though he'd thought of everyone that way from his godlike position. Everyone but heavyweights like Gable and Cooper . . . Christ, they were both *dead!* Why did he have to run dead men's names through his mind? There were plenty of living heavyweights! There was Wayne, and Mitchum, and . . .

Joy-Joy called again. He raised his voice. "I'm thinking, dammit!"

She shut up.

Time to trade her in anyway. There was the script girl he'd met at Universal when taping a guest spot on a TV special. She'd come on straight and strong—said she was looking to live with someone "special" for a while—and she was total knockout.

Goddamn it, ass wasn't the order of business to be considered! Work was! Getting back on top was!

And Freddy, sounding stoned, had said tomorrow he'd put something into Rob's hands that would make him *"Number one!* I swear to you, Rob, it'll put you on top of the whole fucking film world!"* He'd refused to explain further; was coming over tomorrow afternoon.

Rob went back into the house. It wasn't quite eleven, but he was depressed, and when he was depressed he wanted to sleep. He didn't invite Joy-Joy to share his bed, thinking she'd take the front bedroom as when he was ill or she was into her period. But she came to him, fresh from the shower, as he was slipping under with the help of a Valium. He mumbled: "I'm sweaty, tacky, babe. Better forget it."

She didn't forget it. She was a short, stacked Eurasian who'd played a bit part in his last film, *Caravans East,* and hung around until he finally split with Adrienne, his fourth wife. Then she moved herself into his house along with her lovely ivory skin, her great ass—which was one hundred percent Chinese, she said—and the one quality he knew he'd miss, because it was so rare, her snap pussy, that velvet milking machine that had kept him satisfied for five months.

She was pulling down his pajama bottoms; she was into her foreplay routine, murmuring about "your great big beautiful tool that's going to stab me to death," and he began to respond because he loved to think of himself as big when he wasn't nearly as big as he wished he were. It had always seemed he'd been cheated. He had everything else in super amounts—height, shoulders, looks, voice—so why the hell not a super penis? Instead, he had six and a half inches, in full throb.

Enough, certainly, and Joy-Joy worshiped it. So had almost every woman he'd ever bedded. And now Joy-Joy was beginning to lick it, to lick under it, around his sweaty testicles, murmuring unintelligibly, obscenely. Finally, she deep-throated him.

It took a while to get to full throb, full hard. The bitch knew the second it happened, and stretched out alongside him, pulling him onto her, putting him into her. She grabbed his ass as he grabbed hers, squirmed until he was fully sheathed, and began milking him, those cunt muscles stroking independently of her hip movements.

He came, hard enough, but not as hard as he once had with Joy-Joy.

She was bucking, gasping, and he gave her a few more jabs and lowered his weight full on her chunky body, knowing from long experience what she needed to come off properly.

He wanted to get right up and shower, but she held him tight, twisting a little, groaning a little. "Jeremiah, another hump for the whore of Babylon?"

He thought a moment. "My strength and my hope is perished from the Lord." Which got her laughing, and he was able to exit to the bathroom.

When he returned she was sleeping soundly. And now he was wide awake, wondering what Freddy had for him. The man had never come on this strong before. Must be something real; something he at least thought was real. But what? Another script? Another role? That wouldn't make him Number One. Had to be a ten-million budget, or more, and they were few and far between. And even one of those might not do it. *Caravans East* had ended at eight-million budget, and bombed.

For the past sixteen months, Rob had been offered nothing but the small stuff, the shit deals. Naturally, he'd turned them all down. But dammit to hell, he'd have to take something soon!

He went to the closet for his gray sweat suit. He put it on as he made his way to the deck and then the beach, tying the drawstring around his waist as he walked over cool sand to the ocean. He let his toes touch the surf; then turned north and began to jog.

He hadn't smoked in eight years, and his wind was excellent. He drank hardly at all, ate carefully, and exercised regularly, so his legs and stomach were hard and strong. But that tranquilizer he'd taken had his knees a little shaky, his mind a little foggy.

That-tranquilizer-he'd-taken was his current area of weakness. Where once it had been booze, butts and twenty-four-hour poker, now it was sleepless nights and Valiums. Plus occasional Quaaludes to knock out anguish over not being able to get back on the track, to avoid realization that he soon would cease being a star.

Being a star was all that mattered!

The thought was nothing new, but now it was phrased differently; now it was a matter of life and death. The thought hit him so hard, he stumbled and almost fell.

He was afraid to pursue it, shook his head to clear it of Valium, and sprinted for perhaps a hundred feet before settling back into a jog.

He thought of 1936; of Utah and the apple orchard where he'd been working and sleeping. Of that frosty morning and Dayle Cowper saying he was going to Hollywood to write and produce movies. "C'mon along with me, kid, and *fuck* apples!"

They'd left the way they'd come, hopping a freight, the only way to travel in those hard, hard times. Cowper, who was thirty to Rob's seventeen, had fucked more than apples . . . he'd fucked Rob, three times in the dark, cold freight train, promising meals from the surprisingly thick wad of bills taped to his side.

In Los Angeles, they'd stayed with a married cousin of Cowper's, who let them share a back bedroom in his house on Cherokee, almost country in those sleepy, orange-grove days. Cowper had used Rob's already mature body, and Rob had gone along for the food and shelter, and for the leadership which Dayle Cowper provided. The man was a mover, a wheeler-dealer, and was soon established in the writing department at Paramount. And soon after that in the front office at Brunswick Studios. And then was able to pay off on his promises, shoving his friend into small parts in small pictures during the day, shoving his cock into Rob's aching ass and not-too-willing mouth at night.

The nighttime shoving came to an end when Rob learned he could land his own parts. He was a natural, tall and handsome and, with a new mustache, older-looking than his years. He went to dramatic school only *after* he'd handled his first supporting role at the tender age of eighteen. At nineteen came *Jeremiah* and fame and money and women, and Cowper had turned his attention to a muscular singer-dancer only too anxious to please a studio VP destined to become Brunswick's chairman of the board.

Dayle had died two years ago at the age of seventy-one. Rob had wept at his funeral. Because they'd climbed the heights together, and remained friends, remembering the apple orchard; remembering the hard Depression-era farm-boy lives before that—Dayle's in Kansas and Rob's in Missouri. They hadn't talked of the sex between them because Rob considered it dangerous to his reputation, and because Dayle was a man's man in every other way.

Christ, how he missed Dayle tonight! How he needed his old friend! His smart, powerful friend, who would have helped him with a movie, a deal . . .

He couldn't jog any longer, wasn't feeling well. That fucking tranquilizer had messed up his breathing. The pills—reds and yellows and Q's and V's, the shit he took to ease his fear of failure—would ruin his health if he didn't quit them. And he would, once he landed an important part; once he could work again, sleep normally again.

He turned back toward the house. He looked out at the sea, but saw instead the farm and his mother striding toward the kitchen where he sat with his grandmother. He saw her tall, raw-boned figure in the shabby mackinaw, her thick work shoes rising and falling as she walked from the fields where she'd put in an afternoon that would kill a modern woman. His mother, who'd been beautiful in the old pictures on the dresser.

He remembered; and he saw the way she had suddenly turned, swooping down on one of the chickens that pecked around the yard, never pausing in her stride, too busy working and feeding her sickly mother, her son, and herself to pause in her stride, wringing the neck of the stewing hen and throwing it aside to run in circles, spouting blood, until it fell dead. By then she was in the kitchen, slicing vegetables into the big pot, into which the chicken would also go.

He would always admire her, and grieve for her because she had died before he could do more than begin to repay her.

She'd been the last of family. When she went, there was no one.

He walked along the dark beach, grieving for his lost family, his lost friend. There was no one to help him; no one to see him as son or friend, maybe not even as human. Only fans now, or ex-fans. All alone on the face of the earth . . .

The next day, when Fred described his *Galt's Island* concept, being so alone was suddenly an advantage.

Three

Friday, May 6,
and Saturday, May 7

Don drove up to Freddy's house at nine-thirty, where
a red-jacketed car-park boy took the Mercedes further
along Bedford, lined on both sides this night by expensive automobiles, the tip-off to a Beverly Hills
party. He walked slowly up the drive, hearing music
and laughter, preparing himself to act surprised, as per
Freddy's instructions, when the crowd shouted Happy
Birthday.

He was alone, not because Cecily had to be among
the greeters, the surprisers, but because they'd had
three bitter conversations about that incredible *Galt's
Island* concept . . . that she wanted to star in!

They'd quarreled Wednesday afternoon, some hours
after Freddy had left, telling Don not to be hasty, to
"think it over, buddy," when there hadn't been anything to think over, no way he'd considered allowing
his book, his name, to be associated with hardcore
porn.

They'd quarreled again on Thursday, in bed, from
which she'd jumped, shouting that he was "never con-
cered with *others'* viewpoints!" She'd added that he
was killing her by blocking "this last big chance," and
run, crying and half-dressed, from his house.

Freddy had called that evening, asking if he could come over. Don had said no, using the excuse that he was feeling poorly, which he was. "All this tension, this stress . . ." So thoughtful Freddy had talked on the phone . . . and talked and talked. And some of the arguments had begun to convince Don: about the money, primarily. "If, as you say, your family back east will feel embarrassment, it'll be more than balanced by the tremendous growth of your estate, in which they have considerable interest, right? And if you insist—though I think it would be a terrible mistake, costing you hundreds of thousands in book sales and future movie deals—we can change the title and eliminate your authorship."

Don and Cecily had fought one last time, this morning, when she'd never even made it to his bed. She'd left after an intense half-hour, saying she couldn't love a man who cared so little about what she wanted most out of life, "Who obviously doesn't care if he never sees me again!"

So there it was. He'd been shocked to the core at the reversal of three years' mutual affection, consideration, and passion; at the possible end of so important a relationship.

What could the woman be thinking of, wanting such a part in such a picture, with Johnny in her life?

He'd been tempted a dozen times since Wednesday to ask what she intended to do about her son while she was fucking before all the world.

Bub opened the door. "Welcome to this house, Mr. Baylis. And Happy Birthday."

Don thanked him, shook his hand, looked through the archway to the jam-packed living room. "You know Cecily Warren, don't you, Bub? Is she here?"

"Arrived early to help set things up. Don't forget to act surprised."

Bub led him to the living room, stopping under the arch. He waved at the pianist, guitarist, and drummer over near the patio doors. The pianist was Freddy himself, taking a turn at his beautiful Schaaf baby grand. Freddy didn't look up, but the guitarist tapped him on the shoulder.

There was a drum roll, some shouted instructions, and people rushing in from other rooms. Finally, the idiocy culminated in about a hundred men and women, most of whom he didn't know, bellowing, *"Surprise!"* and singing "Happy Birthday to You."

Don did his part, grinning and shaking his head, and was hurtled into the crowd for introductions. A few minutes later, he spotted Rob Dennings's famous face across the room, bent to Cecily's rapt, attentive face. Two men he didn't recognize were part of the group.

"Berry and Pandaro," Freddy murmured, following the direction of his eyes, then introduced him to a large, heavy-set man Don had met at an earlier Gower bash or two.

"You remember Otis Daimler, Don. Otis might be scripting your novel."

They went on through the crowd, Don shaking hands and smiling a cover-all smile, knowing a few faces here and there, knowing not one *person*, really.

Freddy was introducing him to another face; a man whose photograph Don had once seen on page four of the *New York Daily News,* and whom he recognized as Freddy said, "Meet Sal Andro." Mr. Andro had been identified in the newspaper as a Mafia Hoodlum; he'd been indicted for assault with intent to kill, but had beaten the rap.

Andro's fleshy face was affability itself as he murmured: "Gladameetya. Happy Birthday. This is Giselle."

Don turned to a small blond downing a tall drink. She said, "Like in the ballet," and screamed laughter. She was bombed.

"Ah, yes, good to meet you two." And he slipped away, leaving Freddy behind.

By the time his host caught up with him, he'd been introduced to three theatrically beautiful girls in various stages of latest-mode undress. Two had their unrestrained breasts showing from the sides; the other had a third of her dramatic derrière exposed by a ridiculously low back. None of them appeared to speak English, confining their comments to nods and giggles and, in one case, after the man introducing them said, "L'isola dei Galt," to a sudden movement into Don with her watermelon breasts. The man smiled at this and said: "I am sorry. She has come for the Signore Pandaro. But the lady Tara," he gestured at the derrière, "she is free."

By then Freddy had him by the arm, leading him back toward "some important people we can't afford to miss."

Don said: "You mean more important than Andro? Ax murderers perhaps, or rapists?"

"For God's sake!" Freddy whispered, and grinned vibrantly in Andro's direction. "Keep it down! If he heard that . . ."

"He'd have us bumped off, correct?"

"Very funny. He's a sensitive guy when it comes to his . . . disadvantaged past."

Don chuckled, but Freddy wasn't joking, and the reason for this became clear in his next statement.

"He occasionally bankrolls a flick. That could be important to the new production company we're going to form once we've finished our end of *Galt's Island.* Which is to say, once the cameras begin to roll."

"*If* they begin to roll."

Freddy shrugged.

Two more stops for multiple introductions. Don wouldn't have been able to attach names to individuals for all those millions Freddy kept dangling in front of him. Waiters circulated with trays of appetizers; a bar on the street or east wall was doing a roaring business; the noise pollution, composed of voices shouting above the trio's music and other voices, was beginning to hurt him.

He stopped as Freddy tried to draw him to the bar for "a small glass of wine. You need to loosen up a little, and I've got your favorite Chambertin hidden away."

"I think I've had it for the moment. I'm going out to the pool for a breather." Freddy began to protest, and Don interrupted. "After all, this *is* my maiden outing."

"All right. But first pay your respects to Dennings and the others."

Don nodded.

"Good. I want to hear you turn down the biggest deal of your life." They began threading their way across the room to the west wall. "I want to hear you say no to millions. And please get one thing straight—I'm not talking about Cecily. If you say so, she's out."

"Aren't there any nonporn roles in this goddamn movie?"

"You know there are, but not for her. She fits the female lead, and the crooked secretary. Otherwise, it's walk-ons and two-liners. I guess I could have the scriptwriter expand one of those two-liners to a page, but Cecily won't be satisfied. She'll never forgive me."

"*You?* It's not you she'll blame."

"Yes," Freddy said. "I know. Think about it. She's been in love with you for three years. Three years of love in *this* town from a woman with *her* looks is something special. Don't lose it. Not for anything."

Don had no chance to reply, because they'd reached the group of Dennings, Cecily, Berry and Pandaro, which other guests, especially women, were attempting to join. Dennings, however, had a defense against outsiders. He concentrated intensely on one person, in this case Cecily, and so kept others away.

Freddy said: "Rob, this is our author, Don Baylis. You're talking to his fiancée."

Cecily said, "Hi, bun. Happy-happy." She stepped forward, pecked his cheek, and stepped back. She didn't really look at him.

Don looked at Rob Dennings; looked *up* at him because five-ten from six-four left much to be desired. And Dennings was bigger than just his height; a big man in every sense of the word, including his personality, what the kids called his *confront,* the way he appeared to dominate those around him. Especially the women, who pressed in from all sides.

Dennings's large, smooth hand engulfed his. Dennings's rich baritone said: "That's one hell of novel you wrote. I read it in ten straight hours, and wanted to go on reading."

Dennings's clear blue eyes, his gentle smile, his big, tanned face—a face Don had seen since childhood, a face that didn't seem old enough for the memories it evoked—enfolded him in warm intimacy. Unable to resist, he smiled back, even as he felt small, sick, and defeated. "Thanks. I couldn't begin to compliment *your* work, nor would it be necessary."

Dennings released his hand. "It's *always* necessary, Don, when speaking to an actor."

Freddy and Cecily laughed. Berry slapped the actor on the back. Pandaro, attempting some sort of parity, smiled and glanced around as if looking for someone. Dennings looked at Don . . . and Don suddenly realized he hadn't responded at all, was simply standing there. And nodded and chuckled and said: "Artists and their egos. We'll have to match stories some day."

Dennings turned to Cecily. "This is a very lovely woman you have, Don." He paused, and appeared to consider his words carefully. "If she becomes my leading lady, I'll be sure never to forget the warm and loving things she's said about you."

It was gracious, also clever, and yet Don was suddenly consumed by jealousy at the thought of this great male creature even kissing his girl, not to say making naked, public love to her!

The moment was so bad, he could handle it only one way, by turning to Cecily and saying, "But we're far from any such decision, aren't we, sweetheart?"

Sweetheart barely nodded; she turned to Dennings and smiled. Dennings was too sharp to return the smile. He said: "Well, you two will decide that in private. But I hope we'll have our author's cooperation in shaping the project."

Cecily finally gave Don her full attention, to see what his answer would be. She was absolutely stunning in a simple black sheath and narrow diamond choker, her dark hair curled slightly, falling to her shoulders, her extravagant body making that simple sheath shout with excitement. He didn't answer.

Freddy then introduced him to Money. He shook hands with Coleman Berry, short and stout, and with Umberto Pandaro, almost as tall as Dennings, almost as handsome, still not in the actor's league. Both men complimented him on his novel, and Berry said: "Filming it as it is written, in all its sexual honesty, will make movie history."

Don murmured: "We'll see." And all the time he was aware of Cecily, of men being aware of Cecily—of her beauty, her sensuality, her desirability.

He hadn't made love to her since Monday. He might never make love to her again. Which seemed the most tragic of possibilities, one he had to avoid at all costs.

And the cost was simply that he allow her to do what she wanted to do.

Looking at Dennings, that cost was impossibly high.

"Haven't you anything else to say?" Freddy prodded.

They were all watching him, waiting. He reached out and grasped Cecily's wrist. "Something important," he murmured, and pulled her to and through the patio doors, onto the flagstones and over to a table near the pool. Where she jerked free.

"That was impolite!"

"As impolite as burping? Or fucking on camera?"

She turned to the house.

"I have to tell you," he began, and was suddenly short of breath, and immediately afterward felt a series of flutterings, of arrhythmatic heartbeats that made him drop into a chair. He gasped for breath, trying to control the spasms, and when they'd diminished was ashamed of his weakness, his sickness. "Was it Hitler who said, 'There is only one disgrace: to be sick'? If so, the bastard was right."

She was facing him again. "Can I get you anything?" The question was cool, remote; an inquisitive acquaintance's, not a lover's.

"I have to tell you that I know about your son."

She paled. She sat down—not beside him, but across the table. Then, showing her usual resiliency, she shrugged. "Okey-doke. So what?"

"So what you're thinking of doing would absolutely destroy him! At the least, your ex-husband will demand and get custody."

She dropped her eyes. "It won't destroy him. I won't let it. He won't find out. He'll have to wait eight years before he's even old enough to see X-rated films. By then I'll be an established star. As for Andy, my ex, he's got a girlfriend with a son of her own and he wouldn't want . . ." She swallowed drily. "Maybe he too won't find out."

He gave a short laugh. Her eyes jerked up; her color rose. "It's possible!"

"Freddy's talking of a million-dollar advertising and promotion campaign over and above the production budget. And I believe it, since that's the handle for this project—making people know they're going to see a great movie star fucking in front of their eyes. So if

Rob Dennings actually allows himself to be used that way, if it goes the way Freddy believes it will, everyone in the *world* will know of it!"

"All right. And know of *me*. Fame, like nothing I ever dreamed of. To make me bigger than any of today's actresses." She leaned forward. "I want it. I'll handle my son, my mother, my ex, any way I can. But I want it."

He tried to argue, and couldn't find words. And she was full of words.

"Forget Johnny, for the moment. It'll be more than a year before we have to face screenings. We'll find ways to handle it, together. For now, think of me, of my life. If you know about Johnny, maybe you know about other things. Anyway, it's not as if I'm just a woman, just a mother, just your lover. I'm dying to become somebody! Somebody important."

Her voice, quiet enough until now, began to rise. "I swear I'd kill for success, if that's what it took! At first I was upset by the porno idea, but thinking it over, I realized that having sex on camera means nothing to me! It's just a way of getting what I want. Every woman uses sex to get what she wants. Besides, with Rob Dennings, it'll be art, it'll be epics, not shlock porn!"

He was exhausted. He'd rested all day for this party, this confrontation, and now, barely an hour after arriving, he was drained, pained, slumping in his chair. "But do you expect me to watch you and Dennings. . . . ?"

"You'll watch nothing. You won't be there when we shoot. And it's just work, like any movie love scene."

He probed her with his eyes.

"Besides, Freddy says my sex scenes will take about fifteen minutes, total, out of a two-hour movie."

He couldn't believe it was really going to happen; that he was going to allow it to happen. "When we saw *Deep Throat*, you couldn't believe a woman would allow herself to be photographed that way—not just nude, not just rolling around with a man, but taking his penis into her, sucking him, fucking him."

She shrugged, looking away.

"And Dennings . . . is he actually ready to sign?"

"Yes. They're waiting on you. And the budget's grown. You'll get five percent of five, maybe six million! They want to make the caper—the invasion of that gambling resort island—big-time. They're going for a name supporting cast. And your producer-percentage of profits . . ." She reached across the table to grasp his hand, her face glowing. "Freddy thinks he's got ten percent for the two of you! He thinks the picture will gross better than a hundred million! You could make five million dollars!" Her fingers meshed with his. "Five *million!*"

He began to catch some of her excitement, though he didn't believe the enormous figures. "Well, a guaranteed five percent of budget for the novel, up-front, is more than I've ever made before. If, as you say, it's grown to five or six million . . ." He smiled. "We'll get that place in Bel Air."

"And I'll buy the Rolls!"

They leaned toward each other; their lips touched.

She jumped up, clapping her hands, consumed by the dream of fame and riches; the Hollywood Dream, the American Dream. The dream he'd once shared, that had proven itself empty when his heart had threatened to stop. Then *people* had proven necessary—Cecily and his children and the letters from his oldest, closest friend, Mel. *People* had provided the means to his survival and recovery.

He wanted to tell her this . . . and knew there was no way.

"I want to be with you," she said. "But as your equal, not your thing. Most women are their men's things. I've been a thing to men all my life. Men like my husband, my agent, the casting directors and producers . . . you don't know!"

He said, "I can guess," needing her, giving in to her, unable to fight her any longer. "And I understand. You'd gain equality and superiority with success. Even such success."

"I'll make it success of the sort you'll be proud of, once I'm a name." She bent to him, pressed her face to his. "Like you with your books. You were reviewed as a dirty writer in your first two novels, you told me. Ahead of your time, you said." She straightened. "Well, this movie is ahead of its time right now. But by the time it's released, you and everyone else will accept it, admire it. And I'll bet that other stars will begin doing hardcore sex scenes in their movies; good stories with the love scenes the way they really are, the way honest writers write them. And critics will speak of you and me and Dennings as *pioneers.*"

"Maybe," he said.

"You'll tell Freddy to go ahead? You'll tell Dennings and the others? You'll say you want *me* opposite Dennings?"

He nodded.

She turned to the house. "I'll get them!" She stopped. "I'm sorry if I gave you a hard time. What I want is you and stardom. I'd have taken you alone, if there'd been no choice. But suddenly there *was* a choice, and it became both or none. Can you understand?"

He said yes, and she ran off. He used the time before the others arrived to breathe deeply, to recover.

Bub was with them and set a bottle of Gevry Chambertin and six glasses on the poolside table. He blocked some guests who tried to join them, then stood guard at the glass doors.

They toasted their project. Cecily clinked glasses with each of them in turn, and Don felt the eyes of those four men on his woman; eyes that saw ahead to

the time when she would have sex naked with Rob Dennings before the cameras. When millions would see her
naked with Rob Dennings on the screen, see Dennings's penis entering her, see her sucking that penis,
see *everything!*

He had a second glass of wine, and became a little
light-headed.

He rose, feeling that he should be sporting antler-
sized horns on that light head, and said: "Gentlemen,
we'll be leaving you now." Cecily took his arm, and
there were good-byes and parting comments. "Please
don't talk about us when we're gone," he half-sang.
There was a sudden hush, and he and Cecily left in
that hush.

Outside, she began to speak, and he said: "Never
discuss that movie with me."

She said, "All right," and they went home to bed.

The party really got going at about eleven-thirty.
Bub had to stock the bar with more gin, vodka, and
white wine, and he hoped the Scotch would hold out.
The sweet aroma of cannabis was cutting through tobacco smoke, and the laughter was changing, taking
on a wilder, sexier sound.

He heard shrieks from the pool area, and hurried
there in case some drunk had fallen in and needed saving. But it was skinny-dipping time, and he watched
appreciatively as the three Italian chicks stripped and
jumped in, joined soon after by Pandaro, his friend
Marco, and Freddy. One of the chicks, with a bumper
like a mule, climbed right out again and tried to shove
Rob Dennings in. He wouldn't play, grasping her
wrists and flipping her back into the water. After
which he left.

Bub, along with about two dozen other spectators,
watched as Pandaro's friend Marco got the chick with
the bumper in shallow water and began a stand-up
hump. Freddy, inspired by this, got a shriek and a tor-

rent of Italian as his chick saw the size of his stiffening weapon. Pandaro swam slowly up and back, a strange look on his face, while his big-jugged chick dove under him, reaching for the brass ring.

Then upwards of twenty people were stripping and jumping in. And while all the bodies—especially some of the older men's—weren't exactly godlike, all were in the mood and it was orgy time.

Bub would have liked to join in, but he had work to do, and not all of it for Freddy and his party.

He went back to the bar, noting that Sal Andro had given up on his blond and was talking to a group near the piano. Andro called himself a real-estate investor and realtor, but his bread came from drugs, prostitution, and gambling. Bub knew he was richer than half the people in Beverly Hills, Holmby Hills, Bel Air. For example: He had a private bank, a holdover from New York where certain moneyed racketeers had kept up to a million in cash in a closet at home.

Andro had one of those closets transformed by steel lining and an inner steel door into a safe where he kept, rumor said, the fabled million in small bills. Bub had been tipped off to it when he'd bartendered at one of Andro's parties and his best customer, the Mafioso's blond playmate, had babbled a drunken story.

Now she was half passed out in an armchair. Earlier, she'd been heaving in the bathroom.

A sad, sloppy little chick who'd once been cute as hell and was now coming apart at the seams, she would soon run out her string with Andro . . . if she hadn't already, from the occasional hard look he was sending her way.

Drink in hand, Andro nodded at something Joe Kruger, the old songwriter, was saying, and caught Bub's eye, and smiled his small wolf's smile. He nodded again, and looked at the blond, and his smile changed, hardened.

Giselle must know she was running out of time.

She'd made her deal; it probably seemed a good one at the time; the manhandling, the slapping around he'd seen Andro give her after that last party, went with the territory. But what would come next was something she might not know, though it was standard enough with discarded Mafia broads. What would come next was one of Andro's Nevada "ranches," whorehouses in the form of trailers clustered around a roadhouse-bar-gambling casino. End of the line for Giselle.

Bub had an idea about the chick and that closet full of money. He'd had it earlier, three months ago at Andro's house, watching the Mafioso sobering her up with the flat of his hand after the guests had left. But until now it was just a random thought. Until now he'd been playing what-if games.

Now . . . now he suddenly saw how he could use her, get her help, work with her to solve both their problems.

And it was still what-if games if he valued his beautiful black hide!

Besides, he'd checked his box at the post office on San Vicente, and there'd been a letter from Brains. Albert was ready to deliver one of his kids the day before they pulled the job. It was up to Bub now—shit or get off the pot. And he'd put off calling Brains, telling himself he had to take care of the party first.

The bartender, a Chinese kid who was faster than Bub had ever been at pouring and mixing but lacked the style, the chatter, necessary to excel at smaller, more intimate affairs, nodded when Bub asked if the sauce was holding out.

Bub then went to the kitchen, where a red-jacket was sitting down and stretching his legs. "They're not interested in canapes anymore," the waiter said. "Carl's handling the dining room and that's about finished, too."

Bub said they could check out as of midnight, which

was in five minutes, then went to the dining room and the table which had held five hot entrees and seven side dishes. There was little left but scraps. One guest was there, accepting a cup of coffee from the red-jacket named Carl.

Bub waited for the guest to leave, and sent Carl to the kitchen to take off with his co-worker.

The eating part of this affair was over. The *normal* part of this affair was over. Bub's part was over. From here on, the guests would amuse themselves . . . and since he couldn't join in, he didn't have to stand by and watch.

But before he cut out, he told the bartender to stick around for at least another hour. "And when you leave, put the bottles and glasses on the bar for self-service." Then he made a quick tour of the house, upstairs as well as downstairs, tennis court and jacuzzi as well as swimming pool, to make sure no one was wrecking or burning the joint.

The jacuzzi, a circular whirlpool tub about fifteen feet past the shallow end of the pool, was steaming in the cool night air, and not just from the hundred-degree water. A threesome consisting of two young men and one not-so-young woman was working a ménage à trois, as Freddy liked to call it; a three-freak-act, as it was known on the street. Bub was surprised when he recognized the woman as Mrs. Lawwence Bates, whose millionaire restaurateur husband was recovering from surgery in Century City Hospital. Not that she wasn't known to take on any and all comers . . . but rarely in public. Then he smelled pot, saw the ashtray with smoldering joints at the side of the tub and about a dozen empty highball glasses, and realized she was bombed out of her mind.

He went on to the tennis court, where the lights were out but where pale-skinned figures seemed to be playing games just the same. He counted two couples . . . and then a third, half-dressed, rose to his left. The man said: "Say there, get us some champagne, will you?"

"Certainly," Bub replied, walking away. And to himself, "Fuck you!"

He returned to the house and went up the stairs. "Get us some champagne," he muttered. It was to escape such shit—though it was a rare guest who pulled it—that he was going to use Brains and Albert.

The master bedroom was locked, Freddy having learned years ago that he'd end up in a puddle of semen if he didn't keep the late-hours guests out. But the two other bedrooms were in use.

Back down again for a last look at the pool, where about thirty people were making the water boil. No use trying to find Freddy in that mob, so he returned to the house, praying that no cigarette was smouldering in couch or chair cushions, in the thick carpeting near the drapes, or anywhere else where it could later burst into flames and fry Bub Kane and his plans to a crisp.

Too many people ended that way in this town, and Freddy had had Bub install smoke detector alarms in every room. But Bub would still set his radio clock for three and do a systematic search of all cushions and drapes. He and Freddy took their chances, all right, but they also took their precautions.

Which was exactly why he was stalling in phoning Brians. He was ready to take his chances in order to get his payoff—but he was also trying to think of every possible precaution.

In his room, he locked the door, opened the closet, and took down the box of dope usually kept under the kitchen sink—but not on party nights. He used Zig-Zag paper and the little cigarette rolling machine to build two thick joints, then took off his shoes and lay back on the bed, sucking reefer deep into his lungs, unwinding, thinking the party had gone well. Freddy would be one sick cat tomorrow—his hangovers were something brutal—but the boss-man would also consider the party a roaring success. Baylis had given in on the big porno flick; the food had been plentiful and good; the same went for the booze and sex.

After five minutes, with a nice, warm high building, he sat up and dialed the number Brains had given in his letter. He let the ring sound ten times before hanging up. The cons must be out on the town. Okay with him. Plenty of time before the game.

Next Friday morning, he'd get one of Albert's sons and take him to the apartment he'd rented for the month; feed him good, then put him to sleep with half a Lude . . . which would keep the kid under for as long as it took Bub to return to Brains and Albert and give them the game plan for the next night. After that it would be simply a matter of keeping the kid happy, or asleep, while Bub established an iron-clad alibi. He had to make certain he was known not to have been at any of the houses that would be robbed that night.

He didn't know exactly which *would* be robbed. There were six on his list, but it all depended on who among the occupants of those houses was away. Saturday night was go-out night, especially for those wealthy, social people who went to so many parties thrown by so many of their friends. By the same standards, they themselves threw many parties—so one or more of their homes might be the center of heavy activity.

But say four were empty, except perhaps for a servant or child. That would be more than enough for a big score, because every one of the houses on his list had valuables ready for the taking.

Two houses could give him that minimum hundred thousand retirement fund. Even *one* house, properly sacked, could do it. And without much personal risk.

The only time he'd be putting his ass on the line would be for the transference of goods from the cons to him—or rather, to the big apartment he'd rented on San Vicente, south near the hospital. Sitcky, baby, but it had to be done. The goods to him, and the kid to Albert. No way to avoid it.

Once past that, he could use his contacts in Vegas for a top fence-off.

He was singeing his fingertips with the roach, but tension fought down the reefer-high. Because he'd done too much thinking. Because now he was facing the danger, the chance that he could land in stir. And there was no way he could survive stir. Twenty-two days in a cell back home had proven that, so he'd left pimping to the rest of the Kane family. Just three weeks in that cell with those scumbags and he'd been ready to kill them and himself. Only a heavy payoff by his father and brother—after he'd threatened to talk—had gotten him out and away from insanity and death.

Twenty-six years ago. He'd fled from New Orleans to Vegas, where contacts had begun pushing him back into the rackets. He'd fled to L.A., and had begun tending bar and living small and sleeping nights. And eight years ago had accepted Freddy's offer to become his Man Friday, and begun living easier, sweeter, if with less cash money in his pocket.

But now he was risking the barred rooms, the slamming metal doors, the trash food, the ass-buggers, the madness of years locked away from everything good.

He sat up, sweat standing out on his forehead. He said: "What the hell you doing, Bub boy!" He thought a while, and *knew* what he was doing; felt the odds were so strong in his favor that it was impossible not to take the risk involved.

And still he didn't use the phone. And still fear immobilized him.

Until he lit up the second joint, and thought of the beautiful women who saw his white jacket and not him; of the men who said, "Say there, get us some champagne, will you?"; of Freddy who would eventually blow everything with his lust for young boys or friends' girls and leave him alone, aging and without a dime. Of everything that a bundle of bread could mean . . . and he lifted the phone.

Albert answered. "Brains is busy now, you-know? We heard the phone before, but we were *both* busy, you-know?"

He was stoned, you-know. Bub said he'd call back in one hour, exactly, and to make sure Brains was available. Then he finished the second joint and thought only good thoughts.

Rob Dennings drove his Rolls Royce west on Wilshire, heading for the coast and home. That Italian broad in the pool hadn't been bad, he thought, but a star couldn't indulge in public sexing.

Then he remembered. *Except before the cameras.*

Cecily Warren had surprised him. Very beautiful, very sensual, very determined. Also very light in the screen-credits department . . . but what was needed for *this* leading part was to be very beautiful, very sensual, very determined. He'd wanted her on sight . . . and that was before he'd learned that he'd be getting her in *Galt's Island.*

Too bad she was so tied to the novelist. Too bad they couldn't establish a close personal relationship *before* the film went into production; like moving her into his house instead of Ellen, the script girl he had decided would take Joy-Joy's place. Too damned bad . . . and not just for the pleasure of Cecily Warren's beautiful self. There was an element of fear, of self-doubt, connected with having sex on camera. And even normally, in private, he performed better in bed after knowing the woman a while.

He drove faster. What he had to do was make Cecily Warren a few times—rehearsals, sort of—before they stepped onto a set together. Otherwise, he might not be able . . .

He cut himself short. *Dangerous!* Keep thinking

that way and he might experience the greatest humiliation a man could conceive of. It was bad enough when you couldn't get it up in private. Imagine having it happen in front of the people who would have to be present for a shooting session on even the most tightly controlled closed set.

He put on the radio. He took a package of sugarless gum from the glove compartment and chewed up two sticks. He thought of the contracts he'd discussed with Freddy; of the enormous payoff he would almost certainly get.

And wondered how his six and a half inches would photograph in living color. And thought of Harry Reems's monstrous penis; of other male porno stars' heavy equipment; of whether Rob Dennings was physically equipped to handle the part.

No one had asked him. These were matters no producer could broach with him . . . though it *had* to have crossed Freddy's, Berry's, and Pandaro's minds.

His stomach began to ache; that fucking nervous cramp. But Jesus H. Christ! He wasn't being hired for his genitals! He was a *star!* His few sex scenes would take no more than fifteen, twenty minutes out of a two-hour blockbuster! Nothing, really . . .

And yet he knew the public would be coming to see Rob Dennings fuck, no matter how delicately Freddy and the two backers put it. Knew there could be no stand-ins for *these* stunts. Knew he stood to make a fortune because of those fifteen, twenty minutes.

And knew he stood to become one of the world's greatest jokes if the cameramen didn't handle certain closeups correctly.

Now he was sweating as well as cramping. Now he was thinking he would never be able to go through with it.

At the same time, he remembered the amount of money his ten percent could represent—ten million for a hundred million grosser! And it could go to three times that; literally thirty million, which for once in his spendthrift life he would find a way to hang onto. And the fame, the incredible fame . . . which meant picking and choosing among the big flicks again.

He was convinced that this picture was the right thing to do, the chance of a lifetime, and that three or four other stars would grab at it if he didn't. It was an idea whose time had come.

His agent would scream. Terrence Boyle always screamed, unless the project was born inside that head of skin that rivaled Telly Savales's. He'd use every argument in the book . . .

Joy-Joy was waiting when he got home. She didn't ask about the party and why she hadn't been taken along. She was used to being left behind at times. She was used to being ignored at times, even here in the home she shared with Rob Dennings. It was understood that he was totally free. It was understood she was his bedmate, at times, with no strings attached.

Tonight he needed his bedmate, to chase away the ghosts of impotence.

Impotence! God, not at *this* point in his career!

Joy-Joy rubbed his neck, his back, his buttocks, easing away the nervous cramps. Joy-Joy kissed his mouth, tenderly. He moved her head down. She kissed his chest, his stomach, his genitals.

Joy-Joy made love to him . . . and he decided she wouldn't be replaced until after *Galt's Island* was safely in the can. She had what he thought of as an Oriental calm and a totally feminine understanding of him.

She might even help bring Cecily Warren to his bed for those "rehearsals" that would end his fear.

At one A.M., Cecily got up and went quietly to the closet where she'd hung her clothes. She began to dress in the light of the bedside lamp, which Donny always left burning since his heart attack. He seemed to be asleep, lying on his right side—no more on his left; his heartbeat disturbed him now—breathing regularly. But then he rolled over to face her, eyes open, and said: "Why so early?"

"Have a nine A.M. appointment at the hairdresser's . . ." Then she remembered that he knew about Johnny. "The sitter's a teenage girl, not the elderly woman I use when I stay till morning."

"Maybe you'll bring Johnny here next Friday and we'll spend the weekend together? Would it disturb him, you think?"

"I guess not." She was hurrying now, anxious to escape this conversation. She wasn't ready for such questions. The whole business of Johnny and Don getting together had come on her too quickly. "We couldn't just hop into bed in front of him."

"Gee, I'd counted on a little sixty-nine."

She'd irritated him. "You know what I mean. It'll take time before he understands how we feel about each other."

His irritation seemed to be growing. "*I* still don't understand."

"C'mon, birthday boy, don't spoil a beautiful evening. You're too grown-up for that kind of crap."

"I guess you could call fifty grown-up. Though I still can't talk to you. I doubt I'll be able to talk to you when I'm a hundred."

"Tacky, tacky," she muttered, slipping into her shoes.

He sat up. "How long do you think it'll be before you tell me about your sister Teresa?"

She was startled. But why, since he'd obviously checked her out when he'd learned about Johnny. She put on her choker, using the mirrored closet doors to adjust and center.

"The one in the mental institution," he said, pushing her.

"Ah, that one. Almost forgot. Want to tell me more things about myself?"

"Didn't you think I'd wonder about the evasions, the running home at odd hours, the lack of conversation about family? The lack of talk on any real adult level between us?"

"I think we talked plenty. I think we're talking too much." She came to the bed, sat down, put her hand under the blanket. She kissed his cheek, and tickled his penis. "Nighty-night, both of you."

"You have one answer to every problem," he said. "Sex."

She stood up. "You never complained before."

"Yes, I did."

He was right. He'd complained often, wanting her to be *something more*, as he put it. Something she wasn't. Something she perhaps could never be.

"All this bullshit," she said sharply. "I want to go home."

"Certainly. You've pressured me into allowing you to make a fuck film. You've given me the reward of your body. And now it's home to bed . . . with Señor Jorge Resordo, perhaps? Or does he still have Tuesday mornings? When we're married, will you switch to a motel—say, the Farmer's Daughter on Fairfax, your photographer's favorite—or will you insist on having him come here?"

"You bastard! You sneaky, spying bastard!" She was close to tears, but fought them, not wanting him to have the satisfaction of seeing her break. "We'll *never* be married!" She turned toward the door, wanting to run, yet afraid to leave this way. All considerations of love aside, he could still kill her chances of getting the female lead in *Galt's Island*.

"I'm sorry," he said. "I'm using pressure myself now; unfair leverage. We both know what kind."

She let the tears flow, because they were burning her eyes, and also because at this point they would help her.

In a moment he was standing beside her, tying his bathrobe, putting his arms around her, saying: "What an odd couple we are, sweetheart. The mismatch of the century. You're so much the natural woman, the free body and almost-free spirit. I'm so fucked up, mentally and physically. God, physically! What right have I to tell you what to do? I can't even be sure I'll be around to love you."

"Don't talk that way." She was hugging him back now, and knew she had won. She also knew this argument would be repeated again, softer, milder, and yet again and again. Each time she would win, and each time the point of it would be further dulled—the point that she took other men and had lied to him about her son and her sister and might lie to him, might do all the things she'd done in the past, even if they were married.

"Did you lay Freddy?" His mouth was right up against her ear; his voice was soft, sweet, reasonable. She had to fight the impulse to drop all pretense and say: "Yes, why not? It has nothing to do with how I feel about you."

She pushed him away, looking him straight in the eyes. "I should slap your face and walk out."

He began to speak, but she overrode him. "If it'll make you happy, I'll admit I was tempted—curiosity, mainly, as we're all curious about attractive, successful men and women. Does that make me guilty?"

His mouth moved upward at the very corners in a small, bad smile. "Would you *swear* to only that temptation?"

"If it'll stop this idiotic argument."

"On your son's life?"

She laughed, shaking her head. "The atheist will accept *that* as proof?"

"I always have, with those who aren't atheists. Just say it."

She kept looking into those probing brown eyes, those unhappy, narrowing eyes. "I swear on Johnny's life that I haven't made love to Freddy."

" 'Made love?' I see an evasion there, a way out. You might distinguish between making love and screwing."

She did indeed, and turned on her heel. "Think what you want! I'm leaving!"

He caught her in the hall. "All right—I'm sorry. Will I see you tomorrow? Maybe you and Johnny?"

"Give me some time." She turned to the door, feeling it was best to keep the family situation from growing too thick . . . until after *Galt's Island* was shot, was finished. "Give Johnny some time."

Standing behind her, he put his arms around her waist, pressed himself into her, cupped both her breasts. "But now that I know about him . . ."

She was in charge again. She would have liked to have thrown his words back at him as he rubbed his stiffening member into her bottom: "You have one answer to every problem—sex." But she couldn't do that to the man who controlled her future, her career.

"Johnny *doesn't* know about you," she said. "I'll need some time."

"All right," he said, voice thickening. His lips nibbled at her earlobe. His arms tightened. He rubbed harder, breathed faster. His right hand dropped from her breast, over her stomach. She twisted away before it could reach her crotch. Because he could set her afire very easily, this complex, difficult man. Because she had to leave with her wins intact. Because she couldn't risk further talk tonight.

She opened the door, stepping into the carport. "And you dare call yourself an M.I. patient!" she said in mock outrage.

"I dared it that third day in Intensive Care, remember?"

"Yes. 'Save my life,' you said."

He was chuckling, moving toward her again. She

reached back inside the door to press the button set into the frame. The electric wrought-iron gate began lifting. She blew him a kiss and ran out to the road and her car.

She almost expected him to follow her, to try and drag her back inside. Once aroused, Mr. Baylis was a very stubborn man. As he had proven at Cedars–Sinai Hospital five months ago.

Half dead, he'd begged her to go into the bathroom of his room in the Cardiac Intensive Care section, pull down her Levis, let him see her "lovely ass—to make the blood move; to let me know I'm still alive; to *save* my life."

It was the third day after what the doctors called his myocardial infarction; his M.I. He was pale as a white-washed wall. He was too weak to sit up unaided, raise a glass of water, lift himself onto a bedpan. He was fed by tubes sticking into his veins; he slept most of the time; he looked at her out of eyes that seemed to have lost all life. The voice with which he asked her to do this crazy thing was a hoarse, croaking whisper.

"But Donny, the nurses keep walking in."

"Wait until the next one checks. You'll have a few minutes . . ." He gasped for breath ". . . until she checks again."

They had told her he was "in a critical phase, far from out of danger." They checked on him night and day; checked on him electronically too, with the help of the cardiac monitoring machines that recorded his heartbeat on a screen above his bed and on a panel of screens at the nurses' station outside. How could she do such a . . . a *normal* thing here?

And then the very thought—*a normal thing*—made her understand what he so desperately wanted. Maybe it would be wrong for another M.I. patient, but not for the Donald Baylis she knew; the man whose need for her body was such an important part of their love.

The nurse came in, fiddled with the bed, looked up

at the screen. She smiled at Cecily. "With such a beautiful girlfriend," she said to Don, "you can't spend too much time here, can you?"

He said, "No," in that whispered croak. And when she'd gone, said: "Let me see you, my beautiful girlfriend."

She went into the bathroom, leaving the door open. She pulled down her jeans and turned completely around in her pale blue panties. She looked at him, and he said: "Panties—off."

She turned her back on him, pulled down the un-underwear, stuck her naked bottom out at him, looked over her shoulder at him.

He was smiling; maybe the first real smile since he'd come here. He said: "Shake it, sweetheart."

She began to *feel* like shaking it. She rotated her bottom, the bottom he'd loved to kiss, to finger, to grab in orgasm. She felt moisture in her cleft, felt hunger for her man. She rotated and jutted and turned, clutching her vagina, sticking her tongue out at him, mouthing: "Fuck me, bun."

Then his eyes darted away, and she had enough warning to close the bathroom door as another nurse entered. This one wanted a urine specimen from his bed bottle, but she also remarked on "the strong activity" on his cardiac monitor.

When Cecily had come out of the bathroom, he'd kissed her with a little of the old vigor instead of the goodbye-forever-pecks he'd been handing out the last three days. He'd even tongued her; put a shaky hand on her breast.

She'd felt then he was going to live.

Johnny liked it better when Mary, his babysitter, wore skirts since most of them were short and he could get looks at her thighs and even her panties. He would sometimes make believe he'd gone to bed and then peek at her when she thought she was alone. Once she'd left the bathroon door open and he'd seen her beaver! Tonight she was wearing Levis and a blouse and still looked great because her figure was so *mature*, as mom said.

Mom used Mary a lot lately, now that he was twelve and she didn't worry as much about him as she used to. She felt she didn't need Mrs. Maillet, who charged more and had been sitting with him as long as he could remember; not unless she was going to be away until morning or later. Then she still used Mrs. Maillet and Johnny would go to sleep a lot earlier because it wasn't any fun with Mrs. Maillet, who looked like Ma Kettle on afternoon TV movies.

Mary looked like one of the girls from the bikini beach party movies! Really *beautiful*, man! Even that fool, Klaus, said she was a "dish" and Klaus hardly seemed to pay attention to girls.

He was in his bedroom . . . for the second time. He'd gone there at eleven when Mary got mad at his excuses. He'd made believe he was asleep, and come out to see if he could catch her peeing or scratching herself or something good. When he couldn't, he said he wanted a glass of water, then brushed against her moonie, as if by mistake, when she bent over to put his glass in the dishwater. She gave him a funny look, and he turned away and went back to bed because his pajamas were bumped out in the front. He'd been getting stiffies for a long time now, but Mary really did it to him!

She was fifteen and three months. He knew when her birthday was, and had wanted to send her a card, get her a present, but was afraid mom would think it was funny and question him and maybe get an idea of what was in his mind. Man, she'd *murder* him!

Or maybe not? Like she hadn't really gotten mad the time he'd drunk half a bottle of wine. All she'd done was laugh when he was sick the next morning.

Mary was singing in the study, along with the radio,

and he touched his pistol, as Mike in school called it, and wished Mary would touch it. He wondered how it would feel. Great, he was sure! Mike said his half-sister had *sucked* his when she thought he was asleep!

Maybe it was a lie.

But there was another kid, older, who said a real grown-up woman, almost thirty, had played with his and sucked his and gotten it to shoot white stuff. Come, they called it, and it was all over the girls' faces in the porno books Mike brought to school.

Oh, oh, how he wanted to shoot white stuff over Mary's face! Though he wasn't sure he could; hadn't yet; just leaked a lot, mostly at night.

He couldn't stay in bed any longer. He had a stiffy. He had to get up and talk to Mary, maybe bump her moonie again if she bent over, maybe brush her chest—her *tits*. Maybe kiss her and tell her he loved her and to please touch his pistol and he'd give her the fifty-dollar bond grandma gave him for his last birth-day, his new camera, anything she wanted.

He got up, and his pajamas bumped out in front. He pulled them down and looked at himself. If Mary walked in, would she scream? Would she laugh? (It might not be right: turned up too much like it was or the wrong color, purple, like it was.) He pulled his pants back up and went down the hall to the bathroom and did what the older kid, Paul, said to do—splashed cold water on it. But he also touched himself and the stiffy stayed tilted up toward his stomach and stayed purple and ached.

Finally, he got up on the closed toilet seat and leaned over the sink and kept lowering himself until he could put the end of his pistol under the faucet. Then the stream of cold water did what Paul said it would do, and the stiffy went away.

He was relieved . . . and yet sorry. Sorry he couldn't do something with it to Mary. If only he could be sure she'd do what the girls in the porno magazines did . . . what mom did with the old man she called Horgey; crazy name, but he was a Mex and they had crazy names. What he'd seen them do for years, when he pushed open the door and peeked. What he would no longer watch since he'd been getting stiffies.

He tried to stop thinking of mom. It got him all mixed up, thinking of mom and having a stiffy for Mary and remembering what mom did with Horgey and remembering what the girls did in the porno magazines and Paul saying all girls, all women, all mothers did those things so as to have babies, except maybe not up the moonie and in the mouth which mothers, Paul said, didn't know about.

Mom did. At least about in the mouth.

He left the bathroom. Made him feel bad to think of mom and Horgey. He went to the study, and when Mary saw him she jumped up from the couch. "Johnny, damn, it's almost one o'clock! Your mother'll . . ."

"It's okay. I slept this afternoon. She won't mind. I want to show you some movies of my vacation at my father's place."

"You napped in the afternoon?" She had her hands on her hips and was making a face that showed she didn't believe him.

"Honest," He kissed his pinkie and waved it to heaven. "Swear to God." He went past her, and suddenly wondered if his fly was closed. And began to feel the stiffy again. He went to the table where the projector stood and looked through the drawer.

"Don't worry about my mom. When I nap she's cool." He glanced at her. She was turned toward him, hands still on hips, face still not believing him. "Remember when we had wine last week, Mary? I sure got a buzz-on, did you?"

She sat down. "No. One glass doesn't get me going. But I'll bet *you* were sorry the next morning."

"What, me? I once drank half a bottle and felt great. I been drinking a long time."

She laughed. "Years and years, right?"

He made believe he didn't care about her laughing. "Well, three or four years. My dad lets me drink because he knows I can hold it. My mom doesn't like me to, because she's . . . well, she's like all moms. Bet yours is the same." ·

He'd scored. She leaned back, nodding. "Went to a party and got a little scootied and she was so mad. For nothing." She laughed. "Wasn't a boy there who knew how to take advantage . . ." Then she stopped, glancing at him.

He filed away that "scootied," even though it might be a girl's word. He quickly said, "Yeah," trying to deepen his voice, toughen his voice. "Same here, with girls my age or a year older. At thirteen you hardly find . . ." he swallowed and hurried on, mumbling ". . . any action at all."

"What?"

He had the reel mounted and went across the room and pulled up the screen, standing on his toes, straining but smiling to cover it. He went to the lamp near the couch. "Lights, camera, action."

"What's that you said before? I couldn't hear." She was staring at him, and that was okay because she wasn't laughing and she was paying attention. He could do what those men did in the porno magazines, he was sure of it, if she were naked and helped put his pistol in the right places.

He turned off the lamp; just in time too because the stiffy was coming back.

"Thirteen?" she said. "You're just barely twelve."

He was twelve and five months, but that wasn't enough to brag about. So he went back to the projector and threw the switch. "This is where my father grows grapes for Gallo. You heard of Gallo, Mary? That's the wine we drank."

She said yes, she knew, and was his father rich?

"He does okay. In two years, when I'm fifteen, I get a lot of bread from him."

"Really? You inherit, you mean?"

"Something like that. In trust, they call it . . ." which they did, and which his father talked about for him when he was twenty-one, *if* he was good until then, which was forever and dad never came through anyway. so who could worry about it.

"How much, Johnny?"

He liked her using his name. He liked her looking at him instead of just at the screen. He liked the feeling that he was starting to become a person to her, not just a baby she had to watch. She wasn't that much older than him. It *could* happen.

His heart was pounding; his mouth was dry; he said: "Let's have some wine, huh?"

"No! It's one-thirty and your mother'll murder us both! Just finish the movie and go to bed!"

He said, "Sure," and then, "I get about fifty thousand in trust."

Her head jerked to him. She laughed. "Oh, come on!"

"Look at those fields," he said, pointing at the screen. "You know what grape ranches like that make? Bet you don't. Plenty! And I'm his only child and I get a share in trust. In two years, when I'm fifteen, I get fifty thousand."

"What if I checked that out with your mother?"

He went cold. "She'd be angry that I told you something personal like that."

"Wow, fifty thousand! You'll be rich. You'll move away, won't you? To Beverly Hills, maybe?"

"Why? We have everything here. Pool and nice street and the best looking girl in the Valley."

For a minute she didn't react; then she laughed. Her

laugh sounded different from before. Her laugh made his heart pound harder, his mouth go drier.

He came to the couch, letting the machine run along on its own. He sat down beside her, not too close. He said, "That's the riding stable," and had to clear his throat. "You like to ride, don't you, Mary?"

"Never get the chance."

"I'll take you."

She turned to him, smiling. She was about five feet two, and he was about five feet, and that wasn't such a big difference standing. But sitting she was much taller . . . because her moonie was so big and round and all.

He stood up, moved past her as if to adjust the machine, then came back and perched on the arm of the couch, right over her. He smelled her perfume.

"You mean you could really take me horseback riding? Your mother would let you take me?"

"Sure. I'm good at it. She'd even drive us to Agoura where there are some great trails. I'll lead your horse until you're used to it."

He didn't know where this conversation was leading him. Only knew that it was important she believe he was grown-up enough to do something for her. And the stiffy was aching and he leaned over her, smelling her perfume and her body, shaking, unable to talk any more because he was sure his voice would shake . . . and he heard the car pull into the driveway.

He raced to the projector and shut it off. "My mom! No use getting her mad. Put on the light." He raced to the bedroom. Where he got under the covers. And where the panic fled.

He began to feel good about how he'd handled himself tonight.

Man! Maybe he'd kiss her next time! Maybe he'd touch her chest . . . her *tits!* And her moonie . . . her *ass!* And her beaver . . . her *cunt!*

God, those words, those dirty words, they drove him wild!

His mother opened the front door, and he closed his eyes. Inside, mixed with the excitement created by Mary, another excitement grew—the one that always accompanied his mother's return.

Then he felt it—wetness, stickiness, flowing onto the front of his pajamas. He'd *leaked*. If mom took the covers off him, rearranged the blankets as she sometimes did, she might see. And be disgusted.

Terrified, he jumped out of bed, tearing off his pajamas, tops as well as bottoms, so as to be able to say he'd been hot and never put them on. He stuffed them into a drawer and got back into bed. And realized his door was open and he always slept with it closed.

Out he jumped and ran across the room and closed the door, hoping he hadn't made too much noise.

In bed again, eyes closed, breathing controlled, he was safe.

He hoped.

Cecily had come off Lookout Mountain onto Laurel Canyon. Traffic had been light, and she'd made it to North Hollywood, and was parked in her driveway at one thirty-five. Before getting out of the Jaguar, she looked around; completely around. A girl one street east had been attacked as she got out of her car at two A.M. of a weekday evening. That had been more than a year ago, but Cecily had never allowed herself to forget it. Three men had raped the eighteen-year-old in her own backyard for over two hours, and then one had kicked her in the face a few times. She still didn't look right, even after all that surgical and dental work. She certainly didn't act right, from what people said, staying home most of the time. She was afraid the men would come back for her because she'd reported the rape, giving descriptions, worked with the police, and the three animals were still on the loose.

Cecily took a deep breath as she opened the door. Any sonofabitch who tried to nail her would get a scream that would wake the sleeping-beauty cops at their station house ten blocks away! That and a knee in the nuts!

She ran for the house, thinking that this was one of the joys of living in the big city—at least in a somewhat rundown part of the big city. And had her key in the door and was inside as she counted: "One, two, three, four . . ."

She closed the door on five, and nodded. She'd made it in four some nights, but five was her average. After a few drinks, or a joint, she'd gone to seven and eight, which in her mental battle against rapists meant possible disaster.

She heard another door close, inside the house. Johnny's door, she figured. An old game of his, to battle the babysitter until all hours . . . or until his mother came home.

She went directly to the study. The cute, dark, high-school girl was sitting on the old sleeper couch, pretending to read the magazine in her lap. But she was a poor liar; she looked guilty as hell.

Cecily saw the movie projector on the table, the screen set up against the wall. She said, "Hi, Mary," and went to the projector. It was hot.

"He wouldn't go to sleep," the girl said. "I tried, Mrs. Warren, but you know how he is."

Cecily nodded. She switched on the projector to see what he'd been showing. His father sprang into life, riding a horse around the corral of the stable they used up near Bethel. A big, handsome man, Andy. An unimaginative, violent man, Andy. She switched him off.

"I dragged him to his room at eleven, Mrs. Warren, but he came out again. What could I do?"

"Try belting him next time," Cecily said, and turned away.

"Oh, I couldn't!"

Cecily went down the hall to Johnny's door and opened it. The lights were out and all was quiet. She threw the switch and saw him in bed, on his side, eyes closed.

She hesitated, wondering whether to hold off the scolding until tomorrow. And then he gave a little snore, overacting as usual.

She was angry, but had to laugh. She always had to laugh at *something* he did. She went to the bed and yanked the covers clean off him, and was surprised to see he wasn't wearing pajamas.

He shrieked and tried to cover his naked body. He rolled and dodged, but she gave him playful slaps and not-too-playful pinches on the bottom, and he jumped out of bed and ran from the room, yelling, "No fair, dammit! That hurt, fool!" She followed in hot pursuit.

In the hallway, he came to a sudden halt, because Mary was coming toward them. The girl said, "Oh!" and froze. He twisted around, bending over, trying to cover himself . . . and suddenly burst into tears.

Cecily said, "I'm sorry, honey," and held out her arms. But he ran by her, back into his room, sobbing.

Cecily paid Mary, and walked her to the door. She stood watching as the teenager hurried across the street and down three houses to where she lived with two older sisters, two younger brothers, and a pair of worn-out parents.

She waited until Mrs. Cherrel waved at her, then went to Johnny's room. He was in his blue terrycloth bathrobe, wiping his eyes with a tissue.

"Why'd you hafta do that? In front of Mary! Bet she was making jokes about me."

"No way, Boy Wonder. She was sorry she embarrassed you." She stroked his hair. "And I could tell she thought you were a knockout."

He blew his nose. "Cut it out! It's not funny!"

She dropped her hand. "Well, serves you right for refusing to go to bed. I told you eleven was your deadline."

"On weekends? What's the point of weekends? . . ."

"You were up at seven this morning and you should be in bed at a decent hour."

"A decent hour," he mimicked. When she didn't take umbrage, he began hamming it up like an English lady, in falsetto over his already high voice. "A decent hour, young man, I say, because you have to grow to eight feet nine and be a great big *fool* like your mommy and daddy."

"Yeah, make jokes." She turned to the door. "Boring the pants off Mary with those movies your father takes . . ."

"Wish I could," he muttered.

"What?"

"The pants off Mary." When she turned on him, truly shocked, he said; "Hey, a joke, big momma! You make jokes, don't you?"

She stared.

He waved his hands, face worried. "Whatever it means, right?"

She nodded, but she suddenly knew that twelve and a half wasn't as young as it had seemed a moment ago.

She tried to think of herself at twelve, thirteen. She recalled knowing, and feeling, quite a bit.

But boys were far behind girls that way, weren't they?

She said, "Keep it up, Boy Wonder, and I'll marry you off."

He brightened immediately at her bantering tone. "Okey-doke. Mary'll do. She's really built."

She made as if to whack him one, and he backed away, yelling: "Kidding! Christ, I'm going to move to dad's! I mean it!"

He didn't say that too often. Tonight it struck a

nerve. Donny thought his father could get custody when *Galt's Island* was released.

"How about tomorrow?" she asked.

He tried to hang tough, shrugging.

"Pack a bag. If you want him, you've got him. You don't listen to me and I've had it up to here."

He was staring at her, lips pressed tight together, ready to cry. She felt like a monster, and dropped to her knees, holding out her arms. He ran to her and they hugged and she said: "Well, we've given each other enough trouble for one night, right?"

"Yes," he said, voice high and weak.

She squeezed him, kissed his face, whispered: "I'm sorry. I love you more than anything in the whole world, you know that, don't you?"

"Yes. Me too." His mouth pressed her cheek. "I wasn't tired, so I started making up stories for Mary. About dad. About how he buys me things and sends us lots of money."

"Maybe God'll hear and make it come true."

Johnny laughed. "It'll take more than God to loosen up dad's wallet."

Which was something *she* always said. Most of the things he said were things she'd said. She'd shaped him, made him the person he was.

It worried her. He needed a man around; a man like Don.

But what a shock for him to have someone so different. Someone so insistent on reading and thinking and going to the museum and ballet and opera . . . and keeping TV at a minimum. Someone on such a definite head trip in charge of Johnny Warren's life.

She wanted it and feared it. Perhaps feared it for herself, too. Perhaps didn't believe it could work.

"Hungry?" she asked.

"For a pizza, yes!"

"I meant a cheese sandwich with lettuce and tomato."

"A frozen pizza's fine, big momma! I'll make it. Please . . . please . . ."

He was tugging her hand, and she knew it wasn't good for him at almost two in the morning. And let him pull her to the kitchen, where she sat and watched as he took the pizza from the freezer compartment and lit the oven.

They ate in the study, while he ran off the film of his father riding around the corral. He joked that, "Dad's moonie is bigger than the horse's," and rewound the film and begged her to let him run off the reel she'd taken of his last birthday party.

They sat together, watching the party film, drinking from the same can of root beer. She was happy, and felt she was making a million mistakes raising him and he'd pay for it some day. But she didn't want to end their freedom; the freedom of two kids playing their way through life. Didn't want it brought under the adult eye of Donald Baylis. Didn't want Cecily and Johnny forced to toe the line.

He dozed off. She got up to turn off the projector. He roused and said: "Hey, that's my job." He'd handled the projector since she'd taught him to at the age of nine. The past year he'd also been shooting some of their home movies, and he'd shot part of the reel featuring his father.

He was a competent boy in many ways, old for his age in many ways, but she knew he was heading for big problems. He didn't really know how to read . . . how to concentrate on reading, that is. He was falling further and further behind each semester, and yet they passed him on as they passed on everyone, including real illiterates. He got better grades than he deserved. He lied, cheated . . .

Just like Cecily Bajorka, back home.

They walked together to his room, and he asked for "a real good story."

He didn't mean one of those in the books she'd

bought him, which he never cracked. He meant some-
that had happened to her during the week.

She sighed. "Three o'clock, Boy Wonder. Well,
there was this party tonight, and who should be there
but Rob Dennings, the movie star."

"From *Caesar's Soldiers?*" he murmured sleepily.

He'd seen it on TV. As had almost everyone in the
country, she guessed, when they made that big two-
parter out of it last year.

"The very same. And we talked about my working
with him in a movie; a starring role." She was dying to
brag about it, but how could she? She decided right
then and there against mentioning Dennings or *Galt's
Island* to him ever again.

"Anyway, my writer friend, Donald Baylis, was also
there, and I told him about you. He said he wanted to
take us to dinner soon."

She saw that his eyes were closed. She murmured his
name, then got up and moved quietly out of the room,
pausing to shut the lights and close the door.

Her little boy . . . though not so little any more,
from what she'd seen, heard, and most of all *sensed*
tonight. The male animal was coming alive there. It
would change things.

But her little boy still, and forever. Her baby. Her
poor little bastard, literally.

In her big, comfortable bed—Resordo had insisted
on buying her a king-size—she remembered the small,
hard bed in which she'd slept the first time with
Andy. *Slept*, hah! The SOB had been on her, in her,
teaching her to use every opening she possessed, all
night long. Not quite eighteen, and hot to trot, Cecily
Bajorka had accepted the instruction gratefully—and
in her innocence had trusted her twenty-two-year-old
lover to protect her.

And trusted to luck, preferring what he called "velvet pussy" to the tight sheath of a condom. Luck
might have worked the first time, even the second and

third times on the small bed in his friend's Bethel apartment, but somewhere around the fourth or fifth times, his luck ran out.

Or rather her luck, since the skipped period caused him to accuse her of "screwing around with high school kids who don't know the score." And he'd decided he wasn't going to see her again.

Until then he'd been talking love and marriage. Until then he'd been delighted at her swearing he had been the one to take her virginity—believable since bleeding was rare in a farm community where all the girls rode horses and most lost their hymens before puberty, and *true* since she certainly didn't consider her father a lover, didn't consider him at all any more as he ignored her and her mother and drifted toward senility.

Indeed, it was no small accomplishment for a girl in their milieu to remain a virgin as long as Cecily had.

Andy Warren, just back from two years of army service preceeded by two years of junior college, had ended that. With his "older man" good looks, his education—"top grades in Agriculture, and Spanish, too, which we need here in California to handle the ranch hands"—and his G.I.-on-the-town experience, he made short work of her resistance.

For the first time since her father had forced her, a man's penis entered her body. And this time brought ecstasy unmarred by fear or guilt; though as it turned out, she could have used both emotions for self-protection.

In her fifth month, her mother said she was turning into "a listless, crying *fool*," and her father muttered she was eating too much and "growing fat as a cow." Cecily knew she either had to confide in her parents, or leave home.

No choice, really, and she left home.

Teresa was by then living in Los Angeles, pursuing an acting career, supporting herself as a checker in a

Ralph's supermarket. That was before she decided that men could pay some of the bills and began to date, as she put it, "financially." And taught the lesson to Cecily, who had arrived full of child and grief.

Cecily would never forget that Teresa had taken her in, fed her, comforted her, begun the financial-type dating because of the increased expense her pregnant sister represented. ("Just as easy to play games with a married businessman who's real grateful for the fun, as with a poor acting student who'll give you nothing but his inexperience.")

Despite this reasoning, Teresa always had a "heavy" for a "real heartthrob." So without consulting Cecily, she'd written Andy half a dozen times, telling him just what a fool he was, saying he'd never find another girl like Cecily ". . . so beautiful she's had three proposals of marriage, big belly and all." He finally came to see her, a day after she'd given birth in the clinic on Franklin.

Johnny—not yet named—had won him over. Johnny, seven pounds of squalling mouth and a few ounces of dark hair. Johnny, so cute he made her glad it had happened!

Andy stayed in town a week, and took her back home. And took a month to marry her. Only then did Cecily bring Johnny to her parents. Her father said, "Before the wedding, huh?" and walked away. Her mother said: "Try blaming *this* on your poor father." So she didn't see them for almost a year. But eventually they all made up and Johnny was a beloved son and grandson.

Andy, however, wasn't a loving husband. He wanted a slave, an adoring servant, not a wife. Certainly not one who dreamed of an acting career. And he continually reminded her of how he'd "saved" her with legitimacy and marriage.

Even so, she might still be Mrs. Andrew Warren, rotting away on the grape ranch, probably with another few kids, except that Andrew Warren began to drink. And with that went bar-hopping and woman-chasing.

Still, she stuck it out, until he began slapping her around. Once, she forgave him. The second time, she used a broom handle to beat him to his knees. As she packed, he said: "Just what I want. Took you long enough, you and that bastard kid who sure as hell isn't mine." He ran then, because she picked up the broom handle. He ran out the front door, and flattened against the wall. When she followed, raging, weeping, he grabbed her, and this time used his fists . . . on her body, where it wouldn't show as much.

She was three weeks recovering, but it had its benefits. She didn't have to agonize over whether or not to forgive him, whether or not to divorce him.

The day he was served with divorce papers, he decided he loved her and his son too much to part with them, and in court gave a convincing performance of a misunderstood husband and father. Cecily laughed out loud. It irritated the judge, an elderly gentleman of Fundamentalist pursuasion who still didn't believe divorce was legal in the truest sense. He punished Cecily by awarding the minimal support in such circumstances—sixty dollars a month—and no alimony whatsoever, this despite medical proof of the severe beating she'd taken from the "loving husband."

Even that didn't end it, because now Andy began pestering her at her parents' place, where she'd moved with her child. He called on her evenings "to make sure you're raising my son right," and to try and slip into her bed.

She refused all his advances.

One night, he attacked her as she walked down to North Lane to post a letter to Teresa. He knocked her half unconscious with a blow to the temple, dragged her into the almond orchard on the other side of the dirt road, and pulled up her housedress. She came fully awake as he was pushing his penis into her, and screamed and fought. He finally backed off, holding up his hand, saying: "Wait, honey, please, I love you! I gotta have you! You're mine! Didn't I give my name to your son?"

She went a little crazy then, trying to tear open the big, square face; trying to rip out the pale blue eyes that peered at her so honestly. And felt she could never trust another man again, certainly never love one of these selfish fools who used women when their cocks were hard and discarded them when their cocks were soft.

Her mother came out to call her then, having heard the faint sounds of her screams. Andy left, pulling up his pants, vowing to make her "sweat for every dime" she got from him. And in this one thing, at least, he had kept his word.

Andy's attack gave her the determination to move herself and Johnny to Los Angeles. Where she found an apartment near Teresa, a job as a receptionist, and the Sunset Actors Lab and Workshop, which offered night and weekend classes.

After two years and eight months of marriage, plus five months of living with her son on her parents' farm, she celebrated her twenty-first birthday by attending drama class. She had no experience, no previous training, and was the oldest neophyte in the group, male or female. But she was happy, truly happy.

She met people, mainly men, "financial dates" who helped her. She landed her first bit part in a movie, and was ecstatic. She received her final divorce papers . . . and a few visits from Andy, generally on Friday nights, when he'd ask innocently if she could "put him up" during his weekend in L.A. She said no three times, and the fourth time he tried forcing his way in. She called the police and filed a complaint, even though he'd already driven back to Bethel.

She dropped the charges only after he swore never to bother her again . . . and he knew his name was now on file in a police station.

Johnny spent several weeks a year with him. After each of these visits, he returned home full of stories about camping trips, but was strangely silent about any conversations he'd had with his father. She finally got him to admit Andy bad-mouthed her whenever he got the chance. And at the same time learned her baby boy didn't believe Word One; loved her as she loved him; depended on her as she depended on him.

Whatever happened, they were a team. Like the marriage vows read, but rarely translated into reality: "For better or for worse, for richer or for poorer, in sickness and in health."

In North Hollywood or in Beverly Hills. In Ohrbach's or in Saks Fifth. In Sambo's or in Chasen's. She and her Johnny boy.

They were so tight, it simply had to mean trouble some day.

But screw "some day"! Screw the problems! Her baby boy was worth it all!

Don was up at six-thirty, still tired, but the pattern of waking early, going to the bathroom, and not being able to fall asleep again was long established. He felt a little undone, a little shaky, a little under the weather . . .

Hell, his heart was out of sync, arrythmatic. A slight off-beat *thump* every two or three beats was putting the edge on his teeth this morning, after a night ruined by thoughts of that damned dirty movie.

He swallowed his daily Lanoxin tablet in the bathroom, then went to the kitchen to take his morning Quinidine and Inderal with several tablespoons of low-fat yogurt to counteract the Quinidine's gut-dissolving qualities. He mixed a teaspoon of Postum with hot water and sipped it black, looking down the canyon, through the slot to the city and the ocean. A grayish haze was forming, early as it was, and soon the Pacific would be hidden behind a wall of smog.

What this place must have been like in the twenties, the thirties, even the forties! A *paradise,* native Californians like Freddy termed it. Orange groves and clear dry air and Sunset Boulevard a rustic street lined from Beverly Hills to the sea by open fields, orchards, an occasional house. All sorts of blossoms scenting the air, and agriculture the main industry. All the sun with none of the noise, the noxious air, the crowds, the traffic jams. The porno movies.

A jetliner hung low over the hazy coastline, getting into traffic pattern for landing at LAX. And Don was suddenly swept by homesickness: by longing for his children, his old friends, his mother, and ex-wife; by nostalgia for the scenes of his childhood, his adulthood, his life until five years ago, all of it just six hours away—if he dared risk the flight, the strain, the excitement. If he dared risk the cabin pressure, which doctors warned could be dangerous.

He turned from the windows and went to the study and the unpaid bills, the unanswered letters. At one time, along with his professional writing, he'd handled them day by day. Now once a week was good; once every ten days average.

His daughter had sent a brief note last Monday: She was going to Martha's Vineyard with her latest boyfriend. She expected to eat "tons of lobster." She hoped he was feeling well. Love and kisses, Mootzie—which was the pet name he'd given her when she was three.

His son's letter had arrived yesterday, after no letters for about a month. School was a drag and work was so-so, "but partying is *real bad,* so who can complain!"

A competent womanizer, his son Marv, at just eighteen. A cautious and selective swinger, his daughter

Rita, at twenty-one. They'd learned the trick of pleasure early, when he hadn't until he was almost forty, if
then. If now.

They were good kids, bright kids, and Rita would
be teaching next fall and Marv would be a sophomore
at Purchase (if he didn't quit to return to the roofing
job he'd held for the past three summers). And who
cared if they'd gone to schools no one had ever heard
of; state colleges and almost free? Because they'd
learned to their capacities.

He was pleased with them both. Whatever they
might or might not accomplish, they were work-
oriented—including his wise-guy son, who'd never
stopped working at one thing or another—and so
many kids, including the overeducated, weren't. Yet
neither had the sweaty drive, the intense ambition,
that had driven their father from grammar school on;
that had shoved him up and out of the East New York
ghetto . . . perhaps into Cedars–Sinai Hospital.

Stress could be the villain. Genetic inheritance could
be the villain. So could steak, hamburger, and lamb
chops, along with milk, eggs, and cheese. As could the
cigarettes he'd smoked, the booze he'd drunk, the city
air he'd breathed.

And it no longer made a difference since the pumping chamber was blown, the scar tissue formed, the arteries narrowed. He wished his children better luck, and
put their letters aside for another morning when
his health wouldn't so strongly affect what he thought
and felt. He was breathing heavily, uncomfortably
aware of his heartbeat, and decided it was time to lie
down and count his blessings. Such as being alive, period.

He dozed. He dreamt. He escaped this sordid city,
this sordid time, for the late 1930s of his Brooklyn
childhood. Dreamt of the East New York ghetto on
those special days when its special life showed—Rosh
Hashanah, Yom Kippur, Passover, Chanukah, the

lesser-known holidays like Purim, Sukkoth, Tisha B'Av. Moved through narrow twilight streets that were the natural settings for these memories; the candle-lit, golden-backlit rooms where relatives and neighbors crowded and came and went. And the shabby rooms seemed beautiful and the mean streets seemed magic and he sighed in his sleep, knowing it hadn't been so for him, knowing it had been so for those who believed.

And awoke to see he'd slept less than an hour. And was still oppressed by that heavy pulse, that awareness of his heartbeat.

He returned to the study to check his desk calendar. He was scheduled to see the doctor Wednesday morning, at which time he would receive soothing conversation, the security of generally favorable ECG reports, a brief lecture on the curative miracles of chemotherapy, by-pass surgery, and saltless diet. He would forget, for a while, that X rays showed that the heart he had borne for forty-nine years was drastically and dangerously deformed, indicating he would indeed die like all men, but sooner rather than later.

He checked the time. Much too early to call Cecily.

He had another cup of Postum while listening to the news on radio. He had a slice of toast and a banana, and felt well enough to dress for his walk through Beverly Hills.

Driving down the canyon, he decided he would have the SL's hardtop removed next week at the dealer's. He would begin enjoying the sunny weather with the convertible's top down.

It made him smile. Convertibles weren't for dying men. Beautiful women weren't for dying men. Movie deals weren't for dying men. And he had all three.

Four

Friday, May 13,
and Saturday, May 14

On page 1 of *Daily Variety* and *The Hollywood Reporter* this particular Friday was a story that ran identically in both trade papers, and started Don's phone ringing.

"Island Corp." Formed For Dennings Flick

A production company has been formed by Berry-Pandero in conjunction with Frederick Gower, Donald Baylis, and Rob Dennings. The film, based on author Baylis's novel, *Galt's Island,* will co-star heavyweight Dennings and newcomer Cecily Warren in what is described as "an uncompromisingly realistic caper-romance." Veteran scripter Otis Daimler and casting director Charles Campbell have joined the team, and location hunters are being sent to Florida, the locale of the novel. A supporting cast of "Academy Award winners and nominees" is being sought, according to Gower, and contracts will be signed before completion of the script.

*　*　*

Don had been shown the release by Berry-Pandaro's publicity girl and told where it would appear, but no one was sure just when. He found out when his phone rang at eight-thirty, very early for people in the Hollywood milieu to bother each other.

"Don? Hope I didn't wake you, but this is a day for you to be up with the sun! Congrats! Can't think of anyone to put your property over the top like Rob Dennings! Listen, I'm at Schwab's. Take you ten minutes and we'll be having breakfast. I'm a little fuzzy on your characters, but as I recall there's one I always wanted to play. Hello? You with me, Don?"

"Not really. Who is this?"

"Eric. Can you make it?"

"Eric?"

"Or would you rather I drove up there? I don't have my address book with me, so give me directions. I'll bring copies of both papers for your scrap book."

"Eric who?" Don said, finally beginning to understand.

"Chester, baby. Eric Chester! Guess I did wake you. Clear the cobwebs and all that and let's get talking turkey."

"I'm sorry, Mr. Chester . . ."

"C'mon, man, *Eric*. We spent hours talking about how we could work together, you as the writer and me as the actor."

"I don't recall it, Eric."

"Freddy Gower's place, a while ago."

"Ah. One of Freddy's parties. How long a while ago?"

Brief chuckle. "I don't keep records, Don. A few months. A year, maybe."

"Maybe two. Maybe three. Maybe never. Because, Eric, I don't know you at all. Besides, I'm not involved in casting."

"I'll tell Freddy you suggested I call him, right?"

"Freddy won't believe you. Because I never suggest

anyone call anyone. I'm a bad contact, Eric. Good-bye."

The man was still talking as he hung up.

The phone rang again a moment later. He allowed it to ring three times, after which the answering machine gave its little message: "Donald Baylis is not at home. At the sound of the tone, please leave your name, phone number, and any brief message, and your call will be returned. Thank you."

"Don, it's Eric. Listen, I'll call Freddy, okay? I'll tell him we chatted and you figured I'd better talk to someone more into the production end. Thanks, buddy."

Don shook his head, reaching for the phone to wake Freddy, if the callers hadn't already done that. And it rang again. Automatically, he lifted it.

"Donny?"

He tried to place the voice.

"Donny, you there?" It was a very sweet, feminine voice.

He sat down, making himself comfortable. "Yes, who is it?"

"Diane. Just read the story in *Variety*. Marvelous for you, dear. You once promised . . . oh, I know it's been a while, but a promise is a promise, correct? You promised that you'd give me a push the next time you were in a position to do so."

"And when did I last . . . uh, push you, Diane?"

She laughed, low and throaty. "Same old Donny. *That* came first and foremost, no matter what the business involved."

The name, and the voice, were both vaguely familiar. "I know we've met, Diane, and from what you say, head on."

Again the throaty laugh. "That too."

"But I can't place you, exactly, so please identify yourself."

"Really?" The disappointment was evident. "Diane

Reardon, Fanny's friend. After you two split—maybe three, three and a half years ago—I came around one night, remember, to get a few things she'd left when she was still too mad to come herself."

"Got it now, Diane. A fun evening. You brought solace to a casualty of love's wars."

"Three or four times, until you met up with Cecily Warren. I see by the story she's co-starring with Rob Dennings! What a push *that* must have been! Did you see 'Barnaby Jones' about a month ago? The one with the drug addict? I was the girl who got killed."

"Missed that one, Diane. And I won't waste your time. I'm not involved in casting. Cecily Warren got the part without any help from me."

"Sure." The word was flat. "Couldn't you just tell the casting director I'm a friend?"

He decided the simplest way out was to accede. "I'll do that, Diane. And you can say you know me."

"Thanks, Donny!" Her voice was sweet again, enthusiastic again, though his promise was worthless, even if carried out. "You know, Fanny and I met at a cattle call last week, and she still talks about getting together with you again."

He said good-bye, and called the big stand on Fairfax where he bought so many softcover books, magazines, out-of-town papers that he was known by name and could get delivery of any item within an hour for a dollar surcharge.

He showered, heard the bathroom phone ringing, and ignored it. He shaved and dressed, and heard the phone again.

It was nine-fifteen, and Cecily occasionally called this early, so he walked to the study and listened to the answering machine:

"Donny? This is Fanny. You there?" She paused to allow him time to pick up the handset. He didn't. "Called to find out how you're feeling, *dahling*." Her "dahling" was a broad Australian thing. She'd erased most other traces of her Melbourne poor-town accent, but kept that one word as a trademark. "Hope your heart isn't giving you any more trouble. Both ways." A little laugh. "Please get back to me when you can. Love you, as always. Bye-bye."

Well, she'd love him pretty good at that, for a while. A blond pixy who'd been dancing in a nude club when he'd first met her, she'd warmed his bed, and his heart, for almost a year before her temper, her late hours, and her inability to consider anyone besides herself wore out his patience and her welcome. The last he'd heard, she was living with a rock composer who snorted more in coke than he earned.

Fanny worked hard at being an actress, and had managed to land a series of small parts in the last few years.

A very pretty girl. Also, very different from Cecily. And he occasionally thought of her, occasionally looked at the old nude photos he kept in the storage bin and remembered her lovemaking and grew desirous.

Cecily had other men, didn't she? The old Mexican, for sure. Freddy, probably. And soon Rob Dennings.

Maybe it was time he renewed his acquaintanceship with Fanny Batcher. She'd always been willing to play a little, if only to prove she could cut in on Cecily. What would she be willing to do if he held out the prospect of her landing the role of the secretary, Candy? She was right for the part, physically, and even if they spotted her accent, it could be written into the script. A plus, actually.

But Candy was the other sexually explicit female role. Fanny had danced nude, true but she'd turned down every hardcore porno offer she'd received, and she'd received plenty during the time she'd worked the Sunset Strip clubs. Some of the offers had involved advances of up to three thousand dollars, and Fanny had been desperate for money. Still, she'd said no. She had family back in Melbourne: a mother, father, two brothers. Also, a cousin who'd emigrated to New York City. She feared one of them finding out.

What would she think of *Galt's Island?*

Little chance of keeping a part in *that* a secret.

Interesting to learn whether she differed from Cecily . . .

He realized he hadn't played back the call he'd received while in the shower. He turned the dial to Rewind, let it hit the end of the tape, put it on Playback. The voice was theatrically sensual and sexy, what he took to be a low-pitched female's.

"*Hello,* Don. So *nice* to speak to you again, though you might not remember. This is *Bobby. Try* to remember. We never made it, but I've always wanted to suck your *huge* cock."

Don laughed, thinking: "No, we certainly didn't make it."

"I give such a great *head,* Don. And it wouldn't cost you a *thing.* Just a little *intro* to that casting director. I'd give *him* some, too. And Freddy Gower, who digs them a little *younger* than me, but the same sex. He can grease *my* rear end for a change."

Don frowned, beginning to recall something.

"It's Robert Aster Vines. Remember now?"

Don remembered, and sighed, reaching out to shut off the voice. Bob Vines was an automobile mechanic Freddy had recommended. Vines was a medium-sized, thick-armed, crew-cut man who talked about his service in "Nam with the Marines" and how he'd had "a brief fling with acting but lucked out when my girl made me quit." He was, as Don recalled, married, with two young children.

He decided to allow the voice to continue the few seconds left on the tape.

"Call me at the gas station, Don. I assure you that I'm even better as an actor . . ."

The cut-off brought blessed silence. Don started for

the bathroom, then detoured to the front door as the bell rang, and got his copies of *Daily Variety* and *The Hollywood Reporter*. He read the items, and wondered how he'd have felt if the movie were going to be free of porno: a big, straight production. Proud, certainly. He'd have called the kids.

He took his medication in the bathroom, and looked at the extension phone, wondering whether to return Fanny's call right now. Or whether to call Cecily and see what was on for today. She still hadn't brought Johnny over. She was slipping, side-stepping, shaking off all his offers like O.J., the Juice himself, on a good Sunday afternoon.

He was suddenly sick of it—and of all the thinking, the emotion, he did over that damned woman!

It would be good for him to see another woman, sleep with another woman, become interested in another woman.

Especially another woman who could be placed in the cast and on the set of *Galt's Island;* who could report to him what was happening between Cecily and Rob Dennings; between Cecily and anyone else.

He didn't particularly like that thought, but it persisted.

He went to the kitchen, and decided that today was a big day. So he soft-boiled two eggs and ate them and their cholesterol with crumbled whole-wheat bread. And didn't stop there, mixing himself a cup of instant Sanka coffee, not nearly as safe, as nourishing, as Postum. "I live for danger," he announced dramatically.

The phone rang. He strolled to the study to allow the answering machine to give its message.

"Donny? Hey, bun, answer! It's Cecily. Your lover. Your superstar! Hello, hello, hello!"

He reached for the phone; then stopped.

For the first time in a long time—certainly since his M.I.—he didn't want to speak to her, didn't want to see her. They'd made love yesterday afternoon, and even that hadn't been up to par.

She waited a good long time, then left a message: "I'll call about one, bunny. Have to meet with the script writer. He wants to see the major actors and actresses; wants to craft our roles specifically to our real personalities. We arranged . . ."

The machine cut her off. He was just as glad.

The scriptwriter would enjoy *crafting* those fuck scenes, all right. Crafting them to the shape and consistency of her tits, her ass. Maybe he'd try for a little run-through, for her career's sake, of course. And she'd agree, for her career's sake. Every filthy thing she did was for her career's sake, the *cunt!*

He was raging. And it was too late to deal with Fanny on any meaningful level, any honest level. Too late for Diane and whoever else might call to ask for "pushes." Because that M.I. had frozen him in place. The books he had written were those he would live with; the woman he had last loved was the one he would remain with. Whoever threatened that balance threatened his chances for survival.

And it was Freddy's long, tanned face, Freddy's swiftly roving eyes, Freddy's easy lecherous smile that came to mind. Freddy who was no stranger, as were the others she'd taken. Freddy who'd come to him in the hospital, seen his weakness, knew his dependency on Cecily. Freddy who was mocking him in a totally intolerable manner!

The phone rang.

He was suddenly very tired and walked away from the ringing to the kitchen. He had another cup of Sanka, and the phone rang. He rinsed out the cup, and the phone rang. His eyes began closing, his mind began shutting down. And the phone rang.

He went to bed fully dressed. He slept, a hot, sticky, troubled sleep. And in it, through it, he grew aware of a new depth of misery, a second stage in his M.I., an

infarction of the brain. And knew he should risk air-
plane travel, train or car or bus travel, and flee this
city, this woman, this vile movie. Knew he had to run
for his life.

But he slept on. He stayed set in place, in L.A.,
where his life would be played out. Where the phone
kept ringing as people left messages begging to be allowed to do whatever he wanted. Where he finally
awoke and called Fanny, leaving a message with her
service, determined to fight back . . . though exactly
against what he wasn't sure, exactly how he wasn't
sure.

The phone began ringing at a quarter to nine. Before Bub could tell some broad whose name and voice
he didn't recognize to call back at a more civilized
hour, Freddy was on the bedroom extension, clearing
his throat. "Okay, Bub, I'll take it." Which was a surprise.

A half-hour later the boss-man was downstairs in his
bathrobe, asking for hotcakes, saying the movie announcement had hit the trades this morning and he
wanted to "field all the action" himself, meaning the
actresses trying for parts.

Three times during breakfast he answered the
counter phone and jotted down names and numbers.
After the third call, he leaned back chuckling. "Better
buy about a dozen cartridges of film, baby. My bed's
going to be *smoking* the next few weeks!"

All well and good, but Bub wasn't thinking of ass.
Bub was thinking he had to meet Brains and Albert
outside the L.A. County Art Museum to pick up one
of Albert's sons, take the kid to the apartment on San
Vicente, and drive to the Santa Monica beach parking
lot where Sunset ended. They'd have their meet inside
Albert's gray station wagon. He'd give them the game
plan for Saturday night and return to the apartment
to make sure the kid was sleeping from half a Lude.

Then home to play houseboy until midnight, when he'd cut out for the day off—Friday evening to Saturday evening—he'd arranged for last week. Might even bring the kid with him to Bedford Drive when establishing his alibi, as Freddy said he'd be out until the wee hours. And finally back to the apartment about two A.M. Sunday to trade the kid for his share of the take.

A simple, airtight plan.

No reason to worry.

He dropped the plate with his own pancakes, and cursed and tossed them into the trash. He said he had to do some shopping.

"You haven't had any breakfast," Freddy said, staring at him.

He was saved by the bell; the phone. Freddy got on it. "Hey, Rob! Good shot in the trades, huh? Your phone's getting a workout? God knows how they get the unlisted numbers. You don't think mine is in the book, do you? But not being America's most desired male body, I'm taking advantage of every hotpants actress . . ."

Bub began to leave the kitchen, waving, as Freddy said: "Cecily Warren? Well, that's sticky, Rob. I didn't say impossible. Sure you have to discuss the way you'll handle your roles. Certainly the situation is unique and requires some agreement, perhaps even some, uh, private rehearsal." A pause. "I'm definitely not being cynical, Rob. Hell, I'd be anxious, too, if I had to hit the cameras cold in an all-out sex scene with a stranger."

Bub smiled to himself, going out the front door. Freddy was lying in his teeth. He balled nothing *but* strangers. And almost always in front of a camera.

He drove north to Wilshire, then east to the museum, slowing, looking across morning traffic to the broad stone steps. And saw Brains and a black kid standing there. No Albert.

He went another block, made his U-turn, and came back on the museum side of Wilshire. He swung to the curb, tapping his horn.

Brains came over, pulling the boy by the hand. "Here's Uncle Bub," he said, smiling his broad-lipped smile.

The boy said: "Why I have to go with him? Why pop take me outta school to go with him? Man, this is crazy!"

He was the older of the two kids whose pictures Albert had carried in his wallet: good-looking, good-sized (at least five feet two or three), showing some of his father in his sullen face, broad shoulders, big hands. And, when Brains shoved him into the Caddy, in his language. "Don't *push*, honky motherfucker!"

Brains chuckled and stepped back, slamming the door. "Have fun." And to Bub, "Noon, the beach, right?"

Bub nodded, and pulled away. "What's your name?" he asked the kid.

"Man, what's *your* name? Why you taking me . . ."

Bub turned and looked at him. "I asked your name."

The kid judged that cold look, that cold voice. "Jason. I mean, why should my father tell me I gotta spend all day today and tomorrow with *you?* I never heard about no Uncle Bub before."

"Your father has to work and asked me to take care of you."

"Yeah? Whyn't he leave me at home, with my mother?"

"Your mother has to go somewhere."

"Then whyn't they leave me with Lily?"

"Lily's busy."

"Lily's *never* busy, man! Lily sits in a wheelchair. She makes her bread looking out for kids . . . and sometimes for bigger cats, like me."

"You are big for twelve." And even before the kid

answered, suspected Albert had made him younger to
make the idea of holding him hostage, ugly, unthinkable.

"Fourteen, man, three weeks ago!"

"Well, happy birthday. Have to get you something.
What is it you'd like?"

"You gonna buy me a chopper, Uncle Bub?"

Bub nodded, smiling. "How about breakfast?"

"I like the Farmer's Market and all the different
kinds of food when I come to Los Angeles."

"Too early," Bub said. "We'll stop at a supermarket
and get whatever you want and I'll show you how I
earn my living."

"You a cook?"

"A chef, baby. The best."

"I like ham steak."

"With eggs? Maybe a ham omelette? Maybe ham
dipped in egg batter and pan-fried? With chocolate
milk?"

"Coffee, man! I'm no baby!"

"Fine. Here's Ralph's."

They shopped for twenty minutes, the kid getting
more and more friendly.

When they reached the two-story apartment building, Bub drove around back, parking near the rear
staircase. He carried the sack of groceries and the kid
ran up ahead and Bub was pleased that they met no
one coming down. The door to Apartment G was in
the brief inner hallway leading to the outer hallway
onto which all the other apartments opened.

"Hey, television and everything!" Jason yelled, rushing inside when Bub unlocked the door.

Bub went right to the kitchen, which was off the
large studio room. There was a good-sized bedroom,
too, through a door opposite the hall door, and beyond that a bathroom. All furnished, for four-fifty a
month. He'd taken it for one month, "on a trial basis,"
and would have gone elsewhere if the manager had

turned him down. But there were four empty apartments out of twelve, and the old man had said, "All right. But no loud parties, hear? This is a family place."

Family place hell. Bub had met two hookers when he'd visited his apartment ten days ago, and they lived next door to a young gay who cruised all week long, the hookers said. They offered to arrange a foursome, since he seemed disinterested in a simple threesome. He didn't like the way the blond kept licking a lip sore, and said he'd look them up after he got settled.

Now he made breakfast, for himself as well as the kid, relaxing a bit as Jason turned the TV on its swivel to face the kitchen table and got a comedy rerun—"I Dream of Jeannie." "Love that Jeannie," the kid said, giving him a sly glance.

Well, he could always keep him happy with one of the hookers.

He took a Quaalude from his pocket tin, broke it along the scoring, and dissolved half in Jason's cup of freeze-dried coffee. The kid watched his blond turn-on in her harem outfit and ate ham steak fried in egg batter and said, "Man, good! You some sort of cook, all right!" He creamed and sugared his coffee heavily and drank it down and asked for another cup.

And ten minutes later was asleep, head on the table.

Bub carried him into the bedroom and pulled off his shoes. He covered him with a light blanket, certain that half a Lude would keep him under at least eight, ten hours.

Still, before leaving the apartment, he wrote a note and put it on the kitchen table:

"Jason, I had to go out for a while. Help yourself to whatever you want in the fridge. Also, snacks in the cabinet under the sink. Watch some TV. I'll be back soon. Uncle Bub."

Not that the kid had a chance in a million of waking before he returned from Santa Monica. But just to be safe.

Otis Daimler was fifty-three, big, much too heavy for his own peace of mind, smoked far too much for his own peace of mind, and was currently involved in a situation that made peace of mind a very academic concept indeed.

Originally an actor—but that had ended twenty years ago—who had struggled through a period of true poverty as a door-to-door photographer, cab driver, and professional borrower from half a dozen friends, he had persisted in writing TV scripts until, miraculously, one had sold to the old black-and-white "Gunsmoke" show. After that he found a decent agent, and by working long hours every day at the typewriter paid off more than seven thousand dollars and regained five or six friends. One of these five friends had been, and still was, Fred Gower.

Which was why Otis was going through his copy of *Galt's Island* for the third time, trying to pull together his thoughts on how to translate an overabundance of story into a financially feasible two-hour screenplay— and at the same time build to those very special "love" scenes Gower had described.

Not that he was inexperienced at screenplays; he'd authored and co-authored seven scripts from novels— *co*-authored because it was SOP in Hollywood to bring in another writer for what was euphemistically termed a "polish," in effect a revision according to the producer's direct instructions. Only with his last script, based on the wordy bestseller, *Woodrow*, had he managed to retain exclusive authorship.

Woodrow had just opened to strong reviews and promised to make some money. Which, along with his knowing Freddy, was responsible for Otis being given the *Galt's Island* assignment. And a solid $75,000 fee.

Scripting was stressful, certainly, but he'd learned to

live with it, and retain a degree of tranquility. Claire's illness, severe for the past two years, had at first shaken him badly, but he now accepted the fact that arthritis could indeed cripple a bright and physically vital woman, a beautiful woman whom he had loved and lusted after for seventeen years; whom he still loved, but whose gradually twisting body had made lust a rare thing. What she needed, she insisted, was a pool to swim in every day, without his having to drive her to a healthclub; a pool and jacuzzi in her own backyard so her pride, her ego, wouldn't be wounded by strangers watching as she struggled to loosen her arthritic joints.

What she needed was the house they'd fallen in love with; the house on the quiet cul-de-sac off Nichols Canyon. It had the pool and spa and four bedrooms and three baths so her mother and his mother and her daughter by a first marriage and his old-maid sister could visit, all at the same time if that unlikely event ever came to pass. The house they'd put a three-thousand-dollar deposit on Wednesday after he got his ten-grand advance from Berry-Pandaro. The house whose $142,000 price tag required they sell their little Sherman Oaks rancher in the broiling San Fernando flats well north of Ventura for the $90,000 their real estate agent said they could get.

But in the process of embarking on all this, his peace of mind had been first diluted, then utterly destroyed. For there was that enormous new mortgage to face, plus closure fees and agent's fees and movers' fees and the inevitable costs of filling that big house with furniture and God knew what else!

All of which led to the big question: What if he didn't land another major assignment after this one, because what if he didn't succeed at this one?

Reading Donald Baylis's novel, awaiting his visitors, he broke into a cold sweat. He regretted, bitterly, having allowed himself to make such violent changes in his life at a time when he needed all his powers of concentration to do what he had always found difficult—write a script. Imagine if he'd had to do an *original!*

He was a hack, competent and with a solid knowledge of motion pictures from all angles, but a hack nonetheless. He only hoped he alone knew this.

He sat in his study, dressed in his new blue slacks and matching sports shirt, which he'd already outgrown, the weight, the *fat*, reaching 280 pounds. Sat and sweated. Next Wednesday Xtra Reality would hold what they called "a caravan," during which all of their salesmen, some thirty-odd, would come through this house and assess its selling price—hopefully that $90,000 the agent of record, Gayne Brown, said it was worth.

And then the following Sunday, an open house, during which more strangers, this time buyers, would come to look and sneer.

Why assume they would sneer? The house was attractive, though it badly needed outside painting.

Gayne thought it would be a good idea to have the painting done before the first open house. Otis had gotten two estimates. The cheaper was thirteen hundred dollars.

And there was that sluggish toilet.

And the warped side door.

And the yard badly needed grass, shrubs . . .

Claire called him. He rose and walked heavily down the short foyer, past the bathroom, to the master bedroom. She was lying on her back, face drawn, but she smiled and said: "Otty, just think, we'll be in that beautiful house in just two months!"

"Could be longer," he said, fear stabbing his vitals, thinking: "What if ours doesn't sell before then? Where do I get twenty percent of $142,000 for a down payment? And those enormous monthly payments!"

"I was daydreaming, Otty. I was thinking I'll fool

the doctors when I can swim twice every day; soak in that boiling spa twice a day."

She was asking for encouragement. He nodded, came to the bed, sat down, and took her hand. It had always been small compared with his. *She* had always been small compared with his six one, his broadness, his thickness that had turned to obesity. Now she was wasted.

Jesus God, how did it happen so fast? His gorgeous blond show-girl. His glamorous Vegas hoofer. His sharp, sexy, always-laughing lover. Who laughed no more.

The rich curves, the full swellings, were gone. As if overnight, gone, along with his lust, his pleasures. She'd grown fragile, almost skeletal . . .

The doorbell rang. He said: "Must be the actors I asked to drop by. It'll be helpful to see who, exactly, I'm writing about." As he left, he closed the door behind him, because she didn't like meeting actors, especially actresses, since the changes began.

The moment he saw Cecily Warren, he understood he was an idiot to waste energy, money, peace of mind, on a new house, no matter what Claire thought it would do for her. Because it wouldn't change the course of her galloping arthritis. She wouldn't be using that pool, or anything but a wheel chair in a year, according to no less than three specialists. And it wouldn't make Otis happy, that "mini estate in a prestige area south of Mulholland," as the real estate agents put it, because it wasn't a house he needed, it was *this!*

A pulse throbbed in his throat as he said: "Come in, Miss Warren."

He saw her beauty, felt her sensuality, visualized her in the two scenes he could build to, the scenes she would "act" with Dennings—and her *availability* struck him like a hammer. His thick hands trembled as he closed the door. He was stricken for a moment,

unable to hide his need, and the bell rang again. He
seized on it, chuckling, nodding, turning away, opening the door. And was shocked.

"Ah, Rob. Hey, an honor!"

He'd known Dennings many years ago; had acted in
a supporting role in one of the star's pictures. He'd
spoken to him a few times in the past few years,
mainly at Fred's parties, when Claire had still gone to
parties. He certainly hadn't expected him to come to
this briefing, though he'd made the invitation, leaving
a message with the woman who answered Dennings's
phone.

Cecily Warren and Ben Bright, who was going to
play the accountant who ran the gang of thieves for
Dennings, he'd expected. Cecily Warren was the only
one he'd actually wanted here.

Because all this was a sham. He could write his
script without ever meeting the actors, which was the
way he'd always worked before. But he'd been curious
to see the woman that would screw before the entire
world.

Dennings came in and said, "Hello, Cecily," and she
said, "No one thought you'd bother to come, Rob,"
and they moved together, touching hands, looking into
each other's faces.

Otis walked ahead of them to the living room, and
offered drinks, and the doorbell rang a third time. He
excused himself, returned to the door, and greeted Ben
Bright, a strong character actor of about fifty, whom
he'd known from both acting and writing stints. He
led him to the living room, where Cecily and Rob
were seated together on the couch, which looked small
and shabby with those two beautiful animals on it.

Bright said yes, he'd have a drink, even if no one
else would.

Otis mixed him a Scotch and water and a stronger
one for himself. He sat down facing his three guests,
trying to keep his stomach from bulging over his

waistband. He wiped at his forehead, his upper lip, his neck, and lit a cigarette. He sucked smoke deep into his lungs, and hated himself for the filthy habit everyone seemed to be shaking, and for the fat everyone seemed to be losing. Cecily and Rob still spoke softly, intimately. She put back her head and pealed laughter. "We could over-rehearse something like that, Rob."

Otis knew what they were talking about. Knew and churned inside, feeling fat and ugly. And he *wasn't* ugly; had been one of the "new crop of matinee-idol prospects" to quote *Silver Screen* of twenty-five years ago. If he got into shape, that actress-whore would jump at the chance to ball him!

She crossed her legs, laughing again, and her yellow dress was slit on the side and her thigh flashed white. Otis told himself he had to stop this, had to play his legitimate role. As hardworking scriptwriter. As husband to the woman he loved. As jolly fat man known for his even temper, his sense of humor, his loyalty to wife and family and friends, his gentleness in all things.

Not as the man who, twenty-*six* years ago, before the second lead in *The Big Reformatory* brought him his one moment of fame, before the *Silver Screen* article made it look as if he would break through to stardom, before he fell apart as an actor, had fallen apart one night as a human being.

He had raped a girl in an empty lot not far from the Pico Boulevard bar where he'd watched her quarrel with her boyfriend; watched and followed and punched her in the temple and dragged her over scraggly grass and debris, shaking with a terrible need.

He'd torn her clothing off, but not in haste. He'd kneeled over her, ripping apart first her dress, then brassiere, then panties. He'd left on the flesh-colored nylons. He'd caressed and kissed her body, happy, it seemed, for the first time since he'd been an eighteen-year-old back home. Which was the last time the beast within him had broken loose.

She'd begun to come around. He'd decided he'd better take off her stockings after all, because he had to use one to disguise himself.

When she'd regained consciousness, he was wearing this stocking mask, and he told her what he would do to her if she resisted. Told her in detail, and meant it. A disfiguring by use of the broken bottle he'd found amidst the debris. A long, painful, disfiguring, and finally a killing.

She'd wept a little, begged a little, but when he pulled her legs apart she gave in, whispering: "You won't hurt me, will you?" He'd melted then, saying no, kissing her—or trying to—through that stocking mask. But he'd grown terribly excited afterward. The fear in her face, her violent trembling, her dry tightness down there, all drove him wild. He'd pulled at her hair, her breasts; pulled and torn and drawn blood. And left her with the other stocking stuffed deep into her mouth, gagging on her tears, her pain, hands tied behind her with strips from her shredded panties.

It was the last time he'd let loose the ravening beast inside him, but that didn't mean the beast was dead.

It was the girl he'd raped who was dead. He'd read about it the next night. He'd stuffed that stocking too far into her mouth, too far down her throat, and she'd strangled on it.

Perhaps he'd meant to do it; known while shoving the nylon down her throat he was killing her. Still, he'd sat in his room, rocking back and forth, hands over his face, mourning the girl. After a while he'd stopped and put it out of his mind, except to check the papers every so often to see whether the case was moving toward a solution.

He never saw mention of it again.

And after meeting and marrying Claire, he never

thought of it again. Never let the beast loose again. Felt he was done with such things.

But sipping his drink, smoking his cigarette, sweating as he watched Cecily Warren and Rob Dennings speaking too softly, too intimately to be overheard, watching that beautiful face turn time and again to laughter, hearing that sensual peal of sound—seeing and feeling and wanting—he remembered the rape. The girl's name had been Andrea Beale. She'd been nineteen and an insurance company receptionist. She'd had brown hair and brown eyes and been described as "plump and appealing."

Yes, plump and appealing. Right for the beast at that time. As Cecily Warren was right for the beast at *this* time. Because he needed more of a woman now; needed more beauty, sensuality, importance in his victim now. Importance that Cecily Warren would attain as queen whore before all the world once *Galt's Island* was shot.

He cleared his throat and laughed at something Bright said about wanting to change roles: "I'd planned on being the government agent who rapes the secretary, but Freddy said I'm a little too mature for the part. And, if he only knew, a little too little." Otis saw Dennings's eyes flick to the character actor in seeming disapproval. Or was it that the great star was wondering whether he also was too mature and too little for the part?

Otis Daimler could handle it better than either of them! Claire had delighted in his penis; his eight thick inches. Cecily Warren would too, if only he could convince . . .

But, of course, he couldn't convince her. So he would have to find some way some day, of removing that simple yellow sundress, or whatever she might be wearing. With luck, he might not have to kill her.

He said: "I thank you for coming, you precursors of a cast of thousands. Well, dozens, anyway."

There were chuckles; and a little smile from the object of the beast's lust, he noted with satisfaction. "You, Amelia, you Galt, you Dilo," he said, using their names from the novel, and began to explain what his thoughts were on how to translate that novel into a first-rate movie.

Dennings asked questions. Dennings might direct, and therefore might became his antagonist—as he already was in competing for Miss Warren's crevices, tubes, juices.

Dennings said; "I believe we might have to drop one or even two of the gang."

"Perhaps. But if we use them briefly, see them only as backdrops to you, Cecily, and the two strong supporting characters—Ben and whoever plays the government agent . . ."

"What about the secretary?" Dennings asked.

"Yes, Candy." He looked at Cecily. "She's needed mainly to be raped by the government agent. In that scene she will be important. But later . . ." He shrugged. "Basically, she's a cheap piece of ass." Cecily's eyes flickered. He added, "As opposed to your role of heiress, lover, romantic."

She smiled.

He continued, growing more and more sure of himself, no longer tormented by her presence.

Because the beast had marked her for his own.

Fanny Batcher was sick of the noise Roy called his music; sick of making excuses for him to the manager of the apartment house on Olympic—the third place they'd lived in since December, and that must be some kind of record!—sick of the hard looks she got from neighbors because of his late-hours playing; sick of Roy himself, truth be known. She'd been thinking of Donny for the past few months anyway; thinking she could get back with him again, and even if he kicked off because of his bad heart, he would put her in his will and she'd come out okay. And then she'd seen that front page item in the *Reporter* and she could have died!

Imagine Cecily Warren, a nobody, getting the lead opposite *Rob Dennings!*

Imagine if she'd stuck with Donny, *she* could have had that lead role!

Roy was starting on the piano again—an eighteen-hundred-dollar spinet and they were still paying and the way he was going *she'd* be paying for that and everything else the rest of their lives.

Except she wouldn't be with him much more of her life. Tall and good-looking with his long Elvis-style face—the way Elvis had looked years ago, not the way he'd looked before he died. Dark hair and dark eyes and a smile she didn't like anymore because she was beginning to see he was so damned low, so damned stupid.

Like the crap song he was trying to write. She wished he'd go to the studio with that black drummer and his other coke-snorting friends and work up a gig and make some bread. But he kept saying he'd write this great song and the bread would roll in. He kept telling her about this rock star and that rock star and what they'd gotten for one little song like "Drift Away," or "Caught in the Middle," or other old tunes he identified with because at thirty-six he was already over the hill, the bonkers clown!

Now he was pounding away at the spinet; same song over and over; called it "Rock and Roll Suicide."

A joke, right? When he'd first sung part of it, she'd laughed, and he'd wanted to murder her!

She was in the bedroom of their two-room apartment, the kitchen being just a corner of the living room with a counter-bar to entertain and eat at. Most of the time they ate out, Roy being a junk-food nut. She was starting to put on weight; starting to get zits from all the sweets and crap. While he stayed lean and clean . . . and broke.

He was in the living room, singing and plunking and working on those retarded lyrics:

> If there's a hell for rockers,
> It's right here on earth,
> So take a pill or bullet,
> And man reverse your birth.
> *Rock* 'n' roll suicide,
> Suicide,
> Suicide,
> *Rock* 'n' Roll suicide
> That's the way to go!"

"Then *do* it already!" she screamed, enraged by his obvious lack of talent, the item in the *Reporter*, awareness that she had blown a year with this junkie freak. "Rock and roll yourself out of my life!"

His answer was to laugh: "Hey, cool it."

She slumped on the bed.

"Get your shit together," he said. "Let's go eat lunch."

She lay down, closing her eyes. She clenched her hands, trying not to explode. She wanted him to leave, but she didn't want a fight.

He came to the doorway. "You crashing this early?"

"Get the hell out."

"Sure. Want me to bring back Chinese?"

"All right," she said wearily.

"Got some bread?"

"My purse is on the counter. Take ten. Just ten, Roy."

"Since when did I ever rip you off, cunt?"

"Since three months ago. Since the last time you played a gig."

"So first I carried you; not you carry me. Soon I'll

get my big hit and we'll just lay back and watch the bread roll in. And smoke and sniff and float away."

She opened her eyes. "Just ten, Roy. I'll need gas for my morning appointment. I'm reading at Metro."

"Fucking at Metro, you mean." He went to the door, long body slouching.

"Roy."

He turned. "Don't bug me any more, lady, or I'll split for good."

"That's what I wanted to ask. Please split for good."

"We'll talk after eating."

"No talk. No eating." She sat up. "Go now, Roy."

He stared at her. "You got it." He went to the counter and opened her purse. She began to come off the bed. He took her wallet with money and ID and Mastercharge and headed for the door. She ran hard, and caught his arm. He turned, fist drawing back.

She let his arm go, stepped around him, opened the hall door. She raised her voice. "You're robbing me. If you walk out this door, I'll call for help. You're a junkie. You're a thief."

He shrugged, and threw the wallet across the room onto the couch. He slouched past her and out the door. And turned and hooked his fist deep into her stomach.

She was on her knees, gasping, for a full minute . . . and had to scramble to the bathroom, where she vomited briefly.

She straightened from over the toilet bowl, wiped tears of pain from her eyes, and took several deep breaths. Then she went to the closet and got his clothes—the suedes and leathers as well as the jeans—and stepped onto the little terrace. She watched for his beat-up Mustang convertible to pull out of the garage, then dropped all the clothing three stories onto the street. He jerked to a stop. She waved, and went to the bedroom and got his bright-colored bikini underwear and shirts and shoes and socks, an arm-load, and returned to the terrace.

He was putting the outfits into his car. A middle-aged couple across the street had stopped to watch. So had a teenage girl near the garage.

"Oh, Roy!" He looked up. She dropped the clothing and went to the stereo cabinet and got his albums—his noisy freak albums—and scaled these at him, one at a time. She got close with two, and he turned up a face full of rage and shook his fist. The teenage girl was laughing. The middle-aged couple looked shocked and began walking.

She leaned over the railing. "I'm going to the Wild-cat Club tonight. I'm telling Abbey you beat up on me. You know what he'll do, don't you?"

Roy picked up the remaining clothing and albums, threw them into the car, and screeched off, burning rubber. Abbey was the bouncer at the nude joint she'd been working in when she'd met Don. Abbey wasn't all there, and he'd purely *loved* little Fanny. The one time he'd met Roy he'd rubbed his big hands together and said: "He gives you trouble, honey, I'll put him away. Just tell me."

She might at that. Though the threat alone should be enough. Roy was a coward, except with chicks. Why she'd ever taken up with him . . .

It was her style. She went for the bad guys, and discarded the good guys. She gave to the musicians, the bartenders, the actors, and took from the businessmen, the professionals, the one writer she'd known. She still hadn't shaken the teenage contempt for squares, johns; the teenage adulation for greasers, rockers, junkers. But Jesus, Fanny-Girl, learn now, learn fast!

She'd be twenty-eight come September twelfth. No longer a kid. She was still tight in the boobs, though they weren't very big; certainly not like that cow, Ceci-ly's. Her legs were still dancer's legs; her face good, though the bags under her eyes . . .

She was in front of the bedroom-door mirror, and fluffed out her short-cropped white-blond hair, and pressed her stomach. Despite everything, she was satisfied with the way she looked. The men still went ape for Fanny-Girl, the name she'd used as a nude dancer.

When she checked her service and learned Don had called while she was out at Burbank Studios, she did a little shimmy of joy; then dialed quickly; then groaned at that long-winded recorder message.

"It's Fanny, *dahling*. Returning your call. Hope you'll call again . . ."

He picked up the phone. "Yes, Fanny. Wanted to make a quick suggestion. That you phone Charlie Campbell and tell him I said you'd be very right for the part of Candy. She's a character in *Galt's Island*."

"I remember the book, Don. Very clearly." (Well, not so clearly, but she *had* read it, hoping even then, more than three years ago, that an option deal he had going with an independent producer would come through.)

"Good." He gave her the number. "It's almost three now. Give me ten minutes to speak to Charlie, then call him."

"Gee, thanks, baby! You're goddam swell!"

He laughed.

She wanted to ask about Cecily, but there was too much envy, too much animosity in her, and she decided against it. Just let Fanny-Girl spend a little time with Mr. Baylis, Esquire, and she'd get his pecker to pecking. He had to be ready for a fling, maybe a romance, after three years with Cecily Warren. Little Fanny knew enough about boy-girl, about life, to bet on tensions, angers, boredom, building up over so long a time. She herself had never managed more than eighteen months.

"Just one thing, Fanny. This picture has an unusual angle. Your role is important to the development of this angle. It might not be what you'll want to do."

She frowned. "Can't think of anything I wouldn't want to do in a big flick, babe. Only thing I ever turned down was porno."

"Yes," he said quietly. "Well, you talk to Campbell. He'll explain. I'll be available afterward, if you want my opinion."

"Always want your opinion, Donny. Call you back soon. To make a date. To reward you, *dahling*, for remembering your Fanny-Girl. *Bye!*"

When Charles Campbell got on the phone, Fanny put together the voice and the name to recall a tinker-bell who'd done casting for one of Warner's production groups two years ago; a very fruity fruit who helped keep the swish stereotypes alive and was disliked by other gays.

"I believe we know each other, Mr. Campbell."

"I believe we do, Miss Batcher. Hot pants and platinum shorty-cut and sexy-schmexy walk. Am I correct?"

She laughed. "Never forget a face, do you?"

"It's not the face you're selling, *dahling*."

This time she forgot to laugh. "Did Don Baylis call?"

"Yes. And for once an author is directly on target in a casting situation. Unless, of course, you've been unwise about calories?"

"Slim as ever."

"Or the mammaries have slipped and now play bouncy-poo with the knees?"

"They'll sock you in the eye."

"How delightful." He paused, and she heard paper rustling. His calendar? "Why don't you come in right now and let me see your book, your résumé? After that, we'll chat. About those special circumstances the author mentioned but didn't fully explain."

"Can't you give me a hint? I'm dying of curiosity."

"Not to be spoken about on the phone. And if you get an okay, not to be spoken about until after commencement of principal photography. And perhaps not even then, since it's going to be a promotion surprise, a promotion blitz. Though you may not want to speak of it anyway."

She dressed conservatively, hoping to reduce what Don had once called her lust-appeal, Campbell's tastes being what they were. But he greeted her from behind his desk at 20th Century with, "Wrong outfit, *dahling*. You still use that marvelous word, don't you?"

She said yes and sorry-about-the-outfit. He went to the door of his office and closed it, shutting off the outer room and a secretary-receptionist. "Remove the pants suit, please."

She blinked, wondering if he'd gone AC-DC or what. He still looked the same: short, slender, brown hair worn long for his mid-forties age.

He caught her reaction, and smiled. "You've got some sort of underwear on, I presume?"

She was wearing pantyhose, no panties. She never wore a brassiere.

She shook her head.

He sighed. "Well then, I'm in for it."

She went to a green leather couch and turned her back on him. She undressed quickly, down to her black pantyhose and silver klunkers. She was never without at least three inches of heel, often as much as six, because of her five three height. Today it was a reasonable four inches, in keeping with the conservative pale green pants suit. Which ended up on the couch.

"Anything more?" she asked.

"That's fine."

She turned, a hand rising automatically to her hair, to fluff it, to bring her breasts into prominence. She knew what she looked like to men-type men—this kind of scene brought them from behind their desks and created either problems or jobs. She selected her *jobs* carefully, and did all right. But with Campbell, it was a different ballgame . . . which was one of the reasons he was an objective and successful casting director. At least with women.

"Walk toward me."

She walked.

"Turn."

She turned her back on him.

"You're rather small in the bottom, my dear."

"I think of it as not big."

"Bend, please."

"What?" She looked over her shoulder at him.

"I said bend over. And give me coital movement."

What sort of tinkerbell turn-on was this?

She hesitated. He said, "Candy is a very strong part. I doubt you've ever had anything approaching it. This entire film represents an opportunity." He paused. "There is a definite sexual bent to two of the female roles, two of the male roles. Yours is one. You get raped."

"By the government agent," she said, remembering. She turned to face him. "You mean we're going with nudity and simulated sex?"

"Simulated, hell, lovey. We're going to show the entire act, in detail, just as the Pussycat and other porno-flick theatres show it."

"Will Dennings allow such scenes?"

"His is one of the two sexually explicit male roles involved. Now do you want to continue, or not?"

She didn't know. "Cecily Warren?" she asked, thinking Don would never allow his girl to do such a thing.

"The other female involved. To sum up, there's you and Warren, Dennings and an as-yet-to-be-cast government agent." He smiled. "We're looking for a big, fat, ugly threatening rapist, *dahling*. Pock-marked, if possible. Freakishly large down there, preferably. You'll have a *marvelous* time."

She stared at him. Then she said, "Union?"

"What do you think this is, schlock? The budget

climbs every day. We're over six million now, and wait until production actually begins."

"Above scale pay?"

"Well above. Hazard pay, you might call it. For that one scene. But you'll have other lines, other work, probably a week."

"A percentage?"

"Good-bye."

She shrugged and turned her back, but didn't bend. She'd never taken a porno offer, and she'd had dozens. But this was only one porno scene, as she understood it, out of a major supporting role. In a Rob Dennings picture!

Her cousin in New York.

Her father in Australia, who'd been driven wild by her posing for a few bikini pictures, one of the reasons she'd left home at seventeen.

Her mother, sick . . . and this could kick her into eternity!

But it would be months before shooting began. At least a year before the release date. And in that time, with this credit, with all the talk it was bound to create in the industry, she could really begin to work.

And why kid herself—she'd been fucking *off* camera to get *on* camera and half of Hollywood knew it. And half the girls in Hollywood did it more often than she did. So why throw away . . .

"I've got another appointment in fifteen minutes, Fanny. Coital action, please."

She bent over and humped and ground, and began to visualize working on Donny. Which really turned her on, and she groaned and put a hand between her thighs, a finger on the division in her pantyhose, and worked down on that hand, that finger.

"Try it on the carpet," Campbell said, and cleared his throat.

She went to her knees, and then over on her back, legs up and around her imaginary Donny. She used that hand, that finger, closing her eyes and moaning, wanting to say "Donny" as she grew truly excited . . . and said instead, "Charlie," thinking the worst she could get was a laugh.

She got another clearing of the throat, from directly above her. She opened her eyes to see him right there, looking down at her. He wasn't laughing. And if that wasn't a bump in his pants, he was carrying an awful lot of slack meat around.

"Turn over, please," he said, voice thick.

She didn't question what was happening. She turned over, giving him the rear.

"Pull down the pantyhouse."

She put her hand around back, but now she had to wonder. He could see everything necessary through the thin nylon. The only thing he couldn't do was touch.

"You're really," he began, and stopped and started again. "You're really very stimulating, very erotic, Fanny. I thought that two years ago, but I wasn't in tune with certain possibilities. I think the combination of brash femininity and a certain . . . boyishness makes you . . . attractive to a wide range of males."

She saw what was coming and groaned inwardly. Her rectum hadn't forgotten Roy's stoned attack three months ago, and she'd been stoned along with him. She needed a muscle relaxant, at least a tranquilizer . . . but she also needed this man on her side, right now. Especially for a good payday.

She pulled the pantyhose about a third down over her rear, to where he could see the beginning of her cheeks, her cleft. She said: "I wonder how they'll determine percentage above scale—that hazard pay for the sex scenes?"

"In the case of Dennings, a matter of contract. Cecily Warren has important friends—Baylis and Fred Gower. You, my dear, have only me." His voice seemed even thicker. "Baylis's call was merely suggestive, not a pulling of rank. Which he won't have much of, by the time principal photography begins."

That remained to be seen, she thought. Still, she needed Charlie, sore ass or not. She pulled the pantyhose down over her buttocks and turned on her side to strip them over legs and feet. But he stopped her.

"That's far enough." He went to the door and locked it with a dead-bolt. He went to his desk and an intercom unit. "Val, I'm not to be disturbed." He came back to where she lay on her side, encumbered by the pantyhose. He motioned for her to get back onto her knees. She did, awkwardly, held by that rolled nylon cloth.

"Like being bound," he whispered. "Helpless thing, exposed to slings and arrows."

She glanced up, and he was dropping his pants. He left on the pale cream jacket, the ocher shirt, and wide brown tie. He left on his shoes and his brown stockings gartered just below the knee. He was wearing a pair of flaming red bikini shorts with *Ferris* embroidered in black down the crotch. She hoped Ferris had trained him to gentleness.

He drew down the red shorts. He was in full erection . . . and she was grateful because he had what her brothers back home called a "pencil-cock"—very thin, and not much over five inches. He bent, tracing her cleft with one finger, until he reached her rectum, where he *pressed*.

She grunted as his index finger went in to the knuckle.

He withdrew, murmuring: "It's going to be fine."

She looked up again, and believed him. He was taking a small tube from his jacket pocket, opening it, squeezing out a thick white jelly.

Then he was crouching over and behind her, adjusting her position with his left arm around her waist, left hand between her legs. Then he was moving that right index finger, now slick with lubricant, back into her rectum.

The penis which followed wasn't much more trouble. He shoved it slowly, steadily into her, and she groaned. But it wasn't bad, had a certain erotic quality, especially when his left hand worked on her vagina. He began to hump, and his breath began to pound, and he was saying: "Dearheart, dearheart."

He knew how to bugger, that gay bastard. She'd never known it could be this painless, not to say this pleasurable. He was going to get her off, she could feel it coming, and she wasn't that easy to get off even in normal sex, even with a man she dug.

Damn, he was good!

She climaxed as his fingers played frantically, and he was close behind her. She moaned and shivered. He grabbed her hair with one hand, not pulling but holding tight. He grabbed her under-thigh with the other, not painfully but strongly. And said, *"Ride,* you gorgeous sonofabitch!" and spasmed inside her rectum and laughed shrilly.

After a moment, he pulled out and whacked her ass twice, sharply, the only time he hurt her. She said, "Ouch!" and turned her head. But he turned it back around with his hand, murmuring: "Just a second longer." And stroked her thighs, her hard dancer's thighs, and gripped her hair, her short-cut, man-cut hair. And she understood his turn-on and understood his not wanting her to show her face, her woman's face.

They used his private John and he went through her book in about two minutes flat. He said, "I think we've found our Candy," and tapped her résumé. "This address and telephone current?" She nodded. "Then I'll be in touch. We'll have a contract made up in about two weeks, but it'll be a while longer before we have a script."

She rose, feeling just a wee bit sore in the behind.

He said: "You'll find I don't renege on my word. You'll also find I won't *audition* you again."

She smiled. "You can, if you'd like."

"A compliment, I presume," he said, the fag bitchiness beginning to return. "You're so right for this part, Fanny."

"A compliment, I presume," she said, and walked out.

At home, she remembered Roy had his key and could come back and fuck up the apartment, beat up on her. If he had the guts, after her threat to sic Abbey on him. Which she doubted. But she called the manager anyway, explaining that she'd had to get rid of her roommate because of the noise, the bother to the other tenants, "the bother to you, Mr. Ivorson."

He was at least seventy, but still had an eye for the girls. He said he'd have her lock changed before the day was over. As for the service charge, "What the landlord don't know won't hurt him, right, Miss Batcher?"

She said right and she'd have to make him breakfast some morning. And hung up before he could ask *what* morning.

She called Don. No answer. She left a message; then lay down for a nap.

She slept. She dreamt. About running down a road with her father driving his Morris Minor alongside her and shouting: "Pick 'em up! Pick 'em up!" Just like it was when he'd tried to make her a scholastic marathon champ. Just before she'd posed for the bikini shots and they'd appeared in a local newspaper and he'd tried to kill her. And she'd gone to Sydney for a while, and then to the States.

She awoke, telling herself it was all behind her; it was the past and the present was bright and the future, with Donny's help, could be *super!*

She called Donny again, even though she knew she should wait for him to return her last call.

He answered. He said he'd taken a drive in his Mercedes. She asked if he'd take her for a ride; she wanted to talk about *Galt's Island.* "I think you know why." He chuckled a little. He said he'd made other plans for the evening. "But perhaps tomorrow afternoon."

"Why not tomorrow night?" she asked, knowing Saturday night and his girl and all that, but testing.

He hesitated. "Maybe. Let's plan on lunch, the Cock 'n Bull, about one-thirty. We'll see what develops from there."

She said, "All right," and meant, *Terrific!* Definite problems in the Baylis-Warren household . . . if they *were* a household. "Want me to come to your place?"

"The restaurant will be fine. See you then."

She made a kissing sound, and he said, "Thank you, baby," the way he used to.

She danced around the living room. No more rock 'n' roll suicides for Fanny-Girl!

The phone rang. It was an actor she'd met at FIWI—Film Industry Workshop, Inc. Tall. Blond. About her age. A doll.

Later that night, clasped in his hard arms, with his hard prick throbbing inside her, with his name a sweetness in her mouth, she whispered, "Love you, Eddie," and meant it. Then they arranged to meet here in her apartment twice a week. They couldn't meet at his place. He was married.

Which was okay, she told herself, since she'd have Don soon to counterbalance Eddie's wife.

Bub didn't return to Jason at the San Vicente apartment until four P.M. because the conference with Brains and Albert had lasted longer than he'd planned. The turkeys just couldn't seem to absorb what was necessary, and neither had had an idea of his own.

He'd had to give them the game down to the smallest detail: They'd wanted to use Brains's Dodge Charger—"because it's hot enough for a getaway," Brains had said—and Bub had to explain that in order to avoid suspicion they'd have to appear as if they had a *reason* for cruising those affluent streets. Either they lifted a luxury car, or a service-type vehicle. Since a luxury car wouldn't suit their appearances, a panel truck, the kind a gardener, repairman, or servant would use, was their best bet.

"And if we can't rip one off?" Brains asked. "After all, we don't have that much time."

"Then put a lawnmower and a few tools in back of Albert's wagon and wear work clothes."

He explained how the electric gates operated at their first stop, Coleman Berry's lower Benedict Canyon estate. "It's a strange house; got kind of a big carport area in front—wrought iron all around—and a grilled gate that lifts up, hinging in the middle, and folds back on top. Looks foolproof, and Berry probably thinks it is, but it's a snap. Just be there at nine and settle down across the way, under some big trees where no one'll ever notice you at night. Berry has a houseboy who lives somewhere else and leaves about nine-thirty. The gate'll lift as he drives out. That's when you jump from the wagon and get ready to run like hell. The China boy'll drive off, using a remote unit to lower the gate. He'll be around the turn before it's a third down, and you'll have about ten seconds to get across the road and under it before it touches bottom."

He assured them it was easy enough to do; he'd even tried it himself the last time he'd worked for Coleman, running back inside the gate as if he'd forgotten something.

"After that, you shouldn't have any trouble. Berry's

a widower; his kids are grown and out of the house; he's never home on Saturday night unless he's giving a party. He's not giving one tomorrow, because he and my . . ." He'd stopped then. He'd almost said, "My boss." He wasn't about to let these two whack-outs know anything about him. He continued: "He's going to a party at his partner's place, which is why I scratched a certain rich Italian's house off our list. And why I added another. Here's the list, six houses, but you have to wing it. If there are too many lights, too many cars, too many people, you go on to the next address."

Brains asked what happened after they got inside Berry's electric gate. "What about alarms, security, dogs?"

"He's got dead bolts on all the doors, and a Morse Signal Alarm System. But if you go around to the right of that big carport, you'll hit on a little alleyway the pool man uses to get in back. All you have to do is unlatch a wooden gate and you'll be walking along the south side of the house. About halfway down, you'll see a window to the kitchen, always left open because the ventilation isn't what it should be."

The turkeys had grinned then, feeling secure. And why shouldn't they? He was giving them windows, skylights, screen doors, gardener's and pool men's tricks of getting around back when the owners weren't home. He was giving them easy entry into six houses, six gold mines. Later, if they wanted to, he'd even fence *their* part of the loot, getting them top dollar. He was practically handing them a few hundred thousand and making the same for himself.

"First thing you go for is Berry's safe, which is in the master bedroom. Like a wall safe, but under a cut section of carpeting, in the floor near a painting of the Madonna and Child."

"We blow it?" Brains asked.

"Not in this house. I've got the combination."

They'd marveled at that, and he'd simply smiled, acting mysterious. Why tell them how easy it had been? Berry's ten-year-old niece had been playing with the safe when Bub was doing one of his casing tours during a break in a party. Uncle Coleman couldn't have known the girl would remember his combination after just one demonstration and brag on it to the friendly bartender.

"Berry's late wife's collection of jade, worth about a hundred grand, is located there. And two, three thousand in cash. Then there's a cabinet with his collection of gold coins. Maybe more than *two* hundred grand worth, and so easy to fence. Don't worry about the Electric Guard sticker on that cabinet. It's a phony; I heard him say so himself. He opens it too often to fuck with alarm cutoffs. After you finish taking everything, you go to the front door, where there's a button on the right side that'll lift the carport gate. There's another in the garage, near the playroom door. So either way, you just bop out with the loot."

He'd gone on to discuss the five other addresses, describing points of entry, telling them what to look for in each house.

He'd also given them the areas of danger, putting these off for last so as not to discourage them, running through the list of alarms and dogs and private-cop patrols quickly. And in reality, there wasn't much to worry about. As long as they watched for activity in supposedly empty houses. As long as they used their heads.

Finally, they'd absorbed what they had to do, and he'd been able to leave. He'd driven quickly, thinking to check out Jason and get back to Freddy's by four-thirty. The kid should sleep until eight or ten, by which time Bub would return to the San Vicente apartment and feed him and put him beddy-bye again. It wouldn't hurt the boy to sleep away two days.

He was climbing the back stairs when he heard the TV from that one apartment on the short hallway, his apartment. When he got inside, the kid was at the table, eating from a can of pork and beans. "Where you been, man? Your note said be-right-back. You been gone hours!"

"How long have you been up?"

"I dunno. Let's see. Caught 'All in the Family' reruns." He turned in his chair. "Hey, man, that means I slept till two-thirty! That's crazy! I slept all last night. How come I sleep another four hours, *bam!*, when I never do that before?"

Bub shrugged. "Change of atmosphere." He went to the kitchen to make coffee, and to put the kid under again. For kids his age, Jason must hold the world's record for shaking off Quaalude.

"How do you feel?" he asked the boy. "Maybe sleeping that way means you have a cold, a virus?"

"Not me, man. I'm like my pop—a bull, he says." He stood up, flexing his muscles. "I'm gonna make the high-school football team when I . . ." He suddenly put a hand on the table, shook his head, sat down. "Feel dizzy, like when I first woke up. It's gone now."

Bub said he'd make coffee for both of them.

"How about a beer?"

"You're too young for beer."

"What, me? You wrong! Old Albert lets me belt a few on Sundays. Old Lisbeth yells, but not too much."

"Lizbeth your mother?"

"Yeah. She yells at old Albert more'n she yells at me." He laughed. "Man, he gave her a *wallop* the other night, and she ain't yelled at no one since. Anyway, she's not my real ma. She's a step-ma. And a bitch."

Bub dissolved half a Lude in Jason's coffee. He brought both cups to the table and sat down. Jason watched television. Bub said, "Drink it while it's hot."

"Not in the mood for coffee."

"Come on. I already mixed in cream and sugar the way you like it."

"How come you got no beer, man? I mean, not even for yourself? You a junkie?"

Bub had to laugh. "How about a Pepsi? You asked for Pepsi in the supermarket. You didn't ask for beer."

"It was morning. We were thinking breakfast. I can think Pepsi anytime, but not beer for breakfast. Sure could go for a few Coors now. Why don't we go down and get some? Take a little drive too? Maybe go to Magic Mountain and hit a few rides? Or Disneyland, right, Uncle Bub?"

Bub got up, laughing again.

"What's so funny, *sucker!* I don't like people laughing . . ."

Bub whirled on him.

Jason leaned away in his chair. "Man, first you laugh and then you wanna murder me! What's wrong with you? You never talked to a kid before?"

Bub's mouth opened, but he had nothing to say. Jason was right. He never had talked to a kid before. Not really. Just a few words to some boss-man's child or relative, usually about what they wanted for lunch.

And this was some kid!

He went to the kitchen. "Milk or Pepsi?"

"I had a Pepsi already. I don't want anything. Except if you buy some Coors. Or Lite, 'cause I'm getting a gut from drinking brew." He stood up, sticking out his stomach. "Big belly, right?" he said proudly.

Bub nodded. Big belly, big ass, big chest, big face. "Old Lizbeth feeds you well."

"Not her. I eat around a lot at friends' houses. We gonna get that beer?"

Bub didn't want to risk even so minimal an amount of alcohol mixing with Quaalude.

"Drink your coffee," he said, "and we'll go for a drive."

"You sure funny, Uncle Bub. You act like coffee *medicine*. People don't tell kids drink-your-coffee."

Jason was instinctively sharp, unlike his old man. "Drink up and we'll talk about Magic Mountain."

"Talk? What's talk, man? I wanna *go*."

"We'll go."

"You swear you die before midnight if we don't go? That the vampire drink your blood if we don't go?"

"Drink your coffee."

"You swear?"

"Yes. Drink up."

The kid sipped, and made a face. "It's cold. Can't I have a hot cup?"

"We don't have time if you want to catch a few of the rides, like the roller coaster."

"Man, the one that loops the loop! Up and over!" He gulped down the coffee. "Let's move!"

"You have to put on your shoes. And I have to go to the bathroom."

"Where my shoes anyway?"

"Near the bed."

Jason went into the bedroom. "Yeah, there they are, but I don't remember taking the mothers off."

Bub lit a cigarette and sipped his coffee. Jason called: "I got that funny feeling again. Dizzy, sort of." He came to the door, one shoe on, face dull. "Maybe I'm sick, like you said."

"Lie down a minute."

"What for? I been lying down two days now." But the spirit was gone out of him; he turned and went back into the bedroom.

By the time Bub finished his smoke, Jason was fast asleep. Bub made him comfortable and returned to the main room and the phone. He called Fred and excused his lateness by saying the Caddy had broken down. Fred complained that he'd had no lunch.

At home, he fed the boss-man, listening to his plans

for using the chicks who'd been calling all day about parts in *Galt's Island*.

"And when're we going to get a *boy* again?" Freddy asked. "It's been four or five months now. Haven't you any prospects?"

"Plenty of gay hustlers. Some around eighteen, nineteen."

"Fuck the hustlers. You know what I want."

Bub knew. "We could drive up to Frisco and see that freckle-assed kid."

"Maybe. But someone fresh, someone new."

Bub ate cold chicken. "I'll ask around."

"Anyone that comes from *asking around* won't be worth shit."

"And anyone who comes to us any other way could be worth ten years in the slammer."

Freddy subsided then, saying he was going over to Rob Denning's Malibu place to discuss business. "And tomorrow I'm going to Umberto Pandaro's party and you had to pick Saturday as your time off and Pandaro gives dress parties and what the hell have I got in the closet?"

Bub chose tonight's outfit and nodded as Freddy looked at him in the mirror. Then he laid out tomorrow's outfit, going with a burgundy jacket and cream slacks, adding a ruffled-front pale pink shirt, black bow tie, and sleek black shoes as accessories to give that not-quite-tuxedo effect. After which he walked Freddy out to the Seville and waved him off.

He could return to Jason now. But there wasn't any need to; not after that second half-Lude. He smoked a joint and watched TV, relaxing the tight nerves. He cleaned up the kitchen and checked out the pantry and both refrigerators, making up a shopping list. Freddy would eat out while Bub was on his day off, but he'd expect gourmet service as usual on Sunday.

He was jotting down wild rice for cossack pilaf, when he found himself thinking about Jason, wondering if it was possible he'd awakened again. He laughed sharply, shaking his head, and returned to his list. And continued thinking about Jason.

He decided to set his mind at ease by calling the San Vincente number. If Jason was properly lullabyed, a cannon wouldn't waken him, not to say a phone ringing in the next room.

Jason answered on the second ring. "Yeah? Who's there?"

Bub said: "Christ!"

"That you, Uncle Bub?"

"Yes. You were sleeping, so I ran a few errands."

"You always running errands, leaving me notes, cutting out! Man, I'm sick of sitting here with the fucking TV! I need some air! You coming back, or do I split on my own? I can make it home to San Diego, you know. I can hitch a ride near the freeway."

"Take it easy. How long have you been up?"

"I don't know, but you don't come here now, man, I'm gone! What time is it anyway?"

Bub said it was almost eleven. Jason said, "I been up since the end of "Classic Horror Films." That means since eight."

That meant the kid had slept only three hours!

"I'll be right over."

"Bring some Coors."

Bub said all right, figuring that if Jason's constitution could resist a full Quaalude with just a few hours sleep, a beer couldn't hurt. Alcohol might, in fact, be just what was required to put the little bull under.

He got a six-pack from the big storage fridge in the garage, rushing, afraid Jason would walk out on the streets where he might become groggy, might pass out somewhere, might get picked up by the cops.

He reached the apartment in twenty minutes. Jason was lying on the couch, the TV turned around, half watching, half dozing. He didn't show much enthusiasm when Bub appeared, but sat up when handed a can of beer. Bub opened one for himself, raised the can, said, "Here's how," and drank.

Jason muttered: "Here's nothing, man. Sleeping and sitting around . . . *shee*it!" He drank deeply.

Bub raised the can again. "You ever chugalug?"

"Sure. You sing and I'll chug."

Bub sang: "Here's to Jason, he's true blue." The kid drank down the can in three chugalugs, and asked for another.

Bub sipped his own beer, and examined him. Seemed all right. Maybe a little sullen, a little dull around the eyes, which could mean he was going under.

He got him a second beer, and the kid drank and belched. "Man, good! Too bad it's so late. Sure would like Magic Mountain and that loop-the-loop. You ever been on it?"

Bub said no, watching him, waiting for him to fall apart, to go under, to finally sleep a Quaalude sleep.

"Can we go tomorrow? You said my pop won't be here till real late."

"Maybe. If I have no business."

Jason drank down the rest of his beer. "Satisfies the old soul!" He leaned back on the couch, looking at the TV, and rubbed his eyes. "Man, I've had it with the tube. Turn it off, huh?"

Bub stepped over and shut the television. "Want to lie down for a while?"

"Lie down? What you think I been doin' since morning? I want some action!"

Bub went to the kitchen to dump the three cans. He was sure the kid would go under soon.

He opened the drawer where he'd put a deck of cards and a checker set. "How about some poker?"

"C'mon, man! I want out!"

"Checkers?"

Jason jumped up and yelled: "Get me the hell out of here!"

"Stop shouting!" If someone heard . . .

"Man, I'm not shouting, I'm begging! Can't we take a little ride, for Chrissakes?"

Bub shut the drawer. "Put on your shoes."

"You got it!" But he stopped in the bedroom doorway, muttering: "Everytime I walk in this fuckin' room, I go to sleep."

Amen, Bub prayed. Jason went in. Bub listened and heard nothing. He was beginning to hope, when the kid came out and said: "Show me where the rich dudes live. The Beverly Hillbillies. The Jacksons. Donny and Marie."

Bub drove west on Santa Monica Boulevard into Beverly Hills, then north into the flats. He cruised up and down the best-known streets—Cañon, Beverly, Rodeo. Finally, he turned onto Bedford, and went right by the house. He was talking, telling Jason about the famous people who lived in this fabulous township within Los Angeles. He also kept glancing at the boy, who'd been silent for quite some time, trying to determine if he was falling asleep. It was after twelve, and Bub could have used some sleep himself.

Just when he was convinced the kid was out with his eyes open, Jason said: "What's this Bel Air? On "Police Story" they had a murder there. In a mansion, man, but it looked like way out in the woods."

So they drove west on Sunset to the gated east entrance to Old Bel Air. At night, it was hard to make out the houses up their curving driveways, hidden behind their trees and shrubbery, but they went slowly along Bellagio Road and into some side roads and Jason got an idea of the incredible wealth secluded here. And even more of an idea when they returned a mile east on Sunset and drove through Holmby Hills, an extension of Bel Air that had grown larger estates than the parent colony.

Again, Jason grew silent. Again, Bub began glancing

at him, judging the way the boy was slumping against the door, head down. "Jason?" he murmured.

No answer.

Bub turned back toward San Vicente and the apartment.

Jason said: "Where next, Uncle Bub?" and stretched.

"It's one-thirty. I thought we'd hit the sack."

Jason sat up straight. "Let's go to the beach."

"What for? It's night."

"To see the ocean; the moon and stars and all that stuff. My teacher says if you can enjoy the sky and the ocean, you a rich man."

Bub didn't know whether to laugh or cry. "I think it's time to call it a day."

"No way I'll go back in that fuckin' bedroom, man!" He was shouting again. "I don't know what's goin' down, but sleepin' so much . . . if my pop was here . . ."

Bub turned west again, toward the coast. "Your teacher's right," he said wearily.

Jason slapped Bub's arm. "You a good cat, Uncle Bub!"

At the Pacific Coast Highway, Bub turned left, toward Santa Monica Beach, figuring they'd be less conspicuous there than right here at the end of Sunset in the well-lighted Will Rogers lot.

A few minutes later, he drove into the huge Santa Monica parking lot, past the fee collection booth, and turned north toward the area near the private club, traditionally the least used section. But it made no difference tonight; he didn't pass a single car.

He parked the Caddy nose-first against the walkway, and they were looking down to the beach and the ocean.

It was a mild, bright, pretty night, and he was surprised at how clearly the ocean showed, and for how far. Jason was getting out. "Let's take off our shoes and walk in the sand."

"Well, up near the parking."

"No, man! Who wants to walk near the parking? Down near the water where it's wet and wild!"

"People get mugged here, Jason. Only two weeks ago a couple was robbed and beaten. The woman died."

"Hey, man, who gonna rob two niggers? I mean—we meet any bad guys, they gonna think *we* the bad guys!"

Bub found himself laughing helplessly.

"I'll take off my shoes, right, Uncle Bub?"

Bub joined him and they walked down to the sea. The kid stared out at the ocean, the waves. "How come they move that way? How come they get to be waves?"

Bub didn't know, and was sorry he didn't. Then he remembered something about the moon and tides, and gave a half-ass explanation.

"That right, Uncle Bub?" The boy was looking at him.

Bub said: "I think so. I'll check it out." But tomorrow he'd see the last of Jason. "Ask your father."

"Pop's a good cat, but don't ever ask him to tell you why something works. *You* let me know, the next time pop leaves me with you."

Bub said he'd do that. They walked along the shore, feet cooled by the wet sand. Finally, Jason stopped and rubbed his face. "I'm getting kind of tired."

Which were about the sweetest words Bub had ever heard!

Jason dozed a bit in the car, but was awake to walk up the stairs to the apartment. It was a quarter to four when Bub got two more beers from the refrigerator, to make certain Jason slept well.

The kid said: "Let's play a few hands of gin. Just while we're sippin' the brew."

Bub didn't bother arguing. They sat at the table, and he decided to take the kid fast in order to discourage further attempts at card-playing.

He lost in ten draws.

He dealt a second hand. This one went almost to the turn-card, and Jason won again.

"One more hand," Bub said.

He finally won, and Jason stretched and said: "Man, now that bedroom seems good to me."

Bub made him wash and use the toothbrush he'd bought for him. "What about your teeth?" the kid asked.

Bub had forgotten to bring a toothbrush for himself. He said: "I'll use my finger and some salt."

In the bathroom, Jason watched with interest.

Bub explained that it had been popular during the Depression, when no one had a dime for a toothbrush or toothpaste. Jason wanted to try it; then made a face and spat salt and water. *"Phew,* man!" He left the bathroom in disgust. Bub washed up and came into the bedroom . . . where Jason was just getting into the double bed, naked.

Bub paused. He hadn't thought this through. He could sleep on the couch.

But why? Men slept with kids. A father and son . . .

He wasn't Jason's father. Neither was he "Uncle Bub." He'd done too many funky things and thought too many funky things, and the kid had looked good to him—a plump young boy, the kind Freddy was dying for.

"C'mon, Uncle Bub," Jason muttered, turned on his side, eyes closed. "Shut the fuckin' lights."

Bub walked across to the door and threw the switch. He went into the main room and over to the couch. He could sleep here . . . but he didn't have an extra blanket, and it got cold at night in Los Angeles, in the desert manner, no matter how warm it was during the day.

He could go back to Bedford. He was sure Jason would sleep through the night.

Well, reasonably sure.

As he'd been before . . . and the kid had awakened . . . and if he awakened again, alone at night, he might be frightened. Because hip-tough act and all, Jason was still a fourteen-year-old child.

Bub returned to the bedroom. "Jason?" No answer. He approached and spoke to the boy's back. "I'm going to sleep in the next room."

Heavy breathing. The kid was flat out at last.

Bub hesitated a moment, then stripped, tossing his clothes onto a plastic chair in the corner. He got into bed and under the covers slowly, carefully, and brushed against Jason's body. He moved away a little. But a little was all he *could* move. The boy was almost dead center of the bed.

He took him by the shoulders and shook him. "Jason, slide over!"

A mumble, but nothing else. Bub pulled back the covers to roll him. One hand went under the boy's hip, the other under his chest. Jason's skin was silky smooth, warm, springy. In touching him, Bub felt a sudden rush of desire. And grasped the bulging bottom.

"Jason?"

Another mumble, but no movement, no awakening. The Quaalude had really grabbed hold. Bub could do whatever he wanted . . . and his hand was caressing Jason's genitals, bringing a lengthening, a tumescence to the thick penis.

Then he stopped, took his hands away. He rolled onto his back and said, "You sonofabitch!" and he was talking to himself. And kept talking, until he fell asleep.

* * *

Cecily had called Don at six Friday evening, saying she had to take Johnny to Boy Scouts and hoped to be over at nine.

She'd called at nine, saying she was taking Johnny to dinner and hoped to be over at eleven.

She called at eleven, saying she was exhausted. "But I'll be over in about half an hour, if you want."

He said, "All right," knowing she expected him to say she shouldn't extend herself. She'd played that game before, without using Johnny. Now that her son's existence was revealed, he expected she would use him quite a bit.

What she'd *actually* done since going to the script-writer's home, he didn't know. And he didn't ask her. He was entering a different area in their relationship, a combative area. They were enemies now, facing each other over a no-man's-land strewn with ruined prospects and dead promises. He wouldn't surrender by closing his eyes to everything. She couldn't surrender, not without exposing her entire life as she really lived it.

He showered, wanting her in spite of everything, growing excited in spite of everything. Her eyes, her lips, her voice, her body, her *sweetness* enthralled him as he blow-dried his hair, trying to make it look thick, full for his woman.

He took his evening medication—a Quinidine and Inderal.

His bowels became loose as he was shaving, the Quinidine, a deadly poison in larger amounts, taking its toll. A blood-thinner, it had always cramped him, hurt him, made him ill. But without it, he'd found his arrhythmia returning, growing, weakening him. So he'd taken it religiously and accepted its debilitating side effects. Tonight, waiting for his lover, those side effects not only sickened but enraged him.

He shat his brains out; lost lust in the weakness of his bowels; pounded his fist into his thigh as he felt his intestines leaking into the toilet. He hated the medication, the situation, himself!

The phone rang.

It was after midnight, so it could only be Cecily.

He couldn't get up. He said, "God, too much!" and listened to the answering machine go on in the study

Ten minutes later, he played back the message. Cecily's voice said: "Johnny's got a fever, bun. Honest. He doesn't feel well and I can't get the sitter and I don't want to leave him alone. I'll be over first thing in the morning to make you breakfast. Okay? You must be in the shower, my squeaky-clean lover . . ." She stopped and spoke away from the phone. When she came back, she said, "You there?" and the tape ended.

Just as well. Sometimes the Quinidine really did him in. Like tonight.

He went to bed.

He didn't know he was going to make the decision, until he suddenly did.

He was through with Quinidine.

He was going to give it up and see what happened. If he got away with it, he'd give up Inderal.

He felt he was being poisoned; that the plusses of chemotherapy were now being overshadowed by the minuses.

And that he was unable to be a man with his woman often enough, freely enough, because of those minuses.

A dangerous reason, that last one. A reason that could lead to serious mistakes. If the body signaled that the poison was no longer useful, that was one thing. If the mind said the poison was making sex difficult, that was another.

He remembered the story Freddy told of the producer who'd fallen in love with Marilyn Monroe when she was just starting out in Hollywood, before her role in *Concrete Jungle* brought her national attention.

The producer, in his late fifties, had suffered a heart attack. He'd recovered quickly, getting out of the hospital after two weeks' treatment in time to keep a weekend date to take Monroe to Palm Springs. He felt fine, he said. He hadn't had a real heart attack, he insisted.

His doctor thought he was wrong. His friends thought he was wrong. But he loved Monroe; wanted to marry her; wanted to prove he was young enough, strong enough, sexual enough to make her a good husband.

What Monroe thought of him no one knew. She'd been fond of the man, but actresses were often fond of many men, sometimes at the same time . . . and Don told himself to remember this, to take the story to heart.

To *heart,* indeed, because the producer had suffered a second M.I. during that emotional, sexual weekend. And died before reaching the hospital.

Freddy had attended his funeral, as had other friends. As had the doctor. Who said that what the producer had done wasn't all that unusual: "A form of suicide indulged in by a certain kind of older male, unmarried, involved with a younger woman."

Don was almost seven months, not two weeks, removed from his M.I. But he was still going through something akin to what that producer had experienced.

He had to make sure he was dropping the medication for himself, not for Cecily and nights of love.

He was awake at seven. He showered again, for the therapeutic effect of hot water beating onto his body. He shaved again, for Cecily. And remembered he had a luncheon date with Fanny.

He considered canceling Fanny. And didn't. Because when Cecily came for a morning, she was usually gone by noon. And he was to meet Fanny at one-thirty.

But he hoped Cecily would force him to cancel; that

she'd give him a full day, as she sometimes did, as she had often enough immediately after his release from the hospital.

She arrived at eight-ten. She made herself eggs and coffee; him a banana mashed with low-fat yogurt, a thin slice of whole-wheat toast, and Postum.

He pushed away the Postum and asked for a cup of regular coffee. She was in the kitchen, looking out at him as he sat at the dinette table. "Are you sure?"

"I'm sure."

She served him the coffee. He drank it black, and trembled with delight. He wanted another cup, but decided to wait, to see what happened as a result of no Quinidine and no morning diuretic and strong coffee.

He said: "How'd it go at Otis Daimler's house yesterday?"

"Fine. I think he'll do a good job with your book."

"A good job isn't important. A good job doesn't mean a profitable movie. Sometimes a lousy job, aesthetically . . ."

"I think he'll do what has to be done," she interrupted, and chewed toast and stared past him, into her thoughts.

"Who else was there?" he asked, accepting the cut-off, the beginning of impatience with intellectual hair-splitting, of impatience with *him* now that he'd served his purpose and given her a shot at stardom. (But he tightened inside, hardened, made her more the enemy, the combatant across no-man's-land.)

"Ben Bright, the character actor you probably remember from that Western TV series . . ."

"I remember him as a brash young sidekick to Gable, to Cooper, to Dennings. You remember him from a Western TV series."

She spread cherry jam on her toast. He said: "May I have a bite?"

"Jam? You haven't . . ."

"And now I will." He reached out, took her toast,

and bit into it. It was delicious. He wanted another bite, but handed it back. *Wait and see.* Wait for the fluttering heartbeats, and pray they don't come. "Who was there besides you and Bright?"

"Dennings."

"Ah. Where did you two go afterwards?"

"*I* went home, to Johnny." Her voice, however, wasn't sharp enough for a contradiction in the usual Warren manner. "Why would I go with Dennings?"

He smiled. She said: "Are we going to bed or what?"

"Or what else is there for us to do, correct? Certainly not talk."

She stood up. "You're in one of your moods. Maybe I'd better leave."

He held himself in check, though the rage was rising, the heartbeat accelerating.

She picked up her purse and started for the door.

He picked up the phone and dialed.

She stopped. "Who're you calling?"

"Freddy."

She came back to the table and pressed down on the buttons, cutting the connection.

"Now why did you do that?" he asked.

"It's eight-thirty. You can't call him so early. He was up late at Dennings's house last . . ." She stopped.

He leaned back, smiling.

"Well, damnit, I know how *narrow* you can be about things! I know I promised to come over last night, but Dennings's girl made lunch for me and Bright, and then he called a few friends for a gathering, and I just stayed."

"You could have told me."

"So I've told you. So you should see your face."

He nodded, looking down to hide that face.

"People like Dennings entertain a lot, bun." She was bending over him now, pressing her cheek to his. "And we're going to be working together. Yes . . . don't say it . . . I know . . . but that makes it even more im-

portant that we get along. I don't expect you to like it,
and that's why I didn't want to tell you, but on Johnny's life, nothing happened!" She moved her lips
around to his lips.

He couldn't help responding. He loved her kisses so.
He loved *her* so, in this uncomplicated flesh-to-flesh
way.

If only Freddy hadn't brought her into the movie.

If only he'd never known Freddy.

If only Freddy would die!

She drew back. "What's wrong? You . . . jerked or
something."

He sighed. "Tell me about the gathering."

"Rob wanted to invite you, but I said he'd better
not. Because I was supposed to be with you, alone. Because of how you feel about the movie and my scenes
with him. So he gave in."

"An understanding man," he murmured.

"Yes, really. And Freddy was worried you'd find out
and be angry." She sat down again. "Why were you
calling him?"

"To tell him how happy I am about all the money
I'm going to make. Millions, isn't it?"

She looked at him, and then she was crying.

He was surprised. He watched the tears, the pain in
her face. She said: "I don't want to lose you. I don't
want to lose my shot. How am I going to keep both,
bun?"

He rose and drew her up out of the chair. "This
way," he said, and began unbuttoning her blouse. She
said to wait until they got to the bedroom. He said:
"No, I want you nude except for your shoes, walking
down the hall in front of me."

As soon as they reached the bed, he got on her, slamming in and deep, exhausting himself as he hadn't
since the M.I., forgoing what he called the "whammo"
position in which she rode him, her face to his feet and

her rear to his eyes—which always got him off fast, *whammo!* with a minimum of exertion.

Today he wanted to be in complete charge. Today he wanted to return to traditional lovemaking, violent lovemaking.

He banged away, gasping for breath, until she came; then gripped her ass and ground into her and came hard. And fell over on his side.

"Bun, you okay?"

He managed the "yes," and she went to the bathroom to douche. He lay still, not at all sure he *was* okay.

But then he caught his breath, sat up, and felt fine.

He came into the bathroom, smiling. "I think I've turned a corner."

"What do you mean?"

"I'm not sure I actually have, but when I am sure, I'll explain. Don't want to jinx it, as we used to say in Brooklyn."

She said she had to get home, and asked if he would mind her leaving right away, "after I make you a zucchini casserole for lunch."

He told her not to bother with the casserole; he was going out to lunch.

She asked with whom.

"An old friend," he replied, knowing he'd given it a shade too much innocence, and not at all displeased about it. After all, they *were* at war.

She stopped buttoning her multicolored knit blouse. "Fanny?"

"Yes. How'd you guess?"

"I figured she'd call as soon as the story hit the trades. Are you going to do something for her?"

"I already have."

"Candy, the secretary?"

"Then you agree she fits the part?"

She turned her back and finished dressing. He

walked down the hall with her. At the front door, she said: "I think it's a mistake, bun. She's a devious chick, a complication. We have all the complications we can handle."

"No complication. Just helping an old friend." He paused. "As I would help you, if we happened to part company."

She opened the door. "I love you Donny. Remember that when you're with your old friend. I don't always know what to do about it, but please believe I love you."

She was gone. And he did believe her, at this moment. Because she obviously meant it, at this moment. With the stimulus of Fanny-Girl Batcher in the background.

Five

Saturday, May 14, evening, and Sunday, May 15

After ten minutes, Don's eyes fully adjusted to the Cock 'n' Bull's moderate dimness. He was sipping a glass of chilled white wine, and enjoying it immensely; enjoying the special feeling of once again sitting at a bar, listening to men talk, watching them drink and smoke.

He recognized a local TV newscaster, and smiled and nodded. The man, whom he'd met at a social club that Freddy had wanted him to join, surprised him by coming over.

"Baylis the novelist, am I correct?"

They shook hands. The newscaster, tall, fortyish, and heavily bearded, said he'd read the *Galt's Island* announcement in the trades. "An agent close to Rob Dennings was reported to have done a lot of bitching in his cups last night at Perrino's. Said the film would ruin his client. Said it was obscene."

"Strange."

"What could he mean?"

"Didn't he say?"

"If he had, I wouldn't be over here, pumping you."

At that moment, Don heard Fanny's voice:

"Hello, *dahling*. And hello there, Mr. Newsman. I know your name . . . just slipped my mind."

They both turned. They both reacted. And they weren't alone. Half the men at the bar were reacting. Fanny Batcher was dressed like a gutsy whore. Whether she deserved two hundred dollars or twenty dollars depended on your fantasies.

"Like the outfit, Donny?" She leaned forward to kiss his cheek. "Thank you so much for the intro. I got the part!" She looked at the newsman. "In *Galt's Island*, Don Baylis's movie."

"My book," he murmured.

The newscaster looked Fanny over. "I have a camera crew picking me up in half an hour. I'd like to do an interview with you about that movie."

She beamed. She said to Don: "I knew you'd be lucky for me. And I knew this outfit would make someone happy. Does it make you happy, too, *dahling?*"

He nodded. It was something out of their past: One of Fanny's great black-print minis, cunt high, with—if he remembered correctly—a teeny pair of lace panties underneath. Cut very low in front to expose considerable unrestrained breast. With a blue cloche hat straight off a Gibson Girl. With black-satin klunkers that looked at least six inches and that suited Fanny's strong legs to perfection, thinning them, sexing them. And in her hand a virginal nosegay of white carnations around a single red rosebud.

There was one more touch that the newsman was pointing at, saying, "Marvelous!"

A blue ribbon pinned to her left breast, reading, "Booby prize."

"Let me buy you a drink," the newsman said.

"Please, no. If you still want that interview when your camera crew arrives, we'll be at our table. I'm twenty minutes late, and starving." She hugged Don's arm, her prize booby massaging his biceps.

"Your name?" the newsman asked her, as Don got off the stool.

Don introduced them.

The newsman used a little pocket notebook, and moved away.

"He's divorced," Don said, "and loaded. Good investments in Orange County real estate."

"He won't ask for my hand in marriage," Fanny replied sweetly, as they followed the hostess to their table in the next room. Less dim here, and people turned to look.

When they sat down, Fanny chose a chair facing the wall. "Better this way, *dahling*. I'm not wearing very much panty."

A waitress arrived. Fanny ordered a Harvey Wallbanger, her usual. He stayed with his glass of white wine.

As soon as the waitress left, Fanny leaned forward to kiss him.

"Thank you, Donny! My one dear friend! My one dependable friend! My *only* friend!"

He laughed. He had to. She'd always been a hell of a come-on, a hell of a put-on, and a great deal of fun. If you don't take her too seriously, or try to live with her.

"Don't laugh, *dahling*." She was oh-so-serious now. "I mean it. I know I've made mistakes with you, but that was years and years ago. I've regretted it every minute."

"Tell me what happened with Charlie Campbell."

She looked at him, that pinkish face, that piggy-blond face that could look so knock-out at times, going into its sad act. "All right, Donny. I'll convince you when we go back to the house. You *are* going to give me a ride in your Mercedes, aren't you, and let me see that new downstairs?"

"Yes."

"And we *are* going out tonight?"

He found himself nodding.

She was beaming. She shook a cigarette from a pack rubber-banded behind the nosegay and lit up, inhaling deeply. Then, still jetting smoke through mouth and nostrils, she said: "Oh, forgot. Maybe you'd like me to put it out? If it's bad for you?" But she was poised to take a second drag.

"Just blow the other way."

"Cecily doesn't smoke, does she?"

"Not tobacco."

"Pot doesn't count. It's organic and healthy."

"According to juvenile mythology."

"You two getting along as well as before?"

"How well was before?"

"I'm serious, Donny."

Indeed she was—pitching for a spot on the team.

Men kept turning to stare at her, that twenty-to-two-hundred-dollar hooker. She excited people; and knowing this, he was pleased to be the one she was with. And remembered feeling even more so those first few months when he'd picked her up each night at the Wildcat Club.

The waitress arrived with Fanny's drink and asked if they would use the buffet table, for which the Cock 'n' Bull was justly famous. Don nodded, and Fanny said she too would take the buffet, and they toasted each other.

"So what happened with Charlie Campbell?"

She told him how fruity Campbell was, which wasn't news. She told him how he'd made her do a scene from the book. She told him he'd spent "an hour" with her portfolio and résumé and asking her questions, and "and then said I was perfect for the part! So I got it, *dahling*, mostly because you called and he respects your opinion. As for the porno . . ." She shrugged. "One little scene. Cecily Warren has much more."

He was suddenly sure she'd balled Campbell. Or come close to it. Yet the man was gay as they came.

He finished his wine. She finished her Wallbanger. They began to rise, to go to the buffet, and he was suddenly close to her ear. "Did he sodomize you, Fanny? I always wanted to. Something vaguely homosexual there, for straights as well as gays. You turn *everyone* on."

She laughed. But she looked shocked, and said, "Did *he* say so?" and then shook her head and laughed again.

So he knew. And was stimulated, excited.

"Well," she murmured, "the audition fits the film."

The newsman came to their table as they were finishing eating: Fanny, a cut of rare roast beef Don planned to try himself, if the next week or two went well; he, a large portion of snapper, boiled potatoes, and baked apple. He was stuffed, happily so, listening to how well his heart was handling the pumping of blood to the stomach to digest that big meal, the biggest since his M.I.

Fanny said: "Excuse me, Donny. Fame awaits!" She walked away on the arm of the newsman, who was saying they'd film up the street near the Crazy Horse Saloon. Then she suddenly turned and ran back, bending over to kiss his cheek. Which caused a roomful of men to see those scanty pants, and several women to laugh sharply, bitchily.

Fanny strutted out with the newsman, smiling an opening-night-at-Grauman's-Chinese smile.

Don sat there, nibbling the remainder of his baked apple, digesting Fanny along with his meal. He found himself comparing her to Cecily, knowing she could never come close to making him feel what Cecily did; that she was a caricature, a scam; that she was acting all the way.

But it was Fanny who was the actress, Fanny who— if either of them made it——would be the star. Fanny who had the guts, the insanity, the raw ability, the little-bit-more that was needed. More talented, he concluded, remembering both of them in small film roles; remembering both of them using him as a rehearsal partner; remembering Fanny's dancing. Remembering, finally, that he had always admired her ability to become part of the dream-life an acting role required; that she had convinced him, even in their own bedroom, when she was doing a part.

He just couldn't say the same of Cecily. It saddened him, he thought, because Cecily would never give up.

Or did it sadden him? Wasn't the real answer that he *wanted* her to fail, so that he wouldn't lose her as one always lost a celebrity, a star?

After a while, Fanny returned with the newsman, he talking earnestly. She said: "Thank you, Mr. Brandon. Does that invitation include Mr. Baylis?"

The newsman was taken aback, but recovered quickly. "Of course. The party is next Friday, my place in Century City. You have my card?"

"I have the address, yes."

Dismissed, the newsman bowed a little and walked away. He glanced back once, at the door to the bar, wetting his lips, raising his hand.

She turned to Don. "Can we go for that ride now?"

"Was the filming a success?"

"*If* it gets on the air. He promised to use it in his people-and-events section, but who knows? We can check tonight."

They took both their cars and he led her little green Pinto to Sunset Plaza and the bank parking lot, where she left it and got into the Mercedes. "Put the roof down, *dahling!* It's a fabulous day!"

He'd had the hardtop taken off Tuesday, but hadn't yet worked up the ambition to put back the soft-top. He did it right then, straining with the chrome release tool, then with packing the top into its fold-down compartment. He was puffing a little when he got back behind the wheel . . . but driving up the canyon road, the day glittering bright, the air growing cleaner, clearer as they climbed higher, he was glad she'd made him do it.

Cecily didn't care for sun and wind in her face. He'd always loved it; at least before November 24th. And he loved it now!

Fanny was leaning back, stroking the red leather seat. "Ummm, baby, this is what Los Angeles is all about. Lucky girl, that Cecily."

He said nothing.

"You never answered my question about how well you two are getting along."

"Well enough."

"Doesn't sound good, *dahling.*"

"*Good* enough," he said sharply.

"Oops, sorry. Shouldn't pry, I know."

"Right. Here we are." He pressed the radio gate control clipped to the Mercedes's sun visor.

"Always loved that gate," she said, watching it rise.

Inside, she walked onto the deck and looked down the spiral staircase. "Can we?"

He said certainly, and followed her to the lower level, which she'd never seen.

"I drove by when they were building it, and I knew it was going to be fantastic! God, Donny, I could live here and you'd never even know it!" She paused for effect. "Except at bedtime."

"And mealtimes. Or have you forgotten how you expected me to whip up . . ."

She interrupted. "I didn't expect, Donny! You insisted!"

He laughed then. She lowered her eyes, acting all the way, and murmured little-girl-contrite: "I'd cook some great meals, *dahling*. I'd be a different girl. If I got a second chance."

"You're a great girl as you are. Now let's go upstairs. I'm tired."

"Want to lie down?" she offered enthusiastically.

"Yes. To rest, Fanny. Don't you remember what I looked like when you visited me at Cedars–Sinai?"

She went ahead of him to the staircase. "Don't think about that. It's over and done with."

"It's never over and done with. The heart never fully recovers. The scar tissue on my X rays would make you sick." He was able to say it, to pour it on, to use it as a weapon . . . which he couldn't do with Cecily. Because he didn't care whether or not this woman saw him as Mr. Wonderful.

It was three-fifteen when they came upstairs. He was overdue for his second set of pills. He was stepping into the kitchen, to the cabinet, when he remembered he was going to skip the Quinidine. But he hadn't taken any Inderal either.

He decided to let it go until the third dosage period, because he felt fine.

Fanny had disappeared.

He went to the bedroom, where she was curled on her side. She said: "Didn't get much sleep last night. C'mon, let's nap."

He lay down beside her. She turned into his arms. He accepted her kiss, but then turned her firmly back over. "Cecily was here this morning. I'm not that much of a Casanova any more."

"Oh," she said, and grew quiet.

He closed his eyes. He smelled her perfume, so different from Cecily's, so much more obvious. As he dozed, it made him dream a sensual dream in which he walked through a park and saw lovers writhing in the distance. They were too far away to make out anything specific. Until one, a woman, came toward him, and was revealed as Fanny in a mini which fell apart as if melting under the sun, leaving her nude except for tiny black panties. She stripped him and went down on him and he was going to come and he had to wake up before he soiled himself . . .

He did wake up.

Fanny had his pants open and was sucking him. He arched his body, grasping her head, feeling the unaccustomed drain of a second orgasm in one day . . . beginning to worry the moment the ecstasy passed.

Unlike Cecily, Fanny swallowed his semen. She wiped her mouth with the back of her hand and lay back on the pillow, smiling. "My turn, tonight."

He was breathing more easily now. And was amazed at how well he felt.

"Turned the corner," he muttered, and went back to sleep.

Umberto Pandaro's house was a rental, since the Italian hadn't yet decided where to buy. But he'd furnished it well, and had told his partner and friend, Coleman Berry, that considering its quality location of Chevy Chase in Beverly Hills, north of Sunset, he might just pay the exorbitant $500,000 the old woman who owned the place was asking. "However, only three bedrooms, so small a pool . . . well, we'll talk at my party."

Now it was the night of the party, and he wouldn't be able to talk with his partner. Because Berry had come down with the flu and had called at eight to say that important guest list or not (a list made up in great part by Fred Gower), he was feeling too miserable to leave his home. "I'm going to bed right now."

Umberto didn't have time to press him; guests were beginning to arrive.

Cecily Warren and Fred Gower arrived together, and Umberto asked about Don Baylis.

"He doesn't care for parties," Gower said; and Cecily, almost at the same time, "He had another appointment." So Umberto smiled and assumed that there was maneuvering going on.

The screenwriter, Otis Daimler, arrived alone. Umberto was prejudiced against fat men; men who lacked the willpower to control their physical appearance. He wanted *strength* in their production group. But Fred and Coleman thought highly of Daimler as a translator of books to scripts, and he had some very impressive credits. Besides, a screenwriter was alway a gamble, and they could eventually go to another if necessary.

He greeted Salvatore Andro, the Mafioso, with a correct bow and handshake. Andro was here because he might be useful in the future. Umberto had always cultivated a few important members of the underworld back home. There were things no decent man could do himself.

"Signore Andro, let me introduce you to some people. If you've met them before, perdone."

Andro replied in Italian: "The women I won't mind meeting again. The men I already forgot."

Umberto chuckled as if the coarseness had wit, and brought him to where Fred Gower, Cecily Warren, and Otis Daimler stood talking. "Mr. Andro is involved in real estate," Umberto said.

"Really?" Daimler said. "I'm involved in real estate myself, at the moment. I'm selling my house."

Andro's blond girlfriend arrived from the bar, glass in hand, in time to hear Daimler's statement. She was introduced by Andro as, "Giselle."

"Like in the ballet," she said, and drank, and looked at Daimler. "Who's selling it for you?"

"Xtra Realty."

She giggled. Andro smiled. She said: "You got the top man right here. He bought into Xtra for a laundry operation."

Andro put his hand on her arm.

She said: "I was kidding."

Umberto didn't understand, but both Daimler and Fred seemed to. Cecily Warren said: "If I were you, Otis, I'd try to get Mr. Andro to take a personal interest in moving your property." She turned to the short, stocky Mafioso. "We were there only yesterday. It was a charming little Valley house."

Umberto watched Daimler smile, and decided the man wasn't pleased. And wondered at it, because it was difficult *not* to be pleased with Cecily Warren, whose looks were stimulating, to say the least.

Umberto had more than enough females to gratify his needs, but he had the normal curiosity about Warren—about every beautiful woman—to wonder what she would be like in bed, and more than normal confidence in himself as a lover, being not only Italiano but Romano, a combination he considered unmatchable, especially by an American.

Except, perhaps, by the man who was now coming in the door; the man he hurried to meet. Rob Dennings created feelings of inadequacy in Umberto Pandaro he had never before experienced. And he'd dealt with many important actors of star quality at Rome's studio complex, Cinecitta.

"Rob, I welcome you to my house." He turned his smile on a Chinese or mixed-breed woman accompanying the actor. "And you, my dear."

Her name was Joy-Joy, and he wondered at these Americans, bringing their prostitutas to social affairs. One had a wife for such things. (Umberto's was in Venice; they were separated.) One kept the demimonde females for the bedroom. He never took his bedmates to important parties . . . though at Fred Gower's the previous week he'd had one provided for him by a friend.

He'd never see that woman again, because he'd indulged with her in public.

Dennings was looking at the group of Daimler, Gower, and Andro . . . or rather at Cecily Warren, who stood aside from the group, chatting with Andro's blond. He excused himself while Joy-Joy was complimenting Umberto on his entry hall, and strode over to Cecily and engaged her in conversation.

The Oriental's voice faltered as she watched Dennings. Umberto said: "Shall we join them?"

"Not right away."

He nodded approvingly. She understood her role.

He took her to the bar where they sipped brandy together. She had a very pronounced backside, and caught his eyes there. He didn't jerk them away guiltily as an American would; simply raised them over her smooth flank and reasonable breast to her face.

She drank, failing to respond. Her eyes went back through the archway to where Dennings was still speaking to Cecily.

Umberto left the Asian slut with a brief bow and went to greet more guests.

Later, he saw Dennings, Cecily, and Joy-Joy talking together, laughing together. Or the two woman were laughing; Dennings looked rather somber, rather tense.

Umberto got an insight, and went to join them. He chatted about *Galt's Island* and broached the subject of the sex scenes.

"It can't be easy approaching such exposure . . ."

Dennings interrupted: "Mr. Pandaro, we prefer not to discuss those matters in public."

Umberto wanted to reply: "Why not, since you will be *accomplishing* those matters in public?" Instead he said: "Of course. Forgive me." And went back to the door and the man who introduced himself as Terrence Boyle, Denning's agent. And to several other people, men and women, whom he greeted, and didn't really see. Because he was engaged in regaining his natural feelings of superiority.

Dennings would soon be involved in coitus before the cameras.

Dennings quite obviously had fears about this.

Dennings was either ill-equipped for public lovemaking or had begun to experience failure in private lovemaking.

Either way, it would be amusing to watch him and Warren on the set.

And watch he would. Coleman might be the line producer, working producer, but he, Pandaro, was the major backer, the major financier, the Money as they phrased it in Hollywood. He would be right there, looking down the barrel of the gun, so to speak. If that barrel was minute, that gun defective . . .

He chuckled, not concerned at the moment with the financial success of the movie. They could always go to a "stand in." Which would be such a *satisfying* joke!

At a quarter to nine, Otis Daimler went to the bathroom. Not the ground-floor guest toilet, but one on the second floor, where guests weren't supposed to venture. He wanted to escape the party.

He sat on the closed toilet seat and smoked and dropped ashes into the sink. And seethed at Cecily Warren; at her patronizing "charming little Valley house."

And that oily thug saying he didn't usually involve himself in "smaller properties" but would "see what could be done"; this with all the condescension of a man petting a dog!

The beast inside Otis Daimler surged. The beast wanted out, but tonight wasn't the night.

Still, he had to be careful. Once awakened, the beast could grab control and pick its own time.

As it had the night he'd raped and killed the girl.

As it had the time before, on the Bronx street, when he'd been eighteen.

And when he'd been fifteen.

And twelve.

And twice that first year of the beast's maturity, only eleven.

Actually, there had been incidents even before then, but the beast hadn't been fully developed; there had been no deaths. At age eight, he'd tried to strangle his six-year-old cousin Ida when she threatened to tell his parents how he forced her into playing doctor. That attempt had been interrupted by his older sister, who explained it away as a "childish prank."

God, how he wanted to fuck Cecily Warren, then rip her apart!

How he wanted to rip the Mafia thug apart!

How he wanted to take his revenge out on someone; take his satisfaction out on someone; let the beast loose on *someone!*

As he had that time at eighteen, coming home from the play at City College in his father's old Plymouth sedan after having dropped his date, a dull and unattractive girl, at her home. Sick inside at having failed to get a girl who excited him—like Imogene Aunhault, who dated Howard Roesten, who had been such a big deal in high school; Howard, who had talked his head off in debating society and run his legs off on the basketball court and looked at Otis with disdain.

Otis had been certain the bastard called him "fatty" behind his back, even though he'd begun to lose weight at the time. He was certain Howard had mocked him to Imogene and that was why she wouldn't come to the "comedic evening" where he'd had the lead in a scholastic version of *Volpone.*

With the beast raging inside him, he'd turned down his street. And there, under a street lamp, was Howard backing his tall, lean body out of *his* father's car, a sporty new Chevy, and turning to cross the street.

Otis wasn't really thinking; he never did when the beast took over; he simply stepped on the gas.

Howard turned his head, opened his mouth, and tried to run.

Otis swung the car to follow the tall boy. He hit him doing thirty-five miles per hour, and kept going.

He drove to a movie, parked near the lighted marquee, and examined the car. The old Plymouth had

had more than its share of dents before the "accident"; it didn't seem noticeably more damaged now.

Otis took a rag from the trunk and went over the bumper, the left fender, the hood where there *was* a fresh dent, caused by Howard's head snapping back and striking it as he was flung aside. The rag showed lots of dirt and a little blood. Otis threw it away and went home. Where, the next morning, his mother said: "Your friend Howard was killed by a dirty hit-run driver, may he burn in hell." His father called the hit-runner "murdering scum."

Otis sweated out a terribly long week. But there'd been no witnesses, and Otis began to realize something; a realization that grew firmer with the years: Only a small percentage of murders was ever solved. It was as safe to kill as to jump a traffic signal on a deserted street.

Of course, there just might be a cop on that deserted street.

He returned to the party, to Cecily Warren and the others, holding tight to the beast's reins. But he could never be sure when it would break free again.

Cecily felt that Dennings and his chick were doing a number on her. Not that the Eurasian was overjoyed at her role. Still, they were both working on her to come home with them, to go to bed with them, or at least with Dennings. Though Cecily would swear to a hint of lesbian delights. She'd felt it last night, too, but there'd been too many people around the Malibu place for anything to happen.

Cecily had never gone that route. Still, if that's what it took to ensure that Rob Dennings stayed happy and gave her shot full play . . .

Joy-Joy was touching her arm, saying, "So, very noisy here. Why not come to Malibu with us? Some filet mignon on the gas barbecue—I make a marvelous sweet sauce—and then we can relax. Just the three of us, unlike yesterday."

Cecily said: "Another night. I've got the curse."

"It's not a curse anymore . . ."

But Dennings interrupted. "When you're ready, Cecily. I hope it'll be soon. But only when you're ready."

She wondered at his seriousness—his lack of smiles, of innuendo, of the gags and fun that usually accompanied a make. And then wondered, and worried, about Don and Fanny. And then about Johnny, who'd been feeling sick to his stomach. Lots of flu around the past week, so she'd gotten Mrs. Maillet to sit with him instead of Mary, in case there was need for mature judgment and a call to bring him home.

Johnny had shocked her with his angry denunciation of the woman he'd known so many years, claiming she'd slapped him around the last few times. Cecily didn't believe that; wondered what kind of scam he was trying to pull.

But then her worries, and curiosity, about Don and Fanny took over, and she excused herself and went to the phone off the entry hall. If Don wanted her, she'd split this scene and go to him. She should have stayed at the cliff house this morning; should have given him more time the past week; should have fought the need to flee him, to put space between them, to push away the approaching one-on-one relationship.

His machine answered and she asked him to answer and he didn't, or wouldn't. She hung up and turned, bumping full into Otis Daimler. "Oh sorry!"

"My pleasure," he murmured, smiling.

But she didn't dig it. She had to force an answering smile. And noticed how big his hands were; how thick; how they hung, long fingers curled . . .

He was asking if she wanted a drink.

"No, thanks. Have to be getting home. Family crisis." She walked off, surprising herself at the need to escape his gaze, to get away from him.

After saying goodnight to Dennings and her host, she headed for the door. Passing through a knot of men and women, she felt her ass kneaded quickly, expertly, and turned to catch Pandaro's Italian friend—the one who'd brought the three Roman beauty-contestant winners to Fred's party—trying to look innocent. Again she surprised herself: "Hope your pasta stays limp tonight, *fool!*"

He was shocked. She was rather shocked herself. This was Hollywood, where a feel wasn't any more out of place than it was in the Italian's home town.

Getting uptight. Finding a fat scriptwriter scary, a feel intolerable, and her Donny oppressive.

Had to grab hold of things.

Mustn't allow the shot at *Galt's Island* to throw her off balance. Or she could lose the shot *and* her man.

If Coleman Berry could have made it to Umberto's party, he would have. Even though his stomach was loose, his legs rubbery, his mouth foul-tasting, he'd showered and begun to dress, hoping to make himself feel better. Because he hated staying home alone.

His son lived in St. Louis, where he was a junior executive for Anheuser-Busch Breweries. His two daughters lived in New York, where they'd married after having attended good eastern schools. They visited once in a while; once in a *long* while, ever since their mother had died of cancer. Veda had been the one to keep the family together. Coleman had always been busy with his films, and his starlets.

Strange that while Veda had lived he'd had an active extracurricular sex life, hungering for the freedom to set up house with one or another of the actresses he'd screwed. But when she'd died, he'd found himself just about impotent. Not that even before her death he hadn't gone soft a few times with some big-jugged beauty, but as long as they went down on him and showed patience, he managed to get into the spirit of things.

That was *then*. Now he'd had about a dozen failures and was gun-shy, no longer willing to involve himself in an affair. Which made for long, lonely nights. Which made him an inveterate party goer, and a frequent entertainer.

After giving in to the flu and phoning Umberto, he dressed in pajamas and bathrobe and began to call for his man to make a pot of hot tea. Then he remembered Wu had left for the night, and settled for water and two aspirins.

He tried watching television in the game room, but even the recliner was uncomfortable; his very bones ached; he felt every one of his fifty-nine years.

He walked through the big house, toward the back and the master bedroom. He walked slowly, sighing, thinking he could die and no one would know. Living alone this way, sleeping alone this way, a man could be murdered in his bed.

Except that the bastards would have their work cut out for them! He got the .38 Colt Trooper loaded with magnums from his nightstand drawer, laying it down beside the electric clock as he did each night. He shut the lights and got into bed, still wearing his bathrobe, feeling chilled, feeling sick to his stomach. And said: "Christ Jesus, is it all over for me? At just fifty-nine? Lord, what do I do now?"

He stared up into the darkness, as if blazing words might appear on the ceiling in answer to his questions, his complaints.

"Be in fucking Hebrew anyway," he muttered. Besides, what did God know about maintaining an erection? What did anyone know about it?

"Except maybe Masters and Johnson," he said, talking louder to fill the empty room, the big empty house. "If I took a girl with me, I could try with sex therapy treatment, get things going again, be happy again."

But he hadn't been all that happy even when he 'd fucked three times a week, sometimes a different beauty each time. He'd lost something *years* ago; wasn't sure just when. He'd lost pleasure in fucking, in Veda, in his children, in collecting, in football.

"Only fun left is making movies, making money," he said, and closed his eyes.

His stomach awakened him less than an hour later. He had to get to the bathroom, fast.

When he returned to bed, he wanted a cigarette. But his mouth still tasted foul. Besides, he'd been cutting down on smoking, trying to reach a point where he could quit entirely. Then back on his diet to lose thirty pounds. Then tennis again. Then maybe his prick would stand up . . .

He froze, hearing a noise.

The icemaker in the kitchen? After he used a lot of ice, it sent cubes clattering into the plastic container.

He hadn't used any ice tonight.

He heard it again and grabbed his gun. He got into his slippers and moved out of the bedroom to the foyer, heart hammering. Someone in the kitchen, knocking over a pot, a plate.

Had Wu returned?

But there was no light at the end of the foyer. Wu would use the lights.

He heard the voice then; the strange voice; the black-accented voice: "No one here anyway, so shut up about it."

Which was when Coleman did a little bumping into things himself—the antique table holding the miniature Venus near the library. He reached out to grap the bronze statue. Too late. It fell with a hell of a racket.

"Back out the window!" another voice said.

Coleman bent over, rubbing his knee, tears of pain

in his eyes, hearing the kitchen window slam up to the frame, hearing that pot or whatever it was clatter once again as they climbed out over the counter.

He limped forward, not satisfied with just scaring them away.

Black bastards invading his home; threatening his property, his life! Threatening the *nation's* property, the *nation's* life!

He hated them! Always had! And they were in his home!

They *weren't* in his home by the time he reached the kitchen.

He ran to the front door, opened it, threw the switch for the carport and entry lights.

He saw the two men emerging from the alleyway on the left; saw them running toward the gate—the *closed* gate.

They were trapped out there. All he had to do was fire a shot in the air so they'd know he had them. All he had to do was tell them to drop their weapons and lie face down on the backtop, then call the police.

He fired twice, but not into the air: aiming at the front figure. Seeing it stumble and fall. Seeing the second, larger figure pass the first, then stop and turn, hands going up. But that could be to raise a gun, to fire at *him*.

He aimed again. He had to fire four times, emptying the gun, the roar drowning out whatever the bastard was yelling, before the figure spun around and toppled onto its back.

Both down, but maybe not dead. And he was out of ammunition.

He ran back toward the bedroom, opening the Trooper's chambers, ejecting casings in the foyer. He got the box of shells from the night table and reloaded the gun, panting heavily. But his hands were steady enough, his nerves steady enough.

Training always told. He'd learned his lesssons well

as a lieutenant of Marines—especially on Iwo Jima—
and he'd kept in practice, rarely missing the monthly
gun club trips to Angelus Range with Captain Bert
Ebberhardt, his buddy in the sheriff's department.

Gun loaded, he returned to the door, crouching in
the darkness to check out his quarries. And congratu-
lated himself for being cautious. The figure farthest
away—the larger one that had spun around and down
on its back as he'd emptied his gun—had crawled to
the gate, was in the act of reaching up to the wrought-
iron bars to pull itself erect.

Coleman walked quickly across the pavement to
where the smaller figure lay. From there, he aimed at
the man struggling to pull himself up. The gun
bucked, roared; the man jerked forward into the bars
and slid down.

Coleman looked at them both. "Don't try
anything," he said, and waited. Then he lowered the
gun, certain the magnum loads had done their job.

And they had. The smaller figure had two entry
holes in his back, modest enough and barely leaking
blood. But Coleman knew what to expect when he
turned him over. Even so, he whistled softly at the
enormous exit wounds in the chest. Half the man's
heart was on his denim shirt. He looked white, though
he could easily be mulatto or Chicano . . . and Coleman devoutly hoped he was. The man still held a
snub-nosed Detective Special.

The larger man was lying with his face—or what
was left of it—in the gate. He had a wound in his upper back, but it was that carefully aimed final shot,
that brain shot, that had killed him. It had caught the
back of his head, and on exiting had carried away his
eyes, nose and half his mouth. He was definitely black,
as could be seen by his muscular arms. His gun, a .45
automatic, lay where he'd first fallen.

Coleman went back inside, heartbeat normalizing,
breath slowing. He used the kitchen phone to call

Bert. "Thank God you're home. I just killed a couple of housebreakers."

Bert asked if they were actually, physically, inside the house when killed.

"They were in the kitchen, but escaped to the carport. That's where I nailed them."

"Shit, Coleman, we've talked about this a dozen times. It's not clear-cut justified unless they're inside the domicile."

"You wouldn't want me to let the black bastards get away, would you?"

"Blacks, huh?"

"One for sure."

"Eleanor's been giving me hell for not talking to you . . ."

"She's assured a walk-on, damn it! Maybe more, if I can find something in the script that fits an older woman."

"Forty isn't old, Coleman!"

"Forty, hell!" He took a deep breath. "Are we going to talk movies and actresses with the two stiffs in my carport? Are you squeezing an old friend at a time when he needs help?"

"I'll be right over," Bert said.

Coleman sat down to wait for the captain, and flu or not, poured himself a stiff Scotch and lit a cigarette. Fact is, he was beginning to feel a lot better. They would drag the bodies inside. Bert would call the station for a couple of his close boys and direct the initial investigation, control the initial report, so that there'd be no problems.

Though even if Coleman admitted to killing them in the carport, even if he went to trial on manslaughter charges, they'd been armed housebreakers and it was *his* carport and he would face no more than a suspended.

Well worth it!

He lit a second cigarette. And suddenly found himself thinking of that big-titted Cecily Warren, of Rob Dennings, of the two fantastic bodies writhing naked, screwing.

He went to the phone and dialed. "Azure? It's Coleman. Yes, it *has* been a while. I was busy putting together a deal."

She said she knew; she'd read about *Galt's Island;* she wondered if there might not be a part in it for her.

"That's a definite possibility. We can talk about it later tonight." He looked at the kitchen clock, figured quickly, said: "Drop over about one-thirty, two A.M."

She laughed. She said it was "unthinkable" after not hearing from him for six months. She said perhaps lunch Monday; theater and dinner next weekend.

She was a very beautiful woman who reminded him of the young Esther Williams. He said: "Fine. I'll call you. But for tonight, I want someone who cares enough about her career to do what has to be done."

He hung up. And waited.

The phone rang.

He raised it and heard Azure's smooth, cool voice.

"I guess it'll be all right. Because it's you, Coleman, and you're special. Kissy-kissy for now."

He knew where some of those kissies would go, and felt a definite stirring down there.

Hell, except for creating a lot of dead bastards, his cure could compete with Masters and Johnson's!

At six, Don took Fanny for another drive: into the Valley this time. They turned west on Ventura to Sherman Oaks and a little Japanese restaurant Fanny said served the best tempura in L.A. She ate the big combination dinner. He had an order of tempura with rice, and felt positively evil eating fried shrimp!

And felt marvelous driving back home, the evening coolness descending, the darkness deepening, the city's lights spreading out beneath the open convertible as they snaked down the high portion of Sunset Plaza to his home.

They sat on the living room floor and played Monopoly, always her favorite game. And he too enjoyed playing, because her mini rested up around her waist, showing those strong dancer's thighs and that wisp of black lace she called panties.

It was impossible to consider more sex! Even before the M.I., two times in one day had been a rarity; three times a vague memory.

The phone rang at nine-fifteen. He excused himself, went into the study and listened to his answering machine.

It was Cecily. "Donny? Christ, you're not answering very much lately, are you?" She waited a moment. "Just wanted to say goodnight." She sounded subdued. "Talk to me, lover. I'm lonely." Another pause. "All right. See you tomorrow."

He stood there after she hung up, feeling guilty, but only a little. Because he'd heard music in the background. And voices. Lonely she might be, but not alone.

He returned to Fanny. She'd put on the TV and was sitting on the couch. He sat beside her. They watched the end of a mystery movie and the beginning of a local news program.

When Brandon, the newscaster, said, "Now for people-and-events," she poked Don with her elbow. A pretty good poke, and he grunted. No one had thought to poke him since his M.I.

When she appeared on the screen, posing saucily in front of Gazarri's Crazy Horse Saloon, she squealed and jumped into his lap, knocking the breath out of him. And jumped up immediately, clapping her hands together. The newsman introduced her as "a rising young actress, soon to appear in the new Rob Dennings film, *Galt's Island*." He asked where she'd gotten her start, "honed your talents." She replied: "Off Broadway, where I appeared in several plays."

"Far off Broadway," she giggled to Don. "Like Sydney, Australia."

She then fielded questions about the "special circumstances rumored to be connected with this movie," and spoke of her admiration for Rob Dennings. "And for Donald Baylis, the author, who in my opinion is responsible for the project getting off the ground; certainly for my being part of it."

Don looked at her, and she was clapping her hands and saying: "True, true! The lady knows what she's talking about!"

The interview ended with a commercial, and she turned the set off and jumped back into his lap. He figured that if the scar tissue didn't tear loose today, it never would.

She nuzzled his cheek. "Want to nap some more?"

"You'll kill me!"

"Never. It's organic. Makes you strong. Like the missing girlfriend can't, because she's not here on Saturday night when lovers should be together. Where is she?"

He shrugged. He figured some party Freddy and his buddies had going; some party they'd conveniently forgotten to mention to him so Dennings and Cecily could grow to know each other. Business, yes, in a way, and perhaps even necessary. And they knew he didn't care for parties; wasn't really ready for them. Or hadn't been, until today.

So nothing to sweat about. Except that he hated the duplicity; the convenience it afforded Freddy the manipulator, the denigrator of serious man-woman relationships.

"You look angry, Donny."

"I think we'll call it a night. I'll drive you to your car."

"I feel so stuffed. Could I weigh myself on your bathroom scale?"

"Of course."

She left the room. He looked out the glass wall to the city. It was growing warmer. Soon summer would be here. Soon he could experiment with swimming.

He leaned back. He was happy. Fanny had made him happy. Turning the corner toward health, toward strength, had made him happy.

Which reminded him—he hadn't taken either his third or fourth set of pills. He'd taken none at all today.

"Donny! You won't believe this!"

Fanny was calling from the master bathroom.

He walked there, and came to a dead stop.

"I gained two whole pounds from our eating!"

"Unbelievable," he murmured.

"Well look! I was one-sixteen this morning! I'm one-eighteen now!"

He looked . . . at her. She'd stripped, except for those sky-high klunkers. Her breasts looked marvelous; much smaller than Cecily's, but beautifully shaped, uptilting, with long nipples now in the erect stage. Proving Fanny had more than weight on her mind.

"Everyone gains a pound or two from morning to evening," he said. And then, to show her he wasn't a complete idiot, "Plus those sexy two-ton shoes."

She looked at him, eyes wide and innocent. And finally broke up, laughing. "You just going to stand there?"

"Twice already . . ." he began.

She turned to examine herself in the mirror. And stroked her backside. And said; "Remember how you used to beg to go up my bottom? Does Cecily play that way?"

He didn't answer. Cecily wouldn't even discuss it.

"I've learned a few things, Donny. I'd like to thank you for being so sweet."

"No need to."

She was bending on those high shoes; bending straight from the waist to the storage cabinet. Her ass was lean, so the cheeks didn't hide much. Her rectum was prominent.

"Where do you keep the Vaseline?" she asked, poking around. "Used to be down here."

"In back," he said, hearing his voice shake. "But I don't . . ."

"Ah, found it," she interrupted, remaining bent over as she handed the jar of petroleum jelly back to him.

"You said it would be *your* turn tonight."

"Got a vibrator?"

He tore his eyes from that brown button and went to the bedroom and the dresser. He got the tubular vibrator and returned to the bathroom. She was still bent over, grasping her ankles with her hands. "Remember when I used to do this on stage?"

He dropped his pants and stroked Vaseline onto his stiffening member. He told himself he was insane. And nothing could have stopped him as she shook her butt, humming some rock song.

He remembered how the customers at the Wildcat had hungered for her cunt, and it was *he* who had gotten it; at least when they hadn't been fighting.

And now he was going to get that ass, that tight brown button.

He remembered the lust on the men's faces, then and today, and stiffened further. He greased her rectum, and was surprised at how easily he entered. She groaned. "So fucking big, Donny. So hard, baby. Please don't split me open."

Which drove him wild. Which made him plunge in and out.

"Easy!" she cried. "Like the bumper stickers the gays use—Easy Does It!"

"Is that what it means," he muttered. He turned on the vibrator and reached around her waist and between her legs, trying to find the right spot.

She took it from him, used it on herself, rocking, helping him to hump gently.

He didn't know whether he would actually come. But come he did, and so hard that he went directly to bed, certain that he'd finally done himself harm.

She turned on the shower, calling: "Want to join me, *dahling?*"

He lay there, catching his breath, waiting for chest pain, for weakness.

Nothing happened. So he joined her.

She scrubbed his back. He scrubbed her back, and boobs. He kneeled to scrub her legs, and she moved her crotch into his mouth. They ended up in bed, where he ate her for half an hour. Where at one A.M. she said: "Maybe all my men should have heart attacks."

He found that the funniest thing he'd ever heard, and laughed until tears came to his eyes.

Because he was proud.

Because he was grateful.

Because he had hope of becoming a complete man again.

She said she had an early appointment with the drama coach she'd used for years; the one Don had gotten for her. "You remember him, don't you, *dahling?* Patrick?"

He did, vaguely.

"I called this morning, because I'll want help sharpening up for the new part. Not the rape scene, but the straight acting, especially the way Candy manipulates Dilo, which can't change too much from book to script since it leads directly to what happens at the caper."

"Did Campbell tell you about the novel?"

"No one told me, Donny. I read the book myself. I've read all your books."

"No one but my agent has read all my books."

"I have. The whole list that's in front of your last one, *Trip-Out.*

"I'm flattered." And he was. "But *Trip-Out* wasn't my last. *Dry Spell,* my one and only L.A. novel, was the last."

"I read that, too. Just forgot which came at the end of the list. Ask me questions and I'll prove it."

He laughed. But on the way down the canyon to the bank parking lot, she insisted. So he asked questions. And she'd obviously read them; all twelve of them. Which meant she'd cared enough to use libraries and second-hand book stores. Which warned him she'd been planning this campaign long before *Galt's Island* hit the trades.

He walked her to her car.

"Bye, *dahling!* Promise you'll see me again real soon? And let me sleep over?"

He said yes, thinking that Cecily had read—or skimmed—just three of his novels. Had been holding a copy of *Trip-Out* for almost a year without opening it. Wasn't interested in his stories, unless they were made into movies.

"We'll have a long discussion of your books next time," Fanny said. "I want to ask about a character in *Trip-Out*—whether it was based on Fanny-Girl."

It had been. He leaned in the open window as she pursed her lips for a kiss, then watched her drive away.

He knew she was a calculating witch who wasn't to be trusted or believed.

But she'd been so much uncomplicated pleasure. And what did he need with love when it brought so much complicated pain?

It had been a long day for Bub Kane, and was turning out to be an even longer night. He began worrying in earnest at one A.M., though Brains and Albert could take this long, and longer, if they hit every house on his list.

At two, he was presented with another worry. Jason, who'd been exhausted after a long Saturday at both Disneyland and Magic Mountain, and been Lullabyed to the bargain, awakened and said he was thirsty. It didn't surprise Bub, considering the kid's track record, though he'd given him a full tablet this time, which along with the day's activity and the eleven P.M. bedtime would have kept a normal child asleep well into Sunday afternoon.

But no use thinking "normal" when it came to Jason. He leaned against the jamb in the bedroom doorway, stark naked, rubbing his eyes with one hand, his balls with the other, muttering: "How about a Coors?"

Bub told him to put on his pants.

"Why, man? No ladies around."

"You'll catch cold," Bub said, and waved him back to the bedroom.

Not that he was aware of Jason sexually at the moment. Just playing safe. With luck, he'd hand the boy over to his father within the hour.

He went to the kitchen to get the beer. He'd given up worrying about Q's and alcohol in the little ox's belly. He was sipping a beer of his own when the kid came to the table. "Turn on the TV, huh, Uncle Bub?"

Bub nodded wearily. They watched an old Gary Cooper film. Jason slumped low in his chair and continued to rub his eyes. Bub didn't care how long he stayed up. The exchange of loot-for-kid should be made any minute now. Any goddamn minute now.

The movie ended at three-thirty. Then came "The Five Star Final News"—a voice over the picture of a spinning globe. Then came the story of "an attempted robbery at the home of well-known producer Coleman Berry."

The kid wasn't interested in the news, wasn't listening, was beginning to doze. Bub raised his voice, asking him to get a pack of cigarettes he'd left on the dresser. Jason rose and shuffled out of the room.

Bub learned Brains and Albert were dead. He shut the television, his hands shaking, his mouth suddenly foul. He murmured, "Jesus," and tried to think and couldn't. Couldn't even react.

Jason came back. "Don't see those cigarettes anywhere, man."

"Here they are. In my shirt pocket. I'm sorry, Jason. Jesus, I'm . . ." He waved his hand.

"Shit, man. You make it sound like you run over my baby brother." He grinned.

Bub lit up and inhaled deeply.

Jason sat down at the table. "Hey, Uncle Bub."

"Yeah."

"How about a smoke?"

But said, "What?" and then, "Don't be stupid."

"I been lighting up for years now. Four or five a day. Pot, too, when I can get it. So why not give me one little smoke?"

"Because it'll rot your lungs out!" Bub snapped, getting up and walking to the kitchen, where he threw his own cigarette in the sink.

"You been smoking steady since I first see you. Now you yell and dump one lousy butt like it means something. Old Albert lets me drag a few."

"I'm not your father!" Bub shouted. "Get your cigarettes and your lectures and your lessons from someone else!"

The boy stared at him.

Bub stamped around some more, then realized he was being stupid. He had to stay cool, get this kid back to San Diego and disappear from his life without making waves. It wouldn't do to have Jason talk about

him to that stepmother too much. Wouldn't do to
have anyone begin to wonder exactly why Jason had
been left with him.

Besides, why the hell should *he* care what the kid
did?

"Sorry, Jason. When I get tired, I get grouchy."

"Okay, man," Jason muttered.

"If your father doesn't mind your smoking . . ." He
drew the pack from his shirt and held it out.

Jason hesitated. "Well, if you think it's bad. You
been great to me today. I mean, Disneyland and Magic
Mountain and everything."

"You want to smoke or not?" Bub said, getting edgy
again.

"Why *you* smoke if it's bad? Let's both quit, okay?"

Bub stared at him. And found himself chuckling.
And then turned abruptly away. Because he felt Jason
reaching out to him.

"We'd better take you back to San Diego," he said.
"With the freeways empty, we can be there in three
hours."

"I thought we were waiting for old Albert?"

Bub headed for the bedroom. "He'll meet us at your
home." He passed close to the boy without looking at
him.

And managed to avoid looking at him during the
trip; managed to avoid any conversation except for a
terse yes or no at the very beginning, after which Jason
turned away, face to the door, and gave in to the
Lude.

Bub had to wake him as they entered the outskirts
of Dago, as the white swabbies had called it back in
the bad old days.

Jason yawned and gave him directions to the shabby
street on the wrong side of town, and then to the end
of that street and a stretch of falling-down one-family
houses.

It was seven A.M. and fully light as Jason pointed to

what seemed the worst of the lot. Bub pulled up. "Well," he said, anxious to get away. "Have to be back at work by noon."

"You never said where you do your chef work, Uncle Bub."

"Restaurant in San Fernando. See you around, Jason."

The boy nodded, opened the door, looked back at Bub. Bub looked away.

Jason got out, but held the door open. "Old Albert gonna leave me with you again some time?"

"Sure. Close the door, will you? I'm late."

Jason shut the door carefully, nodding, about to say something into the window. Bub swung around and into a dirt driveway on the other side of misnamed Gold Drive, then backed out and pulled quickly away. But he couldn't help glancing into his rearview mirror. Jason was still standing there, hand half-raised in a farewell wave.

Bub tried blasting him out with music, edging him out with plans to hit Sal Andro's million-dollar closet, outrunning him by speeding. But nothing could push Jason's image from his mind.

BOOK
TWO

Six

Monday, August 29, to Wednesday, August 31, morning

A Santa Ana had descended on Southern California. With temperatures reaching a hundred during the day and not falling much below eighty-five because of cloud inversion during the normally cool evenings, it wasn't doing anyone any good, especially the old and the sick.

Don Baylis should have been included among this group, but the change that had begun taking place in mid-May had continued, though not without periods of reversion. One such had been experienced two weeks ago, brought on, he suspected, by his first weekend with Cecily's son. She'd left Johnny with him when she'd gone home to the grape "ranch" because of her mother's sudden illness. The woman had recovered overnight from what had first appeared to be a stroke and later turned out to be a massive hangover atop a heavy cold. But Don had taken a full week to convert from arrhythmia to a steady heartbeat after two incredibly long days with a boy he'd met four times previously for brief lunches and dinners. The kid was one thing with his mother around, something else entirely when away from her.

Don didn't know whether he could live with Johnny

Warren. Which meant he didn't know whether he could live with Cecily Warren, since the two were inseparable. Unless, of course, he could convince her to send Johnny to a good boarding school.

Johnny did need more than ordinary public school training and discipline, and much more than Don could give him.

Still, Don had regained rhythmic heartbeat, and equilibrium, in time to take on the heat wave, and the script of *Galt's Island* sent him by a worried Fred Gower. "Something's wrong, Don. I don't know what, and neither do Berry and Pandaro. If you could spare the few hours to read it, we'd appreciate your opinion."

Don could spare a few days, or weeks for that matter. He had no work, or plans for work. His life remained one long recuperation, with time out for involvement with Cecily, Johnny, and Fanny. A gamey soap opera, as he saw it, and with that incredible movie looming closer, changing everything. Certainly changing Cecily, his fading hope for the future.

But he wouldn't have to think of that this hot Monday morning. Because a messenger had brought the script to his home at nine-thirty and he was seated in his lower-level room, facing the glass walls and a hawk circling high in a glaring, gray-haze sky.

He watched the bird, imagining what it was like to float up there, eyes telescopically sharp and focused on the scrub below for any movement of mouse, rabbit, squirrel.

When the hawk suddenly dived, he gasped, feeling vertigo, feeling the plunge.

He laughed. It had been a while since he'd experienced that transference, that feat of imagination, that putting himself into someone else's, or something else's, state of being. Quite a while; not since completing his last novel.

He turned the script's title page and began to read.

He was happy. He was comforted by purposeful activity after so long a hiatus, even though it was only a slight job, a few hours' reading with nothing expected of him beyond an opinion. And he didn't anticipate having much of an opinion; never had, when reading the other treatments and scripts that had been based on his novels.

By Page 50 of the two-hundred-page script, his pleasure was gone. He raised his eyes and looked out the window, searching for the hawk. He didn't find it. Nor did he find his previous feeling of comforting detachment.

His novel had been built around an ex-governor of an eastern state's need to regain power and wealth after being ruined by a payoff scandal involving his two closest friends—a crime he himself had known nothing about, but which had nevertheless left him financially ruined as well as politically suspect. Now, using thieves acting as business partners and employees, he prepared to abduct and rob people he'd once called friends, without himself ever coming into the open. The complex plot to raid an island gambling resort used exclusively by these members of the political moneyed, the Rockefeller-Kennedy-Harriman class, had in the protagonist's mind been a sort of business venture-cum-game-cum-intellectual revenge, devoid of any true violence. But he hadn't reckoned with the personalities of his accomplices, and with the way events tended to diverge from scenarios. "The best laid plans," and so on.

A rape. The deaths of a secret service agent, an entertainer, and one of his group. These brought home to him, finally, the enormity of what he'd set in motion. And changed his personality, his priorities, forever, even though he managed to escape punishment. In fact, he accomplished part of his goal, regaining entry to upper-echelon government work by marrying into one of the great political families he'd sought to victimize—actually was forced into the marriage by a woman who discovered what he'd done, and cared only that he'd gotten away with it.

A novel with some meaning beyond the plot, the sex, the violence. A novel ending in a tight-lipped, cynical smile.

And it was being turned into a movie built around the rape, the murder, the killings—in that order. A movie in which women were things to be fucked and butchered—at the least, discarded. A movie with an undertone that upset him, ending as it did in a loose-lipped lecherous leer.

But the pornography would be enhanced by this, wouldn't it? So why should Fred be distressed?

Don put the script aside. He was getting involved. He wanted to use an editorial pencil—change things, cut things, add things.

He wanted to do this script another way entirely. If the sex had to be explicit, he wanted it to be erotica, not snuff-film pornography.

He checked the time. Eleven-thirty.

He dialed Fred's number. Bub answered. "He's just leaving for a lunch date. Hold on."

A moment later, Fred said, "You read any of it yet?"

"I have. I don't like it. But I didn't expect to. Why don't you like it? It's as callous, as brutal a fuck film as you can hope to make. 'Sensational' is the Hollywood word for it."

"Then I was right. I don't want sensationalism, Don. Not beyond those three sex scenes . . . and even those he cheapened. Not for a major production. Not for *Rob Dennings*. I want the reviewers to have something to admire—solid professionalism, believable plot and characterization, some sort of message—so they can accept the explicit sex."

"I'm afraid you have a problem, Freddy."

"*We* have a problem, Don! Don't forget the two hundred thousand I handed you a month ago! You owe the project . . ." He stopped, took a deep breath, went back to being steady Freddy. "I want what was in your book. Dennings' role has lost all its subtlety, its sympathy. Daimler's gone way off. We can use maybe half his script, if that much. A polish won't do the job. It has to be rewritten."

"So he'll do it. His contract covers revision as well as polish. As long as he's being paid for it with a no-cutoff clause . . ."

"Yeah, but once a writer shows a weak hand . . . listen, can you join me for lunch? I'm meeting Berry and Pandaro. We can talk it through. Remember your stake in this."

"I know. Millions. And my girl fucking in Cinema-scope."

"Jesus, Donny, we've been through all that! I'd put my mother and sister in a straight-out fuck film for two hundred grand cash, not to say in a major studio production! Not to say for the payoff you'll get if we can put this thing into the theaters!"

"You don't have a sister. I doubt you have a mother."

There was a long silence. When he spoke, Freddy's voice was tightly controlled. "That two hundred thousand was based on a primary budget estimate of four million, which will climb to six million by the end of principal photography. Which means three hundred thousand just for the rights to your . . ." He swallowed a word, and Don smiled, knowing it was "fucking."

"Just for the rights to your novel. And that's only the beginning." The control began to slip. "How many times do I have to spell it out for you? So we didn't get ten percent of gross profits. So we got seven—three and a half each. Three and a half million each out of a hundred million profit! If *Jaws* could go over that—if *Godfather* and *Star Wars* and half a dozen others—we'll go over *two* hundred million!

Maybe three! They'll break down the doors to see Rob Dennings's fuck! We could end up with five, seven, maybe nine million dollars each!" He took a breath. "Play the big-time novelist with someone else, baby. For God's sake, even the two hundred thousand— *even*, I'm saying!—is the biggest payoff you ever got for a movie property. Admit it, dammit, and start showing some enthusiasm!"

"It's the biggest payoff I ever got for a movie property, by about twenty-five thousand."

Fred began to answer. Don said: "And it promises to be something almost unbelievable in terms of an author's earnings."

"Of anyone's earnings, including the chairman of G.M.!"

"So I admit it."

"You admit it," Freddy mumbled. "And not a word when I brought you the check for two hundred thousand."

"I said thanks."

"He said thanks."

"I could do some spelling out for *you*," Don said. "About my having enough money without this deal to continue living the way I now live for the rest of my life. About not paying as much attention to deals as I used to. About being willing to trade all those millions for an unmarred heart." He wanted to add, "And an unmarred girlfriend."

"Okay. We've had our little shouting match."

"I don't recall shouting."

"Okay! We've had our little discussion! Now join me for lunch. And before it comes to your mind, yes, there will be payment made for any script work you do. You know the Scandia on Sunset? Ask for the captain for Berry's table."

"Not unless you're there for lunch tomorrow. Not until I finish the script. I don't have a producer's special gift for judging material by its title and three random sentences."

"Very funny," Fred sighed. "I don't know what the hell you're so sour about lately."

"Don't you, now?" Don murmured, and hung up.

Fred was right about a lot of things, but he was wrong in thinking Don hadn't reacted to that cashier's check for two hundred thousand dollars. He'd kept a cool face and voice for Freddy, because he would reveal nothing of himself to that man any longer.

But he had felt wonder, exultation, childlike joy at receiving that pale blue check. Felt as he always felt when receiving large sums of money for his work. Felt like talking to his father, who'd died before the first of his novels had been published; who'd known nothing of the rewards America could bestow on its chosen. "Look, dad, two hundred thousand dollars!"

He'd once stood in an empty storeroom off his agent's office, holding a check for eighty thousand, his half of the reprint sale on his fourth novel, and spoken to his father. As he'd managed to stand somewhere after each sale and speak to his father, whether aloud or in his thoughts. "Look, dad, all this money!" When his father had never earned more than fifty dollars in any one week.

His poor father.

His mother had wanted everything, and gotten nothing, and turned her disappointment on his poor father. Don had never forgiven her the cruelty, the contempt, the abuse she'd heaped on the man. And had never been able to enjoy sharing his success with her, though he'd gone through the motions.

Now she was too old, too sick, too far adrift mentally to be involved.

Now he was alone with his triumphs, his successes. Cecily was too involved with her own drive toward success. The kids were too accustomed to such things.

And, like Cecily, they had never known real poverty; couldn't possibly value money the way the child of poor immigrant parents did.

But his father! His father would have danced a kizotsky! His father would have swept him in circles, weeping, laughing, planning *cases* of Celery Tonic, knishes by the gross, days—"no, make that *weeks!*" as he would say when he fantasized for his son—in the Catskill Mountains. "Maybe not Grossinger's . . . wait, why *not* Grossinger's!"

Don had waited until Fred had left, and spoken to his father.

And had wondered what Meyer Bayalichofsky would have thought of Los Angeles, of Cecily, of the house hanging over space, of the Mercedes, of this aging, ailing son.

He had taken the check to the bank and put away feelings of triumph, of joy. Nothing had changed, except his children's estate. He would go on no spending sprees, because he had all he wanted. He would give no diamonds, no furs, no cars to Cecily—as he might have—because he refused to *buy* one iota of her affections. He would live exactly as he had the day before receiving that check.

But what, he'd had to ask himself, if those incredible millions materialized? They were beyond the ability of a Meyer Bayalichofsky to understand, and of a Don Baylis to explain. They were mind-blowers, life-changers. If they came to him, what then?

The concept had been frightening as well as exciting.

It still was.

Don left the desk and the phone. He returned to his chair and the script. He made notes as he read. He thought as he read. He worked for the first time in nine months. He sweated, though the room was pleasantly air-conditioned. He strained, and without pausing to consider it, tightened in the stomach, the chest.

At the end, he was breathing heavily, actually panting.

He put the script on the floor at his feet and looked at the spiral pad—at the six closely written pages of notes. Then he went to the couch against the wall and lay down, because he had to. As he didn't after finishing lovemaking. As he didn't after his morning walks, which he'd lengthened to several miles; which he'd added to with brief periods of downhill jogging.

He was shaking.

He'd done something he'd never thought to do again, accelerated recovery or not, Fred's thoughts on the subject or not. He'd worked at his craft, his trade. He'd engaged in one portion of the discipline of writing—preparation for revision.

And wondered what would happen if he took on a real job of writing. A novel.

Motion-picture scripts had never been writing to him. Scripts based on his own novels. Scripts in which all the true creation had already been done.

He might be able to handle such a script; might adjust to it and reduce, if not eliminate, this terrible exhaustion.

But a novel?

He sat up, shaking his head.

He hadn't thought to risk even as much as he'd done today. A novel would be suicide! Novels had helped bring him to his M.I.—the stress, the strain, the long intense hours. One more could put him under the green at Forest Lawn.

He went back to the chair and got the script and the notes. He went to his desk and dialed Fred's number. Only then did he think to check the time.

Four-fifteen. And he hadn't had lunch, or missed it.

"Arbeit," Freud had said, when asked his definition of happiness. "Work."

It certainly made life pass more quickly.

Freddy wasn't home, Bub informed him. Freddy would return his call as soon as he walked in the door.

Don went upstairs and used the microwave oven to poach a salmon steak. It took exactly ten minutes; and six minutes before that he was eating the ear of corn he'd put in at the same time. The bachelor's friend and companion, that Sharp oven. Far superior to girl-friends like Cecily Warren.

At which point the phone rang, and Cecily said: "Can I come over?"

"For what purpose?" he asked . . . playfully, he told himself.

"To suck your pickle, what else?"

"Ah. As long as you retain your dedication to Eros, your ideals of lust, the answer is yes."

"You left out my ideals of love, main man."

"Deliberately. Because pickles all over this town are being sucked. From Beverly Hills to Malibu."

"Which means?"

"That Freud was right. And that pickle-sucking is your *Arbeit.*"

"You've lost me."

"I know."

She sighed. "Donny, Christ, you're too damn much. Too damn heavy. I just want some fun-time with my lover."

"Which means that after pickle-sucking, you won't want to talk about my weekend with Johnny? *Still* won't want to talk about it?"

"I know what you're going to say. You began to say it a week ago. I stopped you because it would only make for uptight feelings. Get to know him better. Let some months pass."

"It seems to me some months *have* passed."

"Do I come over or don't I?" she interrupted sharply.

He knew it was time to back off, and couldn't. "Not much to be lost, or gained, either way. Just good old groin action. And we both get that from other people in other places, don't we?"

She was quiet.

He said: "Listen, I'm rather tired. I finally did some work, and it knocked me out."

She remained quiet.

"But if you'd like to come over anyway . . . ?"

No reply.

"Where's Johnny?"

"At the Y," she said, voice weak. "You know, that camp thing."

She'd told him about it. The children swam, played ball, learned crafts, were kept out of their parents' hair from eight to five, or anytime in between, for a modest fee.

"Won't he be coming home shortly?"

"He made a new friend. Boy named Abie. They trade off dinners at each other's homes. It's Abie's turn to stand treat."

"I had a friend named Abie, back in Brooklyn. Unless it's suddenly become fashionable among gentiles, the name is specifically Jewish."

"Yes, Abie's Jewish."

"From what I learned about Johnny, he's not too fond of ethnic or minority types."

"Since when are Jews ethnic or minority types?"

He laughed, thinking she was joking. But there was no answering laugh, and she said, irritably: "Wake up will you? This isn't the Brooklyn of your childhood. Jews are the elite in this town; certainly in movies and TV. Hitler's dead."

He understood her point. He'd heard it in far greater detail from far greater intellects. And still hadn't been convinced. "That's debatable," he said. "And this little enclave isn't America. It certainly isn't the world. I think . . ."

"Oh, shit! If you don't want me to come over, say it flat out! If your slut Fanny's expected . . ."

"Not expected. And not any more of a slut than some of my closest friends. Present company excepted, of course." His irony was heavy-handed. He'd been seeing Fanny on the average of once a week, using her to control the need, the pain, the growing sense of loss at the continuing deterioration of the Cecily-Donny connection. "But you're probably expected somewhere. At your co-star's bed and board, or El Señor Resordo's office." He took a deep breath. "So let's not throw the first slut, shall we?"

"I'm going to say good-bye, Donny. You're into your high-tone insults. I'll call tomorrow, or would you rather I waited a few days—let you get over your blues?"

He'd been all right up until now. Bitchy, yet aware of it and in full control. But *her* control was too evident. Her ability to say good-bye without pain too obvious.

He began to seethe. (And at the same time, perversely, began to want her.)

"A few days might be best, Cecily. That work I mentioned, which you didn't bother to inquire about, since you care nothing for *my* work, for anything but that degraded so-called career . . ." His voice had begun to rise, to thicken. His hand had begun to tighten on the phone, to sweat and tremble. He was standing, and couldn't recall getting up from the table.

He sat down. "Sorry."

"I'm glad you got angry. Maybe you still care a little. Lately all I've gotten are those high-toned insults."

"They counter the low-tone insults to my intelligence in your explanations of where you spend so many of your afternoons and evenings."

"Good-bye, Donny."

"Good-bye, Cecily. A few days will allow me to decide on what changes to make in Daimler's script. I might revise it entirely; even junk it. I'll certainly downgrade some roles, upgrade others. Call me Wednesday or Thursday."

"Wait. Otis handed in his script?"

"I can't believe our mutual friend Fred didn't tell you. He's certainly been advising Dennings, and *he* would have told you."

"I knew Otis was close to finishing." She paused. "I thought you were going to stay out of it?"

"So did I. But Freddy felt Daimler bombed. So he gave it to me to read. And Daimler *has* bombed. And I'm considering doing the revision myself."

She switched directions like the pro she was. "Fantastic! If you're able to do the script, then you'll be able to get back to your novels! You said you were finished as a writer, but I never accepted it. We have to celebrate! I'll be there in half an hour, so cancel the slut."

He almost believed her laughter, her pleasure. Almost forgot that he'd mentioned the script the way he had to threaten her with reduction, perhaps even loss, of her lead role. For the past four months *that,* not love, had been the hold he'd exerted over her.

Still, he went to the bathroom to shower, to shave his five-o'clock-shadow, to make himself attractive for his woman. Whom he loved even more than he had seven months ago, when he'd been a whole man. More than he had three and a half years ago when they'd met. More than he had that first month, when he'd felt so much growing inside him so quickly, he'd been afraid of it.

Lust he handled well. Love was something else again. He generally picked the wrong girl, and ended by losing that girl. Starting with his first love in Brooklyn, who married a Marine after promising to "wait forever" when Don went into the air force. Continuing through his marriage to Norma, who deteriorated both physically and mentally and ended by having three distinct nervous breakdowns compounded by alcoholism. He'd left her on advice of a psychiatrist who said they'd both do better apart, and Norma certainly had. She no longer drank; she had maintained a five-year romantic liaison; she'd raised Rita and Marv well enough with little help from him except of the financial variety.

Then there was Gilda, who thought only twenty-two had been mature enough, intelligent enough, seemingly stable enough, to keep him enthralled and in St. Louis for three months when he'd come there for a two-week research job on the Masters and Johnson sex clinic. She'd returned to New York with him for a trial live-in before marriage. They'd taken an apartment in an East-Side Manhattan high-rise, and she methodically begun fucking her way from their twenty-third-floor penthouse down to and including the basement garage (where she exhausted the aging black attendant to the point that he quit his job, writing Don a letter that made him understand he was just about the last man in that house to know what Gilda was).

It was actually funny. A locker-room gag. But he'd come close to killing her—after confirming what was in the letter by following her when he was supposed to be at his agent's. His anguish had been intense. So had Gilda's. Later that night, she'd attempted suicide by means of Scotch and sleeping pills. It was another month before he could take her back to St. Louis and deliver her into the care of an older sister . . . who came to his hotel room later in the evening and attempted to seduce him "because I heard so much about you from Gilda."

Fanny he'd enjoyed, and lost without pain, because Fanny he'd never loved. And the same went for several other women he'd known since his divorce. Women he'd enjoyed because he'd asked nothing of them beyond their bodies.

But when he loved, he was a one-woman man, intensely. Whose goal was the perfect marriage. This a gut reaction, an emotion too deeply implanted to be dislodged. Even as his cynic's mind mocked the entire concept; especially with the kind of women he chose as prospects.

Cecily was his deepest love, his most dangerous love in terms of the violence she aroused in him. That gun remained in the Mercedes's glove compartment, and not just because of worries about street jocks and criminal assault. For the last month, he'd been fantasizing following her, breaking in on her, catching her in the act with Freddy, Dennings, even the previously acceptable Resordo. And the fantasies were explicit.

He would see the man's mouth on her breast. He would see her mouth on the man's organ. He would see her plant that organ in her body and moan and hump and achieve orgasm. Then he would enter and put the gun to where they joined and blow their genitals into bloody fragments.

He dressed carefully, even though he would strip almost as soon as she arrived. He put on new slacks and sports shirt and raised the air-conditioning, as the heat began getting to him. Or was it the tension, the expectation?

The phone rang. He shook his head, thinking she was canceling out.

But almost at the same time, the door chimes sounded.

He lifted the phone. It was Freddy. Don said: "Call you back later tonight. Maybe tomorrow morning."

"Did you finish the script?"

"I've got company."

"Don't you understand how important . . . ?"

"Not as important as my company."

He hung up, went to the door, let Cecily in. They hugged. She wore high heels, tight blue jeans, and a man's short-sleeved white shirt. She had her hair in pigtails, exposing her slender neck, her beautiful ears. He kissed them, and her. She walked directly to the bedroom. He began to joke about it, then changed his mind. No more talk. At least for now. Now he would claim the prize he'd won with his success, his persistence, his ability to absorb punishment and overlook deviousness.

They were in bed, caressing each other, kissing. She grasped his penis. He gripped her swelling backside. He forgot the past, forgot deviousness, and said: "You mentioned something about pickle-sucking."

"So I did. You didn't mention anything about lickety-splitting."

He had to laugh. "A fine turn of phrase."

"Forget about turning phrases. Turn yourself. Around."

He did. And sixty-nine was a thousand and sixty-nine with his beautiful woman. Everything they did was more.

For him, that is.

He couldn't tell what went on behind those greenish-gray eyes, behind that full-lipped smile.

They stayed in bed until eight-thirty, when she surprised and delighted him: She was spending the night. Which meant that Freddy would have to wait to discuss the multi-million-dollar script. Which meant everything would have to wait while Don Baylis savored what was, to him, one of life's greatest pleasures—the simple act of sleeping with his woman.

The cliché had it that without trust there could be no lasting relationship, no real love.

Yet he had lasted.

Yet he loved.

And knowing that, also knew it must end badly.

It was their third meeting, if Bub counted the party he'd done for Sal Andro in June. That was when he'd first broached the subject of hitting the Mafioso's million-dollar-closet to Giselle, Andro's girl. She'd been drunk, as usual, and he'd been extremely cautious, speaking to her while clearing a table by the pool, but she'd quickly picked up on his meaning. And agreed to meet him "sometime soon."

He'd had trouble setting up a meet, because he'd had trouble reaching her. Twice, Andro answered the phone himself, and Bub had to hang up. Which, Giselle informed him when they finally did meet, caused Andro to suspect she had another lover. "I took some good shots for those calls, baby, so I want to collect from the bastard even more than I did before!"

They were finally able to get together in the parking lot of a Studio City shopping center at nine P.M. on July 4th, because Andro had flown to New Jersey to spend the long weekend with his two daughters.

Giselle told Bub she'd been introduced to Andro by the owner of Xtra Realty, who'd been induced to sell a half-share in his company by a reasonable amount of money and a broken left wrist, which, he'd been assured, could become two broken legs in a hurry. Andro had a continuing inflow of cash that needed laundering and investing.

Bub had asked if Giselle knew what had happened to her predecessors.

"He never said. But I figure one of his friends, or a cat house. The cat house sooner or later."

"Then I don't have to sell you on your only way out—grab enough bread and split the country."

"Yes. I been in Spain, Malaga, with a guy. I liked it, and I still like the guy. But if Sal ever found me, I'd be dead, the hard way. And did you ever think what would happen if he found out about you? Which he would, ten minutes after he got his hands on me. I'm not good at keeping secrets when my arms and legs are being broken."

"No one is, but he's not that big in the rackets any more. He won't have much help finding you. If you leave the country, you'll be safe. As for me, I'll take my chances. The odds are with us."

"Maybe. I'm still scared. You don't know what an animal he is. You can't tell at parties. But when he's alone, or with his old friends, God!"

And that's where Bub's plan had stalled—on her fear.

Tonight, seven weeks later, they were in his car, driving up the coast toward Oxnard. Andro was in Century City Hospital for a checkup and a few days rest. The reason for this he wanted kept secret, Giselle said. Then she proceeded to tell Bub about it, and they both cracked up, and Bub now knew exactly how much Andro kept in that "million-dollar-closet." Considerably under a million, but still enough to provide them both with the payoff they needed.

Giselle told her story with vindictive energy and relish, and with all the detail a shaken Andro had passed on to her.

Friday morning, a call had been received at the offices of Xtra Realty for Andro. It had been transferred to his home, because it seemed important enough to warrant his personal attention. Two gentlemen from the Sudan were interested in a home that every agent in Los Angeles had been trying to move for the past year: an estate in probate that seemed destined to stay unsold.

The white elephant was on nine acres in Crossly Hills, north of Tarzana. It had cost a fortune to build, to maintain, and now the children of the wildcat oil millionaire who'd lived in it for forty-six years, until the day of his death, were bound by his will to sell it for no less than three million dollars, fair enough in terms of what had been put into the estate, but unrealistic because it was out of the high-value Basin areas. To keep the open listing active, and the agents' interest high, the estate was offering a point bonus over the usual six percent commission.

Seven percent of three million was two hundred and ten thousand dollars, and on hearing of the opportu-

nity Andro had snapped: "So why aren't you out there
with the spooks, nailing it down?"

His partner, the erstwhile sole owner of Xtra
Realty, one Marty Fein, explained that the two Sudanese insisted on dealing with the top man, the president of the corporation, and that title now belonged to
Sal Andro.

Andro had called the number given him, which was
the Beverly Hilton, been connected with a suite, and
spoken to a deep-voiced man with "a kind of French
accent," as he'd described it to Giselle. The Sudanese
said he and his partner were political refugees and
that they wished to settle quickly, establish residence
for themselves and families, and file for citizenship.
"All will be paid for in cash."

Skeptical about this last, Andro had reminded him
that the price was *three million*.

"Yes. In American bank notes. Tonight, if we can
conclude our business and sign contracts."

Andro had arranged to meet them at the estate at
six P.M., since they had other business to conduct during the day. He'd promised to have the sale contracts
with him, and because of the cash deal, to arrange
their moving in immediately, even though escrow
would, under the best of circumstances, not close for
thirty days. "I'll handle everything," he'd assured
them, and turned grinning to Giselle. "Put down the
glass, lush, and drive me to the office. I'm going to
make a fast two hundred grand tonight. Xtra's sold
some rich paisans, lots of Arabs, chinks of all kinds,
but these are our first Africans with money."

The rest of the story Giselle had gotten when Andro
had her pick him up, which wasn't until the following
morning at which time he was a sadder and much an-
grier man.

He had arrived at the estate at a few minutes before
six, unlocked the gates, and driven up the long, curving driveway to a large parking area before the ante-

bellum mansion. There were still some two hours of daylight remaining as he unlocked the front door. He heard a car approaching, and turned to see a silver Mercedes limousine driven by a black chauffeur pull to a stop behind his Caddy. A moment later, the chauffeur opened the back door to allow two very large, very black, very colorfully dressed men to get out.

The passengers introduced themselves as Mr. Bahi El Salem and Mr. Muhmahd Kadik. They wore "long blue and red and white striped nightgowns" and Kadik, who Andro said was slightly the smaller and had a scar on his left cheek, carried a valise which he tapped. "The payment, Mr. Andro, if all is correct."

So Andro led them into the house, showed them through all eighteen rooms, not counting twelve bathrooms and separate servants' quarters over a six-car garage, and was about to lead them out to the double tennis courts and pool with cabañas that could be used as quarters for five guests, when Kadik stopped him near the back doors, put down his valise, and said, "That would appear to be enough, monsieur. We are satisfied."

El Salem then grabbed Andro around the neck from behind and, his French accent gone, said, "No noise, motherfucker."

Choking, Andro hadn't the slightest chance of making "noise." He was tied hand and foot with rope Kadik brought out of the valise, and shoved into a chair near a phone table with antique French phone. He was stripped of wallet, watch, ring, keys. His clothes were torn open "in case this honky wears a money belt or stash tape." The chauffeur arrived to take the keys and to ask Andro to identify those for his Cadillac. Then he left.

Kadik lifted the phone. "This isn't working. One phone better be working!"

Andro said he didn't know. He was punched in the

face, the stomach, his head jerked back by the hair. He said he thought there was a business phone for probate officers' and real estate agents' use in the kitchen, on the wall. He got another shot in the stomach for "holding out," and was dragged to the kitchen. Where he was told that his "lousy hundred sixty dollars, watch, ring, and Caddy" wouldn't do much more than cover their rental of the Mercedes limousine, their suite at the Hilton, their costumes.

Andro said the ring was worth three thousand, the Caddy twelve. Kadik smiled contemptuously. "We sell 'em quick, man." He removed the ropes from Andro's wrists. "It'll take three million to save your life."

Andro laughed. He got a stomach shot for his trouble. And gasped: "No way I can raise that much."

"You own Xtra Realty," the towering El Salem said. "You're Mafia, with whores and dope."

"I used to be Mafia, and I'm not worth half a million."

"Then we kill you," El Salem said, and drew what Andro described to Giselle as "the biggest fucking switchblade I ever seen; maybe a foot long!" But despite the beating, the knife, their obvious willingness to kill for what they wanted, Andro wasn't afraid for his life . . . not at this stage. They would take whatever ransom they could get. Only after the payoff would he be in danger.

"I can raise a hundred grand," he said.

"Five hundred grand," Kadik said.

"Impossible."

"Then we'll take the hundred grand, and a little piece of *you*."

Kadik unbuckled Andro's belt. His pants were pulled down, his shorts followed, and a big black hand grasped his genitals. "You'll make a great harem slave," El Salem said, and pushed the knife between Andro's legs.

"I won't be able to talk on the phone!"

"True," El Salem said. "We'll wait until after we get the cut-rate payoff before cutting you."

At which point Andro decided to give in, and said he would try to raise the half million. He was handed the phone and told by El Salem to "be very careful. Don't discuss where you are. Just say to have the money dropped in the trash can on the northeast corner of Pico and Doheny, where our man's waiting. Any games, and you die. We got nothing to lose. We have so many life sentences . . ."

Kadik said: "C'mon! No more shit! The bread, to-night!"

Andro had made two calls. The first was to the active head of the rackets on the West Coast, whom he called Larry. He begged for an immediate loan of five hundred thousand, "which I'll pay back tomorrow."

"If you can pay it back tomorrow," Larry said, "you can raise it tonight."

Andro pleaded it would take longer, and El Salem got on the phone. "Half a million, man, or we finish your friend."

"Finish him then," Larry said, and hung up.

Kadik glared at Andro. "I think you're fucking us around. I think we should take care of you and split."

El Salem looked angry, too, nodding, bending close.

Andro said: "I've got the money! At home! Let's go there."

"No," Kadik said, rubbing his scar. "We don't leave here. That's the safety angle. We never leave here, till the money's picked out of the trash can on Pico. We forget it first. We go on to the next job. But we keep our word with you, dead man."

Andro had believed them. And called his home. Where Giselle answered. Andro told her she had to open his closet safe, take out five hundred thousand, and bring it to the drop point. El Salem took the phone. "Don't bother counting. Bring it all, hear?

He'll have a better chance of being a together dude, if you get my meaning."

"I got his meaning, all right," Giselle said to Bud, as they turned back before reaching Oxnard. "I really wanted to tell that man to do his worst. I really wanted to get Sal killed. But I couldn't be sure it wasn't a joke, a test, some sort of scam. And even if it was for real, I couldn't take the chance he'd get out of it and come home. So I said I'd do what Sal wanted."

Only it wasn't that simple. She *couldn't* do what Sal wanted. He could give her the location of the safe (which he didn't think she knew), and he could give her the combination, but he had a safety device found on only the very best safes, the very newest security systems. He had a voice-activated final lock attuned to his voice only.

He wanted her to try and imitate his voice, to speak the series of numbers he gave her, and finish with, "Open, please!" spoken sharply, in the hope it would somehow work.

It didn't.

Then he wanted her to contact a safe cracker who lived in Santa Monica. But El Salem took the phone from his hand and said, "No third parties, lady. You do it yourself, or you don't do it."

Now Andro was shaking, sweating, in fear of his life. Because if these men wouldn't deviate from their plan, he'd be unable to get the money.

"Half a million!" he said. "Just let me give her the name of someone who can blow that box."

"Not worth our lives, man. You gotta figure another way."

Andro's mind froze in panic. It was Kadik who said: "Have her bring a phone to the safe. Then you give it a good yell. Say those numbers, whatever, and get it open!"

They tried. Andro shouted, screamed, over and over, and nothing happened.

Finally, El Salem hung up the phone. He and Kadik walked to a corner of the room and whispered. When they came back, Kadik was holding an automatic pistol. El Salem tied Andro's hands behind him again. Kadik said: "You got anyone else you can call?" voice quiet.

Andro shook his head, tears burning his eyes. "Just trust me! Half a million . . . make that six hundred fifty thousand! Six hundred fifty thousand could set you up for life!"

El Salem laughed. "Shit, man, we spent more'n that since April—over seven hundred C's from our Denver score. We're the biggest, the best in the business. Worldwide."

"Parlez vous français?" Kadik asked. *"Non? Vous êtes un grand turkey!"* He lowered the gun to Andro's head.

"Habla español?" El Salem asked. *"Sprechen Sie Deutsch?"*

"Try Italian on him," Kadik said, pulling back the action on the automatic, which brought Andro a tightened finger away from a bullet in the brain. "Ask him to say good-bye in Italian."

"Please, please," Andro sobbed . . . and the two men turned and walked out of the kitchen. Andro heard a car start, and drive off. He waited, unable to believe it was over. But then his own professionalism asserted itself, and he realized the blacks were indeed top pros, not swayed from their scenarios by risky payoffs, no matter how big. And not willing to kill without profit.

He began to work at his bonds, but it was almost ten hours later, four-fifteen in the morning, before he got his hands free. By then his wrists were so raw from working them against the ropes, his arms and shoulders so agonized from their pulled-back position, his general condition so debilitated by the long struggle, that he fell into a half-sleep half-faint for two hours;

after which he freed his ankles and called Giselle to come get him.

"You should have seen him," Giselle said to Bub. "He was like a whipped dog, that capo bastard who just last week made me do things to his friends under the dinner table. Three of them, stinking old New York crooks, and he made me crawl under the table while they were eating and blow them." She bared her teeth in a death's-head grin. "You should have seen him Saturday morning, leaning on me and crying and telling me how he'd suffered; telling me *all* of it like he would a wife, expecting me to feel sorry for him like a wife, when he's treated me like shit, treated everyone like shit all his life, robbing people and forcing people and killing people." She gasped for breath. "Oh Christ, how I wished those black guys had finished him off!"

She went on a while about hiding her pleasure, about taking Andro home, about his deciding to go into the hospital that same afternoon, about his staying until next Thursday.

Bub finally interrupted to get to the nitty-gritty. "About our taking that safe."

"I wrote down the combination," she said, "and what he has to say to operate the voice activator." She dug into her purse and got a slip of paper. He shoved it into his shirt pocket without looking at it.

She brought out a pint bottle and offered it to him. He sipped California brandy. She retrieved the bottle and took a long belt.

"You didn't even look at that combination," she said. "You'd better, Bub. He'll change it once he gets out of the hospital, and the voice activator numbers, too, because I know them now."

He glanced from the road at her. She was nodding, pleased with herself. She was no longer frightened, as she'd been during their first meeting. And it made sense to be frightened, right through their pulling the job, and for as long afterward as Andro had a chance of nailing them.

"Then you want me to open the safe before he comes home from the hospital? Before he changes the numbers? Before Thursday?"

"How can you?" she asked. She took a quick drink. "That voice activator . . ."

"Right. So why give me a piece of paper with combinations? What do you expect me to do?"

"I . . . I'm not sure. I thought you'd want all the information."

"So I can stick it up my ass?" he snapped.

"That's not nice!" She looked away, pouting. (Prettily, he had to admit. She had very full lips, Cupid's bow lips, and he could imagine them moving over his body.) "Not nice at all, Bub. I just . . ."

"You just wanted a little excitement, a little dream."

"Well, yes." She turned to him, smiling, and put a hand on his arm. "Don't be angry. At the beginning, I thought we might do it. But then I saw there was no way, and I guess I wanted to keep seeing you. It's fun to be with someone decent for a change."

"Flattering," he said (and inside he *was* flattered). "But there is a way. I never planned to use combinations and secret information. What I want from you is *timing:* when I can get into the house, when you're prepared to leave the country."

She offered him the bottle, murmuring: "I still don't see *what* way."

He pressed the electric window button, threw the bottle out, closed the window against the hot Santa Ana night.

"I'm going to drill that safe, then nitro it."

She was staring at him. "You threw . . ." And then, "Make explosions in Sal Andro's house? You're crazy! I'm not risking *my* neck!"

He reached out for her hand. She jerked it away from him. "Suicide!"

"You're going to have to work up some guts, Giselle, or you'll be sucking cock for Andro and his friends until you're sixty."

She flung herself away, up against the door, shouting: "Now you sound like him and I don't want to be with you! Take me back to my car!"

He nodded tersely.

They drove in silence. Finally, she said: "You shouldn't have thrown my bottle away." Her voice was small. "You can't solve other people's problems like that."

She was right. "I'm sorry. We'll stop at a store and get another."

"No. I've had enough. Am I going home?"

He glanced at her. She was looking down at her lap. Again he reached for her hand. This time she gave it to him. He stroked the fingers—surprisingly small, childlike, thin. He turned her hand over, kissed her palm, kissed her wrist, kissed her forearm.

She giggled. "If you're going to travel that route, we'd better get someplace where I can unfold the road map."

He drove to a motel in Santa Monica. It was midnight when they checked in. He threw on the lights and closed the door. He didn't bother looking at the room. It had a bed, that's all he cared about. He looked at Giselle, who was a small chick with small breasts. Where she was large was in the hips, the rear. Where she was much woman was in the strong legs on their high heels. And with that baby face, those full bow lips, a pair of sad, smokey-brown eyes . . .

In bed, caressing her, examining her, he was amazed at how delicately she was formed, how beautiful a woman she was. It didn't show too well when she was boozed up at parties.

"No wonder Andro hangs onto you."

Her hand stroked his penis; her little hand that made him feel enormous; her white hand that made him feel an undercurrent of anger, of cruelty, of soon-to-be exacted racial revenge.

"I love a spade in the hand," she murmured. "Been a long time, too. Sal's a jealous sonofabitch, except when *he* gives me to someone. A real trashy being."

"Yet you went to him, didn't you?"

"Sort of. I had a personal tragedy; family matter." She grew quiet a moment; her hand stopped moving a moment.

He was holding her firm, bulging ass, and gripped it hard, and said: "And?"

She began to make the right moves again. "And I was Marty's secretary when Sal saw me in the office."

"Marty?" he asked, feeling it would be so easy to let her jerk him off, so pleasant. But he wanted to score points with her sexually, for later.

"Marty Fein, president of Xtra Realty. He'd been after me for almost a year. I was sort of straight at the time—about two and a half years ago. Then my brother died in a car accident; we'd been real close. Then I didn't give a damn for a while, and let Marty set me up in an apartment. It was easy . . . he wasn't around much . . . I was free . . ." She was beginning to gasp as he fingered her vagina, her anus, kissed her small, round breasts. "Then Sal took over Marty's job; me with it."

Bub pushed her onto her back. He grasped her ankles and pressed them up and back past her shoulders, down around her ears. Her body lay helplessly open before him now, and that vengeful streak made his face harden. His cock, too, until it throbbed like a kid's.

He looked down at her slit, and moved her ankles further and further apart, and watched the slit widen.

She began groaning as he spread those legs to their

limit. "Don't hurt me, baby," she whimpered. "Be gentle."

"Gentle, *shit!* he snarled, and positioned his cock at that gaping slit and slammed in as hard as he could.

"Killing me, darling," she moaned, and she was enjoying it; it was a game. So the cruelty, the need for racial revenge, dissipated.

They made love in as many ways as he could manage. He gave her as many orgasms as he could manage, before he spent himself and fell sweetly asleep.

The next thing he knew she was shaking him, saying it was after three A.M. She had to get back home. "Sal might call early. I could say I turned off my phone to get some sleep, but I don't want the hassle."

In the car on the way to the dark road off Doheny where her Corvette was parked, he said: "You'll always have the hassle. Until I bust that safe."

She looked away. "We'll talk about it next time."

"With or without you, Giselle, I'm going to do it."

"But . . . he could blame me anyway!" She was staring at him. "You know that, Bub! You wouldn't do that to me!"

"I'd do that *for* you. Time to stop playing games. I want to set a date. I want to free you, like Lincoln freed the slaves."

"I'd rather be a slave than dead!" she shouted. "I could tell Sal what you said!"

"And he'd ask how we happened to talk about such a thing." He tried to change the mood. "And you'd never get my loving again, which would destroy you, right, baby?" He smiled at her.

"I don't want trouble," she said, voice unsteady. "I was just talking. The booze was talking. Please, Bub, don't scare me." She began to cry, head down, shoulders shaking.

He sighed. He said to take it easy. He stroked her head and said they'd talk again.

She looked up, those beautiful lips puffy and trembling. "You're going to force me into it. I can feel it. You're going to get me killed."

He thought of Brains and Albert then, and said: "Don't be stupid!"

He drove too fast, and she fumbled for her safety belt.

He slowed down.

She said: "What would your son do if something went wrong, if Sal found out? Who'd take care of him?"

He chuckled. "You got the wrong daddy. I don't have a son. Where'd you get the idea anyway?"

"The picture in your wallet. I found it while you were sleeping."

He shot her a hard look.

"It was just curiosity, Bub. I wanted to know about you. I really dig you, honey."

She'd seen the picture of Jason. He'd thrown away the younger boy's and meant to throw Jason's away too, but just hadn't gotten around to it. He'd do it tonight. Right now, in fact!

He reached into his back pocket. "Friend's kid. Didn't even know I had it." He handed her the wallet. "Take it out. Throw it away. I keep too much junk."

"No! You don't throw pictures away! You should at least put it in a drawer!"

He muttered, "Forget it," and jammed the wallet back in his pocket. He'd throw it away as soon as he left her.

But he was so tired when he got home, he just didn't think of it.

He didn't dream too often, and even when he did rarely remembered anything. This time he dreamed and remembered everything.

He was driving away from Jason, the way he actually had, only the kid was standing on a large skateboard which was tied to the back of the Caddy. So no matter how fast Bub drove, there stood Jason, right behind him, reflected in the rearview, hand upraised, sad, lost look on his face. Finally Bub took a sharp turn, and heard the boy scream, *"Uncle Bub!"* and tried to straighten out, to keep Jason from spinning off the road at sixty miles an hour. But it was too late and he woke up twitching, choking, "God no!"

He washed, dressed, and went to the kitchen to prepare Freddy's breakfast. And wondered at himself. If he had to dream, it seemed it would be about Andro's six hundred fifty grand, or about Giselle's fine white thighs . . . not about some goddamn kid he'd never see again!

The beast within Otis Daimler had been tearing at the bonds of his self-control. For many reasons. Not the least of which was that he and Claire had moved into their new house on July 15th, and his old house hadn't even *sold* until that same week. It hadn't closed escrow—which meant he hadn't received the money for it—until just last Wednesday, giving him an impossible five weeks of borrowing against the $82,000 he eventually got, manipulating bills and arranging several humiliating loans, one from Fred Gower who'd said, "I thought you'd finished with all this crap, Otis," before handing him the twelve-hundred-dollar check needed to keep the Daimlers afloat one final week.

The debts were paid off now except for the enormous mortgage, but the shorts were going to stay for quite a while. And there were other areas of tension.

It seemed he had never been so angry in all his life, while continuing to show his smiling, fat-man's face to all the world. It seemed he had never wanted to let the beast take over so badly before, while knowing it was not the time, that he could be destroyed if he let go of the reins too early.

He struggled with the world, and mainly with the

House, which had, for him, taken on a special personality. The House, drawing admiration and even envy from friends who came to see it, yet growing daily more deadly in its effect on him.

In his old house, small though it was, on a street crowded with similar houses, Otis hadn't been particularly aware of neighbors. They came and they went, moved in or out, causing barely a ripple beyond the immediate house or two on either side, this very much in the Los Angeles manner. He and his wife had stayed on, long beyond the average time of Southern California home owners who were modern-day gypsies, moving on the average of once every two and a half to three years. They had exchanged occasional nods or brief words and otherwise largely ignored the others on their street, and been ignored, this, too, in the Los Angeles manner.

While the brevity and rarity of nods and words didn't change in Nichols Canyon, the proximity, the awareness of at least one neighbor did: the cul-de-sac's celebrity, Letty Drang, anchorperson on a local news program. Or rather the awareness of her dogs, which were kept in the alleyway beyond the fence she and Otis shared to the south of Otis's house.

There wasn't that much room between houses on the south side, where his own alleyway was a narrow footpath leading to the back and the pool, though the houses themselves, and especially Otis's modern Spanish villa, were large. Much too large for one man, with a crippled wife, to handle alone.

Otis didn't have an extra dime for gardeners, pool men, and handymen. He himself had to plant and trim and feed and water. Had to test the pool twice a week and add chemicals and check the heater and filter and jacuzzi and keep the pool-sweep on a proper course and scoop bugs and leaves from the surface. Had to wash an incredible number of glass walls and windows, as the huge living room looked out on the pool and three of the four bedrooms had floor-to-ceiling glass walls and windows looking onto a walled-in-patio. Had to paint and repair and maintain and—because there wasn't even the few extra dollars for their longtime cleaning lady, and Claire's deteriorating condition didn't allow her to help—had to dust furniture and clean sinks and toilets and vacuum over three thousand square feet of carpeting. And shop. And take Claire to the doctor. And, lately, prepare most of the meals.

He struggled with all this in a kind of numb wonder that he had allowed it to happen. And each night seethed, needing an explosion, an outlet for the pressure building up inside him.

Needed Cecily Warren; her body writhing under his; her stifled shrieks. No longer lied to himself about sparing her life; saw her beautiful neck between his big hands.

And could find no way to do it without weakening, certainly holding back, the *Galt's Island* film from which he had high hopes of making a worldwide reputation. He also had one percent of a hundred percent producer's's share of profits, which promised an eventual way out of mortgage indebtedness and the shorts, which in turn would bring gardeners and pool men and handymen and cleaning ladies, maybe even a housekeeper, to his rescue.

In the meantime, there was no rescue. And there was newly added tension. His agent hadn't been able to get a single straight answer from Berry, Pandaro, or even Freddy, since Otis had handed in his script Friday morning. And he knew they'd rush to read their copies.

Which meant big trouble. And which he had partly anticipated because of the way he'd worked on this script.

From the beginning, the beast had colored his outlook; the need for Cecily Warren had manipulated certain scenes.

And then there was working under the pressure of the move, starting when Xtra Realty began bringing droves of people through the old house while he tried to write. They'd done their job well, under orders from Sal Andro, who'd promised Cecily Warren to produce a buyer. The Mafioso wanted to impress her; and who knew if the bitch wouldn't *be* impressed and hand out favors.

That train of thought always led to more tension, more need. (Later, he promised himself, he would actually dwell on it, as a spur, a goad. When the picture was finished. When her death would bring even more notoriety, even more producers' profits.)

The last two weeks of writing had been done in a sort of exhausted frenzy as he maintained his new home, and at the same time put in long hours at the typewriter. And listened to the roaring of the two huge animals next door.

They woke him at seven-ten this Tuesday morning. They were dogs, yes, but their sounds couldn't be called barks. Barks had a certain lightness. Even a Doberman's. Even a German shepherd's, or collie's, or boxer's, or any of the others categorized as medium and large breeds.

Great Danes *roared*. And when they were badly trained by owners who cared little what they did while those owners were away, and badly treated in the sense that they were never allowed to run, never walked on a leash, and taken into the house only a few hours a day, they became frustrated pests.

A frustrated poodle is one thing; its yips can be distracting but largely ignored. A frustrated lion—or pair of Great Danes—is another.

Claire groaned and turned over. "Otis, can't you talk to that woman?"

He said he had, and would again, and knew it was

no use. Letty Drang was a busy careerist, attractive in
a hard, blond, dykie way, with a very obvious sense of
her own importance. He had approached her once as
she'd headed for her car.

"Good morning. You must be Letty Drang. I'm
your new neighbor, Otis Daimler."

She had nodded, and opened the door of her
Porsche. She couldn't have been more than twenty-
five, twenty-six, but the plastic sheen of her hair, the
rigid lines of her eyes and mouth, indicated premature
aging. Which made him, if anything, sympathetic to
her, because he well knew the pressures of working for
the tube.

"I've wanted to ask about your dogs. Isn't there . . .
uh, something you can do about their barking? I've
heard that certain organizations—obedience schools,
they're called . . ."

"I'd love to chat with you," the plasticized anchorperson interrupted sharply, "but I'm due on the air in
fifteen minutes."

She'd entered her car and started the engine. Otis
had moved back and aside, trying to maintain his
friendly-neighbor smile.

During the following days, he'd tried controlling the
dogs with the shouted command: *"Quiet!"* Which
aroused a frenzy of roaring.

He'd banged a pot, hoping to shock them. They'd
paused to listen; then gone wild for half an hour.

He'd sprayed the fence with his garden hose, pretending to be watering a section of ivy, and thought
they'd break through the slats to attack whatever was
assaulting their domain.

Now he took out the ear plugs for Claire and himself, and they went back to sleep. Or she did. He dozed
fitfully, miserably, head throbbing.

At nine, with Claire still asleep, he got up, and realized he would have to use the air conditioning again.
He hated to do it. He was trying to keep down the gas,

water, and electric bills. But it felt like another scorcher, and Claire couldn't take extremes in temperature. Cold stiffened her to near paralysis; heat weakened and nauseated her.

He'd asked the doctor during their last visit if there was anything to be done. "After all, arthritis isn't cancer!"

The doctor had said: "It's every bit as agonizing, if not as deadly, in its extreme stages. And your wife has a very bad case."

Euthanasia. Mercy killing. It would free her, and him. He could do it easily enough right this moment with a pillow over her face. But he loved her still, though the love was changed, was now just a memory of the one person who had kept the beast dormant. Besides, a husband was always the first suspected in the death of a wife, especially a physically disabled wife.

He went down the long corridor, past his paneled study and the guest bedrooms, through the living room—which still looked empty after having swallowed all their old furniture—and out to the thirty-eight-foot-long irregular-shaped pool and attached four-seat jacuzzi whirlpool bath. The water gleamed clean and green under the sun. All was quiet, the filter not set to start for another hour.

Otis walked to the heating and pump equipment against the wall near the south-side alleyway and threw the manual switch. The dogs began to roar. He tried to close his ears, and mind, to the noise—*the tormenting noise!*—and couldn't. And couldn't shut away the memory of that plasticized bitch's patronizing and insulting response to his legitimate complaint; his so-softly-phrased complaint.

He dived into the pool and swam up and back for as long as his wind held out, a respectable twenty-three laps. He climbed out and sank onto the lounge, panting, feeling good, not bothering with the towel as the

sun warmed and dried his body. And saw Claire at the
glass doors, watching, as she often watched when he
swam, her face drawn to skull-like dimensions, her
body stooped, her hands contracted into claws. She
turned away, unable to hide her anguish, her resent-
ment of his health, while she died by inches.

He said: "Hey, honey!"

She turned again, slowly. God, she looked ninety instead of fifty—stooped, her housedress hanging on her
wasted frame, her hair loose and lank and graying rapidly.

"Why not take a swim?" he said, smiling for her,
nodding for her . . . dying inside for her. "Just a few
laps." And even before the sharp little laugh came—a
reminder, this, of better times, when her quick wit, her
warm sense of humor, had kept them both laughing—
knew she wouldn't.

She'd gone swimming exactly once, on July 16th, the
day after they'd moved in, and almost drowned. She'd
wept after he'd pulled her out, and refused to go in
again though he'd said he would keep his arms under
her, would help her every inch of the way.

The jacuzzi she'd used almost every day, but was
skipping even that the past week, disappointed that
the swirling, heated water didn't loosen her arthritic
joints as she'd hoped it would.

Now she said she felt well enough to make breakfast, and walked away. He called out to her, raising his
voice to say that he wanted grapefruit rather than orange juice. And the dogs picked up on it, as they
picked up on anything—car, animal, human—that entered or moved or made sounds in their cul-de-sac, and
began their wild roaring once again.

Otis went into the house. He had to give the beast
within him *something*, a crumb to assuage its hunger.
Which meant the Great Danes.

Killing them by tossing poisoned meat over the
fence was the obvious way to go; too obvious, and too

small a matter to risk bringing himself under the eye of the law. Especially with what he had planned for Cecily Warren.

Something other than killing. Something that would punish not only the howling mutts, but the plasticized bitch as well.

It wasn't until he was dressed and seated at the kitchen table that the method presented itself to him.

Claire had a glass of prune juice in front of her. She didn't like the taste, but since her mobility had been reduced, she'd begun suffering from constipation. So she drank prune juice, ate stewed prunes, occasionally took Ex-Lax.

Otis smiled. She said: "What is it?" He shook his head, murmuring, "Nothing," and began to eat the oatmeal she'd prepared. And said he had to shop for a few items.

He returned in less than an hour, and left a small brown paper bag in the garage. Then he went on with his day's activities, working around the house, spending three hours at the typewriter on a TV series idea, preparing lunch for Claire and himself, doing some cleaning, calling his agent to learn there was still no response from the producers on his script, putting up a lamb stew for dinner, and finally going out to the garage to putter around with his three-year-old Plymouth sedan.

He added a quart of oil. He checked the fan belt for looseness. He used a Kozak dustcloth on the pale blue paint. He listened to the Great Danes roar . . . and listened for another roar, that of Letty Drang's Porsche.

At six-thirty, the dogs began a heavy whining as they anticipated their mistress's imminent arrival. It was the high point of their day, when Letty drove into the garage and within five minutes let them into the house. Where they would stay for anywhere from a few hours to the night, depending on whether she had guests. The delicate-looking network executive who was her current boyfriend didn't come under the heading of guest; he had to share Letty with the dogs.

She would be out of the house at seven-thirty A.M.; on the air from five to six P.M.; home again at six-thirty, unless she didn't show at all, in which case a rather unhappy-looking black cleaning lady would arrive at seven P.M. to shove huge bowls of food out the side door to the animals.

Otis got his paper bag and took out two large-sized packages of Ex-Lax chocolate laxative. He broke the bittersweet chocolate slabs into double-sized portions and waited for Letty to come home. Because she had to be here. He had to feed the chocolate to the dogs immediately before she let them into the house. They had to do their business in what he'd heard was a lavishly furnished, professionally decorated home.

He moved out of the garage and opened the gate to the walled-in patio. He turned left and walked along the pink stone terrace. The dogs roared furiously a few feet in front of him, beyond the tall grape-stake fence.

He checked the time—six-forty. She was late, or not coming home tonight. He looked into his open hands. The chocolate was beginning to soften, to melt. He would have to put it down in a moment.

He heard the Porsche.

Instantly, the roars ended, the plaintive, heavy whining recommenced.

He couldn't hear the garage door open or close, but the Porsche rasped in low gear, and died.

He carefully threw one handful of chocolate over the fence.

The whining stopped. He heard chomping sounds, and then growling as the dogs quarreled over a last piece. He transferred the melting chocolate from his left hand to his right, and threw that too over the fence.

More chomping sounds. More growling. And then they again whined to be let into the house.

Otis wiped his hands on a tissue. A moment later, he heard the side door to Letty Drang's house open; heard the strong, well-modulated voice say, "Harry, Barbara, down! Easy, damn it!" There were scurrying sounds, and the door closed.

Otis went inside and got a diet cola. Sipping, he went out back to check the ivy and ice plants on the slope behind the pool. Still sipping, he went through the house and out the front door, checking the gold-leaf and tall fern along the atrium entry, beginning to listen now for sounds from his neighbor's house. He finished the cola, but some twenty minutes had passed and he didn't want to go back inside to throw the can away, not if it meant missing what was going to happen.

He went back to the walled-in patio, back to his position near the grape-stake fence. And waited patiently for perhaps another ten minutes. And heard what could only be described as howls—human howls. The door beyond the fence banged open, obviously hitting the wall with force. Letty Drang's voice, no longer well-modulated, screamed: "Get outa here you fucking horrors! Christ, Christ! The carpet! The Persian rug!"

And then came the accolade, the pinnacle: Letty Drang began to sob hysterically.

The door closed. The dogs whined. They weighed about two hundred pounds each. That should mean a considerable amount of loose shit spread around Letty's house.

It soon became evident they had some left; the smell wafting over the fence drove Otis indoors. Where he checked his lamb stew, changed into bathing trunks, and took a leisurely soak in the jacuzzi, without any Great Dane noise to disturb him.

He decided he would lay in a supply of Ex-Lax for

the next time the roaring became too much and the beast within him strained at the bonds.

A fun way to placate it until Cecily Warren and the real thing.

Johnny Warren was discouraged. He was sick of going to the Y and listening to Mr. Bennecke talk about making the Olympic swimming team if he practiced every day. "Practice" to Mr. Bennecke meant twenty-five to thirty laps, fast as you could do them. Of the nine kids attending regular, only Juan and Harold could do thirty laps. Juan was a black Mex, half Negro, and Harold was a Jew who thought he was Mark Spitz. Those kinds of kids always tried harder.

As Jack DeKuyper, a friend at the Y, said yesterday: "They have to try harder, they're so shitty by birth!"

Anyway, he hated going to the Y now, but mom wouldn't let him stop. She said he never finished anything he started. She'd smacked him last week when he said he wasn't going. So he went. Because it was scary, the way her face whitened. Like grandma's when she had too much wine and something bugged her. Like Aunt Teresa, a long time ago, before she got the job at the hospital and didn't come around any more. One smack in the face that almost knocked him down, and two more misses as he ran for the door and the Y.

She was down on him for everything lately. He wished he could go away for a while. Like to the grape ranch. Grandma wasn't down on him. Grandma said he had "a great head for thinking, just like your grandfather, may he rest in peace."

The grape ranch was better for summer vacations than L.A., even with grandma drinking too much and getting white-faced too much, which stopped mom from sending him there this summer. At least grandma didn't give him any hassle about school or reading, like mom, and like that writer-friend of mom's, Don Baylis.

All those books . . . he *wrote* them. And while he
was okay at the Bel Air Hotel for lunch and then the
beach, he got uptight about a few jokes. Like the Monopoly game: He caught Johnny kidding around and
said he didn't see the point of playing if one of them
was going to cheat. When Johnny said, wide-eyed and
innocent the way he always made mom laugh, "You
mean *you* were cheating?" Don folded up the board,
just when Johnny was going to build houses on Board-
walk and Park Place.

And then the business with the wallet, which got
Don real hot.

Still, he was sure he could get along with Don, once
Don got less uptight about kidding around. And once
he stopped the questions about school and reading.
He'd made Johnny read a section of a kid's book he'd
bought just for their weekend together. He'd nodded
when Johnny finished, but Johnny knew how slow,
how bad he'd read.

He could handle that, too, handle Don Baylis even
if mom decided to marry him, which she'd hinted at.
Because he'd met other boyfriends of mom's. Not for
a long while now, true, but he remembered how it
was. First the men, like that accountant, would pay a
lot of attention to Johnny and bug him about school
and reading and *career*. Then they'd forget about him
and concentrate on mom.

He hadn't liked the accountant and the man who
sold foreign cars, which was where mom got her classic
Jag. He didn't remember the rock musician too well,
but that was one boyfriend who didn't even bother
looking at Johnny.

He liked Don all right; maybe best of all. Don had
more money than the other boyfriends—those books
must've made him rich. Johnny thought he recognized
the name of one that had been made into a movie;
thought he'd seen the movie on television; was going
to watch for it.

And Don would change like the others. He wanted mom, not Johnny. He wanted what the old Mex with the crazy name of Horgey got.

He could never think about that for too long. It upset him in a funny way. It almost always got him to thinking about Mary and doing to her what Horgey did to mom, what maybe Don did to mom, what maybe other boyfriends did, too.

Funny feeling. Bad feeling. Better to think of Mary without thinking of mom.

Though there wasn't much to think about Mary lately. One of the worst parts of this summer was that Johnny hadn't had Mary sit for him since the beginning of May. Mom had used Mrs. Maillet because first Johnny had been sick on and off, and then mom had begun staying out real late and until morning. Which she was still doing; something about a big movie and getting her shot, Johnny wasn't sure exactly what since she didn't really talk about it.

After that, Johnny went to spend three weeks with dad in the San Joaquin, and it wasn't too good. Dad kept arguing with his girlfriend and complaining about the drought and they went to a lot of movies and he slept a lot.

By the time he came home, Mary had gone to visit relatives in New York. She didn't return until just last week. He'd seen her in front of her house, helping her mother carry groceries from their old station wagon. She'd looked terrific; even more grown-up than before; even prettier than before. But they hadn't talked.

So a bummer summer, man . . . and when he came home at five, mom was there and told him she was going out again tonight. He nodded glumly and went to the study and looked through his *TV Guide*. Mostly re-runs, but thank God for the tube anyway. Mom wasn't hardly around since she'd landed that part. Hardly any shopping and not many meals out and Klaus away at camp and nothing to do at night.

She called to him from her room. He wandered listlessly to the hallway.

"Mary's coming over to sit with you. She'll be able to tell you about her trip to New York." Before he could respond, she ran out across the hall and into his room, saying: "Where's that Scotch Tape I gave you?" She was wearing pantyhose and boots with high heels and a push-up brassiere and nothing else.

He said: "On my dresser."

He waited for her to come out again. She finally did, walking slowly, looking down at her right hand. "Split my thumbnail. Maybe the tape will hold it until I can find time to buy a paste-on." She came to a stop in the hallway, working on the finger. He looked at her long legs in the dark pantyhose and black suede boots, at her swelling moonie, and turned away, horrified at himself for getting a stiffie.

He was looking through the refrigerator when she came into the kitchen, dressed in her blue suede outfit with vest over a red blouse. Her hair was curled and she looked fantastic and he was proud of her. But when she raised her arms and turned for him, asking, "Well?" all he did was shrug.

"What's that mean, Boy Wonder?"

He closed the refrigerator. "I can't find any dinner."

"Aw, poor baby can't find dinner." She tickled him and chased him and he yelled: "Cut it out, fool! I'm hungry and you're never . . ." He stopped.

"I'm never what?"

He shrugged. He was sure she knew he was going to say: "You're never around." He *wanted* her to know.

She said: "I told Mary to bring over a Chinese dinner from Luck Sun on Viress. Your favorite—pepper steak, spare ribs, and shrimp fried rice."

He brightened. "Fortune cookies?"

Mom nodded. "You mad at me, Boy Wonder? I been neglecting you?"

"Not really, big momma. It's just that I can't wait for school to start so I won't have to drown every day."

She laughed. "You must really hate the Y."

He laughed with her and they shared a diet root beer and she kissed him and said she'd try to get back as early as possible, maybe even before he sent to sleep.

Thinking of Mary and of ways he might warm her up, he said: "Don't spoil your date, big momma. Anyway, I won't wait up for *you*."

"I'll bet," she said, smiling cynically. But she hugged him on her way to the door.

The minute the Jag drove away, he dashed to the bathroom. Where he washed real good, brushed and combed his hair real good, and splashed on the Old Spice aftershave mom had given him last Christmas. Smelled super, and he opened his pants, pulled aside his shorts, and splashed a handful onto his pistol. Where it burned like hell!

He jumped around, yelling: "Christ, Christ, make it stop!"

In a minute it went from hot to warm, and then tingled a little. He examined himself in the full-length door mirror, and sighed in relief.

Anyway, it smelled nice now, so if Mary ever got around to touching . . .

The doorbell rang. He fumbled with his pants and yelled, "In a minute!" and looked in the mirror and ran.

They ate in the study, on the old coffee table, watching TV. He waited until they were almost finished to get the bottle of chilled white wine from the fridge. She said, "I don't know if we should," and he said, "Just one," and poured and raised his glass. "Welcome back to Los Angeles, world traveler."

She laughed. "You got the rap all right, Johnny, 'specially for a kid."

He let that go, and pushed her to empty her glass. She wouldn't, and he didn't either, because he didn't want to get loopy; not before the card game anyway.

They cleared away the dishes. He kept making jokes and thinking up sharp conversation, feeling good when she laughed.

Back in the study, he got her to finish her wine by promising he wouldn't pour any more. "You play poker, Mary?"

She leaned back on the couch, crossing her legs, looking at the TV. "I've been known to," she said, which was what mom called a "line."

He laughed to make her feel good, and poured her another half-glass. When she said, "You promised, Johnny!" he said, "Christ, I forgot, sorry, honest."

She said not to take the Lord's name in vain, and he again said he was sorry. "Look, I'm putting the wine away." He brought the bottle to the kitchen, and when he came back to the study she was sipping from her glass, watching a movie.

He said he'd get a deck of cards and they'd play a few hands. She nodded. "I really dig Rock Hudson," she said.

He went to his room for the deck, and fixed it by putting aces every second card from the top. Then he went to the closet and took down the little treasure chest Dad had given him with twenty-five dollars in five-dollar bills as his summer spending money. He put the bills in his pocket and walked into the study, zipping the cards on the side, as if he'd been shuffling them. "Five-card stud, okay?"

She nodded. Her glass was empty and she was smiling at the TV. "Good movie, Johnny."

"We can watch and play at the same time. But let's make it interesting."

She glanced questioningly at him.

"A little bet." He took out his five-dollar bills and laid them on the table.

"I'm not betting *my* hard-earned money!"

"I don't want you to. I'll bet money and you bet something else."

She'd begun to watch the movie again, but a commercial came on. "You bet money and I bet something else?" She seemed a little dopey, and he hoped the wine had gotten to her. "Like what?"

He shrugged. "A kiss."

She put back her head and laughed real hard. Her boobs pushed out against her yellow short-sleeved blouse and she stamped both feet on the floor and her cutoff jeans were short and showed the roundness, the smoothness of her strong white thighs. And her red mouth was open and her hair, dark like mom's, rippled to her shoulders and she was beautiful and he *loved* her and had to touch her. And looked down at the cards so as not to make any dumb moves. "Five dollars against a kiss," he said, keeping his voice steady.

She kept laughing, but finally said, "Five dollars? Your mother would kill you if you lost."

"This is money my dad gave me when I went to see him. Five dollars is nothing to him, or me. I told you about my fifty-thousand trust, remember? Anyway, my mom said I can do whatever I want with this twenty-five dollars. She thinks I already spent half of it, but I didn't. You win, no one'll know. You lose, same thing."

She looked at the money and looked at him and wet her lips.

"Not that any girl can beat me at poker," he said. "My dad says I'm better than some professionals. He also says that poker's one game women never really learn how to play."

That last part got her mad. "Okay! Five dollars against a kiss on the cheek!"

"On the lips. One dollar against on the cheek."

She looked at the fives. Her family was big and it

was poor and mom said Mary would never have made
it to New York if her aunt and uncle hadn't paid her
way.

She nodded again, her face flushed. "You got it."

Hurrying before she could change her mind, he
dealt her one card and dealt himself one card and her
the third card and himself the fourth card and so on.
Which meant he had three aces, and two other cards
he didn't care about.

She discarded three. He discarded one, holding onto
the king the way his father had taught him to. She
said, "Trying for a straight or flush? Well, start saying
good-bye to your five dollars!"

To make it look good, he acted worried as he dealt
her and himself.

He drew a ten. She arranged her hand and leaned
back, pressing the cards to her chest. "Oh baby, are
you going to be sorry you started this game!"

"Sure," he said, suddenly afraid she might have
lucked into a full house; maybe even four of a kind.

She spread out two pair—jacks and sixes.

He put his cards on the table. "You played smart,
Mary. You almost made it."

"Gee," she muttered.

They were sitting side by side. He knew he had to
do this fast or he would never do it at all. He also
knew he had to do it right, not like a baby. "You'll get
another chance to win the five," he said, and slid over
until their sides touched. He felt himself trembling
and turned toward her and put his right arm around
her waist from the front and his left around her
shoulders. With his left hand he drew her head down
to him and kissed her lips and opened his mouth and
pushed with his tongue the way Jack DeKuyper said
he kissed his fourteen-year-old cousin who would
squeeze his pistol through his pants if he forced her
hand there.

Mary pulled back a little. Johnny held on tightly, desperately, licking at her closed mouth. And raised his hand a little from her waist toward her breast.

She pulled back harder. But now he had an erection and he tasted this girl and he smelled her and his hand from around her waist was pressing the bottom of her breast.

Surprisingly, she stopped pulling away, and opened her mouth. She made a sighing sound under his lips, and moved in such a way that his hand rose freely over the swelling of her left boob. He squeezed it and her tongue touched his and his erection throbbed and he didn't know what to do next. He tried to think of what the boys in school and at the Y had said about sex.

He took his hand from Mary's breast and fumbled for *her* hand. He found instead the electric silkiness of her bare thigh below the cut-off shorts. He stroked, caressed, and she moved again, opening her legs a little.

Excitement was making him gasp for breath, and the kiss was taking away some of that needed breath, and yet he couldn't stop even for a moment. Because if he allowed her to draw back and look at him, to use her mouth to talk, she would surely end this.

He found her hand at her side. He drew it to his lap, and to his erection. She jerked it away, but she didn't break the embrace, the kiss.

He stroked her thigh, stroked up to where the clothed thighs joined. Her hand came to stop him, but not too strongly. He pressed against her hand, and for one instant she allowed him to press his fingers to the place where, under the denim, he knew the beaver lay, the slit lay—the *cunt!*

His chest was full of drums; his pulse hammered in his throat, his temples, throughout his body. When she pushed his hand back this time, he gave in. He took her hand again and brought it gently to his lap again; then used a sudden burst of strength to press it against his throbbing erection.

And she grasped the tube of flesh under his clothes. She rubbed. She squeezed.

He couldn't breathe with the ecstasy infusing his lower body. He gasped as their tongues licked each other. He felt something almost painful, something too much to bear. He pulled back his head, forgeting about the kiss. He gulped air, and put his face in her neck, her hair. He gasped: "Mary, wait."

And had his first full ejaculation, coming in his pants.

He was not quite thirteen. He was a child. He was also a North Hollywood baby who'd learned much from his beautiful big momma, from his friends, from the porno books. And rising from the couch, gasping, he was putting it all together. This orgasm was his coming of age, his ritual of manhood. And so he lied like a man.

"I've had three girls, but no one like you, Mary. You're the most beautiful, the smartest. And you wouldn't give in, like they did."

She was looking away, beginning the return to Mary-the-sitter who would become angry, upset with herself; who would classify him once again as a child.

But he'd interrupted that process, and she looked at him. "You had three girls?"

"Up at my Dad's—Mexican girl. And at my aunt's, here in L.A., neighbor girl your age. And . . ." he ran out of inventiveness ". . . the neighbor girl again."

"You mean like this?"

"No, all the way. You know."

"But you're such a kid."

"Not as long as I can come."

He turned away then, in case she got upset at the word, and said he was going to wash up.

He changed underwear and pants, throwing the

sticky stuff into the washer, putting it under some other clothes, knowing mom wouldn't sort them out once they were already in there. He came back to the study, and Mary was watching TV. She didn't look at him, and her face was glum.

He sat down beside her. "You get much action in New York?"

"You want true confessions?"

"Why not? We're good friends, aren't we?" He reached for her hand.

She moved it away, but just a little. So he moved closer and grabbed it.

She cleared her throat. "My cousin in New York fixed me up with a boy, my age, maybe a little younger, and he . . ." She giggled.

"C'mon, Mary." He was excited, and he was upset. A world full of older boys, and Mary out there looking so good, and if he could get her to play this way, what couldn't they do?

"We were making out. He was begging me and he promised me a gold locket. But the funny part . . ." She covered her mouth with her free hand. "I guess I had too much beer, which he and his friend, my cousin's date, brought along in the car. We were in a dark place, in the back seat, and he . . ." She giggled and shook her head.

"Took your panties off?" he said, trying to be cool.

She nodded, giggling, covering her mouth. "Then when it was going into me, you know, he couldn't hold out and made a mess." She leaned back, laughing. "So I'm still a good Catholic, and a virgin."

He said: "Would've been me, you'd have to go to confession and say Hail Marys and stuff."

Which cracked her up again.

And he drew her close again.

And they began all over again.

He worked at her cutoffs, trying to open them up, and managed to unzip the side vent and get his hand inside, under the smooth panties, onto the hot flesh of her hip, her bulging bottom.

But she wouldn't let him work around to her front, even though he pleaded, saying, "For *you*, Mary. I had mine," and she whispered that he was "sweet."

Still, she was gasping, kissing him all over his face, and when he brought her hand to his fly, she didn't fight. And when he opened the zipper, she put her hand right in.

Remembering her laughter at the New York boy who'd come too soon, he tried to prove he wouldn't be like that, tried to think of terrible things—dead animals and people and school and drowning in the Y pool. But when her hand grasped his penis, when she drew it out and stopped kissing him to look at it, he simply couldn't stop.

He warned her with, "Watch it!" and she twisted it away from herself and up and back onto him. Which made him come harder, longer.

He only had one more clean pair of regular pants left, but at least his underwear didn't need changing. He dressed and came out and she turned from the TV and said: "You sit on the chair!" But she smiled right away. "I'm gonna raise my rates when your mother asks me to sit with you again. I hear that girls in massage parlors get twenty dollars for what I did."

"But they do something else, too."

"What?"

"You know." He touched his mouth.

"You're bad, Johnny Warren!" But again, she was smiling. Then her smile went away. "Hey, you wouldn't talk about this, would you?"

He sat down at the end of the couch, even though she pointed at the chair. He said: "Twice in one night's my limit, until I reach sixteen. And am I some sort of nut to talk about you when my mother would find out about *me?*"

"Guess so." She checked the *TV Guide* "Turn to Channel 2, will you? At ten they've got a special."

He got up, though he was really, *tired*, man. He wanted to go to sleep, but he didn't want her to know that. He changed the channel, and they watched a bit of the special. She didn't like it because it had old songs from Bing Crosby and she'd thought it would also have Elvis.

So he got up again, really drag-assing, and found a movie for her.

They watched, and she talked, and he came up with a few lines, fighting to keep his eyes open. He even patted her bottom when she got up to go to the bathroom. She slapped his hand away, saying, "No more! Your mother will be home soon."

"Gee, that's right. And I promised I'd be in bed by ten. I was up at six-thirty this morning—wanted to finish a book I was reading—and she gets real uptight about my not getting what she thinks is enough sleep."

"Then change into your jammies."

He acted like he didn't want to.

"C'mon, Johnny, I don't want her getting steamed at *me*."

He stood up, but he didn't want her suspecting he wasn't full of grown-up desire. "Well, if you come to my room for a goodnight kiss."

She put her hands on her hips.

He sat down again.

"All right," she said.

In his room, he got into pajamas and lay down on the top of the blankets. It was so warm, he'd have slept naked if Mary wasn't around. He still didn't want her seeing him without clothes; felt too small, too weak, compared with the muscular high-school boys.

She came in from the bathroom. He held out his arms as she sat down at the edge of the bed. "Just a little good-night peck," she said, but opened her mouth when he opened his.

He ran his hands over her bottom and squeezed her boobs and felt her up real good and got another stiffie.

She said, "You'll make yourself sick," but she was breathing hard.

He couldn't believe he wanted to do it again, but he did.

At the same time, he was worried about his mother maybe coming back early.

He said: "Just look at it."

Her eyes darted to his crotch, where the thin pajama cloth was sticking up, tentlike.

He threw caution to the wind and yanked down his bottoms.

She gasped. "It's . . . pretty big."

"Would you kiss it?" he whispered, loving the way her eyes stayed fixed on it.

"No way!" And still, her eyes stayed fixed on it.

He'd learned so much tonight, come so far tonight, that he was emboldened to try something else. His money lay on the dresser. He said: "Take one of the fives, Mary . . . and kiss it."

"Hey, that's like, you know, hookers." She giggled and shook her head.

"Take *two* fives, ten dollars."

"Your mother'll ask about the money."

"I told you, she doesn't know how much I have. I swear to God."

She didn't answer for a while, still looking at his throbbing penis; then spoke so fast he barely made out the words. "I need thirty-seven dollars for two new outfits for school and with some baby-sitting money and twenty from you . . ."

He said, "Take it," thinking she was wiping him out.

"You sure?"

He was sure he wanted her mouth on his pistol. "Yes, but more than a kiss, you know."

She took four of the fives and put them into the back pocket of her cutoffs. She sat down again and took his penis in her hand and without any hesitation or fumbling bent and kissed it. And licked it and took it into her mouth and began to move her head up and back.

In the split second he had for rational thought, he realized she'd done it before. Then he was enveloped in ecstasy for the third time that night. This time he took longer to climax, much longer, and he was glad because it felt so good and looked so good.

He gasped a warning at the end, but she kept sucking and he was horrified and it almost ruined his pleasure. But then nothing could ruin the incredible feeling of shooting his stuff into her mouth.

She left and he heard the water running in the bathroom.

When she came back, he hoped she wouldn't try to kiss him on the lips.

She didn't kiss him at all, just said, "Good night, sex maniac," and something he didn't understand. "Lucky it's all over or we'd have to get married." She shut the lights and the door.

Now he knew what it was Horgey felt doing it with mom.

What the others felt doing it with mom.

Cecily was glad this particular gathering of the *Galt's Island* clan, as Freddy called their inner group, was meeting at his house and not at Rob Dennings's Malibu place. Too many gatherings and parties there, for too many late hours, which required too many lies to Donny because he just refused to believe she could be straight.

She barely believed it herself. But she'd held out against all the pressure by Rob and Joy-Joy to get it on.

Sex between her and Rob would be too damned exposed, and since he hadn't gotten real heavy about it, hadn't made it a condition of their continuing to be friends and co-stars, she was beginning to feel she could hold out.

"It's better, really," she'd told him tonight, when he'd again suggested they "rehearse" their sex scenes. "It'll keep us fresh; maintain the excitement the characters are supposed to feel for each other since it's the very first time they make love. It should be our first time, too, shouldn't it?"

She doubted that she'd convinced him. She'd seen him talking to Freddy, and Freddy had come over to her about half an hour ago and suggested that unless she made it with Dennings, "there might be some hard feelings later on. You wouldn't want that, Cecily, for your future career as well as for the success of this film."

Bub had been nearby, serving drinks, and must have heard because when Freddy left, he'd sung softly: "It ain't necessarily so."

She'd smiled, agreeing with him. She hadn't seen any signs of hard feelings. Freddy was just a natural pimp who would push his own daughter, if he'd had one, into bed with a friend. Besides, it made no sense for Rob to have hard feelings. He'd get her eventually, even if it was in front of the cameras. (He was supposed to come all over her belly, as she understood it, in porno-film fashion so that the audience would have no doubts that they were seeing their super-star hero in a real, all-out fuck.)

He'd get his kicks then, though there was some worry, she guessed from all the hinting at "rehearsals," that he might not be able to perform because of the pressure of technicians and cameras. She herself felt it would turn out just fine. Sex was one area where she had total confidence in her ability to make men perform.

So tonight was fun, with a feeling that she was going

to be able to handle this chance at stardom in a way Don wouldn't disapprove of too much . . . once those porn scenes were out of the way. And that later she'd be able to give him what he most wanted—a faithful woman. Because with the five-thousand-dollar advance on her forty-thousand contract she no longer had to run all over town for bit parts and accept the occasional sex action that went with them, or depend on Jorge Resordo.

She felt badly about Jorge. She'd canceled him last night, when she'd slept over at Don's. She'd canceled him three other times in the past two months. She'd promised to call him today, if an opportunity arose for her to have him over tonight, but she hadn't called and now it was too late.

She no longer needed Jorge's three hundred a week, though the truth was she hated to give up such easy money. And Jorge, seeing a withdrawal, sensing an end, had insisted on mailing her the money anyway, which only reinforced her liking for the man; which made her realize how much she regretted giving him up.

She sighed, seeing Freddy coming toward her once more, that stern, lecturing expression on his face. She braced herself for the shit-storm, and saw Fanny Batcher intercept him, giving him the big eyes and boob-contact and *dahling*.

Fanny's presence here tonight was one good reason for Cecily's splitting. Other reasons were: She'd had a lovely buffet dinner, her safe limit of two cocktails, and wanted to get a decent eight hours of sleep for a change. It was after eleven and she'd been here since seven—a respectable showing.

Also, she wanted to call Don before it got too late.

She moved toward the archway to the hall and the door, thinking she'd speak to Freddy tomorrow and say she'd left because of sudden illness.

And not care whether he believed it. He was a slick

item, Mr. Fred Gower, and bad news for women. Still, she owed him a lot—this shot at stardom, actually—and because of it forgave him much.

She was keeping her eyes straight ahead, trying not to have to see anyone who might stop her, when a hand grasped her arm from behind. Freddy said: "Not without having a nightcap with your host, you don't."

She turned, saying she really didn't feel like more booze. But he was holding two large bell glasses of wine, one red which was half gone, and one white which was full. She said: "I'll take the short order."

He sipped from the red, handing her the white. "You wouldn't want to risk catching something, would you?"

"I've already risked it, twice."

He chuckled and led her past the front door to the staircase. She stopped. "Not another gig with you, Bub, and the camera?"

He chuckled again. "Bub's busy. I've given up, for myself. You know what I think you should do to set Rob's mind at ease." He shrugged. "But that's not what I want to talk about. We have trouble with the script, as you probably know from Don. I've been trying to speak to him since last night. First, I gather, you were there . . ."

Someone called him from the living room. He called back. "Be right with you," and, to Cecily, "Let's get out of this for five minutes. You have to help me with Don." Holding her arm, he drew her up the stairs.

"I was sure he'd call you when I left," she said, as they reached the second-floor landing. She shook her head as he moved toward his bedroom. "You have two other rooms up here. Let's use one of them."

"All right!" he said irritably, and steered her into the room beside the master. He sat down at the edge of the double bed and waved her to a corner chair. Then he took a deep breath. "I'm uptight about this script business." He raised his glass. "To *Galt's Island* and our getting into production before I die of aggravated tension!"

She smiled and drank a little.

He looked at his glass. "This red is a Rothschild, forty dollars a bottle." He looked across at her. "Your white is Margaux at perhaps sixty a bottle. I've served no more than two bottles all night, to Dennings, Pandaro, Berry, you, and me. And you're warming that chilled nectar like a buck-fifty Chablis."

She said sorry. She drank again, more deeply, and frowned. "I think my taste runs more to buck-fifty Chablis. This stuff is bitter."

"About Don," he said. "Did he discuss the script with you?"

"A little, this morning. He dislikes it. He wants to rewrite it, but he's afraid of taking on the work. His health, you know."

"His health is better than mine," Fred snapped, and raised his glass. "Here's to our being as healthy as Donny."

She drank with him, and said: "I just don't like your expensive wine." She put her glass on the floor.

He looked at it. He seemed to be measuring what was left. She said, "So I owe you five dollars," and yawned and leaned back, dead tired. "Can we finish this discussion, Freddy? Your guests are waiting, and so is my son."

"Yeah, your son. Imagine keeping him under wraps all this time. What did you hope to gain?"

"I was simply keeping him out of an actress's rather untidy life. Now what is it you were saying about Don and the script?"

"That I want him to rewrite it. That I want you to help him decide to rewrite it."

"I've already told him . . ." She stopped and looked at Freddy. Something about the way he was talking; the time-wasting way he was talking.

"I want you to call him *now*," he said quickly. Too quickly, as if he'd read her sudden suspicion.

But suspicion of what?

She stood up. "I'll call him when I get home." She turned to the door, and was suddenly loose in the hips, the knees. She put out a hand to steady herself against the wall. Freddy was there to help her.

"You all right?"

She looked into his face. "Am I?" she asked, feeling things recede, feeling a drug high, or low, coming over her. She'd taken enough shit on her own to know she was going under something. "Freddy, you wouldn't . . . ?" She began to draw her strength together, to claw at him, to fight him.

"We'd better get someone to drive you home," he said. "Lot of flu going around, and with a few drinks it can really put you down."

She wanted to believe that. And he was taking her out of the room, not to the bed, so it was all right.

Two cocktails and almost a full bell-glass of wine and maybe a flu bug . . .

They were on the landing. She put her head on his shoulder; her eyes closed; her brain clouded over.

She was resting. It felt marvelous. She was lying down and someone was helping her out of her clothes.

She forced her eyes open. It was a man. "Freddy, stop," she mumbled.

Warmth lapped between her legs. She couldn't help enjoying it.

She was being had. She was being taken. She had to fight.

A voice spoke to her, and it was Rob Dennings's deep, rich baritone, telling her he'd wanted her for three months, and was so pleased she'd decided to accept him. "I need this, Cecily, for self-assurance. I need to be certain all will go well in front of the cameras."

His large hands moved over her body. His lips pressed here and there, and returned between her legs.

It was something to have Rob Dennings, super-star, perform cunnilingus on you, wasn't it? The thought, slipping through the layers of cotton packing her brain, excited her. And the sexual stimulation . . . and then the penis entering her . . . and then his gasping, his coming, the blurred view of that famous face sinking to her breast. And his thanking her, thanking her.

She was alone for a time. Then Dennings was back. No, it was Freddy. She was being turned over. Freddy was saying she'd "helped the project stabilize." And despite the fuzzy senses, the cotton packing her brain, she felt pain. She groaned, begging him to stop, but he kept pushing with that enormous penis of his and the pain in her rectum grew until she didn't think she could stand it.

And had to stand it as he plunged in and out, calling her "a big-assed whore" and "gorgeous ass-fuck" and she was being pounded in a debased, meaningless piece of drugged flesh and again her control had been stripped from her and again her life was shaky.

Alone. Wondering how late it was as she sat up and gasped at the pain in her rectum. Finding her clothes and stumbling around, crying, hating Freddy and knowing she could do nothing to him or to Dennings; knowing she would have to forget this, make believe it had never happened.

Her watch read almost five. She looked at the windows, and faint light was growing there.

The windows were in Freddy's bedroom. She remembered that Bub had a camera. And Fanny Batcher had been downstairs. And Johnny was being watched by Mary who wasn't supposed to stay past one or two.

And she hadn't called Donny. She hadn't told him how she'd loved being with him last night and this morning; how close she'd felt then to becoming the woman he wanted.

She dressed and tried to make herself look right in

the mirror. Her hair was gummy, sticky, and she tried brushing it out and said, "God!" and gave up. She opened the door and stepped into the hall. She heard voices—Freddy's and Bub's. In the end room. Bub was saying, ". . . hell of a stupid thing!"

She walked there. Freddy was in bed, looking as if he'd been asleep. Bub was in a brown bathrobe, and he spoke to her: "Can you drive home?"

"I think so."

"Want me to follow you, just to make sure?"

She swayed. "Yes." And to both of them: "Good clean fun, right?" and couldn't help crying, standing there and holding onto the door jamb. "Christ, couldn't you let it go? Was it that important?"

"No," Freddy said, sounding annoyed. "It wasn't that important. And it isn't that important. So forget it. Rob feels reassured and we can move ahead."

"Do *you* feel reassured?"

"You could say that. At least I got it out of my system, wanting to do that to you." He waved his hand. "Go on home now. I'll see you get a second advance on your contract—first thing tomorrow. Doesn't that deserve a smile?"

She couldn't tell him what that deserved. She couldn't tell him what he'd made of her. Maybe it wouldn't have felt this bad before Donny. But now, tonight, with her life beginning to change . . .

She went to the stairs. Bub came after her, and took her arm. She shook it loose, saying, "I'm surprised you didn't get into me, too. Or did I pass out during your trick? Or were you too busy with the camera?"

"I didn't know a thing about it until I made my regular early-morning fire-check. I was a little late, and I found you in Fred's bedroom. I was just learning what happened from him when you walked in."

She wanted to believe him, but her anger, her reduction, was too intense. "Did you use Quaaludes?" she asked, holding to the banister as she walked.

"I didn't use anything. But that's what he'd use to get you that far under. You'll be a little out of it for some hours, yet. I don't think you should drive."

"What's the difference? There're lots of big-titted pieces of ass around Hollywood. What's one more or less?"

He didn't answer, and they walked outside to where her car was at the curb. She got behind the wheel, reached for her little black purse, and realized she didn't have it. And also realized she couldn't drive five blocks, to say nothing of all the way to the Valley and home.

She looked up at Bub, who was at the window. She told him about her purse. He said to slide over and wait.

She got into the passenger's seat. Later, she opened her eyes, and Bub was dressed and behind the wheel. They were driving.

Her head sagged against the door. Again she cried, trying to keep it quiet.

Bub said: "God damn him, he just doesn't know who to pick on. He's really not the bastard he seems to be."

"Oh yes he is! You just don't want to admit it because you're his friend."

"I'm his servant, lady."

"His friend. Maybe his only friend. Because he's the worst. Someone's got to punish him."

"Don't think of telling Don Baylis. You'll blow a few lives if you do, including Baylis's."

"So your friend'll go on. Raping. Because that's what it is, you know."

He said nothing.

"Or that's what it would be, if I was the kind who could claim rape, right?"

He didn't quarrel with her. He said: "Think of what would happen to the movie."

She let it go at that. They were almost home. She

told him where to turn. "Thank you, Bub. Will you call a cab from my place?"

He said the cab was already waiting . . . and pointed . . . and it was right in front of her house. He'd ordered it when he got her purse.

He was gone, waving, and she was inside, pulling herself together to face Mary.

She needn't have bothered. The girl was asleep on the couch in the study. Cecily woke her and paid her double, apologizing, saying she hoped Mrs. Cherrel wouldn't be too upset at the hour, but that she'd had car trouble.

Mary looked at the money, and smiled sleepily. "It's okay."

Cecily watched her run across the street to her home; then looked in on Johnny; then went to her room.

And felt *filthy*.

Fighting the Quaalude, she forced herself to undress and get into the shower. Where she scrubbed herself front and back, and refused to cry when the tears welled up inside her.

"I'll get even," she said, face turned up into the stream of hot water. "I swear I will, when I'm a star."

Seven

Wednesday, August 31, and Thursday, September 1

Fanny couldn't wait to call Don!

She was up at nine, though she'd slept barely three hours . . . because she'd waited down the street from Fred Gower's house until Cecily Warren had come out with the black houseboy. Probably made it with him, too—Fred and Rob Dennings for sure—and Fanny hoped she'd enjoyed it since it was going to be the most expensive night of her life.

She dressed carefully, not too much turn-on, but teeny-weeny-bikini panties of wispy pink lace, Frederick's of Hollywood's best, for when the casual pants suit came off. And her highest klunker shoes, to get that show-girl height when she stripped down for action. She needed all the erotic help she could get with Don.

She'd been seeing him about once a week since that first date in May, and nothing much had happened. Sure, they were making it, but he wasn't all that hot for bed with her. And it wasn't developing, wasn't growing the way she'd thought it would. She wasn't gaining on Cecily Warren, and had recently begun to feel she would lose out entirely.

For one thing, Don hadn't made the slightest move

to spend any part of the two hundred thousand he'd gotten for his movie rights; at least not on her.

God! *Two hundred thousand dollars!* And the few times he took her out it was to Dupars where he liked the pancakes, or to some fish house for broiled salmon. She'd hinted at Chasen's, Le Bistro, Perrino's. Also Saks Fifth, Broadway, I. Magnin's, this for starters, certain she could eventually lead him to Rodeo Drive and Beverly Hills' Million-Dollar Strip. But he smiled and said nothing and did nothing. And she knew he wouldn't raise a finger to stop her if she threatened to head for the exit.

If he'd been anyone else, she'd have given herself the satisfaction of telling him to fuck off!

But he wasn't anyone else. He was Don Baylis. He was, from the talk at Fred Gower's party last night, going to rewrite Daimler's script, thus saving little Fanny from having to pitch the fatso, which she'd planned on doing when the scriptwriter entered the polish stage where he could add lines and action to various parts, including hers. Now it was Don who would be doing the adding and the subtracting. Don who could suggest a change in lead actresses if he were to decide Cecily Warren was no longer right for his revised version of Amelia.

She sang as she dressed. At nine-thirty, she went to the phone to call Don. She just had to get this show on the road! She figured that by noon she'd be well on her way to moving into his life and bank account. This time she'd know how to handle it. This time she'd last long enough to establish legal rights, and wouldn't leave without heavy bread.

As for immediate profit, she couldn't help but pick up more lines, more action for Candy's role in *Galt's Island,* and she was hopeful for the lead before the week was out.

Don asked her to come right over when she said she had "some interesting news about Cecily and a party at Fred Gower's last night," and she was in his living room by ten, sitting beside him on the couch. All the while she talked, he nodded, encouraging her, telling her not to "spare" him, telling her he "appreciated her help." And why not? It didn't take ESP to know that he'd set her up for this very thing, a spy job, by putting her in the same movie with his loving cow, Cecily. Hadn't he said several times that he'd "like to hear what goes on at the meetings and parties and later, on the set."

So his sudden change when she finished really caught her by surprise. He sank back in the couch, growing terribly pale. He breathed heavily, and she began to ask if he was all right. He interrupted with:

"Would you mind leaving? I have work to do."

His voice was cold and his face like stone.

She decided she was getting a bad deal, and put it right on the line: "C'mon, *dahling*, this is what you wanted from me. This is what you suspected. All I've done is confirm your suspicions."

He stood up, looking at her with dead-fish eyes. "Yes, I knew you were right for the job. I thought you'd be reporting incidents during production, but you've beaten your schedule. You've earned your role in the movie, and I'll do my best to improve that role."

"You make it sound as if I were *working* for you—so cut and dried."

"When all the time you've loved me madly."

In that dead voice, it wasn't funny; it was harsh and insulting.

But she kept her temper. "I'll call tomorrow."

"If you wish."

She rose and stepped forward to kiss him. He moved away.

She decided she was hurt enough to cry, and began bringing up tears, sobs.

He said: "Don't strain my credulity."

She wasn't sure what "credulity" meant, but there was no mistaking his growing anger.

She left and drove back down to Sunset. It took fifteen minutes, and she insulted him every minute of the way with every name she could think of, beginning with fucking kike bastard. Her father had always said Jews weren't to be trusted. But that was a bad rule to try and live by in *this* town.

Don phoned Cecily the moment Fanny drove off. Her service answered and he left word for her to call him as soon as possible. "Tell her it concerns her role in *Galt's Island*." Which should have brought a response within the hour.

So when the phone rang ten minutes later, he picked it up without first checking it out over his answering machine. And it was a mistake.

Freddy said: "How long are you going to keep us waiting for a meeting on the script?" He sounded irritated.

Don grinned a death's-head grin. The man had balls.

He decided it wasn't time yet to bring things into the open. Perhaps it would never be time—at least not with words. Fred Gower couldn't be punished by words.

He gave him an honest answer. "I want to put together more than critical notes. I want to be ready to suggest detailed revision; in some cases new scenes."

"Yeah, but when? We want to get into production."

"This kind of revision wouldn't take me long, should I decide to do it. A month at most. I'd say two weeks."

"Should you decide to do it? Listen, Donny . . ."

He didn't like Gower using his first name, especially the diminutive, this morning after. It made his face flush, his fists clench. He suddenly saw Freddy's bragged-about nine inches sticking into his woman, and he said, voice rising, "Don't call me on this any-more. I'll be in touch with your or one of the other producers when I'm ready."

He hung up. And was sorry he'd lost control. He didn't want to worry Fred Gower. He didn't want him on his guard. Until *after* his punishment had been concluded. And that might not be for some time yet. It would take much thought.

He went through the house, gathering up the four photographs Cecily had given him, and was wounded by each—by her beauty; by the love he'd invested. He tried to throw them out the back door, into the gar-bage, and couldn't, and put them on a closet shelf.

She didn't call until two, and even then sounded groggy, half-asleep. She asked if they couldn't discuss whatever it was on the phone.

"No. This requires face-to-face. I'll expect you in half an hour." He hung up.

He'd spent the past three and a half hours rehears-ing how he'd slowly, methodically, entrap her in her own lies. He'd paced about, wanting to take a walk and not being willing to risk missing her call.

Now he went out to Sunset Plaza and walked uphill, around right and left hand bends, continuing along the corkscrew road in blazing sunshine. He was perspir-ing heavily, breathing heavily, when he reached Appian Way, a road considerably shorter and less im-portant than the ancient one that had run from Rome to Brindisi. But it did have a brief stretch between Sunset Plaza and Lookout Mountain, perhaps two city blocks in length, where the houses were beautiful, some of them historically valuable in the Hollywood sense—such as Errol Flynn's cliffside castle.

He realized he was no longer planning entrapments; no longer full of rage and hatred. The long walk had stablized him.

And made him realize something else: A long trip, by bus or train if not plane, back to New York for

example, would stabilize him even further in terms of
Cecily; would perhaps wipe her from his mind as he
was going to wipe her from his life; would be easy
enough for him to make now that his physical condition had so improved. He was still off the poisonous
medication, and his doctor agreed it was working out.
If he so decided, he could return east for good.

He'd almost lost touch with his children.

He hadn't called or written his mother at the nurs-
ing home in three months.

His agent had given up on him, as had his old
friends, including Mel, who had written twice since
Don confessed the heart attack, and whom he hadn't
answered.

It was just that he felt there was nothing more to
say to those people back there.

He walked further, and a large tan dog, part boxer,
came out of a garage to challenge him. A woman
shouted at the dog, and he recognized her as a character actor on one of the TV situation comedies, handsome in person despite her zany, eccentric television
role. Perhaps thirty-five, with a strong smile and
strong voice, and she gave him both, saying, "Sorry
about Claudius." She was quite tall, quite lean, but
with appropriate curves and bulges, and she wore tight
denim shorts and a red halter this low-nineties afternoon.

The dog was slinking away, looking apprehensively
at his mistress.

"Claudius?" Don chuckled. "Well, you do live on
Appian Way, but I'm not sure whether Robert Graves
would have appreciated the honor, not to say the em-
peror himself."

She gave him a big smile. "They'll have to forgive
me, because I named my pup for the British television
series."

"Yes, I recall," he said. No way Graves could compete with television; even with himself on television. "But you definitely should read the book."

"You wouldn't happen to be our resident novelist?" she said, as he began walking by her. "Donald Baylis?"

He said yes, and was pleased. She seemed to want to talk. She seemed open to friendship. He recalled reading she'd been divorced. If he stopped, something might develop; something that could make entrapment of Cecily, revenge on Freddy, long trips to the cold east unnecessary.

"You'll have to drop by this Sunday," she said. "I'm having an open house in honor of the Labor Day weekend. Bread, cheese, beer, and wine, to fit the proletarian occasion."

He said thanks and he'd try to make it. But he didn't stop walking.

"I promise not to ask questions," the TV actress called after him, "about that mysterious movie."

So that was why he was becoming known on Sunset Plaza Drive. And elsewhere. Because of the trade papers and their bandying about of certain juicy rumors. He doubted she had ever heard of him from his books.

He turned back at Lookout Mountain Road. He walked more quickly, but only because it was downhill, not because he was worried about missing Cecily. She had a gate-lift control and keys to his house. Besides, this was the road she would have to use.

At that moment, the Jaguar pulled alongside, and Cecily said: "Want a lift?"

He got in with the TV actress watching from her garage, and they drove off.

He wiped at his face and neck with a handkerchief. "When's this Santa Ana supposed to break?"

"I don't know. Why don't you go swimming at your friend Barry Salvadore's pool? You said you'd enjoyed it last week, and it wasn't nearly as hot then as now."

"Yes, I might do that. Or I could drive to the ocean."

"Not too smart an idea. You should stick to pools, with someone like Barry around who knows enough to watch you. Even a mild attack while swimming could be curtains."

"Curtains. I think you learned that expression from me."

"I've dated other old boys," she said, and turned her head to smile at him. It wasn't a convincing smile. She looked ill. Hungover, probably. Bruised and worn by that orgy.

He looked away from her. They rode in silence a while; then she said: "What's this about my role in the movie?"

He didn't answer.

"You using pressure to make me put out for you?" And since he still didn't answer, still didn't look at her, she laughed for him.

They were approaching the house. "How was the party last night?" he asked.

She sighed. "All right."

That sigh. She knew he knew.

"You look as if you stayed late," he said, and somehow the rage was dissipated, the desire to entrap her gone. What it boiled down to was that he had a choice—keep her, or let her go.

"I outstayed Fanny," she said, "if that's what you mean."

"I'm afraid you didn't. She waited outside until Bub drove you home, after five A.M."

Another sigh. They were at the house. She took the electronic gate-lift unit from her door flap and pressed it. The gate rose. She began to put the unit back in the door, but he held out his hand.

She gave it to him.

He allowed her to open the front door; then removed his keys from her ring.

She went directly to the bathroom. She stayed there about ten minutes, and came out looking green.

"Orgying doesn't agree with you," he said.

She was looking at the fireplace mantle where one of her photos had stood.

He didn't want to lose her.

He couldn't keep her after what she'd done last night.

Unless she hadn't done it.

"You know what Fanny told me," he said.

"Yes, the spying bitch!"

"If you swear on Johnny's life that you didn't have sex with Fred, or with Dennings, I'll believe you."

She went to the kitchen and opened the refrigerator. She brought out orange juice, poured a glass, gulped thirstily. "I've given up swearing on my son's life." She drank again. "But I'll give you my word I didn't do anything last night you would have disapproved of."

"How about before last night?"

She drank. "You mean my whole life before last night?" She smiled wanly.

"How about with Freddy, before he suggested you for the part of Amelia?"

She said, voice shaky: "Are you going to destroy me completely—take away my part?"

"Certainly not. You're perfect for those fuck scenes. And I do have three and a half percent of profits."

She leaned on the kitchen counter and looked somewhere beyond him. He thought he saw tears glistening in her eyes, but she didn't cry. She said: "Is that all?"

"No. I want to tell you about Johnny. It's important that you know, and try to do something to change him."

"I already know. I don't want to hear it. If I leave now, will you punish me . . . ?"

He interrupted with a sharp, "No."

She began to walk around the counter. He said:

"How can you trust me to keep my word?"

She kept walking. "I've always trusted you. That's the whole point with Cecily and Donny. Good-bye now."

He wanted to let her leave, and couldn't. "Johnny stole fifty dollars from my wallet."

She stopped. "Are you sure?"

"I had four fifties. I left the wallet on my dresser. I was in the bathroom and he was getting ready for bed in the study. I heard something, and came out, and the wallet was turned around, in a different position. I checked it, and there were only three fifties. I went into the study and he was in bed and asleep, or so he wanted me to think."

"Maybe he was," she said. "Maybe you're wrong."

"I'd had unhappy feelings about him since you left us alone Friday night. I'd seen him cheat at games and heard him make racial slurs. And he's a liar, you know, in almost everything. An accomplished liar at that. When I slid my hand under his pillow and found the fifty, he made out he'd awakened to find me putting it there."

She smiled grimly. "I know him when his back is against the wall. He'll insist that's what you were doing when I brace him about it."

"Yes. Back against the wall. Lies and cheating. Stealing. Exhibitionism. Where did he learn it all, Cecily, if not from you?"

"I don't know. I guess from me, but I don't do all that." She paused. Her face looked oily, worn. "Do I?"

"I don't know the full story of your life. I know a child so close to his mother . . ."

"Excuse me," she said, and ran down the foyer to the small bathroom. He heard her retching.

He went to the glass walls and the view.

She came back. Her face looked better; she'd washed it. Her voice was firmer. "Are we going to see each other again?"

"What for?"

"For fun. I won't expect you to deal with Johnny. We won't think of the day after tomorrow." She came closer. "But I want to keep seeing you, lover."

The word hurt. He shrugged and said: "Why not?" and knew it wouldn't work, not for Donald Baylis who needed marriage-and-forever plans with a woman he loved.

"Can I stay now?" she asked.

He nodded, and was aware of her body behind the light-weight cream pants and old *Stars Wars* T-shirt. He wanted her in his arms, but it wouldn't be like Monday night; never again like Monday night.

The sense of loss was so great that rage returned, and he stepped close to her and almost shouted: "Did you make love to Fred and Dennings? To Bud?"

"Fred and Dennings made love to me," she replied instantly. "I was so far out of it, I didn't know or care who was there. Could have been Bud, too, but he wasn't."

So there it was, and pain was intense. Yet he calmed. "Fanny said you were cold sober when you went up to the bedroom."

"I wasn't a short time later."

He would have questioned her further, but she said she couldn't take anymore; she would leave and come back later if he needed time.

He replied that later he was going to begin outlining script changes.

He hadn't known he was going to say that, or do that, but it was the truth. He said he'd be working during the Labor Day weekend and she was free to make plans excluding him.

She nodded solemnly.

He went to the couch and sat down. "I guess this is what they mean by an adult reaction, an adult solution. Beats shooting people, doesn't it?"

She surprised him. "I don't know," she said, voice bitter. "Some people deserve shooting."

With that he wanted to ask about Freddy, about the details of last night's sex. Knew without proof she'd been manipulated, as he'd known for months and months that Freddy had slept with her.

"Make love to me," she said, coming to the couch. "No more talk, Donny. Just make love to me."

They went to bed.

He didn't know what he expected, but it wasn't such incredible eroticism. Because what he most hated about her life—the other men in it—was at the same time a tremendous turn-on. That marvelous body, that beautifully shaped vagina, had drained two men last night. And who knew how many more in the last month, the last year.

Afterwards, she dressed while he lay resting, both of them in silence.

She got her bag and looked at him and he nodded. She turned and went out of the room.

He heard the garage gate lift. He heard her car start, back out, roar up the road.

He was empty. He didn't know what to make of his life.

He must have dozed. He heard door chimes. He got up, slipped into a bathrobe, went to the door.

Cecily came inside, looking back at the road. A car drove by, slowly. She closed the door. "I haven't been seeing Jorge Resordo lately. He's outside, driving up and back. He must have followed me."

He turned to the bedroom. "I'll dress and see you home."

She said: "No. He's not dangerous. It's just that I don't want him bothering you. He might . . . well, try and discuss things."

"Like the wages of sin?"

"I guess so." She paused. "I'm just worried about

what you might think about Resordo. Especially now."

"Now? Now we're an insoluble quantity. Nothing can break us apart. You can't break . . ." He let it go with a smile. She knew the rest anyway. They couldn't be broken up any more, because they were no longer really together.

She left.

He showered and dressed and went downstairs to his chair facing the void. He worked on Otis Daimler's script. He made notes, and wanted to start the actual revision.

As a novelist, he'd always done his best work during weekend holidays when other people were traveling, partying, enjoying themselves. A sense of rejection, of isolation, of apartness from mankind had been the sharpest goad to his talent, his energies. Now Labor Day was approaching, and as during so many other periods of his life he and his woman were drifting apart, his pleasure goals were diminishing, all that was left was work.

The phone rang. He went to the desk to answer it.

"Mr. Baylis?" (It sounded more like *Meestair Baylees*, and he was suddenly alert.)

"Yes."

"You don't know me. My name is Jorge Resordo. I am what you might call . . ." Resordo cleared his throat, steadied his voice, ". . . I am Cecily Warren's lover."

It was so strange hearing that. So sad, too. Because this was an old man, a gentle man, a man losing something of vital importance in his life. As important as what Don had lost today.

"I see."

Resordo had obviously expected some heat, some anger. He pushed on, trying to get it. "She is playing us both, I am afraid, for fools."

"Well, Mr. Resordo, I don't know what she's doing with you, but I don't feel like a fool. And I don't really understand what it is you expect of me."

"If you give her money . . . ?"

"Never."

"Ah." Resordo was confused.

"Besides, she's got her own money now," Don said, and began trying to help the old man. "She's also much busier now than she's ever been in her life, getting ready for a starring role in a movie. Has she told you about it?"

"A little. Are you . . . an associate in that movie?"

"Yes."

"And that is how you know each other?"

"Yes." Why hurt someone bound to be hurt enough by Cecily? "In fact, I'm working right now."

"My apologies for disturbing you," Resordo said quickly. "If . . . I . . ." And then, mumbling, "Forgive this nonsense. I'm not well." The line clicked.

Don returned to his chair.

He wondered where he would be, in terms of love, of desire, at Resordo's age, assuming his heart would carry him that long.

It could be a very tough thing, old age, Gray Panthers notwithstanding.

"I can't understand it," Freddy said, shaking his head. "I've made him two hundred thousand. I'm going to make him millions, if he ever gets his ass off the dime and starts writing. And the man actually seems to dislike me!"

Bub served veal scallopini and mixed green salad, then sat down. They had hot sourdough bread and icy-cold beer, and with the tube showing the Dodgers going into the eighth inning in Cincinnati leading by two, it could have been a fantastic meal.

Could have been, except for Fred's insanity.

"Are you saying you don't understand why Baylis could hate you?"

"You're referring to Cecily, but she'd never tell him."

"There were other people at that party, Fred! You must've been crazy . . ." He took a deep breath; he took himself in hand; he drank beer and settled back in his chair. "None of my business," he muttered. "You didn't ask my advice then and you won't get it now."

"You're turning cubelike lately," Freddy said, looking across the table at him. "Next you'll be getting married and settling down to raise kids, attend church, and share-crop."

"Why the fuck would I share-crop?" Bub snapped.

Freddy laughed. "Sorry about the old stereotype. How about running a poverty program and playing basketball?"

Bub smiled a little, but he was deeply bothered, had been for some time now, because the boss-man didn't know how to protect himself at all anymore.

As if determined to prove the point, Freddy said: "This should cheer you up. I got us a chicken for the weekend."

A chicken was a young boy.

"About fifteen and young for his age. Soft and plump. A real sissy type. Bet he doesn't even know he's a natural queen."

"He doesn't? Then how are you going to get him for the weekend?"

Fred ate and watched a Dodger infielder make an error. "They're going to blow it."

"About this chicken?" Bud said.

"His mother's a date. She's going to spend Friday and Saturday nights here." He grinned his wide, innocent grin. "Can you dig it? She expects to get stuffed all night, and she will, at least twice, including you.

We'll go the regular route, with the camera. But *then* . . ." He leaned across to Bub and laughed. "Does the Lord provide or does he ever?"

"The kid doesn't know anything about gay action?"

"Not as far as I can tell. We can break him in right. And I'll be sure to treat the mother especially well, so she'll spend more weekends with us. You'll have to start taking double doses of E, baby. Now tell the boss-man how great he is."

Bub said yeah-great, and ate and watched the Dodgers blow their game. And thought Freddy would blow his, too, pretty soon. The way he was operating, it was only a question of who was going to try to kill him first. Which made him decide he couldn't allow Giselle the cooling-off time he'd thought to give her.

But right now it was poker with Freddy.

The boss-man described Sergio, the kid who was his mark for this weekend. "Helped her tuck him in," he said, discarding three cards. "When she left for a minute, I made believe I was rearranging the blanket and got it off him. What with the heat wave, he was naked. Christ, we're going to have fun! Fat little chicken with big balls! The penis didn't show much, but it'll grow under proper stimulus."

Bub gave him the required grin. "Look, Fred, it sounds great. But one little thing—they can send you up forever for raping a child."

"Rape? Who said anything . . ."

"I know. He'll be sedated and quiet and no bruises and I've heard it all before. The fact remains it's rape, statutory if you're lucky, and homosexual to boot. What if he tells his mother?"

Fred spread his cards impatiently. "Three jacks."

Bub tossed in his hand.

"And he won't tell his mother."

"Like no one told Baylis about Cecily last night?"

"Nothing to tell, because no one actually *saw* us."

"Like you haven't had your ass on the line a dozen times over some broad? This could really tear it."

Fred stood up. "God damn it, I'm sick of your cry-baby act! You want out, you're out! I can handle it myself. I would've liked film, but I don't need it, like I didn't need it last night."

Bub said: "Yes, I want out."

"Fine!" He strode to the sideboard, poured a brandy and gulped it. "You got some joints?"

Bub went to the kitchen and the dope-box under the sink. When he returned, they lit up. Freddy calmed quickly. "You haven't seen the mother, Arabella. A Spanish beauty. I mean Madrid, man, not Tijuana. Aristocratic. You'll never get a crack at anything like that. Ducal bloodline. Small features and small high tits and an ass that begs to be ridden like a pure-blood mare's. She's barely thirty—married at fourteen, can you believe it? Rich husband dead in an auto-racing accident. No action for more than a year, and now she's left her widow's weeds back in Spain and come to L.A. to rip and tear."

"Sounds good. I'll go for *that*. Have to be crazy not to."

"They're a package deal—Arabella and Sergio. You can't have one without the other."

"Then I'll pass." He picked up the cards. "We playing poker or not?"

Freddy sat down. "We got around to some intimate talk in the Polo Lounge. She's never had a black. Never even considered it. Bet she'll go ape when you slip that ebony dick into her ass."

Bub sucked reefer. "Bet I'll go ape when some cellmate slips his dick into my ass. When I'm doing twenty for juvenile, homosexual rape. Maybe it'll be *your* dick, if Arabella doesn't have us killed."

Fred made an explosive sound and jumped up. He went to the sideboard and poured and drank. Then he turned. "We're just not having the fun we used to."

Bub looked down at the cards.

"You've changed, Bub. Grown too cautious."

"I don't think so, boss. I think you've changed. Begun to take too many chances; begun to play very long odds."

"Didn't we have boys before?"

"Only those who knew the score."

"No use talking to you, is there?"

"I don't think so, Fred." He raised his eyes. "Want me to split? I mean for good."

Fred stared at him for a long moment. "Who'd take my pictures, develop the film in the tennis shed, cook those great meals? And you—where would you get the kicks, the fine ass, the great food? Where would either of us find the . . . the . . ." He moved his lips, and didn't seem able to finish.

Bub took a chance. "The friendship?"

Fred nodded.

Bub said: "Nowhere, boss-man. Ass and food and the rest I can duplicate—a reasonable facsimile thereof. But not the friendship."

Freddy sank back into his chair. "Play poker."

They played three hands. Fred played badly, losing two when he could have won all three. He finally said: "We'll forget Sergio."

Bub smiled then, began to speak then, and Fred quickly added: "Your part in Sergio. I'm going ahead."

Bub nodded and handed the deck to Freddy, who dealt seven-card. He decided he wouldn't be around this weekend, aristocratic Spanish ass or not. He didn't want any part of what might come down as a result of screwing that boy. They'd soon be lining up to take their shots at old Freddy!

He threw in his hand and said that a headache was really bugging him. "Maybe I'll take a little walk."

"What, in Beverly Hills, at night, with *your* complexion?"

Which wasn't really a joke when you knew how the cops cruised around here, and how they'd jump on a black.

"Thought I'd drive down to the Strip and walk through a few massage parlors. You can do miles and miles, if you don't drop your pants."

He left Freddy laughing, and called Giselle. She sounded ready for a dry-out ward. But he wanted to score points, get her ready, and said he'd pick her up a block from Andro's house, at the corner of Olympic. "*Walk*," he said.

He got there in half an hour, and she was sitting on the curb.

He took her to a motel, where she half-passed out, half-fell asleep. But she'd hugged him, cried in his arms, said he was the only thing holding her together.

Toward morning, she awoke and they made it.

Then they talked about Andro's safe. Then she began to sound as if she was going to pick a date to do it. And finally she told him Andro would be away again, Sunday night to Tuesday morning. "His daughter Violet's meeting him in Las Vegas."

They looked at each other, and he said, quietly: "All right. Make sure that passport you used last year is still good. I'll take care of the rest."

Cecily's phone rang, and she rolled over and reached to the nightstand. She was saying hello before she realized it was still dark.

"Cecily," the trembling voice whispered, "please don't be angry at the hour. You can't know how I've missed you."

"Jorge? What time is it?"

"Four o'clock. I'm at home, in the kitchen. I just had to speak to you."

"Like you just had to follow me yesterday."

"Yes, I had to! It's *infierno!* Hell! Please let me come over now."

She didn't hesitate. "No." She simply couldn't. Too much sex. Too much confusion over sex. Especially the last twenty-four hours.

"Querida, por favor . . ." His voice had risen, and he stopped and began again, in English. "If you're upset because that friend Baylis has told you of my call . . ."

"You called Donald Baylis?"

The sharpness of her voice threw him into a panic. "But just . . . I wanted to know . . . I asked if you were all right."

"Don't lie to me, Jorge! Or I'll never speak to you again!"

"Have pity," he whispered.

She softened. She had pity, all right. Maybe more than pity. "How did you get his name, his number?"

"There was mail in his box when I stopped, after seeing your car park inside his gate. I called Information."

She thought Don would have to change his number and go unlisted. Not because of Jorge, but because that movie would soon be making headlines.

Which brought something else to mind, something she'd been putting off: What to do about Johnny when the shit hit the fan. School in Mexico, maybe. Jorge knew about a very good one where American and English diplomats, corporate executives, such people sent their kids. She'd have the money. And even though she'd miss her baby, it might solve certain problems with Don.

"Querida, I beg you not to discard me this way."

She would discuss the school with Jorge. But she couldn't see him now; she needed a few days to get herself together. And to work out an explanation of why she wouldn't be seeing him afterward. Perhaps another two, three meetings, and he'd be able to accept an ending.

"Are you going away for the Labor Day weekend?" she asked.

"Just on Friday, and only to Venice, to see Mrs. Martinez, an old employee who is bedridden."

"Then I'll see you on Saturday or Sunday."

"Saturday or Sunday? Which?" He now sounded dull, despairing, as if he didn't believe her.

"Call me when you get back Friday. I'll know my schedule then." When he still failed to respond, she added: "We'll definitely be together one of those nights, our usual time."

That did it. He said, "Ai, gracias! Thank you, my beauty!"

The explosive joy wounded her, made her remember how much she had valued this man, beyond the obvious value of his three hundred a week.

He sent her kisses, endearments in both Spanish and English, wounded her further as she understood that no matter how well she explained, how many visits she allowed him in preparation, the ending would still be cruel and painful.

Otis left Doctors Hospital at eleven Thursday morning, exhausted. Claire was resting comfortably, under sedation, and he wished he could say the same for himself. He'd been up with her since nine Wednesday evening, when the ordeal had begun.

An attack, you could call it. Actually, a buildup of rheumatoid arthritic pain, culminating in such agony infesting her knuckles, wrists, elbows, shoulders, neck, hips, knees, ankles, toes—every major and minor joint in her body—that she went slightly mad. Her shrieks had set the Great Danes to roaring in their pen (where they were confined because Letty had guests), which set other neighborhood dogs to barking, which caused the hidden but still considerable coyote population of the canyon to join in with their strangely piercing *yip-yip-yips*.

A mad world, he'd thought, waiting for the ambulance since Claire couldn't get out of bed.

But now all was peaceful, and he was on his way home for bed and bottle. And if those Great Danes dared open their mouths, he'd stuff them with Ex-Lax, all six boxes he had in the medicine chest, and make them shit themselves to death!

The phone was ringing as he opened the door. It was Avery Sanford, his agent. "Still no definite word on what they think of your script." He paused. "But prepare yourself for some chickenshit. The novelist, Baylis, is expected to do a revision."

"So what?" Otis said. "We've been paid. What about that meet with network people on the mystery series deal?"

"It'll take time." Again he paused. "And I doubt they'll go for another cop show. I'm trying to line up a feature at Goldwyn. Independent producer who just moved from Warners. Small budget, but he has a property, a novel that'll be tough to translate into screenplay. Right up your alley, and we might work him for a good price."

He went on a while and Otis said fine and they said good-bye.

And it wasn't fine. It was goddamn awful.

The novelist would rewrite his script, and Cecily Warren would think even less of Otis than she already obviously did. She couldn't talk to him for more than a minute without running away, for which she'd pay.

But maybe that was because she sensed something? Maybe he should think twice about letting the beast loose on her? Everything pointed to this being too dangerous.

He smoked three cigarettes, and drank three Scotches, and showered and walked to the bed. And didn't get in.

He went to the closet for fresh clothing, and to the garage for the car. Then to Mulholland, and Laurel

Canyon, and down into the Valley to North Hollywood and the street on which Cecily Warren lived.

He wondered if she knew his car—if she'd ever seen
it, or could connect it with him. It would be smart to
have another car.

Because with Claire in the hospital, and going to
stay there for weeks, perhaps months, according to her
doctor, he would have the opportunity to play this
game over and over, nights as well as days.

How exciting it was! His heart was pounding, his
hands damp on the steering wheel as he drove past the
modest frame house on the street of modest frame
houses, past the driveway—there was no garage—with
the old green Jaguar parked near the front door.

The Jaguar indicated she was inside that house
right now, behind those windows right now. Those
windows left open to catch what little breeze stirred
this Santa Ana heat.

She had a son. If the boy wasn't home, she could be
alone.

And even if she wasn't alone. Even if the boy was
there. Even if the novelist, her lover of record, was
there. Even so, he could smash a child and a sick man
and take her in her own home, her own bed.

Insane! He'd have to silence them all, kill them all!

He turned and drove back past the house more
quickly, forcing his eyes to remain on the road, because the temptation was so great he couldn't risk another look at those windows, those open portals . . .

At home, he had two drinks while sitting in the jacuzzi; smoked and drank and soaked.

And realized he was horny, had an erection, needed
a woman.

The pool area was secluded, fenced in, "skinny-
dipping territory" as the cutesy real-estate copy had
described it. He pulled off his shorts and spread his
legs. He looked down at himself, at the organ bobbing
thick and red in the bubbling water. And saw his

bulging stomach, his massive thighs, the flabbiness of his thick arms and big chest—all the weight that he'd accumulated in frustration, in repression, in misery. All the weight needed to seal in the beast all these years.

He would crush Cecily Warren with that weight; crush the life out of her with that weight! Even as he filled her with his semen!

He was grasping the thick red organ under water, jerking it madly under water.

And came copiously under water.

He climbed out, upset now that the frenzy was past. He'd fouled the sparkling hot water. He'd have to use the net, a fine sieve, perhaps his hands to scoop out the congealed scum.

What he eventually used was a porous cloth Claire had bought as a lint-free duster for their mirrors. It took quite a while, and was disgusting work, and he blamed it on Cecily Warren.

The bitch would answer for it!

He decided to drive by her house again tonight, and many nights while Claire was away.

But the possibility that she knew his car bothered him.

If she mentioned to Baylis or Gower or anyone else connected with the picture that he'd been coming by her home, it would cause comment. And later, when she died, it would cause suspicion.

He couldn't afford to buy a second car. And even if he could, *one* more car wouldn't be enough, because if she noticed and began watching, it would be the same one-more-car each time.

The solution was simple. He would rent from that cheapie place on lower Vine. He could get a different car for each trip to Warren's home, and the chances of arousing suspicion would be minimal. And the joy of stalking her would be maximal!

He realized that he was planning details, which meant he was allowing the beast to take over.

He hoped it didn't mean he would lose control before the safe time, after production was completed.

Teresa refused to forgive Cecily for not visiting her the past month. And the phone calls didn't change anything, including the one this morning, because they had to be taken at the nurse's station with that big dyke Rose watching her and listening to her and who could talk like that?

So Cecily begged to be forgiven because she was busy, did she? Goddamn cheat! Always that way! Always taking from Teresa!

When Teresa innocently asked what Cecily was busy *with*, the bitch farted around with Johnny this and going-on-vacation that and it was all bullshit! Because Teresa wasn't innocent about Cecily. Hell no!

Cecily thought that because Teresa didn't have any money, she wouldn't be able to get the trades. Cecily thought that because she was in the nuthatch she would forget about her career. Well, Cecily didn't know how sharp big sister was!

Teresa had gotten that new nurse, Tansy, to supply her with copies of *Variety* and the *Hollywood Reporter*, which Cecily hadn't been bringing since the end of April. Teresa knew that the new nurses always treated you nice; that they thought they could change things and help the patients get well, at least during their first few months on the job. Then they found out that the system didn't work that way, and they got like the rest of the staff—hard-ass.

Tansy hadn't reached that stage yet, so Teresa had read that first announcement in the trades about *Galt's Island*, "which will co-star heavyweight Rob Dennings and newcomer Cecily Warren." Had read it and not believed it! And waited for Cecily to say something when she came for her next visit.

That next visit had been almost two months later—
at the end of June. And Cecily hadn't said Word One
about the movie, and neither had big sister, who was
too sharp to let on that she knew what was being done
to her. Because if she let on, Cecily would run for the
door and never come back.

She'd waited until the end of July for the next visit
and gotten the bullshit about "forgot the *Variety*s,
hon" and still not a word about the ripoff of big sister.

It hadn't been easy, but Teresa had held onto her
temper; had managed to smile a little and talk a little,
and mainly act drugged and dopey like she was supposed to be with all the medication they'd been feeding her since early May when she'd lit into the rapist-
pig attendant, Matt. She had to fight back a smile
every time she saw him, because his left eye still
looked like Muhammad Ali had belted it.

Anyway, Teresa had been reading the trades regular—the two front-page stories and all the rumors in
Hank Grant and Army Archerd about this going to be
Rob Denning's first X-rating, Hollywood's first big-
budget sex film. And the descriptions of "voluptuous Cecily Warren who should turn heads and hearts all over
the world." Cecily Warren "who will attain a level of
stardom unmatched since Marilyn left us, according to
producers Berry and Pandaro." Cecily Warren "who
has been partying with Rob Dennings often enough to
cause talk that the hottest part of their relationship
may not be *on* the screen." Cecily Warren this and Cecily Warren that! All over the trades and also in the
L.A. *Times* and the *Examiner* which someone brought
in and left in her room, underlined, probably Rose,
because Rose knew Cecily was her sister.

Her sister? Her goddamn *murderer!* She'd stolen everything from Teresa! Pop's love and having a child
and now becoming a star! And she didn't talk about
pop and she didn't bring Johnny and she was trying to

keep it secret about becoming a star. Wanted to keep Teresa dumb and sedated and locked away so no one would know that it was Teresa not her snot-nosed kid sister who was the one with the looks, the training, the talent. Because once Rob Dennings met Teri Barker he'd know which sister to choose as his co-star and that's what Cecily was afraid of.

And that's what would happen! Maybe tomorrow night, which was Friday, the start of the Labor Day weekend, because she'd heard Matt the attendant say there'd be a "skeleton staff" over the long weekend.

Teresa had learned, finally, how to bust out of here. And remembered, most of the time, where Cecily lived. And had an address label from one of Cecily's trade papers in case she forgot.

She was in her room and the door was open the way Rose insisted it always be since Teresa had let Matt have it. She was sitting in her chair, looking drugged and dopey the way she was supposed to look, thinking that Cecily could have gotten her out of here years ago and hadn't and that was the same as if she had locked her in and thrown away the key.

But Teresa had the key now!

She looked at the pale green padding on the walls, a plastic that she'd heard was used in prisons as well as nuthouses. A plastic she'd found impossible to tear, and there was nothing to cut it with. A plastic the staff said was "almost indestructible."

Almost.

She wondered how many people knew it would burn.

She smoked one or two cigarettes a day . . . or had. Now she smoked more, so as to be able to ask Rose for a butt and a light every hour or so; or ask whoever took Rose's place on days off and holidays. Like the black nurse, Viola. Or Tansy, who might head up the ward this weekend because of the "skeleton staff." And Teresa was always careful about putting out the cigarette in the ashtray provided her; always careful to make sure they saw that drugged or not, she was a safe smoker.

Oh, they had a long way to go before they could figure out big sister!

She had touched a cigarette to the wall, low and behind the bed where no one could see. The hole had grown from a pinpoint to a half-dollar in a split second and smoked heavily with a grayish choking stink and she'd had to put it out fast with the paper cup half-filled with water left over from her last medication period.

That was another thing—she'd been faking taking her medication, tucking it away behind her tongue where most of the time it wouldn't wash down with the water. The few times Rose, who was wise when it came to looneys, made her open her mouth for an examination, she managed to swallow the pills rather than get caught with them. Now that Tansy handled her, she was even able to palm them once in a while. And down the toilet they went, to make the fish dopey.

Still another thing: Tansy had a little red Datsun she'd bought since getting this job; talked about it and showed Teresa pictures of it and last week parked it close enough to the west fence, where only the doctors were supposed to park, so Teresa could see it from her window. She kept the keys in her wallet, and her wallet in her uniform pocket. And she and her keys and her car were scheduled to be here over the holiday weekend.

So there'd be a fire and stinking gray smoke and people running around yelling and not enough staff. And if Teri Barker didn't burn up or choke to death, she'd be out and driving to North Hollywood in that little red Datsun. To give kid sister a *big* surprise!

* * *

Johnny knew mom had two parties for the weekend—he'd heard her on the phone this afternoon. The
first was tomorrow night, Friday, and the next was on
Saturday. But she didn't seem happy or excited like
she always was with parties. And she didn't mention
Don Baylis.

When Johnny asked about Don, she turned on him.
"You actually have the nerve to talk about him?"

He shrugged and made believe he didn't understand
and got outside fast.

So Baylis had told her about the fifty dollars. Jew
snitch! Too bad Johnny hadn't gotten right up that
night when Baylis went to sleep and taken the fifty
again, the way he'd thought to do, because Baylis
would never have expected him to have that much
nerve and wouldn't have counted his money again.

Anyway, mom hadn't followed and belted him, so
she couldn't care too much. Maybe she'd broken up
with Baylis.

Sure, that must be it. Like she broke up with every
man, in time.

Good deal! Now they'd get back to the way it had
been before, with eating out and shopping and seeing
shows!

Well, as soon as she finished this movie, anyway.

But he had something even better to look forward
to tomorrow night and Saturday, Mary!

What he needed to make *sure* he had a great time
was money. He had about ten, and maybe another
three in change from his piggy bank. If he could get
ten or fifteen more, she'd use her mouth again, he was
sure of it.

Even without money, maybe he'd get on top of her,
put it in her . . . which reminded him that he had to
get hold of rubbers.

He could walk to the drug store. No problem getting there. The problem was whether the clerk would
sell him the things. And sometimes a lady worked the

counter. He didn't think he could make himself ask a lady.

He was sorry he hadn't thought of it earlier today, at the Y. Maybe one of the older kids, who carried rubbers in their wallets, would've sold him a packet.

Okey-doke. He had tomorrow, Friday, after swimming, to see if he could find the right kid. It wouldn't be easy because lots of families were taking off early for the weekend. Jack DeKuyper had already left for San Francisco with his parents and sister. And Klaus was on a camping trip with his father.

He went back into the house, feeling a little down, a little lonely, thinking mom must've cooled off by now.

But while she didn't yell, she was cold, unsmiling.

"Hey, big momma, how about eating out?"

"Don't call me that."

They were in the study, where she was reading a book. A book yet!

He bent over and read the cover. *"Trip . . . Out. By . . . Donald . . . Baylis."* He straightened. "Hey, the old Jew-baby."

She surprised him with a slap. He never had the chance to dodge. She caught him across the left cheek and it staggered him and she was getting up to come after him, her face white and crazy like he hadn't seen it in a long time.

He screamed, "I was kidding! You . . . damn . . . I was . . ." And couldn't hold back the tears.

She stopped. He cried, touching his cheek, which felt on fire. He hated her! Like on that TV movie, the mother running around all the time and the kid left alone and finding out she had supernatural powers to start fires and make walls and ceilings crack and kill people.

He concentrated as hard as he could on the ceiling, willing it to crack and fall on her.

She went back to the couch. "Get a book," she said.

"It's almost six. I'm starving."

"We'll eat at seven. After we read for an hour."

"I was at the Y all day . . ."

"Get a book!"

He went to his room and those nothing presents she'd given him—six books lined up on his dresser between black elephant bookends. Looked nice, but he hadn't read even one. And he couldn't remember the last time he'd seen *her* reading before this.

Make that seven books on his dresser because Don Baylis had bought him one when they'd spent their weekend together.

He took Baylis's present, thinking it would help make up to her for that Jew-baby. He came to the study and began to sit down in the wicker chair. She said, "Sit here."

He came over beside her. He opened his book, and she closed hers. "Read aloud."

Not again, he thought. Baylis had made him read aloud from a hard section in the middle.

"Can't I read to myself? I don't ask you to read aloud, do I? I'll bet you wouldn't do too good."

She was getting that white face again. He was madder than hell himself! He wanted to plan how to get money, how to get rubbers, how to get Mary, and he had to play school!

He began to read.

"Louder. Clearer."

"Yes, mein Führer."

She snorted then, choking back quick laughter, but right afterward said: "Don't push me tonight, Johnny."

No Boy Wonder. No big momma. She got this way sometimes. She wanted to change everything in five minutes sometimes.

"England . . . is an *is*-land."

"Island," she corrected.

"That too," he said, trying to make her laugh again.

She poked him in the shoulder with those sharp nails.

"Cut it!" he yelled.

"Read."

"England is an . . . island. Not very . . . large, but its . . . history . . . is a . . . proud one."

"Can't you read smoother? You make each word separate. How can you understand sentences when you break them up that way?"

He began again. He made the part he'd read smoother. But then he came to new stuff and had to slow down, read each word separately again. She said, "Enough!" and shut the book on his hand.

He wondered what was coming next.

What came next surprised him as much as the slap. She began to cry. "I've done such a lousy job with you," she sobbed. "I'm so sorry, honey."

He put his hand in hers. "That's all right," he soothed. "You did much worse with yourself."

Which was taking a big chance, but it paid off. She broke up completely, crying and laughing. And grabbed him and hugged him and gave him salty kisses.

"Now can we eat?" he asked.

She nodded, wiping her eyes with a tissue.

He figured he had her on the ropes. "In a good place for a change? I think I deserve it, big momma. You've been away a lot, right? And tomorrow and Saturday . . ."

"Your ears are like radar. Okey-doke. We'll go to Knight's and you can have a steak."

"Now you're talking!" He jumped up.

"Where are you going?"

"Gotta get some decent clothes—a jacket and my yachting cap."

Half an hour later they were in Knight's and he was

having a ball, laughing his head off while trying to eat a great steak, because big momma was talking about the two schmucks at the bar trying to give her the eye and not let Johnny see.

"Smooth," she mocked.

"Like Felix in *The Odd Couple*, right?"

"More like Igor in *Frankenstein*."

Which got them both to laughing.

She said her steak was the best she'd ever had, and her onion rings were better than her steak, and they kept taking things from each other's plates and having fun. He figured now was the time to hit her for ten dollars.

"What for?" she asked.

"Surprise," he said, smiling mysteriously, like he did when he was planning to buy her something.

"Don't you have some money your father gave you?"

"A little. But with ten more . . ." He raised his eyebrows and widened his smile.

She asked: "Why can't you tell me?"

"Does Macy's tell Gimbels?"

"What does that mean?"

"*Miracle on Thirty-Fourth Street*. About New York. They show it every Christmas on the local channels, and this old man . . ."

"I surrender! You got the ten."

"Hey, you won't be sorry!" He'd worry about a gift for her when she remembered it, which might be never.

Then he said, "What time will Mary be coming over tomorrow to sit?" and she said, "Mary can't come. Mrs. Maillet is coming."

He wanted to yell his head off, but held back. He put a piece of steak in his mouth and chewed and swallowed before asking, "How about Saturday?"

"Same thing. Mary's moving. Didn't she tell you when she sat with you Tuesday?"

He shook his head, stunned.

And then he remembered the last thing Mary had said to him that night: "Lucky it's all over or we'd have to get married." He hadn't understood. Now he did.

Mom was talking and he began listening again. . . . don't own their house like we do. They rent, and their landlord found a buyer and asked if they'd move fast. He made it worth their while, giving them August rent-free, so they're getting out by Tuesday, the day after Labor Day, which is really the beginning of the new month."

"So they're moving. I still don't see why she can't sit like before."

"They're moving to Oxnard, hours up the coast."

He couldn't believe it! "But we ought to say good-bye or something. I mean, why can't she sit once more?"

"They're busy packing. A move's a real mess. Forget the pretty sitter and accept the old one. It shouldn't make too much difference at your age."

He made believe he was laughing with her. He ate. He was numb.

Then he thought of something. "I told you about Mrs. Maillet losing her temper and slapping me, didn't I?"

"I don't believe it," she said sharply. "And if you ever mention it again, we'll all three sit down and discuss it."

"Who needs the hassle," he muttered, knowing she knew he was lying. "But anyway, with Mary, just this last time. I mean, ask her just for tomorrow night. Like a farewell party, right?"

She was staring at him. "What have you two . . . ?"

He stopped her with: "Forget it! I just want to say good-bye to someone we've known for years and you have a heart of stone."

"Touching," she muttered. "I save my heart for those close to me. You'd better do the same."

"Right. Cool. Teach the boy to step on people."

"I'll teach the boy to close his mouth!"

So that was that.

Forget the rubbers.

Great weekend coming. Mrs. Maillet had a mustache and bad breath.

Well, there were some good TV specials. And his old favorites in re-runs. He ate an onion ring. Thank God for the tube.

Eight

Saturday, September 3, and Sunday, September 4

Freddy slipped out of Arabella's arms, moving gently even though she'd had a Quaalude with her coffee, and even though they'd already done everything he'd wanted to do. Some people recovered from, or resisted, Q's a lot better than others . . . and she might be a little distressed about the back-door action.

A fine piece, nice and tight in all departments, though her rhythm was poor. Needed practice, the Spanish widow did.

Now it was time to visit her son down the hall. Sergio had absorbed his half-Q in a Coke, and was fast asleep, as he was supposed to be.

Freddy had done the doping himself, not even asking Bub to help. Because Bub had kept a closed face, a remote and respectful demeanor, with lots of yes-sirs thrown in for the company. Not so much as a glance at the aristocratic beauty's sleek ass. And right after the dishes were cleared away and mother and son getting sleepy, Bub had split, saying he had a date.

Now it was one A.M. Saturday. Now Fred had rested a few hours from his labors with the mother and was ready for the son.

He left the master bedroom, nude, walking into the

hall and pausing at the stairs. Maybe Bub had come home. Maybe he'd changed his mind about Sergio.

He went down the stairs and through the kitchen. It was a hot night, the Santa Ana persisting. Even the kitchen floor, made of rocklike plastic squares, was warm to his bare feet.

He came to Bub's door, which was closed. He knocked and tried to open it. Locked.

He couldn't recall Bub locking his door before.

It bothered him, and he knocked again, harder.

Still no answer, and he said: "I know you're in there, Bub. You wouldn't lock your door from the outside, right? Listen, go upstairs and take Arabella. She's relaxed just right from Q, baby. You don't have to bother with Sergio. But if you change your mind, he's in the end bedroom."

Nothing.

He got angry then and returned to the kitchen for the flashlight. He went through the living room and out the sliding glass doors and along the pool and into the alleyway and past the kitchen window to Bub's window. He bent forward and flashed the light through the glass onto the bed, ready to shout for Bub to open up.

The bed was empty. The room was empty.

An insult, that locked door! Bub was really changing!

He went inside and put away the flashlight. He started back up the stairs, and his anger died and he had to admit something to himself: It wasn't nearly as much fun without Bub.

But then he was at the landing. Then he was at the end bedroom and threw the light on. The dark-haired, olive-complexioned boy slept heavily. He was under a summer-weight blanket, but a quick step forward, a jerk of the wrist, and the blanket was off. The boy was naked, lying on his side, his ass to Fred.

He stroked that ass, fingered it, tested to see how

tight the anus would be when he went up it. The boy grunted, and turned onto his back, making Fred withdraw his hand. Fred reached between Sergio's legs and cuddled his testicles and penis. Sergio sighed, and opened his eyes.

"Mr. Gower?" he mumbled. He rubbed his face.

Fred leaned over him, and gently squeezed those genitals.

The boy's eyes blinked and cleared. His penis swelled. He reached up and put his hand on Fred's hip. He slid that hand down and around a little and his thumb touched Fred's cock. His own cock was now quivering rock-hard, purple-hard.

"Mr. Gower," he said softly, and smiled.

So there was no seduction.

Sergio explained that he knew it all. He'd been in a boy's school in Switzerland since his father had died. He spoke Spanish, Italian, and English equally well. He spoke French reasonably well. He'd made love with boys of all four nationalities for eighteen months, rarely missing a night. He was a confirmed, dedicated homosexual.

And he managed to do something no one had ever done to Fred Gower. He sodomized him, leading him into it with tongue action, with play and pleas and little-boy endearments. A new thrill for the old master, even though it had elements of pain.

Plenty of fun and plenty of action. But on balance, Fred was disappointed that he didn't have an innocent here.

And because he'd been fooled, because he was used as much as user, he took particular delight in the boy's moans, in his stifled cries of pain as he rammed his nine inches home.

Sergio wept softly afterward. Fred petted him and slept with him. Until five-thirty, when a sound awoke him and he want downstairs to see what it was.

Bub was in the kitchen, drinking beer from the can,

looking clean and fresh and disgustingly undissipated.

"Strike out?" Fred asked.

"Not at all. How'd it go for you?"

"Fantastic. You cheated yourself for nothing. The boy knows it all. He's the biggest faggot in the bunch."

"Glad to hear it, boss-man. You'll live another few weeks."

"Funny." He got himself a beer from the refrigerator and took a long swallow. "Go on upstairs."

"No, thanks. I slept with a little Jap massage-girl. Got all I needed."

"Arabella's no massage girl. Just take a look. And the boy's *beautiful.*"

"I'll look." He got up.

"Would you shoot some film of my second go-round with Sergio?"

Bub sat down again. "Think I'll sack out a few more hours."

"Forget the film," Fred sighed. "Forget everything." But a moment later he said, "Let's go," and led Bub to the stairs. They began to climb, and his excitement grew because his friend was here to share with him, and he whispered descriptions of mother's and son's best points. "Remember, they'll be here for another night, so don't run away again."

Bub finally smiled, and it was a beautiful thing! Fred threw his arm around his shoulders, and Bub looked at him and said: "You ain't fucking *this* old boy, baby."

Fred laughed, realizing he was naked and it was strange. But what they had between them was deeper than sex, and the strangeness disappeared. "Who first, Arabella or Sergio?"

"The widow," Bub said. "But just to look."

They talked right over her naked form. Fred turned her onto her side, onto her stomach, onto her back, and all she did was sigh a little and smile a little and try to sleep. He ran his hands over this part and that, and finally got Bub to do the same. After that, it was only a matter of time until Bub sat down at the edge of the bed.

Fred grinned and started for the door. "I'll have another portion of fruitcake."

He enjoyed sixty-nining with the boy more this second time than anything they'd done the first, because Sergio was completely out from under the Quaalude . . . and also because Bub was down the hall.

Later, Bub came in, and Sergio said: "Ai, negro! I never had one before!" And Fred was able to watch while Sergio blew his friend and jerked his friend and did everything to his friend . . . but couldn't make him come.

"I don't please you?" Sergio asked, leaning back, exhausted.

Bub said: "You please me plenty. I'm just plain fucked out."

The boy shrugged and turned on his side and fell dead asleep.

Downstairs, in bathrobes, they ate eggs and bacon. Fred even made the coffee, he was so happy. Everything was getting back to where it had been and the good times were rolling and he had his friend again.

They shared a joint out near the pool, watching the sun illuminate the palms and roofs of Beverly Hills. He asked Bub about locking his door.

"Did I? Didn't mean to."

He asked Bub about Arabella.

"Nice."

"Just nice?"

Bub shrugged. "Cunt's cunt."

Fred dragged and passed the joint. "I guess. But to me, each one's something *terrific!* I tell you, Bub, whatever the cost, each experience is worth it."

"Was Cecily Warren worth it? The last time I mean, with the Q, with someone tipping Baylis."

"There's no proof anyone told Don."

"The proof's in the way he's talked to you since then. Or hasn't talked to you. Have you heard about whether he'll do the script?"

"He called Berry Thursday morning. Said he'd do it."

"Berry? When did he ever talk business with Berry before?"

"All right. Say he knows. The answer is yes—it was worth it. Cecily's ass! That perfect ass! Raising it up and getting ready and knowing I'd fed her to Dennings, I could feed her to any bum on the street if I wanted to, I *owned* her, and no one, Don Baylis or her parents or God himself, could stop me from doing what I wanted! And then fucking her in that tight unwilling hole! Hearing her groans, her yells! Plowing her and finishing and wiping my dripping cock in her hair!"

He was panting. Bub looked away from him, out to the palms of Bedford. Freddy said he was thirsty and went inside. And worried that Bub would think he was nuts.

Bub came in with the ashtray and dumped the roach down the disposal, shredding it as he always did. Freddy said, "A real sex maniac, huh?" laughing to take the curse off.

Bub said: "Hey, boss-man, I dig it. This isn't the Reverend Sun Moon Coon you're talking to."

Freddy had to laugh. Bub went on, and soon Fred's laughter was gone.

"You know me. I'll go all ways all days as long as the balls hold out. But that's only if I don't hurt people, or risk my neck. And the second usually goes with the first. Look at Roman Polanski."

Fred was going to answer, but Bub held up his hand.

"If we push it, boss-man, we'll end up with no place to go but in different directions. I'm not ready for that, if you're not."

Fred left the kitchen and went upstairs. He showered and got into bed in the middle guest room, the one with the camera slots. Too bad he couldn't use his own room—he'd have loved to run off those films of Cecily and himself taken in May. Talking about her had revived his appetite.

He went through a few scenarios, but it was Bub he ended up thinking about before falling asleep.

What was wrong with the man anyway? He couldn't understand him lately.

Hurt people?

When the hell had Fred Gower ever hurt anyone!

Bub waited until he heard the shower before going out to his car. The small wooden box was on the floor under the front passenger's seat, propped so it wouldn't move. He removed it carefully and carried it into the garage and past Freddy's tan Seville; carried it slowly, gingerly, because inside that box, wrapped in heavy wood batting, was a tiny glass tube of clear, slightly yellowish liquid—nitroglycerin.

Unstable element, nitro. Best to keep it cool, immobile, and not around for long, since it tended to spoil. And when it spoiled, it tended to go off for no damned reason.

He'd gotten this information, plus expert instructions on how to use the explosive and the high-intensity drill which was in his room, from the cat known as Voodoo, his long-time contact for buys ranging from marijuana and cocaine through the current heavy items. Voodoo had been surprised, saying, "I never figured you for the dumb plays, Bub." Bub had assured him it was for a "friend," and Voodoo had grinned. "Always is, man, always is."

Made Bub feel stupid.

But then again, Voodoo didn't know about the six hundred fifty thousand.

Neither did he know the mark was a Mafioso.

No time to think of that now. He and Giselle were
on for either Sunday or Monday night, the choice to
be made according to how she read the scene. With the
pickup of the drill yesterday and the nitro tonight,
Bub was ready. The safe should blow easily; Giselle
should be out of the country within two hours; Bub
should pocket three hundred twenty-five thousand.

He placed the box gently inside the large storage refrigerator that Freddy never touched; that no one ever
touched but Bub Kane. Even so, he removed eight six-
packs of beer and cola in order to put the wooden box
far in back on the bottom shelf; then replaced the
drinks, effectively burying the nitro.

Now if Freddy didn't go blind and drive into that
fridge, everything would work out.

Bub smiled a little as he closed the heavy door . . .
yet knew he would sweat until Sunday or Monday, until that nitro was out of here. Two years ago, when
Freddy'd had the car Bub now drove, he had come
home bombed and stoned and forgotten to use the
electric lift control and run smack into the closed garage door.

Which was something Bub didn't want to dwell on
tonight!

He went to his room and the locked door; locked
because of that special drill in the black leather carrying case stored in the closet. An expensive item, and
one that would create curiosity if Freddy ever came
across it; that would create more than curiosity once
news got out that Andro's safe had been drilled and
blown.

He unlocked the door, went inside, locked the door
again.

In bed, he assured himself all would go well. This
time he wasn't using two clowns who couldn't get anything right. He was handling it himself, and Giselle
only had to let him in and stand back.

Thinking about those "two clowns" gave him a bad

feeling. And led to his recalling Jason as he'd last seen him, standing outside that San Diego shack.

Finally, he promised himself that once he had the three hundred twenty-five thousand, he'd find out how to put thirty or forty grand into Jason's name, in trust until he reached the age of eighteen.

With that, he was able to sleep.

"Fred set up this introduction," Coleman Berry said to Cecily Warren and the woman who wanted to become her new agent, "and then he cuts out of my party. Something to do with Spanish nobility."

Lise Apner, the agent, said she and Cecily could discuss the matter without Fred Gower. Cecily said she preferred it that way, and Coleman figured Fred had pulled one of his raw stunts with her. He didn't know how many actresses refused to deal with Freddy.

Now it was Cecily's turn. And that call from Don Baylis about the script indicated the novelist was also pulling back from Gower, trying to avoid working with him. And they'd been the original partners in getting *Galt's Island* off the ground.

It made no difference to him and Pandaro, because all the production contracts were signed, the studio lined up, the major cast under contract, the location sets chosen and cleared—everything ready to go, once Baylis put the script into shape.

Freddy and Pandaro had both reacted violently to Daimler's script, pointing out the excess brutality and the many changes from the novel, but Coleman hadn't thought it all that bad. In fact, he rather liked it. An extra killing or two, a little more action, never hurt the box office. At least in his experience with non-X-rated films. Perhaps this was different, so he'd deferred to their opinions.

He moved among his guests, saw Bert Ebberhardt and his wife, Eleanor, off to his right, and shifted left to avoid them. Had to invite Bert, even though he hadn't really wanted to; hadn't felt the old friendship for the sheriff's department officer since the night Coleman had nailed those two would-be thieves in his carport area. Bert had been too cocksure of himself with Coleman since that night. As he'd put it the last time they'd gone to the shooting range, "Guess you owe me one, Coleman. A big one."

Coleman had introduced Eleanor to the casting director personally, and all it had led to was a two-liner. Coleman was unhappy about still owing Bert that "big one." And Coleman was unhappy about something else . . . which Bert unwittingly reminded him of every time he called or came around.

The big thief, the black, had shouted something as he raised his hands, right after Coleman had killed his partner, just before Coleman shot and wounded him. Coleman hadn't really heard him, or so he'd thought. Since then, however, the words had come back to him, had come crystal-clear to him.

"Don't kill me, man, I've got two sons!" And Coleman had reloaded and killed him.

He felt the hand on his arm, and turned to see Bert's sun and wind-lined face. "Great party, buddy. Listen, Eleanor wants to meet Rob Dennings. I wouldn't mind myself. We're great fans of his." He belted down an on-the-rocks drink.

Coleman said of course; maybe a little later since Dennings was joining Cecily Warren and Lise Apner and they'd be talking business. Bert said: "Oh, I don't think they'd mind, Coleman. And if Eleanor has another Manhattan, she'll have to be *carried* over to meet him."

He laughed, and Coleman wanted to throw him out on his ass and laughed with him. "Let me check first."

The pushy bastard!

He went across the room, in time to have Warren and Dennings step abruptly from Apner, almost into Coleman. And heard Dennings say; ". . . hadn't the faintest idea drugs were . . . ," and heard Cecily say, "Here's Coleman."

Obviously a bad moment, but he went right ahead and asked if they'd mind meeting a friend of his, thus giving them a chance to disengage.

Dennings was tight-lipped and pale. Cecily was smiling her usual sexpot smile, but her eyes were jumpy, her hands unsteady.

"Not now," Dennings said bluntly, and took her by the arm and walked her into a corner. Where they jawed at each other in very animated fashion. Coleman went over to Lise Apner.

"Any idea what that's all about?"

"Saturday night in Hollywood, Coleman."

"You can do better than that."

She smiled and didn't seem about to answer. He was turning away when she spoke.

"I dearly love Freddy, because he's sent several clients my way. But if I were you, Coleman, I'd get this picture before the cameras as soon as possible. Mr. Gower is having his usual divisive effect on any and all male-female relationships."

"Fucking around again, is he?"

"Yes, though the height to which the man has raised the art requires some special terminology."

Lise was about forty, a big woman who had been married twice. But talk was that these had been covers at a time when gays had preferred to remain in their closets. Now she was more or less in the open, a lesbian with several revolving relationships, none of which were with current clients.

"How long," Lise asked, "before you can begin principal photography?"

"The week we get the shooting script."

"That well set-up, are you? And when do you expect the script?"

"Don Baylis assures me he'll complete his revision in two weeks. Then he and Dennings, who'll direct, will get together for at most another week's work. Assuming, of course, the script is in shape. That will give us the white copy, or shooting script, which we'll hand out to the actors. Say a week later, we'll be in the studio for the closed set scenes, which I want to conclude first and lock away from prying media eyes. After that we'll appear to be shooting a more-or-less standard action movie." He thought a moment. "Our target is a total of eight weeks to conclusion."

"Including location?"

"Hopefully. We've got an island in the Florida Gulf Stream, and unless an early storm hits, we should be in and out of there in a week. All within the eight weeks' schedule."

Lise was watching Warren and Dennings. "Wrapping it up twelve weeks from today?" He nodded. She said: "That might save it. Otherwise, those two aren't going to be able to talk to each other, not to say make hard-core love before the cameras."

"You exaggerate," Coleman said.

"Probably. It's an agent's failing in social circumstances, and strength in business situations."

And a lesbian's wishful thinking, he thought. Because Cecily Warren wasn't a star and would do everything to become one, including swallowing whatever shit Freddy had raised between her and Rob Dennings.

Bert and Eleanor were at his elbow again. He introduced them to Lise. She nodded at them, and turned to a waiter with a tray of drinks.

"Who does she think *she* is?" Bert muttered, looking as if he'd had more than his share of the sauce.

Coleman felt the question more aptly applied to Bert and Eleanor, and ambled away. Big favor or not, this was the last party of his they attended. What could the captain do anyway, say he'd faked a crime-scene report for a friend? He'd go up for a lot longer than Coleman!

Coleman went over to Warren and Dennings. They didn't seem happy to see him, but actors had never particularly bothered or impressed him, and he said: "Would you two like the producer's good offices as mediator? Because a reminder of what's at stake here might be appropriate. Fame . . ."

"Infamy," Dennings said, "is the word."

"And fortune," Coleman concluded. "Even infamy and fortune ain't bad," he cracked, but got no laughs.

Cecily Warren, however, was calmer now. "Sorry if I said anything out of line, Rob."

Rob looked at her, and his anger changed direction. "Well, it's a hell of an accusation. I've never had to stoop . . ." He glanced quickly at Coleman, who knew he was intruding and stayed right where he was. "I'll speak to Freddy. If it's true, he'll learn never to do anything like that again—not with *me* as part of it anyway!"

Coleman said: "See, I've worked my magic, healed the rift, and now offer you two the master bedroom for rehearsals." He realized the joke had bombed very badly. "Or, as has been said of better men than me: A producer is the expert who comes on the set to approve the actors' shoes."

Which finally got a laugh, and he was able to stroll off without egg on his face. Back to Lise. Who was again eying Cecily Warren.

"I thought you layed off clients," Coleman said, bold because he'd known Lise a long, long time—fifteen years, back to when she'd worked for MCA.

"Without this film, Warren hasn't a prayer of making it, or being my client."

"I don't see your point. She *is* in the film. She therefore will make it . . . if not like Bette Davis, then a cross between Monroe and Lovelace. And unless you dislike money, she'll be your client."

"For all our sakes, old acquaintance, I hope you're right. But the venture is a funky one. The chances for slips between cups and lips many." She shook her head. "Maybe you'll make your fortune, finally. Or maybe *Galt's Island* will end up dead in the can, unfit for major distribution."

"Bite your tongue, woman." He shivered in mock horror, but fled to another group of guests because part of that horror was real. The growing ban by newspapers on advertising of X-rated films was a real problem. He hoped that *Galt's Island* would break the ban because of its stature, its star, its "redeeming social value" in the form of ninety percent story as opposed to ten percent explicit sex.

He heard a commotion off to his right, near the front hallway, and saw a woman on the floor. It was the blond actress, Fanny Batcher, who was cast for the part of Candy, the secretary who gets raped. He was about to rush over—they needed that body well and unmarked!—when she was helped up by a man he recognized as a local newscaster. Fanny was glaring after Cecily Warren, who was walking to the door. Fanny was shouting something, the newscaster was trying to calm and quiet her, and everyone was staring. Cecily Warren opened the front door and turned and waved at Fanny. The blond then tried to break free of the newsman and go for her.

Cecily waited a moment, but when the newsman didn't release Fanny, she left.

Coleman had a glass of champagne with Pandaro, who was amused by the incident between the two women. "The blond claims she was tripped by the brunette." He smiled aloofly. "Such *quality* actresses. Perhaps we should let them fight it out on the screen, nude, of course."

Coleman wasn't in the mood for his partner's European class-snobbism. He excused himself and had a second glass of champagne with Grant Vasper, who'd just arrived from another party at his agent's home where he'd been celebrating landing the role of Rorke, the brutal government agent who rapes Candy. Grant was a massive ex-wrestler, six-feet three and about three hundred pounds, who fit the description of Rorke right down to his shaved cannon-ball head and pockmarked face. But under it all, he was a sweet, unassuming man, and he was asking to be introduced to his co-workers—Dennings and Warren and Ben Bright, and especially Fanny Batcher.

"Never thought I'd be doing a trick in front of the camera," he said, shaking his head slowly, grinning slowly. "I've wrestled in shorts, but to let it all hang out, and *use* what's hanging out! If it wasn't for Arthur getting me such a fat price, I'd have been thinking it over at least a year." He looked around. "Which one do I trick with?"

Coleman pointed out Fanny.

"Well, maybe I'd have thought it over a little less than a year, say ten minutes, if they'd showed me *her!*"

Coleman really didn't want to introduce them tonight; not with Fanny still steaming over her run-in with Cecily. Because when she got a look at Grant, she'd have a fit.

But he had no choice.

The crowd parted before Grant and Coleman a lot easier than it had for Coleman alone, and they soon stood before Fanny and the newsman, whom she introduced as Amos Brandon. As she spoke, she was staring at the massive, *monstrous* figure of Granite Mountain Vasper, who waited patiently for his turn in the introductions.

Finally, Coleman had to do it. "Fanny, Mr. Brandon, this is Grant Vasper."

The newsman shook hands with Grant, and said: "I know you, sir, but the name doesn't quite . . ."

"Granite Mountain," Vasper offered.

The newsman shook his hand again, enthusiastically. "I'm a wrestling buff, Mr. Vasper, and the arena lost perhaps its most exciting champion when you left the profession!"

"A wrestler?" Fanny said. She began to relax, and offered Grant her hand.

He bent from the waist, looking rather like a giant redwood beginning to topple, and kissed her wrist. He looked up at her from under heavy brows, and spoke to the newsman.

"I didn't really leave the profession, Mr. Brandon. I was an actor then, and I'm an actor now. Except now I'm a member of SAG."

Fanny withdrew her hand. She looked at Coleman as if to say: "Don't tell me!"

He told her. "Grant has signed to play the part of Rorke, the secret service agent."

Fanny wet her lips, eyes fixing on Grant. He said; "Don't let it worry you, Miss Batcher. Remember what they say about judging books by covers."

Because of the newsman's presence, not much more could be said. And Brandon began asking questions.

"Do you two have scenes together? Could any of them be classified as love scenes? They wouldn't be part of those rumors we've all heard, would they?"

Fanny said; "You agreed not to talk about the movie, Amos."

"But surely these are innocuous questions."

"Or would you rather I asked someone else to take me home?"

Brandon smiled and gave up, but Coleman wondered for how long. The people-and-events portion of his broadcast was noted for show-biz scoops. He wouldn't be able to resist probing, no matter how much he wanted Fanny. Unless she really threw a hook into his sexy little heart.

Coleman took Fanny aside. She said: "God! Is that Frankenstein for real?"

"A very gentle person. Nothing to worry about."

"How about broken ribs and a ruptured . . ." She searched for an acceptable word.

"Pelvis?" he offered.

"Mr. Berry, he *scares* me!"

"You have more to fear from Amos Brandon and his news show. If he gets hard evidence about our sex scenes, he could cause us a great deal of trouble, even put the production in jeopardy. We can't have a premature release of that information, Fanny. For one thing, it'll cause blue-nose reaction—pressure on all major studios to deny us use of their facilities. And I'm sure the bad publicity will cause us to lose our location leases. Perhaps worst of all, the media will descend like a plague of locusts, trying to get into our closed sets, hounding our stars, making life impossible for us all."

She was nodding.

"At best," he continued, "it'll blow our promotion campaign. We're not having previews for reviewers. They'll get passes to opening nights in the major cities. This will give the public the chance to start attending before anyone can make them feel guilty about it. And once they do, word of mouth will take over. So if you could handle Mr. Brandon, who obviously is taken with you, perhaps bend yourself to his will a little . . . ?"

"I was bending anyway," she interrupted dryly. Then she grew angry. "Bending with a stiff back and sore hip, because of Cecily Warren!"

"I like to stay out of personal conflicts, Fanny. If you'll excuse me." He turned to go.

"Wait a minute. Forget Warren. About Vasper. Am I really expected to make love to that . . . *mountain*? He's going to get very rough with me; at least according to the book. I mean, have you read what he does to Candy?"

"You might find you'll like it," he murmured, and left before she could reply.

What the hell did she expect anyway? Since when could actors pick their partners, their love-scene opposites? That went for porn stars, too. Besides, Grant was a heavyweight in more than physique. He'd had five busy years in features, and some very selective TV roles. He'd won an Emmy two years ago, and been nominated for an Academy Award as Best Supporting Actor for that villainous hillbilly in *Back of the Woods*. He outclassed Fanny Batcher in all ways, and Coleman would let her go if she refused to work with Grant. They could always get another blond to screw on camera . . .

More commotion, this time from the dining room where the buffet was set up. He moved to the left, to where he could see through the archway, and couldn't believe his eyes. It was Bert, being restrained by his wife, Eleanor, from trying to grab a woman, from actually swinging at a woman!

And when he saw who was standing beside that woman, acting like her escort, he moaned, "What *is* it tonight!" and rushed forward.

The woman was a light-skinned black, young and very pretty. And very angry.

"I don't care if he does have a badge," she said, voice shaking, "and I don't care if he is a guest here, he's a dirty racist pig!"

"Damned Mandy punched my face!" Bert said, trying to get around Eleanor, who was doing a fantastic job jumping in front of him and pushing against him. "I informed her I was an officer, and she assaulted me!"

"*Mandy!*" the woman said. "You see, Tony?" She turned to her escort, a popular white singer, and tears trickled down her cheeks. "Was I wrong? Was I?"

The singer, whom Coleman had counted as a coup when he'd accepted the invitation, said, "You weren't wrong," voice very tight, very controlled. "If he gets by his wife, I promise to fracture his larynx."

Coleman said, "Tony, sorry about this!" and quickly moved in front of Bert, taking Eleanor's place. She stepped away, shaking her head, putting her hands to her face. Coleman dropped his voice. "I want you to walk away, Bert. She's Tony Wyanda's date. *The* Tony Wyanda. The singer. And my honored guest."

"He's a Mandy lover!" Bert said, raging, pushing against Coleman. "Get your fat gut out of my way! She assaulted me and I'm gonna run her in. Assaulting an officer is a felony."

"You're not an officer here!" Coleman said, sweating as he considered Tony Wyanda's history of night-club brawls, and Bert Ebberhardt's habit of carrying an off-duty weapon.

Coleman turned to offer more soothing apologies to Wyanda. "My God, Tony, I don't know what to say! Please ignore the fool! I'll have him out of here . . ."

Bert broke past Coleman. Tony went into a Karate stance. Eleanor shouted: "Stop them, someone, please!"

And someone did. Granite Mountain Vasper had been standing there, watching, and now grabbed Bert from behind, enfolding him, pinioning his arms, holding him helpless.

"You're under arrest!" Bert shouted, face crazed and white and oily. He always drank more than his share, but tonight he'd gone overboard. He began to kick and struggle, spewing obscenities.

Grant tightened his hold a little. Bert's obscenities came to a choking conclusion.

Grant said to Eleanor: "If you'll lead the way to your car."

She began to walk. Grant simply lifted the hundred-eighty-pound sheriff's deputy up off the floor and walked with her.

Coleman followed. By the time they reached the Ebberhardts' Pontiac and he was released, Bert stood quietly. But he still said: "I'm going to make that felony arrest. And include you, Coleman, and you, whoever you are, for interfering with an officer in performance of his duty."

Coleman said, "Not when you sober up," and Eleanor said, "Let's go home, Bert," and Coleman left with Granite Mountain Vasper.

"Can't thank you enough, Grant."

Grant was looking across the crowded room at Fanny. "I still owe you, Coleman. For that. Though I almost wish I wasn't going to get her in the movie, so I could try on my own."

"No law against trying on your own, afterward."

"She seems turned-off at the moment. I have that effect on some ladies." He smiled a little. "For the picture's sake as well as my own, I hope I can change her opinion."

Which was a problem Coleman couldn't consider right now. He tossed off a third glass of champagne, and went to soothe Tony. Who told him Bert had entered the buffet room, approached Tony's expensively gowned and diamond-bedecked date—Arnetta Lyle, a recording artist in her own right—and said: "Get me some beef and salad, missy." And patted her on the rump.

Tony had been off in a corner chatting with someone. She'd turned to look for him, stunned, and Bert had said, "Move it, Mandy," and patted again.

He was obviously drunk, but it was too much for Arnetta. She'd slapped Bert in the face; which was when he'd flashed his badge and tried to arrest her for assaulting an officer.

"You should pick you guests more carefully, Coleman," Tony said, and headed for the door with his girl.

Coleman didn't think he'd be seeing Tony at his house again. And didn't blame him, because Tony was right.

Not only should he pick his guests more carefully,

but also his friends, as that's what Bert had been; perhaps his closest friend. And boorish attitude or not, Bert had really come through for him. So why was he now so deep-down ashamed of him, and not just for that idiotic drunken-man's scene? Why did he want him out of his sight, out of his life, *forever?*

He surprised himself by knowing the answer. It was because he and Bert were alike.

Coleman had never really thought of blacks as people. He had blocked them out except as criminal menaces—rapists and robbers and killers—this, despite years of dealing with them in show biz. He had never had a single black friend, and most of the whites he knew were the same. He didn't even have a black acquaintance, had invited no blacks to this party; only Tony had brought one as a date.

And now Albert Dunster's ghost-voice had given him a few uneasy moments, and he had been made to see his attitudes, himself, in an old friend. His thinking tonight was a process of growth, of liberalization, finally entered upon three weeks from his sixtieth birthday. A beginning, a questioning . . .

And it was interrupted by still another commotion. He said, "Damned party is jinxed!" and turned. To look again into Bert's crazed white face. To see him rocking back and forth, as much with frenzy as with booze. To hear him shouting a most incredible phrase here in a lower Benedict Canyon mansion.

"Nigger lover!"

Coleman hadn't punched anyone in years, but he drew back his fist.

And Captain Bert Ebberhardt drew a thick-snout revolver from under his jacket. "Not only helping assault an officer, but attempting assault yourself! You're under arrest! Put your hands on your head!"

Coleman said: "The hell I will!"

Bert pulled back the hammer and aimed directly at

Coleman's chest. "I won't warn you again," he said, voice shaking.

People were shouting, and Coleman could see Grant making his way through the crowd behind Bert.

Coleman raised his hands to his head, because that cocked gun could go off if Bert *sneezed*. "Put the gun away. I'll go wherever you want."

"You bet you will!" The crazed white face swung back and forth as Bert looked around at the guests. Coleman prayed he wouldn't see Grant. And he didn't, because Granite Mountain was almost directly behind him now. "I want the Wop singer! And his nigger bitch! And that big ox! All of you, for assaulting an officer of the sheriff's department."

Coleman had his hands clasped firmly on his head. "All right," he said. "Just uncock the revolver."

"You'd like that, wouldn't you? Ungrateful, double-crossing . . ."

His voice choked off as Grant duplicated his act of fifteen minutes ago, reaching around to pinion Bert's arms to his sides.

Coleman let his breath out in a long sigh, and began to lower his hands. Bert had gone too far this time. He'd drawn his gun in a room full of people and would have to be turned over to the L.A.P.D. It couldn't be *just* the result of alcohol. Bert was unbalanced. Perhaps enough so that he'd talk about the shootings in the carport. But it had to be risked.

He was about to ask if anyone had called the police, when Bert's right hand jerked up from the wrist; when the gun went off; when the .38-caliber bullet entered Coleman's mouth, smashing lips and teeth, slanting sharply upward into the head.

He didn't have time to feel surprise, fright, even pain. Because he had caught a brain shot. Like the ones he'd tried for as a Marine lieutenant on Iwo Jima, but hadn't been able to confirm. Like the one he'd carefully placed into Albert Dunster's head as he lay helpless against the carport gate.

The fact that *this* brain shot was a mistake, an accident caused more by Grant's actions than Bert's, made no difference. Because a brain shot allowed for no excuses, re-enactments, corrections.

It was, quite simply, lights out.

Fanny was still shaken, sickened, unable to accept what had happened even three hours later, when Amos Brandon finally finished putting together the feature on Coleman Berry's death for his station's "Sunday at Noon" show. This was one story that wouldn't keep until his own show Monday evening.

They'd taped an interview at the Sepulveda Boulevard TV studio with Morey Blair, the "Noon" host, in which Fanny more or less said "me-too" as Brandon described the party and "the tragedy, so much in the Hollywood tradition, that has struck down producer Coleman Berry, fifty-nine years old and involved in *Galt's Island*, a film shrouded in mystery. A violent and sexual film, it is rumored, which has the aura of a jinx about it."

She'd remembered Coleman's warning about not giving the media any hard evidence, and stopped saying me-too. When the camera and the host's questions turned to her, she said, "Not any more violent and sexual than most movies. As for the mystery part," she thought fast, "we're just trying to keep some tricky plotting under wraps."

Brandon had pointed out that the novel was available.

Fanny smiled prettily, remembering finally that murders or no, she was on camera. "But the script is different."

It was after five when they got into Brandon's Alfa convertible. He said; "I know it's been a bad night and you probably want to sleep . . ."

"Not alone," she whispered, shivering.

What she wanted was a hot bath, and a man's protective arms.

She got the hot bath at Brandon's Century City apartment. And when she came out of the bathroom, wearing his robe, found Brandon lying on the bed, wearing pajama tops, stroking his erect penis.

"Hope you don't mind the honesty in advertising," he said, voice thick.

She thought that rather cute. Also his prick, which was on the small side.

She came to him and began to reach for that cute prick.

He pushed her hand away. "I'm not an ordinary man," he said. "I don't have ordinary tastes."

Mother-of-God, she thought, what next tonight?

Next was that he brought out a black leather dominance costume of spike-heeled boots, shorts, and jacket, the boots large enough to fit all, the shorts and jacket with rubber stretch insets, and asked her to wear it. She said, "All right, but if you try to beat up on me, Amos . . ."

"Don't be silly," he said, handing her a riding whip. "I don't care to do anything to *you*. I want you to do everything to *me*."

Which could have been worse, she thought, as she let him have it on the ass with that riding crop, wondering that he could enjoy the welts she was raising. But enjoy it he did, saying things about being a good boy if she'd only stop, she picking up the cues, saying he was a very bad boy and had to be taught a lesson.

She had, of course, heard about masochism and female dominance, but it was her first actual experience. And when he began to hump against the mattress, began to come, she realized he was as much a loser as Roy, composer of "Rock 'n' Roll Suicide," even with his career and his Century City condo. As useless to her, despite his postorgasmic promises of publicity and other help.

Because he lived on freak street. Because he offered no shelter from the storm. Because he could flip out at any time, as could the junkies, the wanderers.

She tried to sleep with one eye open, as her father used to say, and didn't sleep at all. She wondered where she would find that man to give her shelter, to give her comfort, to give her bread until she made it big on her own.

Damn, if only she could get a handle on Don! Cecily must have taken a fall with him because of Fanny's information. Why else would she have done what she did tonight—stuck out her foot and shoved Fanny over it?

Fanny was glad Brandon had stopped her from fighting. Bad scene, losing your cool that way. Let Cecily lose hers. Let Cecily go for revenge, give herself ulcers, get a hard-ass rep.

Little Fanny would lie back and watch. If she learned Don was still tight with the whore, still seeing her, she'd find something else to pass on to him. Cecily was bound to play around again. Anyone who took on two men at a crowded Beverly Hills party was what the rock musicians called a come-freak—a nympho, unable to control her appetites for long.

Don might hate the messenger bringing bad news, temporarily, but once Cecily was gone, he'd need someone to fill the vacancy.

She sighed morosely. With all her planning, she no longer had confidence in Don Baylis as the long-range lover, the main man.

And look what she had to face—Granite Mountain Vasper!

She shuddered, and turned to Brandon's arms. But he slept in a tight, self-contained knot, and there was no room for her.

She wished he would take her home.

Finally, she dozed off. And dreamed about Coleman Berry's smashed, bloody mouth. And awoke twitching . . . to find Brandon stroking his rigid cock, the leather costume laid out for a second go-round.

Johnny woke her at the ungodly hour of nine A.M., excited by something he'd seen on an early news program he sometimes watched because it preceded his weekend cartoon shows.

"Coleman Berry," he said, shaking her. "You went to his party last night, didn't you?"

She said never to wake her again on a Sunday morning.

"Did you see him get shot?" he said, sitting on the floor so as to look into her face.

"Shot? What kind of stories are you making up now?"

He got angry then, and scrambled erect.

She said: "Johnny, wait. I left the party about eleven-thirty. It must've gone on for two or three hours more. What happened?"

"Coleman Berry, the producer, was shot by some drunken sheriff. They had a picture of him lying on the floor."

She sat up. "He isn't dead?"

"Yes!" He was excited again. "Shot dead in his own home, they said, by a drunken deputy."

She got up and went to the bathroom. She showered . . . and didn't believe it. She returned to the bedroom and laid out clothing. And then just had to talk to someone who would know what had happened, and what it would mean to the movie.

Who was there but Freddy?

She'd made up her mind never to speak to him again, except in the strictest line of *Galt's Island* business.

And didn't this fit?

She dialed his number, sitting at the edge of the bed, controlling a feeling of rage, of hatred.

Bub answered. She asked for Freddy.

"Is it about Coleman Berry?"

She said yes. He said it was true and that Freddy was at Berry's home right now, along with Pandaro. They had talked at six A.M. and decided to remove anything having to do with *Galt's Island.*

"What about Coleman's family? And what if they— his estate—don't want to do such a movie?"

"The way I got it, each of the producers, including Freddy, is insured by the production company for half a million, which goes into his estate in place of rights in the production. No one can take over Coleman's rights but Pandaro, who put up most of the money. If Freddy died, same thing. If Pandaro died, the studio would take over and the movie could still get made."

"You sure about that?"

Bub chuckled. "No. Neither was Freddy. But they've got a lawyer with them."

They talked a while longer and she was comforted, but only a little.

While she dressed, she turned the clock-radio to the all-news station. And heard the story of Coleman Berry's senseless killing. The newscaster stated Coleman was overheard saying "jinxed" just before he was shot.

"Could this be one of those jinxed productions that fail to make it into the theaters for reasons not always connected with the budget? Orson Welles's *Don Quixote* was one. The Charles Laughton–Merle Oberon *I, Claudius* another." He went on to name movies she'd never heard of, because they'd never been released. Movies from the one Fatty Arbuckle was going to star in until a girl died in his bed, to a production which was to include the ill-fated Sharon Tate.

"And there has been industry talk about this film going beyond any previous major studio production in nudity, or sex, or brutality, or perhaps all three—no one is certain. What *is* certain is that one of the producers, Coleman Berry, was murdered at a party attended by almost all the principals involved in *Galt's Island*, and for no reason the police have been able to uncover. Bert Ebberhardt insists he was joking while under the influence of alcohol, and that his gun went off accidentally when he was grabbed from behind. This is the same Captain Ebberhardt of the sheriff's department who was the investigating officer when Coleman Berry shot and killed two would-be robbers in his home four months ago. So the *Galt's Island* jinx may have been working even longer than anyone suspects." Little laugh. "But as we all know, jinxes are nothing but superstition. And none of us, I'm certain, believes in that. But aren't you glad *you* aren't associated with that movie?"

Which led into a commercial.

And left Cecily confused and frightened.

Because she'd felt like killing someone connected with the movie herself last night. Fanny Batcher, whom she'd tripped and shoved, unable to restrain herself as she was leaving the party. A few more drinks, a few more thoughts about what that blond trash had cost her with Don, and she might have put one of Coleman's beautiful buffet carving knives between the bitch's siliconed tits.

And lucky that animal Freddy hadn't been present!
Jinxed?

She finished dressing and went to the study. Johnny was watching cartoons. No place for him to go today. Labor Day weekend and his friends were away.

She couldn't leave him. Mrs. Maillet was unavailable today and Monday: Her children were coming in from Utah for one of their rare visits. And no Mary.

She could call one of the services and get another high-school kid. But it would be a stranger. And Johnny hadn't seen much of his mother lately.

She was jumpy, scared, unhappy. She wanted to go

to Donny; have him talk away the nonsense about jinxes and give her his opinion on whether the movie was in danger of being stopped by Berry's family.

She could ask him to come here.

They could all three talk together.

But he was working, and they weren't as before, and he didn't care for her son.

She couldn't sit still. She told Johnny to get dressed, they were going out for breakfast and then to a movie.

He jumped up. "Yay! Pancakes and bacon for me, big momma! And can we see that new space-travel movie?"

She said yes, and he ran to his room. She picked up the phone extension and dialed Don's number. Just to say hello. Just to ask if he'd heard about Berry. Maybe to invite him to join them for breakfast—not the movies; not more than an hour away from his work; not too much of Johnny.

Not too much to ask, but he didn't answer and his machine went on and she identified herself and he still didn't answer. So that was that. She was alone. Without Donny, she was really alone in the world.

Not a sudden realization. She'd known for a long time how much more than any other man he meant to her. But she also knew *he* didn't know it. And there was no way now to convince him of it.

She'd put off calling Jorge. He'd be waiting anxiously, and she'd promised, but she'd kept putting it off.

Now she dialed his service. "I'd like to leave a message for Mr. Resordo."

When she finished, she knew she'd be seeing him tonight. Rather five A.M. Monday morning, his usual time if not his usual day.

It comforted her. An old friend. Someone who cared. Even if he couldn't give her what Donny had.

* * *

Fred called Don at ten, telling him "not to worry about the production" and that "Coleman's death won't change a thing."

Don hadn't been worried; hadn't known anything about Coleman Berry's death, even though he listened to the radio news every morning. He listened to National Public Radio, which gave a half-hour of commercial-free news at nine A.M., and while there was a portion devoted to local stories, it wasn't crime-oriented. So he'd heard the governor's latest diatribe against atomic energy plants, and the various sigal-erts—a term coined to cover problems for the L.A. car commuter—but nothing about rapes and murders, which he would catch on the five o'clock TV news, if he had nothing better to do.

He'd *had* something better to do the past three days. He'd been working, and working beautifully. There'd no longer been any doubt in his mind that he could give Coleman Berry a completely revised script within the two weeks he'd promised. And he'd been feeling only moderate strain.

Now he had to give that script to someone else.

Freddy said: "Listen, I don't know what's bugging you, but I heard you arranged to work with Coleman on the script."

"You *do* know what's bugging me," Don said coldly. "And I'm busy now. I want to finish the job and collect the thirty-five thousand dollars Coleman–Pandaro agreed to pay. I have a promissory letter, if you're interested."

"Pandaro told me. It's fine. But I'd've gotten you fifty."

Don ignored that. "I'm sorry about Coleman, though I really knew nothing about him. I know nothing about Pandaro, but I'll deliver the script to him now that Berry's gone."

"A waste of time. He'll only have to give it to me.

He's not capable of judging a script and discussing changes with you."

"He was capable of judging a novel and investing in it for a film."

"That's a general kind of thing. He saw a way to go, and his partner and I took over. But he has a language problem. He talks English well enough, but he really doesn't have . . . I don't know what to call it, but he can't make decisions about a shooting script. I'm the one who'll have to do that. And Dennings, in his role as director."

"Then Pandaro will give it to you. Good-bye."

"Wait. It'll only waste time. You and I have to sit down and go over that script. Then you and Dennings and I. And finally, Dennings and I. Because with Coleman gone, Pandaro's made me line producer. Which means I'll do all the real work putting this thing together. I probably would have done most of it anyway, but now I'm alone and now it's official."

Don was silent. Fred Gower was making hard sense.

"I won't try to clear up whatever misconceptions you have about me . . ."

Don gave him a dry chuckle.

"Okay, whatever, but if you want this film to be right, we have to work together."

Don said nothing.

Fred said: "I'll take your silence for agreement."

Again Don said nothing, thereby confirming the agreement.

"Stay well, Donny."

"You, too," Don said.

"Me? I'm healthy as they come."

"So was Coleman, I gather."

Freddy laughed; rather unconvincingly, Don felt, and he hung up on the laugh.

A moment later, as he was sitting down to go over yesterday's pages of script, the phone rang again. He didn't answer, and didn't bother going to the study to

listen in on the machine. It no longer mattered if Cecily called. And anyone else could wait.

At one, he decided to take a walk, to unwind and
think certain plot problems through. He planned to
have lunch when he returned . . . and then remembered the TV actress's party. She'd looked up his number and called yesterday to remind him. Her name was
Candida. Lovely name, if probably her agent's creation rather than her parents'. Candida Orwell.

If he dressed a little less casually than his knockabout jeans and T-shirt, he could have his walk *and*
lunch with Candida and her guests, thereby wasting
very little time.

He changed into a light-weight linen pants-and-
jacket combination and a pair of crepe-soled blue loafers. And brushed his hair. Then decided to shower
again, as one never knew where one would end up
when attending a Hollywood party.

He ended up following Candida on a tour of the
little red-bricked Mediterranean hacienda, of which
she was justly proud. There were a few good paintings,
lots of books, some decent objets d'art, and tasteful
furnishings. Her guests—downstairs and out back on
the *terrazza*—were a rather tasteful collection, too. Candida Orwell had it all together.

They were standing in a white-washed, airy, second-
floor bedroom, looking out a plate-glass window at a
city view equal to the one at Don's house, when Candida took his hand and murmured: "I'm truly pleased
you're here."

She wore an outfit of white linen, see-through
weight, and he'd seen through it several times as they'd
passed sun-filled windows. And he'd felt it was lovely,
just as it was now with her hand squeezing his.

But when he did what he knew he was expected to
do—drew her into his arms and kissed her and ran his
hands over her body—there was no real excitement.
On her part, yes, judging from the way she pressed

against him, then pulled away, trembling, whispering, "My guests."

And Don? He was comparing her with Cecily: Her hands were large, strong, where Cecily's were small, delicate. Her hair lacked that soft curl. Her body was leaner . . .

They were different people. They each had areas of charm. Intellectually he knew this, and also knew that in time he could appreciate Candida's "areas." But for now, the differences chilled him, made him want to run.

Because the one-woman man made that one woman the ideal, the paragon of beauty. Nothing else would do.

Still, he didn't run. He walked downstairs hand in hand with the actress. He joined her guests, ate and drank a little, returned her frequent smiles, her meaningful glances . . . and found he was perspiring heavily.

When he said he had to leave, she walked him to the road. She kissed him there, and murmured she hoped she'd be seeing him soon. And held to his hand as he stepped away, so that he had to turn again and kiss her again and say: "Yes, very soon."

At last he was able to leave. He was grateful it was a downhill walk, because he was a very tired man. Far more tired than he'd been after making love to Cecily, or Fanny.

It was draining to spend hours telling lies with voice and body.

Back in the cliffside house, he changed into his knockabout jeans and T-shirt, and was shocked to see it was only two o'clock! Just one hour, including the walk up and back!

The phone rang. He left the bedroom and went to the study to the answering machine.

As his voice droned on about not-being-at-home, he

remembered the earlier call that he hadn't answered downstairs.

This call was from Fanny. "Just wanted to say hello, *dahling*. Feeling rather down. I was at Coleman Berry's home last night when he was shot. Terrible! But that's not the only reason I'm down. Feel so awful about making you unhappy—I mean by telling you about Cecily. If I'd known . . . but it's done, and I don't understand why it should change things between *us*."

It hasn't changed things between us, he thought. There was never anything between us but lust. Which can return and still be nothing.

"Stay well, *dahling*. Please give me a call one of these days. Just to let me know I'm welcome again."

He put the machine on rewind; then played the earlier call. "Cecily, bun." Her voice was restrained, quiet. "Would like to talk to you. But I guess you're busy." She waited. "Bye now."

He ached for her. He wanted to call and tell her she was the only woman in the world for him. Candida had helped prove it.

He repeated to himself what was becoming a litany—that his need for her would weaken, his love for her dissolve in the shabbiness, the sordidness of her life.

He went downstairs and worked and didn't answer the phone when it rang at four and again at six.

At eight, he broke for a light dinner of salmon salad. Then read through what he'd typed. Then sat down with a novel he'd started reading a week ago.

At eleven, he closed the book and turned on the television for the news. He saw and heard the Coleman Berry story.

At eleven-thirty, he started for the bedroom. He didn't want to admit it, but his chest hurt a bit. He'd put in a very long day. He had to build a new tolerance for work.

The chimes sounded.

He turned and opened the sliding door to the carport. Cecily's Jaguar was standing outside the closed gate. She'd pressed the bell and was back inside her car.

It was raining. The storm the weather report had promised was moving in. But promised rain had bypassed Los Angeles so often the past three years, no one believed the forecasts any more.

It came down harder, even as he stepped into the carport, even as he told himself she had no right to come here without first calling.

Even as his heart leaped in greeting. "Want to come in?"

"Yes, thank you. I called a few times . . ." She let it go at that.

He opened the gate. She got out and ran. And then she was hugging him, hair damp and sweet, head down in his chest, saying nothing, as he said nothing, because what was there to say?

They didn't go to bed. He made no moves in that direction, feeling the slight irregularity in heartbeat, the growing exhaustion. And she didn't suggest it or play sexy; she sat down on the couch and asked for a glass of white wine.

He poured for her, but not for himself. He sat with her, and she drank and said: "You know about Berry?"

"Yes."

"You hear what they're saying about the movie being jinxed?" She smiled, because she knew his impatience with hunches and horoscopes and superstitions.

And he understood that she wanted him to smash the jinx concept. "I heard."

"It's pure nonsense, isn't it? Just a silly drunken brawl that ended up . . . bad. A mistake. Never happen again in a thousand years, right?"

He said: "Not right. Not a mistake. Not an isolated incident. Part of a pattern."

She didn't want to hear that. "You're kidding! You just want to scare me. Punish me."

"Then we won't talk about it."

She emptied her glass and asked for a refill. Rain rattled against the glass windows and walls, and he closed the sliding panels to the sundeck. The heat wave was dying under the lash of wind-driven water. The temperature was dropping by the minute.

He filled her glass. She drank half of it in one swallow. And said; "I want to talk about it. Tell me."

He told her. "This is a violent city. More so than New York. New York is very violent, but in a different way. New York is racially violent. Los Angeles is socially, historically, more broadly violent. Especially Hollywood, that cover-all label for the movie industry wherever it resides.

"Hollywood has always been violent. It's always dealt in bodies. Hot bodies and cold bodies. You're a hot body; and Fanny, when she dies in the movie, will be a cold body."

She made a laughing sound, but she wasn't laughing. She looked through the rain-streaked windows. The view was gone. The city's lights were gone. The wind, the rain, the sounds they made, increased. The storm began shouting.

"That's what movies are," he said, knowing he was frightening her, using it as revenge. "Hot bodies and cold bodies. Kisses and shootings. Love leading to hate and death.

"Books deal with the same material, but they're different. They can stop and think. Movies have to keep going. The frames keep racing by. *Movies*. The bodies keep moving, and falling. They have to, or the audience would lose interest. It's a captive audience by nature of the theater and the element of time. It can't close the feature, suspend the feature, and open it again later. So movies have to move, faster and faster. Can you imagine a film stopping the forward action for one tenth or more of its length to think, to assess, to ruminate what it and life is about?"

She said: "Some movies are thoughtful."

"Are they? Well, perhaps one or two a year. Some years not even one. Movies are rooted in the silents, still solidly based on the silents—the chases, the heroes and heroines, the dangers and rescues. The extreme face of all this. And when they use a novel or play, they almost have to reduce that novel or play to a skeleton and reflesh the skeleton with extremes."

"You never told me you don't like movies."

"I was raised on movies, like you. I'm a product of movies, like everyone. But I've diluted their unreality with books and education, and so joined a minority far more persecuted than blacks, Hispanics, American Indians. We have our minds, our very reason, attacked every day. And if we ever admit this, we're considered snobs, eggheads, dangerous subversives, or more likely contemptible pansies." He chuckled.

"You're putting me on, Donny."

Perhaps he was. He didn't know.

He did know that whether she liked what she heard or not, this is what she wanted from him. Talk. What she'd always asked for and taken away with her. His opinions, serious or not.

She said: "God, listen to that storm! Hope I can get home all right."

"You can stay the night, if you want."

"No. Johnny's asleep, but he's alone. I never leave him alone all night."

He wondered if she would discuss Johnny now; tell him what the boy had said and done when faced with her knowledge of the fifty dollars taken from Don't wallet.

She was silent a while, then said: "But can a movie be *jinxed?*" She quickly laughed.

"Of course."

"Oh, come on now! You're going back on everything you believe in!"

"No. I'm still using reason. A movie can be jinxed if the people in and around it are jinxed. Like Fred Gower."

She finished her wine.

"Like you, Fanny, Dennings, whoever plays the government agent."

She put down her glass and rose. "I'd better get going." She stepped around the coffee table and paused. "Why us? Why the actors?"

"The actors. The fucking actors."

"But it's only another kind of acting, of art . . ."

He smiled then. She stopped speaking. He realized it was an unfair stopper, that caustic smile. A movie trick. She deserved a real answer.

He said: "It *is* acting, *is* art, if you believe it is."

She went to the door, giving him a little wave.

"And you don't believe it. Neither do any of the others. Because the truly free souls are a very rare breed—a species of monster, actually—and I haven't met any yet at Freddy's parties. Certainly not you and Fanny. Now Freddy himself requires closer examination."

She said: "Goodnight, I really have to run."

He said: "Most of us know when we're rolling in the mud. So the movie is full of self-destructive people, and perhaps one true monster. So the movie is full of jinxed people. So the movie is jinxed."

She ran from him, leaving the door open behind her.

Thunder rolled. A sheet of water struck the house, making the cantilever structure shudder. He got up and went to the door. The Jag had just completed a U-turn, and was disappearing up the hill.

He pressed the gate button and closed the door.

He'd written a movie-type scene tonight, feeding Ce-

cily guilt, fear, extremes of black and white. He should
be ashamed of himself. But he wasn't.

He locked up and shut the lights.

He went to bed. His heart didn't beat quite right.
He knew it, could feel it, but the arrhythmia wasn't
marked enough to keep him awake. Still, it was regres-
sion.

Bub was alone in the Bedford Street house. Coleman
Berry's death had changed all plans.

Freddy was at Pandaro's for a late-session meeting
with the studio lawyers. No time for the Spanish
mother and son; lots to do to make sure the movie
could go ahead. But, as he'd put it to Bub, "The deal
looks clear."

Now if only *his* deal would clear up, Bub thought,
hovering around the phone, sweating over not hearing
from Giselle when they'd been supposed to decide
whether to blow the safe tonight or tomorrow.

Andro should have flown out of L.A. for Las Vegas
at six. So where the hell was Giselle?

He had the drill in the trunk of his Caddy. He was
ready to put the box with the nitro under the front
passenger's seat. He would prefer to do the job tonight, because too much waiting brought too much
thinking. And the thinking was all bad; all about
what could go wrong.

But whether they did it tonight or tomorrow, what
he wanted now was to hear the phone ring! She'd
promised to call as soon as she returned from taking
Andro to the airport—"no later than eight."

Say traffic had been bad. Say another hour on the
freeway. It still didn't explain why she hadn't called
by midnight!

He heard the rain whipping down on the pool, that
splashy water-on-water sound he'd always liked.

He didn't like it now! Motherfucking rain could
have held up flights.

But it hadn't started until ten-thirty, eleven. Andro's flight had left four to five hours sooner.

With or without Andro?

Bub had to know. Because if the job was postponed—indefinitely postponed—that nitro was going to be a real problem. Voodoo said it could be stored a long time if kept still and cool, "But sometimes it changes, man, and when it does, look out! Me, I wouldn't keep it around, period."

He picked up the phone and dialed.

His heart hammered as he listened to the ring at the other end. Six. Seven.

Giselle answered on the eighth ring. "All alone, on the telephone," she sang, and giggled. "Compliments of Salvatore's Golden Oldies."

Drunk, the bitch!

"It's Bub. You're drinking!"

"Mr. Andro's in the shower," she said, and dropped her voice. "Yes, I've had a few. Wouldn't you, after playing his dirty games in bed? And don't tell me I'm no Virgin Mary and such crap. He still makes it filthy."

"What happened? His daughter's waiting in Vegas, isn't she?"

"They changed their plans. She's coming here to-morrow, if the rain stops. If not, the next day. But he's staying home. I'd've phoned you in a few minutes . . ." She stopped, then whispered: "He's calling. Likes me to scrub his balls, on my knees, while I'm singing one of those old songs he taught me. Remind me to sing one for you next time. Like *Baby Face,* or *Ain't She Sweet,* or . . ."

"You'd better go." He hung up so as not to keep her; not to make Andro come out of that shower looking for her; not to fuck her up like he'd fucked up Albert and Brains . . . and Jason.

He went out to the garage, where the sound of rain on the uninsulated roof was a heavy drumming. He opened the storage fridge and stooped and looked over the six-packs to that wooden box. He sighed and closed the door. He took the drill from the trunk of his car, brought it back to his closet, then went to bed. The rain kept coming down, harder and harder. Not since May had they had a real storm, and now that there was no hope of doing the job, he began to enjoy it, began to feel the coolness, sensed the drought-parched earth soaking up moisture.

Thought of himself as a kid running around in the summer rain with his friends. Went back in time with the help of the sweet, wet-greenery odor pouring through his window. Kept remembering the past, so as not to think of the present. A present dominated right now by that box which could blow this house to hell if Freddy nudged the storage fridge with his car, or maybe even his shoulder.

Nine

Monday, September 5

Coming at any other time, the storm would have been welcomed by most Angelinos, rain-starved as they were. But this was the Labor Day weekend with many of them on the road, and driving became a horror. Also, thousands were camping and hiking, and their campsites were flooded. Lawn and pool parties ended early Sunday evening instead of carrying on into the wee hours, and movement was generally curtailed on this hectically active weekend.

Otis Daimler, however, didn't mind. True, he was in a car—one of Verity Trans. Inc.'s terminal vehicles, a five-year-old Volkswagen—and true he had to practically crawl as he approached Cecily Warren's house. But he'd planned to slow down at Cecily's house anyhow. Also, the lashing rain reduced the chances of his being seen, this time, or the first time he'd come by.

The first time had been at midnight, with the storm already sweeping the streets clear of cars and pedestrians. Cecily hadn't been here—at least her car hadn't—and there was no pleasure in casing an empty house. So he'd gone home, caught a few hours of sleep, and come back again at five-forty A.M., with the town ghostlike under the continuing, increasing tempest.

He came to a full stop near the driveway in which her Jaguar was now parked. He checked the house windows, three of them facing the street, and sure enough one was open. Just a few inches from the bottom, but enough to allow him entry, should he suddenly give the beast its freedom, its will.

It was a marvelous feeling, well worth the trouble of the two trips, knowing he could be inside that house and on her in about a minute. Though he wouldn't, of course, use an exposed front window; would go around back and try to find a duplicate entry.

A tremendous temptation, that, to satisfy himself and gain revenge for what all of them connected with the movie were doing to him.

It was official—they had decided to revise his script. And who was already in the process of doing it? The novelist, Baylis. Cecily Warren's stud; her cardiac-arrest sweetheart.

How he hated the man!

How superior he must feel, getting his story back to do with as he pleased. How amused, to be getting equal screen credit for tinkering with it a few weeks when Otis had slaved over it for months.

And Otis was unable to present any defense of his work. He was cut off from the producers and actors; from the entire movie. His agent said he was to "consider the relationship severed." Severed, indeed! He hadn't even been given the courtesy of an invitation to Denning's party on Friday, or Berry's on Saturday.

He accelerated and went to the east end of the street, and smiled. Berry had been punished by someone else's beast. Delightful touch, the killer being a cop and one of Berry's closest friends. How he wished he could have been there to see it! How he resented not being there to see it!

Well, something else for which he would punish Cecily, and through her Don Baylis and the others. She would be a long time dying, and screwing.

He had U-turned and was heading back toward her house when he saw car lights swing around the corner. Seemed to be going excessively fast, and he pulled over to the curb and stopped. *Was* going fast, and erratically, the lights winging from side to side, then far to one side. Finally, one light tilted up.

For a moment, it didn't make sense. Then he was able to see what had happened.

A small Japanese car—Toyota or Datsun—had stopped half on the sidewalk directly in front of Cecily Warren's house. Another car, a large American sedan, was parked at the curb. The Japanese car had almost run into it, necessitating the sudden stop, and probably a skid and swerve onto the sidewalk.

The car lights died. A figure got out and ran into the driveway. It hesitated near the front door, then ran past Cecily's Jaguar, into the back.

A woman, he thought, though he couldn't be sure at this distance and through heavy rain. Might even have been Cecily herself, though why she would be driving the Japanese car and not her Jaguar . . .

He began moving again, slowly passing her house, examining the car—a Datsun two-door. He went to the intersection and turned right and pulled to the curb. He backed up until he could see along the street. Now he was only a quarter of a block from Cecily Warren's house, and on the opposite side. Now he could see house and cars and everything clearly; could fantasize his break-in and attack clearly.

Fantasized so well the details of clutching and tearing and penetrating those tantalizingly camouflaged tubes and crevices that he became uncomfortably tight in the crotch, had to open his fly and free his erection. And then had to hold it, to squeeze it, to begin masturbating.

But he didn't finish. Because that figure was back at the Datsun. Because lights went on in Cecily Warren's house, including a front outside light, illuminating the figure reaching for the Datsun's door.

It was a woman, not unlike Cecily Warren, though he didn't think . . . couldn't be sure . . .

She was inside the car. The engine and lights came alive and the Datsun lurched backward and stopped, seeming to stall. And turned and went across the street and up on the opposite sidewalk. And jerked back, straightening, stalling again, then accelerated madly forward, up the street toward the corner on which Otis was parked.

He didn't have time to put his organ back in his pants. Nor could he have. It wouldn't go down, because the beast was beginning to break free, was demanding satisfaction.

Otis Daimler hoped the woman in the Datsun *wasn't* Ceily Warren. Because that would mean taking her before she was famous for her role in *Galt's Island*—notorious, recognizable, sought-after—before she was the prey to end all preys.

It would also risk hurting his chances of earning top money for his percentage of the film.

And it was spur-of-the-moment; went against his vow not to do anything without solid planning.

But he was backing out into the intersection and swinging around and driving after the Datsun. And he had only to glance down and see his rigid organ sticking up out of his trousers, tingling in the cool night air, quivering in anticipation, to know that this was something Otis Daimler wouldn't do.

Otis Daimler stepped back inside himself and watched as the Datsun reached Laurel Canyon and turned left toward the Basin. And skidded in its turn. And only just managed to straighten instead of hitting a lamppost.

The Datsun slowed. The beast was able to slow. Otis Daimler sighed in relief.

* * *

Because of the storm, Jorge had arrived half an hour later than his usual time of five A.M., this despite his leaving Santa Monica early in order to give himself leeway.

"Impossible!" he said. "Skidding, crawling, *inundacion*—flood—at some corners. I admit it, I felt my age while driving those long miles. Ai, Cecily, I need your *caricia*—soft caress."

And so they didn't talk the way Cecily had planned to. About her changing life, her changing circumstances, her changing needs in men. Step One, she'd thought, to be taken the moment he came in. Step One, to dampen his ardor. And again, the next time they met, and the next . . . and it would be finished.

But he was so worn, so anxious to relax in her arms, she couldn't deny him.

Worn or not, within minutes he was kissing her breasts, grasping her bottom, telling her in a mixture of fervent English and Spanish how much he had missed her. And then he was turning his body, maneuvering hers, so that they could perform sixty-nine. But more than anything today he wanted to mount her, to make love to her "in traditional fashion, *un hombre con una mujer,* a man with a woman, which is to say the man on top. Forgive the macho, *querida,* but I have the need."

He mounted her. He was strong in his need, the old man; rampant and exciting. She trembled as he began taking her. She loved it as he stroked deliberately; slowly and lovingly and deeply. She grasped his arms, his shoulders. She whispered: "What a man you are. What a man you must have been." And thought how difficult it would be when he finished and she began speaking of the end for Cecily and Jorge. Thought how hurt he would be.

And needn't have bothered worrying. Because he was spared all hurt in one tremendous hurt that began as she heard footsteps in the hallway outside the bedroom door. Her first thought was, *Johnny?* Then she knew it couldn't be him because the steps were so loud, they rushed and pounded so.

As she froze, and as Jorge felt it and began to ask, "What . . . ?" the door flew open, all the way, hitting the wall, and a figure stood there, fumbling for the switch.

The lights went on. It was Teresa in a gold raincoat from beneath which her long gray hospital dress showed. Her hair was dripping, her mouth a garish red smear of lipstick, her cheeks heavily, clownishly, rouged. Her eyes were fixed on the bed and on the nude figures still linked in coitus.

A doll, Cecily thought, shocked into paralysis. *A wide-eyed painted doll.*

And then the doll shrieked, *"Pop, no, you promised!"* and rushed at the bed with hands extended clawlike; rushed at Jorge Resordo, who choked and fell away from her and curled up and choked again and rolled across the bed and onto the floor.

"You'll never stop!" Teresa screamed, coming around the bed after him. *"You'll keep fucking us, fucking us!"*

And then she stopped. Then she backed up a step. Then Cecily was able to get off the bed and into the bathroom, where she locked the door in terror of her madwoman sister and got her bathrobe off the door hook and sat trembling on the closed toilet seat.

Then she heard Johnny's voice. "Mom? What's going on? Who're you? Where's . . . ?"

He cried out. Cecily leaped up and opened the door, ready to kill her sister if she hurt her son.

Teresa was gone.

"Where is she?"

Johnny was looking down at the floor on the other side of the bed. "She ran right over me. Your friend Horgey's passed out."

She couldn't see Jorge, but Johnny could. Johnny

was looking at him as he lay naked on the bedroom floor. Johnny knew his name.

But she had no time for Johnny now, or for Jorge, Teresa was running around somewhere, maybe still in the house.

"Let's find Aunt Teresa," she said, and came to him and began to turn him toward the door . . . and finally looked at Jorge.

"God!" she said; and then, "Johnny, look around and see if Aunt Teresa's still here."

"I heard the front door close."

"Make sure."

As soon as he was gone, she dropped to her knees beside the old man, who looked so terrible with his purple face, bulging eyes, gaping mouth, and protruding tongue. As if he'd been choked to death, or frightened to death.

Some sort of stroke? Shock when Teresa had come screaming at him? And a blood vessel had burst in that just-turned-seventy-two-year-old brain. And her dear friend was a purple-faced corpse.

She was sure he was dead. But she bent her ear to his chest, and heard nothing. She took his wrist and moved her fingers around, trying to find a pulse, and failed. She put her ear to his mouth, to catch any whisper of breath, and there was no breath. She shook him and said: "Jorge!"

Johnny was coming back. She ran out the door and closed it behind her.

"No one's here, mom. I put on all the lights and I saw someone outside getting in a car. Was that Aunt Teresa? She looked . . . you know, with her mouth and cheeks painted up."

"Stage play," she said, the first thing she could think of. "Go back to bed now."

"But Horgey's passed out in your room."

"He got up and went home. Go to bed."

"How could he go home? I was at the front door."

"He went out the back, past the pool and down the alley. He was ashamed, you know, to see you."

"How'd he get dressed so fast?"

"He just put on a raincoat and carried his clothes."

"There's a big car—I think it's a Buick—parked out front. I seen it before. I think it's Horgey's. So how'd he . . . ?"

"Go to bed!" she shouted.

"Okay!" he shouted back, and ran across the hall to his room.

She said, "Johnny," and he said, "Yeah, sure, you're sorry," and slammed the door.

She nodded slowly. She *was* sorry. For many things.

She took herself in hand. She had to do something about Jorge.

Call the police, an ambulance, the paramedics?

What for? He was dead. His wife would be humiliated. Jorge's memory would be humiliated. Cecily Warren and Johnny Warren would be humiliated.

She had to move Jorge somewhere else.

She went back to her room and dressed, not looking at him, though once she called softly, hoping it was all a terrible mistake, "Jorge, let's go."

After dressing, she sat down on her bed and picked up the phone. It would probably finish things for good with Don. But then again, he already knew about Jorge Resordo. More important, she had no choice.

She dialed, and heard the recorded voice, and said: "Of course. He won't be awake. He won't answer me even if he is awake. Like yesterday when he wouldn't answer."

She was crying when his voice ended and the beep sounded and it was time to leave her message. "Donny," she wept, "help me. Jinxed, Donny, you were right." She lay down and tried to think of who else to call. And there was no one else. She had to do it

alone—dress him and put him in his car and drive him
to his office and take a cab back.

Someone might see her. The cab driver would see
her. In L.A. you had to call a cab; they didn't cruise.
There'd be a record and maybe she'd get in trouble
and maybe it would all come out and Johnny, her
screwed up Johnny, her victim son . . .

The phone rang.

She sat up. "Please God," she prayed, and lifted the
handset.

God was good. "What is it?" Donny asked. "What's
happened?"

She told him. He understood immediately. "You
can't have him found in your home," he said. "Does
Johnny know?"

She said, "Yes," and he said, "We'll talk when I get
there," and she said, "Are you sure you feel well
enough? Maybe you have a friend . . . ?"

He gave a little laugh. "There's no friend for anything like this."

She went into the hall and stopped at Johnny's
door. She heard nothing and wanted to walk in and
see if he was asleep. She had never hesitated to do exactly what she wanted with her son, but now she hesitated. Now she was afraid, ashamed, to open his door.

She moved a chair over to the window and looked
out at the street. A quarter after six and still nighttime
dark because of the black clouds and continuing
downpour.

She looked at Jorge's Oldsmobile—Johnny had been
wrong to call it a Buick—which he'd maintained so
beautifully. He loved his car, he'd said, only a little
less than he loved her. "Always, *querida*, I've had
Oldsmobiles. Since the LaSalle, a car you will not remember, went out of business, I have had Oldsmobiles.
I do not change cars. I do not change wives. And, my
dearest child, I do not change lovers."

Faithful unto death, she thought. That's what they could say at his funeral . . . if she got him out of here and somewhere safe for his reputation.

She stopped thinking of him. He was gone. She stopped thinking of herself and her son. Donny would take care of them.

She thought of Teresa out in this wild storm.

Johnny said he'd seen her getting into a car. She hadn't driven since entering Restwell four and a half years ago.

She should call the police, the hospital.

But then officials would be involved. Then Teresa might be found tonight, tomorrow, and talk about Jorge and it would all come out.

Teresa had done this thing to Jorge and now she was on her own. If enough time passed before she was found, she would forget about tonight as she forgot so many things.

And maybe she wouldn't be found. Maybe she'd leave L.A. and start over again someplace else. Maybe someone was driving for her, a man, taking care of her.

She certainly couldn't drive alone after all that time, especially on such a terrible night!

But on second thought, knowing Teresa, if she'd managed to bust out, she could just as well have managed to take a car. As for driving, they said you never forgot how, like roller skating or riding a bike. And nothing had ever scared that Bajorka but her own past, her own nightmares. So even if she was on her own, she might just make it all right.

Besides, sending her back to that hospital, to the sedated days, months, years, was like burying her alive.

Cecily prayed for her sister, for her sister's safety, and tried to block the thought that the jinx was spreading.

* * *

Teresa drove, shouting, "It wasn't pop! Of course it wasn't! She's gonna call the cops on me because he fell down and his face . . . Christ, his face!"

She rocked in her seat, peering through the wiper-smeared windshield, through the rain-distorted night, to the semiflooded road.

"All night, damm it! All night this way! It's gotta end!"

It didn't end. She drove past Ventura Boulevard, remembering coming here with Huey, her boyfriend, to shop and look in store windows and drive from his Studio City place to a restaurant in Sherman Oaks. She remembered eating steak and drinking Margueritas and driving back to Laurel and then to Mulholland. Where they would look at the Valley view from one of the many parking spaces, at the miles of Valley lights, and kiss and make out, sometimes all the way when she'd open his pants and straddle him and watch his face.

"Where are you?" she asked Huey. "I didn't mean to hurt you, baby. It was *pop*."

It was always pop, and it was always someone else who got hurt.

Like the old man fucking Cecily tonight.

Like Tansy, the new nurse back at Restwell.

She moaned a little then, and saw the traffic signal change to red, and was afraid to slam on the brakes. She'd skid like she had so many times tonight.

"Tansy, you *fool*," she moaned, and went through the red signal, and didn't want to think of Tansy and did.

She'd set fire to her room at a little after midnight, and it had gone even better than she'd hoped. That plastic wall covering had blazed up so fast and spread so fast the staff had opened every door in the place and used the P.A. system to tell everyone to run.

But Tansy had come to make sure her patients all got out. Teresa hadn't even had to look for her; Tansy had met her in the hall and begun leading her through that stinking gray smoke and Teresa had simply put a hand in her pocket and taken the wallet. And said: "I'm all right, but some of the others aren't leaving."

So of course the dummy'd gone back to help, when all the patients were gone because the fire and choking smoke was everywhere and they weren't *that* crazy.

Teresa had gone to the parking lot and the red Datsun and started it up easily enough. Then began this endless night of driving. Then began the bucking and stalling and skidding and swerving, and if there'd been more than just a handful of cars on the road, she'd have run into one for sure.

As it was, she'd spent almost an hour locating the Las Virgenes entrance to the slick, partially flooded road that was the Ventura Freeway. And on the freeway had stopped at the side five or six times to rest, to control her shaking, to gather her scattered thoughts.

During the second rest, she'd put on the radio. The hourly news had reported the fire, "and one tragic death, Nurse Tansy McHardy, due to smoke inhalation."

Teresa had shrieked laughter, and driven back on the road.

"Not my fault," she said, remembering that moment with pain, navigating the upward portion of Laurel more and more slowly. "No one but a *fool* would go back."

She saw the red light in plenty of time, but went through it because she wanted to get to the top of the hill without skidding, without sliding, without stopping. And no one around anyway. And soon, as she remembered, she'd reach the top of Laurel, the road at the crest of the long ridge separating the San Fernando Valley from the Los Angeles Basin—Mulholland Drive, famous as a lovers' parking place, where she and Huey . . .

"God," she said, "I'm tired."

She'd been on the road from Restwell to Cecily's house almost five hours. Not only because of the storm and her inexperience as a driver, but she'd forgotten her routes and gotten lost and had to backtrack and stop to ask a gas station attendant directions. And had to go to the toilet, but didn't want to get out of the car wearing that hospital dress. Also, the Datsun's gas gauge read almost empty.

She'd had money. Poor Tansy's money.

She'd told the attendant, "Fill 'er up," and looked in the back seat for something to wear, and there was nothing.

So she'd paid and driven out and back onto the freeway. A while later, she'd stopped to make behind the car, then remembered the trunk. She'd opened it and found the gold raincoat, small because Tansy had been small.

Now she saw headlights in her rearview mirror, but not very close. Nothing in front and nothing anywhere else, so again she passed a red light. She turned left and drove along winding, curving Mulholland, and the rain was unbelievable!

She saw the parking place across the road on her left, on the Valley side, and stopped dead. Was it the one Huey had taken her to?

Behind her, headlights showed around a turn, and she thought she'd get a blare of horn. But no, the other car just stopped, waiting.

Teresa swung across the road and onto the dirt parking spot. She cut lights and engine and leaned back and closed her eyes. Nothing to see anyway—the view was blotted out tonight. But she wanted to be where Huey had taken her for what had been one of her last nights of love. And wondered if he would still be hot for her if he saw her now.

She switched on the interior lights and turned the rearview mirror so as to see her face.

Hard to tell if she'd used enough makeup.

Best to be safe, and she added a bit more of the lipstick and blush she'd found in the glove compartment; then switched off the light.

If anyone saw her now, she'd be ready.

If she met Rob Dennings tonight, she'd be ready. And he'd know which one of the Bajorka sisters had the looks, the sex appeal, the talent.

She'd forgotten her rage because of what had happened in Cecily's bedroom. But damned if she'd forget it for long!

Tomorrow, first thing, when this goddamn rain stopped, she'd return to Cecily's and tell her the score! Tomorrow she'd give her a choice: work big sister into the movie, or by Jesus . . .

The door opened; the interior light flashed on.

She cried out, leaning away from the big face bending toward her.

"Is everything all right, miss? I saw your car and thought you might need assistance."

"Oh!" She put her hand to her heart, theatrically, to show how he'd startled her. And laughed, to show she was now relieved of fear. And saw he was big, heavy, but not bad looking. A man, damn it, and not old like Cecily's, or like pop. Strong looking. And *kind* to want to help her.

"No, I'm quite all right." She drew the gold raincoat close around her in an attempt to hide the ugly hospital gown. "But you're getting all wet!" She gave him the big vamp smile. "I *was* frightened by the storm, and I *could* use a little company."

He said, "Fine," and, "Why don't you move over?" and she wondered briefly why he didn't go around to the other side. But then again the door was already open and he wasn't wearing a raincoat; not even a jacket.

But then she saw he was *holding* a jacket, a Windbreaker. She slid over and he got behind the wheel, the Windbreaker in his lap.

The door closed. It was dark. She let go of her raincoat. "On clear nights," she said, "this spot has the most beautiful view."

"Yes, I know. I live in the vicinity. Nichols Canyon, just about ten minutes from here, on the Basin side."

"Exclusive area, isn't it?"

"Expensive, anyway."

She pealed laughter. "You're witty, Mr. . . ." And then, with hand back at her breast, "Goodness, we haven't been introduced."

He smiled then. A very wide smile. "My name is Otis Daimler."

"French? Ah, *bon appetit*."

He laughed. "The same to you."

She figured she'd blown the line somehow, but joined him in laughing, and said: "We're both witty."

He put his arm up on the top of the seat. His hand was hanging down near her shoulder; a very big hand.

"*Your* name?" he asked.

"How silly of me!" But she found it hard to put on the big act now. She was breathing fast, and that hand, those thick, long fingers, moved further along the seat. She shivered as they brushed the back of her neck.

"Teri Barker."

"You remind me of someone," he said. "An actress. A friend named Cecily Warren."

Her eyes jerked to his. "Really! But what a gas! I'm her sister! Warren's her married name. Barker's my stage name. We're really the Bajorka sisters."

"I'm delighted to meet you," he said, and bent his head and kissed her on the mouth.

She was speechless.

She wanted some action, yes, but he'd moved so . . . so *unexpectedly*.

But then he withdrew and spoke casually, and she figured what-the-hell.

"Are you an actress like your sister?"

"A lot better than my sister. And I sing, dance, do specialties."

"Fuck?"

"What?" It had come at her from nowhere.

"I said, do you fuck?"

"Not lately," she answered, plenty angry . . . but even more excited.

"Then why waste time?" he said, and moved in on her and wrapped her in his arms and began doing things to her clothes. His mouth pressed over hers, wide open and sucking so that she could hardly breathe. And his fingers dug into her crotch, pulling the white cotton panties aside.

She couldn't stop him. He was all over her, so big and so heavy and those hands so terribly strong.

Those fingers in her crotch kept digging. Before she knew it, her thighs parted and her head went back and she felt her breasts being torn from their brassiere and squeezed so hard she wailed. And came.

He raised his head and smiled. He flung the Windbreaker off his lap and said, *"Bon appetit."* One hand was on the back of her neck and she had no choice but to go down.

That's when she saw his fly was wide open and his tool sticking straight up.

Since she was no longer on fire, she said: "Wait a minute!"

His hand tightened. "Don't be selfish. I did you, now you do me."

She could barely breathe. His fingers were so long, they almost enveloped her neck. "You're . . . right," she gasped.

He let up.

She took his tool in her hand, and he sighed and leaned back. She licked it, like she used to Huey's, and he said, "Suck it now," not asking like Huey used to. *Ordering!*

She figured she'd bite the bastard a good one and be outside and running . . .

The hand was tightening again. "Don't even *scrape* it."

She knew then she had to do as he said. She knew then he could hurt her.

And what the hell, hadn't she dreamed of sucking a big cock, fucking a big cock? And wasn't this a beauty?

She got to work. He moaned and panted, and she wondered if he'd warn her before he came. And tried to judge for herself so she could pull back.

He began to spasm. She began to pull back. The hand on her neck tightened, paralyzing her, and his come filled her mouth and throat, choking her. And he didn't let up, saying, "Swallow, bitch!" until she did.

He let her go. He leaned back and stretched. His cock had gone down, but not all the way. He said: "Play with it."

"I have to get home."

He slapped her. With that big, meaty hand. She went into the door and bounced and reached for his face, screaming, "Dirty son of a bitch!"

He slapped her again, even harder. She saw stars and got groggy.

He said: "Be a good girl now, Cecily. Play with it."

She wanted to say she was Teresa, not Cecily, but his hand drew back again and she trembled with fear of a man for the first time in her life. Not even pop had scared her. Sickened and enraged her, yes, but not scared her. And she was a woman now, not a kid. She was as tough as they came now, and still she trembled.

"All right. But no more hitting."

The third slap must have put her out of it for a while, because the next thing she knew he was going over her face with a wet handkerchief. "Have to get this paint off your face, Cecily, so you'll look right for our mating."

He was scrubbing her, and she was glad when he stopped. But then he reached down and tore her rain-coat up the buttons, and ripped open her dress, and pulled her panties down over her knees to her ankles. "Kick them off," he said. "Too bad this car is so small. Mine is even smaller. But we'll make do, won't we, Cecily?"

She understood now why he'd wanted her out from behind the wheel. He'd known he was going to fuck her, do what he wanted to her, from the very begin-ning.

She thought then of the Hillside Strangler who'd raped and killed a dozen or more women in L.A. and who had set off a series of copycat killings, and she had to fight against hysteria. If he was one of those, if he was going to kill her . . .

"You won't hurt . . ." she began.

He pulled back that big hand.

She grabbed his cock and stroked it and bent when he pressed down on her head and sucked until it was hard.

He got her on his lap, facing him, straddling him.

"You're not moving," he said, and his hand went to her throat and pushed until her head pressed the windshield and squeezed until she couldn't breathe.

Choking, she humped his dick.

He released his grip, a little, so she could suck in a breath.

She humped as hard as she could, ground as hard as she could, so he wouldn't tighten that hand again.

Teresa Bajorka was gasping, actually sobbing and trying to hide it, terrified because this man was no Huey. This man, this animal . . .

He kept calling her "Cecily, bitch, cunt, whore-of-whores," until he finally came.

Then he said: "You're lucky. You're not her. I won't drag it out."

"Thank . . ." she began, thinking that meant he was leaving.

Instead, the hand on her throat tightened and shoved, and at the same instant he rammed the heel of his other hand under her nose . . . both with enormous strength and purpose. So that her head didn't just shatter the windshield but went through it. So that her neck wasn't just torn but also broken. So that she died of two massive injuries—neck and brain—simultaneously.

So that she finished her life on a note of hope, with the beginnings of a smile; the proverbial happy ending.

As usual, Otis had to clean up after the beast.

He got out of the car and adjusted his clothing and put on his Windbreaker. He leaned into the open door and pulled her around and behind the wheel. He turned the key in the ignition.

The rain had eased up somewhat, but he was still soaked before he got the engine started and the shift-lever into drive. Then he pushed the Datsun over the edge and down the cliffside.

He watched for an explosion, for fire, and sure enough there was a flash and a dull *thump* as the gas tank went. Then some reddish flickering through the murk of rain and mist, and continued sounds of grinding, sliding, crunching. Then just the smell of burning oil and rubber rising from below.

Car lights on Mulholland reminded him that he wasn't alone in the world.

He hurried back past a clump of brush and drought-stunted eucalyptus to the smaller parking area where he'd left the Volkswagen.

He drove onto Mulholland and proceeded carefully along the rain-slick road for about five minutes before finding his turn onto Nichols Canyon. Another five minutes and he was parked in his garage, using the electric eye unit to shut the door behind him.

He sat still a moment, trying to think of areas of danger, and could find none.

He went inside, and into the shower. He was out in record time and in bed before seven of a very dark, dismal morning. But he was far from displeased with either the morning or the night which had preceded it. He could now visit his wife, write his scripts, maintain his house.

It would be a while before the beast began pushing again.

They dressed Jorge Resordo together, after first lifting him onto the bed. It was unpleasant, and difficult, and Don sent Cecily twice to make sure Johnny didn't leave his room.

The second time she said: "I think he knows. But if he stays in there until after we leave, he can't be sure. His window faces the back."

Don finished buckling Resordo's belt and began tying his shoelaces.

Such a terrible face, he thought. So twisted, distorted. He wished he could straighten it out.

The hardest part was putting on the tie. He finally had to pull Resordo into a sitting position and get behind him so as to duplicate the way he made a knot. And then, when he'd almost finished, Cecily said: "That's wrong. He always wore a Windsor—the thick knot. He was a sharp dresser."

So he had to pull it out and start again. And do it over three times before getting the Windsor correct, a knot he hadn't used since his boyhood in Brooklyn.

By the time they were ready to leave, he had to sit down a moment, had to catch his breath. Cecily came over to him, timidly touched his face. "Are you all right?"

He nodded. But he wasn't. He wasn't getting enough breath. He'd been working long hours, hard hours, and now this.

He decided he would see the doctor within the week . . . reassure himself.

But he knew what he'd be told: Less work, less stress, stricter diet.

And no hauling of your girlfriend's dead lovers around Los Angeles.

He smiled. Cecily said: "Wish *I* could think of something funny."

He got up. "Pull your Jag out of the driveway. Drive Resordo's Olds in so the passenger's side will face your kitchen door. I'd do it for you, but it's best we create less possibility of notice, of talk. Your neighbors know you; they don't know me."

She took the keys he handed her; the keys he'd found in Resordo's raincoat pocket. She began to leave; then looked back at Resordo, now propped against the headboard. "His hair."

"I'll take care of it," he said.

He found a brush in the bathroom and used it on the corpse's thinning gray hair. All that remained now was to put him into his raincoat.

Which he and Cecily did together after she returned, struggling to keep him erect.

They rested a moment, Resordo sagging between them, then they started out of the room.

The door across the hall opened and Johnny stood there.

"Drunk." Cecily said. "We're taking him home."

The boy said: "Hi, Mr. Baylis."

Don said: "Hi. Why don't you change out of those pajamas—get dressed—so that when we come back, we can all go out to breakfast?"

Johnny smiled, nodding, but his eyes remained on Resordo's face, that twisted, apoplectic face; that obviously dead face. "Okay. Where'll we go?"

Don saw that Cecily was about to shout, and quickly said: "We'll let you pick it."

"Great! Even a big hotel?"

"Only if you're dressed when we get back."

The boy turned and ran into his room.

"You did that well," Cecily said, as they began moving down the hall toward the kitchen and the front door. "You don't really dislike him, do you?"

He was straining to carry his side of the body, and gasped: "Later."

The rain had lessened considerably; the skies had lightened. It was only seven-fifteen and a legal holiday, so no one was on the street as they moved to the Olds.

They got Resordo in, then quickly closed the front passenger's door, allowing him to sag against it. Cecily went around the other side and Don went in the back, and between them they propped him firmly into a corner.

"He had a hat," Cecily said, and ran into the house.

She emerged a moment later with a tan rainhat. Don put it on Resordo's head, pushing it low over his eyes, as might be worn by a man trying to sleep.

"Anything else?" he asked. "Think carefully now. Once we leave him near his office, it'll be too late. Watch, rings?"

"He never took them off when he . . ." She stopped.

He turned to walk to his Mercedes, parked at the corner. "I'll follow," he said.

She drove slowly, and he could see her look at Resordo every time she took a turn, especially a left turn, which could dislodge him from his corner.

They went via Laurel to Sunset, and here traffic was more noticeable. Then down LaBrea to Wilshire, and east all the way to Western and a few blocks beyond. Traffic was a little heavier, but still incredibly light by normal standards.

There was no problem finding a space on the side street where Resordo usually parked. Don was right behind her, and got out and walked to the Olds, looking around. Still no pedestrians; no one to show any interest in them.

"Leave the key in the ignition," he said, when from force of habit she reached for it.

She got out, pulling Resordo across the seat so that he was behind the wheel. She began propping him up.

"No," Don said, and stepped in. He gave Resordo a gentle push, allowing him to topple onto his side, then shut the door and took her arm. "He'd fall in his death spasms."

"Shouldn't we wipe the handles, the steering wheel?"

He kept walking. "There's no reason for anyone to check for fingerprints. It's obvious he died of a stroke—cerebral rupture or occlusion. Any medical examiner will be able to see that."

A moment later, they pulled out past the parked Oldsmobile. They couldn't see Jorge Resordo . . . and probably no one else would, at least from a car. Eventually, a pedestrian would notice. Or, after Mrs. Resordo began worrying, she or relatives would drive down and look around, since Jorge had told her he was working; always used work as a cover for his early morning trysts with Cecily.

They were back in Cecily's house at eight-twenty, just an hour and five minutes from the time they'd left.

"Seems longer," she said, going to the range to put up water for coffee.

"We're eating out, remember?"

"He's watching television," she said, jerking her head at a doorway. Don could hear the sound of shouts, shots. "We'll have time for coffee. Or do you want tea, juice . . . ?"

"Coffee's fine," he said, opening his raincoat and sinking into a chair at the table.

The TV went off. Don looked up, and Johnny was coming into the room. "Hi, ready for the Bel Air Hotel?" He was carrying a book.

Don smiled a little. "I don't think they serve breakfast."

"I'm sure I saw it on that menu board when we went there. But okay. Make it the main dining room at the Century Plaza."

Cecily said: "How about the main dining room at Denny's?"

"He promised!"

"I promised," Don said. "And I keep my promises. What's that book?"

Johnny turned it around and held it up. *"Trip-Out,* by a writer near and dear to all of us."

Cecily was watching, and Don wondered why her expression was so bleak. He himself had to smile. "Read any of it?"

"Almost half." He turned the book around, riffling pages. "Ask me questions."

"That's not necessary. If you've read it, you're the gainer. I mean for having read *any* book, though that one is a little beyond your age level."

"Sexy-schmexy, you mean."

Again Don had to smile. Again he wondered at Cecily's bleak expression; at the way she kept watching the boy. She said: "I'll ask you some questions."

"You didn't finish it, mom."

"I'll ask only about the first half; the half we both read. Ready?"

The boy was smiling, nodding, but his eyes were jumpy. And Don understood. He lied even about pointless things like this. He was hotdogging; scoring points.

"Let's forget it," Don said. "And turn off the range. We'll have coffee out."

"The Century Plaza," Johnny said, putting the book down on a counter and moving away; disassociating himself from it, Don thought.

"I'm not dressed for that formal a place," Don said, spreading open his raincoat to reveal tan slacks and a cross-striped rugby-style sport shirt. "I don't even have a jacket."

"Why didn't you take Horgey's? He won't be needing it."

Cecily said: "God!"

Johnny quickly laughed. "Just kidding."

Don was beginning to feel those chest pains again. Too much tension here. Too big a problem here.

And yet when the boy smiled, really smiled, he was attractive. When he didn't push, sweat, deal, cheat . . .

Don wanted to tell him that it was so much easier, so much more pleasurable, not to hustle your way through life.

But you couldn't simply say such a thing to such a boy. You had to demonstrate it over and over, day by day.

He stood up. "I really didn't think it through, Johnny, when I promised you any restaurant you wanted. I forgot about my clothes. But I know a very fine place in Westwood that serves breakfasts on Saturdays, Sundays, and holidays, and they don't mind casual dress. You can order eggs any way you've ever heard of—Benedict, for example, or omelettes to your own specifications. And hot cakes and waffles and croissants and ham steaks and sausage and Canadian bacon . . ."

"You got it!" the kid yelled, grinning and waving his hands in stop-signals.

"And you get a rain check," Don said, "on that hotel dining room."

"Fair enough!"

Don looked at Cecily. She made a smile for him. "I'll go freshen up."

"I'll get my jacket and yachting cap!"

"The tweed jacket and no yachting cap," Cecily said. "You've worn that outfit to death."

"Aw, but I look great in it."

"You look great in everything, Boy Wonder." Her smile was finally relaxed and real. "Get moving."

"Aye, aye, Captain Bligh."

He ran to beat her to the doorway. She bent and slapped his bottom. They disappeared, laughing and running.

Don walked into the study and looked around. A large-screen TV set, and what his mother had called "chatchkas" on the bookshelves—gimcrackery; little glass and ceramic animal figures and ashtrays and dishes. And mementos like coconuts that had held Polynesian drinks. And several kinds of candles. And a painting on the wall, a sailing ship—slick, romanticized, awful even by Starving Artists' standards.

He went down the hall and came to Johnny's room and looked in and the boy wasn't there. A group of books on the dresser. Three pictures of his mother; one of a sullen-looking man, probably his father; another of a couple dressed in a fashion of the past, an old, yellowed photograph. Another awful painting, a landscape, but better because it was smaller.

He went to Cecily's room. Their voices came from the bathroom, where Johnny was *ouching* and complaining as she washed his face. Don had been here an hour ago, but Resordo had filled the room, dominated the room.

Now he saw the shelves against the left wall, empty except for five of his books that he'd given her early in their relationship.

Pictures on the dresser, one of them his. And one a blond woman, quite handsome, reminiscent of Cecily in eyes and mouth, but stronger looking, harder looking. The sister, Teresa.

Cecily's mother and father in another old picture, a

different pose, the father with big mustaches and a rigid smile; the mother solemn and worn-looking.

He walked to the closet and pulled open the folding doors. Jam packed with clothing, wall to wall, including her mink and several full-length suedes.

On the wall, a small Van Gogh print, overpowered by a gaudy gold metal frame.

Standard dingbat digs, he thought, as he returned to the kitchen.

The refrigerator held a goodly percentage of standard dingbat food—peanut butter and jam and Cool Whip and snack-type cheeses; the freezer was full of frozen pizzas and TV dinners.

The cabinets held more of the same—crackers and cookies and candies and potato chips and taco chips and pretzels.

He heard them coming, and moved to the table.

None of his business. He wasn't going to take on the job of turning that boy around, of living with Cecily's promiscuity, bad taste, and so-called career. Maybe a lifetime ago, before the heart attack. And even then, it would have been a ball-breaker.

They went to Westwood. The rain was now a drizzle, and cars were beginning to make this look like L.A. again, home of the county-to-county traffic jam.

Jeremy's had a good crowd, mainly families, but there were still tables available, and soon they were being served an enormous breakfast.

Or Cecily and Johnny were; he limited himself to fruit and Jeremy's great hot cereal—a blend of five whole grains—though he refused to pass up the superb chicoried coffee. The table was covered with ham and bacon and waffles and hotcakes, and the Warrens were demolishing everything in sight.

Don smiled. His mother would have forgiven almost anything in people who ate like this. Watching them, talking with them, laughing with them, feeling Cecily's hand press his thigh every so often, seeing Johnny

lean back and smother a burp and begin eating
again—being in this family group among other family
groups—he realized how isolated he'd become.

And despite Resordo, despite all his criticism of
mother and son, despite a feeling of weakness and exhaustion, despite a host of negatives, he was enjoying
himself more than he had in a long time.

He looked at Cecily, and he loved her, chatchkas
and dingbat food and bad art and promiscuity notwithstanding. That was the plain truth of it, the ir-
reducible nut at the heart of it: He loved her. And
now knew he would as long as he didn't launch a life-
wrenching battle against it.

And Johnny was part of her.

He would love the boy, too, in time.

"What's wrong?" Cecily asked, leaning close and
taking his hand. "Aren't you feeling well?" She'd obviously misread his change of expression, his sudden
realization.

"He's okay," Johnny said, but stopped eating.
"You're okay, aren't you, Don?"

Not Mr. Baylis. Don. The warmth was spreading.

Love could spread, too; not just jinxes.

"I'm fine," he said, and in fact the discomfort in his
chest had lifted. He was still tired, but he was no
longer worried about it. He had to get back to work
on the script, but another hour or two wouldn't matter.

He took her hand. He raised it and kissed it, and
Johnny watched as he drank the coffee he'd insisted
on having. He spoke to the boy. "I know you love
your mother. Do you know that *I* love her?"

Johnny grinned and shrugged. "Doesn't everyone?"

It was a catch-phrase, a one-liner, a joke. It was also
a shocker, and revealing as hell. Cecily froze; then decided to laugh.

"Not the way I do," Don said.

"Just kidding," the boy said, attacking the remains

of his ham steak. And sneaked a sly, worried-but-amused look at his mother; a vengeful little look.

Which cut in on the warmth. Which reintroduced a reality other than love.

Still, Don kissed her hand again, and said: "We've got to make some sort of arrangement. We've got to start doing this kind of thing regularly."

"After I finish the movie," she murmured.

The remainder of which further slowed things, yet he nodded and pushed ahead. "And we have to go on to something more."

Her smile was tentative. "I didn't think you wanted . . . you've been so cool . . . to do this for me and Johnny."

"I'm not doing it for you and Johnny. I'm doing it for me."

"Are you sure?"

He nodded vigorously, but of course he wasn't sure.

Johnny said: "So when do we put a lock on the TV, and me in military school?"

He was grinning, and he was frightened.

"He understands everything," Cecily said, apologetically.

Don spoke to the boy. "We're just talking. But say we all get together. There won't be any sudden change in your life. You'll hardly notice it."

"As Mr. Lion said to Mr. Lamb before the big *crunch*."

Cecily smothered a laugh. Don gave them the obligatory smile, and returned to his cereal.

Johnny was subdued from then on.

So was Don.

Back at the house, Johnny went inside; Don and Cecily spoke on the sidewalk near the Mercedes. The rain had stopped; the sky was beginning to clear.

"I wish I knew where Teresa was," she said.

"Perhaps she returned to the hospital."

"Never. She hates it. It's just a prison for her anyway—she's not getting any better there." She thought a moment. "Now that the rain's stopped, she might have gone home—to the ranch, I mean." Another pause. "But I doubt it. Nothing for her there either. I'll call my mother later anyway."

"Why do you think she came here?"

"I'm all she has, unless someone helped her break out of Restwell. Or she heard about the movie . . ." She stopped.

"Yes?"

"Nothing," Cecily muttered. "Little sisterly rivalry, at least on her part." Then she said: "But it could have been because she wanted to see me and Johnny. I hope that was it! I hope she remembered the *good* things. Maybe if Jorge hadn't been here . . ."

Don said not to dwell on it.

She said: "Yes. Teresa will be all right. The odds favor it. How many terrible things can happen in one weekend anyway, even with a jinx?"

"I have to apologize for that jinx lecture."

She put a finger to his lips. "We'll never mention the word again."

But she did mention it again, weeping, nearly hysterical, when she called three hours later to say she'd been contacted by someone at Restwell, who'd been contacted by the L.A. police, who'd traced the license plates on a wrecked Datsun to a nurse named Tansy McHardy.

"Teresa's dead—all smashed up and burned in a car accident! That jinx, Donny! Coleman and Jorge and now Teresa! That damned jinx! Just like you said—spreading out from the movie and the people working on the movie!"

He said he was coming right over. She was to call her doctor and to "forget that nonsense!"

Yet counting the bodies, he almost believed in the jinx himself.

* * *

Freddy was out again, at Dennings's Malibu place this time, meeting there with the actor-director and Pandaro. They'd been together at the Fox lot earlier, and then at Tajunga Studios where, Freddy told Bub when he came home to shower and have a quick bite to eat, they were going to transfer the production. "Pandaro has stock in Tajunga and can get a break on everything from stage rentals to postproduction equipment and technicians."

"The porno angle wouldn't have anything to do with it, right?"

Freddy had grinned. "You've got a devious mind, man." Then, "We anticipated problems after a meeting with Fox executives. One kept asking if there was any truth to the rumors we'd be shooting sex scenes on closed sets. I said that even bare boobs were shot on closed sets, but the questions kept coming. When we were told they'd prefer to 'monitor' our shootings, we knew it would be more trouble than it was worth."

"And Tajunga won't be trouble?"

"Pandaro has the chairman in his pocket. And since he's inherited Berry's points, he can afford to hand out maybe a half point, maybe one, as grease."

Bub was alone at nine-thirty watching the tube in the living room, when the phone rang. He answered it in his best houseboy manner, because it hadn't come in on his private number. "Mr. Gower's residence."

"It's Giselle. I tried your number but no answer. Can you talk?"

"Yes."

"He's gone for the night. He and his sister are visiting another relative in San Diego. He said they won't be back until tomorrow afternoon."

"Then we can do it! I'll get going!"

"No! The sister came with someone; a friend. She's upstairs right now, setting her hair."

He was quiet for a moment. "Always something, Giselle. I get the feeling you're back to where you were at the beginning—stalling, faking, keeping it going for the fun, the fantasy."

"I swear . . . !"

"I've got a tube of nitro sitting in the garage, and I'm not sleeping well, and I told you I'll do it myself if you back out."

"But I'm *not* faking!"

He went right on, as if she hadn't spoken. "I won't wait too much longer. I'll case the place myself, come in when he's gone, whether you help or not."

"You don't give a damn about me! You don't care if you get me killed!"

But he did. Because he'd already gotten Brains and Albert killed. He softened his voice. "Let's get together tonight."

She was breathing heavily. "The way you talk," she whispered thickly, "I'm beginning to think you'll cheat me anyway."

He marveled at that, even in such an amateur.

"How could I cheat you, when you know me, could name me, could get me killed in a minute? Just as you can't cheat me, because I could get you killed. We're both protected—like insurance, Giselle—because we both have our asses on the line." He paused. "And speaking of asses, are we going to meet tonight?"

She laughed briefly. "I'd sure like to. He told his sister I'm a Girl Friday—a maid and secretary and go-for. The friend is upstairs, a ritzy New York bitch who keeps asking me to get her drinks and food, and I'm ready to scream!"

"You know how to get even. How about tonight?"

"I guess I can meet you. I guess a servant can sleep out, as long as she's back in time to make breakfast. She won't think anything of it, won't tell Sal. Even if she does, I'll say I went to a late movie. He knows how pissed . . ."

"Let's save something to talk about at the motel."

But they didn't talk, they made love. Twice within the hour, and she was asleep in his arms by eleven.

He examined her face—pouting, frowning—and kissed her forehead and stroked the smooth swell of her hip. Her eyelids fluttered and she murmured something about "wedding."

He kissed her cheek, and felt a surge of affection. Getting used to this little chick. Getting to know her, as the song went.

Getting to dig her more and more, especially when she didn't drink like she hadn't tonight, because of the guest in Andro's house.

And then something came to mind, something he'd been avoiding since early Saturday morning, when he'd made the Spanish chick and tried to make it with her son.

Sergio had all the equipment he dug in a boy.

Except he wasn't digging boys that much lately.

In fact, he hadn't dug Sergio at all; would have walked away from the whole thing if Freddy hadn't been there, watching.

And it made no sense. For most of his adult life, he'd been able to enjoy boys. Not men, true, like most AC-DC's, but an occasional boy had been a great turn-on.

So what the hell was happening?

Growing older, that was for sure.

But growing older in a few weeks, a few months?

He thought of Jason, and the night he'd stopped himself from sexing the child.

And he was using the word "child" lately, and he never had before when thinking of a make. If you thought the word "child," how could you use them, *fuck* them?

Using a child, fucking a child, was hurting people. But Sergio knew it all, had tried it all . . .

To hell with it! Something had happened to his

head, like it had when he'd given up pimping. Something had changed, and he didn't want children, male or female. And he'd never wanted men. What he wanted he had, right here.

He bent his head and kissed her lips. He stroked down over her full buttocks.

She laughed softly, startling him. "You like it," she said. "You like it a lot."

"Not *it*," he said, annoyed. "*You*."

"That's nice," she whispered. Her hand came to his head; her fingers threaded through his hair. "Sal's always talking about coons and calling it wool and making jokes, and it's so nice, so curly." She pulled him down for a kiss. "I'm sorry I said you'd cheat me, get me killed. I trust you, honey."

That really tore it; really turned his whirling head around.

He got up, put on the lights, and lit a cigarette. He walked to the window and said: "Damn!"

"What's wrong?"

Without turning, he said: "Maybe you're right. Maybe we will get killed. I'm not going to push it anymore. You want it, you let me know. You don't, fuck it! I'm tired of hustling people!"

"Come back to bed," she said, voice worried.

"I'm smoking, can't you see that, woman?"

"Bub, he'll be away a whole week in October. I heard his sister talking about a wedding—one of his cousins, I think—and he said he'd go and stay at her house and they'd have a real family reunion."

He still didn't turn. "So?" he said, unwilling to bite again and have her tell him something else was wrong.

"He's going to take me along and put me up at a hotel. The house will be empty, except for those days the cleaning lady comes and the pool man and the gardener. And no one inside at night and I can tell you when the private patrol usually checks. And give you my keys for the door and the dead bolt and the alarm system, to make copies."

He put out the cigarette and the lights and returned to bed.

"I'll be safe," she said, coming into his arms. "I'll be with him and he won't be able to blame me, suspect me, right?"

Not right. Andro was hip enough to consider an inside setup even with jimmy marks and other red herrings Bub would plant, including a complete ransacking as if the thief had come across the safe by accident. Andro would eventually suspect her, but with a fast payoff, she'd be away before he could do anything about it.

"October when?" he asked, wondering what he would do about the nitro. It wasn't that easy to get. Voodoo was his only source, and had already informed him he wouldn't go for another pickup to his supplier in Simi Valley, and certainly wouldn't divulge the supplier's name. "I get a lousy fender-bender bump on the freeway," the fat, aging dealer had said, "and I'm *gone.* I hand out his name, he comes after me and I'm gone a lot slower. One pickup for an old friend, okay, I sweated it. But no more. Just hold onto what you got, keep it nice and cool, and maybe you'll get lucky."

"I don't have the exact dates, Bub. Maybe I'll find out tomorrow. Long before we go, anyway." She snuggled against him. "You feel better about me now, honey?"

They kissed, and she went to sleep. He tried to make plans, to consider options, but October was too far off. Depending on the date, it could be two months. A month minimum.

He'd have to live with the nitro all that time, and hope he didn't die with it.

BOOK
THREE

Ten

Monday, October 3,
to Wednesday, October 5

Don was up at seven of a warm, Indian Summer morning, which in Southern California fashion promised to
reach into the high eighties by mid-afternoon. He'd
slept badly. He *felt* bad, though he'd finished his
script, as promised, in two weeks, and satisfied Dennings, Pandaro, and Freddy to such an extent that the
so-called polish took about five hours and the script
was retyped, copied, and distributed to all concerned
in two more days. So that by the 25th of September,
the actors were studying their lines, the director was
conferring with his cinematographer, the producers
were setting up shooting schedules at Tajunga Studios
and had a two-man crew preparing Sanibel and Cap-
tiva islands in the Florida Gulf Stream for on-location
work.

The normal foul-ups of clearing a union crew, of
getting the principals agreed, of signing every last paper referring to the studio's responsibilities and equity,
of satisfying opposing sets of lawyers and quibbling
agents, and finally, of applying for insurance coverage
in case of a dropped production, took another week.

Pandaro decided against the insurance, though he
stood to lose as much as the studio . . . more, since he

was the studio; at least thirty-two percent of it. There were too many questions the insurance people wanted answered, and sworn to. And he, Freddy, and Dennings agreed they couldn't allow anyone outside their tight group, which included the casting director, the four actors involved, the two writers, chief cameraman, head grip, and perhaps three others who would have to be there either before or during the shootings, to know what those closed sets entailed. At least until the X-rated material was safely in the can, in a bank vault, and the normal production underway.

All this Don had been informed of by Pandaro, and also by Freddy, who continued to act as if there was no reason he and Don couldn't go back to being close friends. All this Don was expected to know, since he would be doing continuing work on the script after the sex scenes were out of the way. His dialogue wouldn't remain inviolate once actors began speaking it, once their own personalities took over and the lines had to be drafted to them as individuals. Changes would become necessary day by day. But none of this concerned Don today—a dismal morning for him, despite the warm, clear weather.

He was seeing the doctor at ten: A complete checkup, with emphasis on the fluttering, irregular heartbeats that had grown more pronounced in the past few weeks; that made it difficult for him to breathe, reduced him to weakness and fear.

It was worse today than it had been since he'd overcome it with the shock treatment called electrocardiac conversion. Because today his tension was incredibly high; his stress, his frustration, his anguish enough to finish him off if he didn't gain some control over his thoughts.

His thoughts that couldn't help turning to a stage at the Tajunga Studios where Rob Dennings and Cecily Warren, along with others necessary to the closed shooting, had gathered at six-thirty A.M. Where they might already be "acting" their scene.

He walked to the glass walls, trying to soothe himself with the view. And pressed a hand to his chest. And told himself not to be a fool; he'd accepted this situation long ago; it would end and he and Cecily would go on.

With those fuck scenes playing theaters all over the country, all over the world! In a year or two they wouldn't be able to go anywhere without her being recognized, leered at, lusted after.

DiMaggio had experienced something like it with Monroe.

But Monroe had never done what Cecily was doing . . . perhaps right at this moment. Freddy would be there, and Pandaro would be there, to watch. And to laugh, as one always laughed at whores even while one made plans to fuck them.

He went to the kitchen, moving as slowly as on the day he'd been released from Cedars–Sinai Hospital. He poured juice, and his hand trembled, and he said, "Idiot!" for being involved with her, with her son, with this awful film that would degrade him along with the others.

And make him a millionaire.

If only he would think of that; think of his father whirling in deliriously happy circles, singing, "Zeindelah, zeindelah, a millionaire!" If only he would think of his children's future. If only he would think of joining that most respected, envied, and miniscule of all American assemblages, he could accept what went with it.

As for the concept of an honored intelligentsia, that he had once believed in, he could forget it; it was a lie. Forget scholars and scientists and teachers and poets and all those to whom Americans paid impatient lip service, and largely ignored.

They didn't ignore their sports stars, entertainment stars, communications or media stars, whom they turned into multimillionaires.

Instead of *In God We Trust,* the motto should read, *If You're So Smart, How Come You Ain't Rich?*

And he *would* be rich. *Filthy* rich, which was just the word for it.

The phone rang. He hoped, suddenly, it was Cecily, calling to tell him . . . what? Not that she had changed her mind. How could she? And why would she, this being her one way to the top?

To tell him she was thinking of him. To tell him that as Dennings's cock went into her vagina, into her mouth, into whatever orifice the actor-director decided would best demonstrate his virility, she'd be thinking of her Donny.

He stretched his lips to show himself it was funny, and walked slowly to the study, where he listened to the machine.

It wasn't Cecily. If she'd been going to call, she'd have done so last night; and she hadn't called since Saturday afternoon; and they hadn't seen each other since the Wednesday before that. She was too smart to present herself, body or voice, to him with what was approaching; with what was now here.

It was Fanny, ready to capitalize as always. "Hi, *dahling.* First X scene being shot today, but, of course, you know that. If you want company, I'll be home until about noon, studying the script. And I can cancel lunch with Amos Brandon . . ."

He lifted the phone. "Hi. Have those lines under control?"

"Lines, yes. But not that rape scene scheduled for Wednesday." She sighed, and he knew she wasn't acting. Pandaro said she'd hinted she'd be a lot happier with someone, *anyone*, in the part of Rorke beside Grant Vasper. "Maybe I've allowed myself to think of it too much."

"You have. Thinking can be destructive, if it's about something you can't change." And he was speaking of himself.

"You're right. Want to pick me up? I'm sick of studying that script, even if it's yours and terrific."

"Part mine. Let's spread the blame evenly."

"C'mon over."

"I'm on my way to the doctor."

"On such a beautiful day? Cancel, like I'll cancel Brandon."

"It's not the same thing. I'm feeling ill."

"Oh. Sorry. Anything I can do?"

She'd already done something—made him realize that talking to her, or anyone else, wouldn't erase those images of Cecily and Dennings.

He said good-bye and started back to the kitchen. The phone rang again.

He listened to the machine.

It was his son Marv; his first call in months.

"Hey, dad. What's happening? You okay? Wanted to check out the old man. That's a joke. With a girl like Cecily, you gotta be younger than springtime." Pause. "I'm not comfortable talking to a machine. Anyway, that's all I got to say. Just hello, hope you're well, and good-bye."

There was a voice in the background.

"Okay," Marv said. "Dad, here's Rita. She says not to waste a call."

His daughter's voice said: "Meant to write you, daddy. But you know how it is. Busy, busy, like all the mad Baylises."

He knew he should pick up the phone, he knew he should speak to his children, and didn't want to.

He was ill. He was unhappy. Some other, better time, he'd call them. (And he'd been saying that for months.)

". . . so I'm still teaching the little ones . . ."

The machine cut her off. He returned to the

kitchen. Clichés about loving one's offspring couldn't help him here. His offspring weren't on his mind. They'd grow rich along with him, but they were no longer part of his life; not really.

Cecily and Johnny were. And the vile mess they were getting into.

His heart fluttered. He sipped his juice. He fought for control. A week since the production schedules had been set. A week of sleeplessness, anguish, increasingly frequent irregular heartbeats. And over what?

What she wanted to do. What he'd agreed in May she *could* do.

But in May it had been a concept; distressing, but just a concept. Now it was real. Now the actual day of shooting had arrived.

Shooting. A very meaningful word in this context, because Rob Dennings's semen would be an integral part of the sex scenes. Only when he spurted over his co-star, only when long shots and medium shots and closeups were properly edited would the millions who lined up to pay five dollars each believe it. And tell their friends and line up again and again to make this the biggest grossing movie of all time.

He couldn't finish the juice. He couldn't stand his inquisitor brain any longer.

And where, he thought, was that jinx now that he needed it to stop the production dead?

His heart fluttered badly. He gasped for breath.

Maybe *he* would be the one to revive the jinx. After all, he was connected with the film and therefore a fitting candidate.

But his death wouldn't stop production the way the death of Dennings or Pandaro would. Though she might have a tear in her eye, Cecily would fuck on.

He called the doctor. The service answered that Goodsand wouldn't be in until nine. He said to inform him that Don Baylis was quite ill, he was leaving right now, would be there before nine and expected the doctor to meet him.

It was eight-ten. He would drive—with extreme caution—to the medical building on Cañon. Alvin Goodsand, M.C., would be there early, and take him before his nine o'clock appointment. Alvin Goodsand had to be careful, being one of the few non-Jewish doctors in the medical building, perhaps in all Beverly Hills.

A joke, that, which had elicited a very thin smile from the young, athletic, too-healthy-to-comfort-his-patients Dr. Goodsand.

Don decided he would repeat the joke today; irritate the good Goodsand; get him to *want* to find something wrong. Then perhaps the doctor would do what Don was beginning to think was the only way out of this spiral of self-destructive thought, rage, jealousy, despair. Admit him back into the hospital.

Cecily sat alone in a corner, on one of the cane-backed chairs provided for that most common of all movie-production occupations—waiting. Rob Dennings and Pete Krianous, the chief cameraman, were moving the big brass bed, talking, setting up the angles for the next scene.

The next scene. The nitty-gritty. What they kept calling "the bed scene."

Well, she was ready. As ready as she'd ever be.

They'd done the brief seduction sequence, the undressing scene, in the corner set that was the sitting room to this bedroom "in the palatial home of heiress Amelia Pearsons."

Not too bad a scene. Because it had elements of real acting, even though she'd been stripped down to panties, his hand cupping one breast and his lips closing over the other.

Then cut and into a bathrobe and now, at nine A.M., she was going to be filmed in just about every sex activity short of sodomy. That was on for her second and last sex scene, tomorrow. Then came Fanny and Grant Vasper, which gave her some satisfaction, since Pandaro had been chuckling about Fanny's "reticence in doing the rough rape sequence with Granite Mountain."

But Pandaro himself gave her no satisfaction. Pandaro and Freddy both, standing off to the side, murmuring and looking at Dennings and the set and her. Mainly at her. Freddy, the bastard, had even waved and begun to walk over to her, but she'd chosen to use the little john at the north end of the stage at that moment. He must have got the message, because he'd stayed away since then.

Why was he here anyway? And Pandaro! They were excess baggage, spectators, lookers, and grinners, and this was a closed set!

They humiliated her!

She calmed herself. Had to get in a loving mood. Unlike Fanny, she wasn't being raped in either of her sex scenes. She was doing what she wanted to do. Though Lord God, since that terrible Labor Day, since Jorge's and Teresa's deaths, she'd felt anything *but* loving. For perhaps the first time in her life, sex wasn't the big turn-on, the best of all possible fun.

Even with Donny . . . though there her gratitude, and the tenderness that had always distinguished her beddings with him from any others in her experience, made it worthwhile. Still, neither of them had sought it out, and there hadn't been much loving in the past month or so.

But once these sex scenes were over with . . .

Then would come some new problems—mainly Johnny.

She couldn't think of it now—of where to send him when the promotion, the screenings, began. She couldn't think of anything but doing the next scene right, fuck scene though it was. Everything she did had to be right; better than right—super!

So she could emerge a star.

And if she had to pay a price with her lover, her son . . .

Again, not to be thought of now. Rob Dennings was looking her way. He too wore a bathrobe, the same drab brown horseblanket provided by Wardrobe, but it was big, long, voluminous, did what it was supposed to do—covered him completely.

She tensed, thinking it was time.

Then he turned away and called to the one other woman on the set, a tall, red-headed script consultant named Dolores Raimon, who had once been an actress, more specifically a porno actress. Her value was obvious. She'd shot a dozen fuck films in her time, and knew the tricks and pitfalls. Charlie Campbell, the casting director, had suggested her, and she'd already proved her worth by stripping off the white bed sheets early this morning and sending to her home for three identical pastel-colored sets.

"You'll need at least two identical sets each day," she'd said. "And white doesn't show skin tones, unless you're shooting with blacks."

When Pandaro asked why more than one set, she'd said: "My dear man, we're all animals, especially in sexual activity. We secrete . . ."

Pandaro had held up his hand. "Sufficient!"

Cecily had laughed.

Now she didn't laugh. Those secretions would be *over* her body instead of inside her body.

"The proof," Dolores had explained to her. "In hardcore films, the proof is the ultimate excitation."

There had been many people on the set for the seduction scene—the full standard crew, which had made Cecily feel as if she were being undressed in Dodger Stadium. Several grips and a sound man with his board and a gaffer, the lighting man, with an assistant, and the cameraman and two camera operators and an assistant director named Logan and two stand-ins and the script consultant and, of course, Freddy and Pandaro.

Yet once Rob gave the nod to Logan, and once Logan shouted, "Quiet on the set! Roll 'em!" she and Rob might well have been alone. Dead silence, no movement, a professional crew doing a professional job.

It had comforted her. But to *screw* in front of so many people?

And then the weeding out process had begun. The sound man, the assistants, the gaffer, the grips, had begun leaving. Until, now, there were only eight people on the set beside Cecily and Dennings, which Dolores, the porno technical expert, had said was a "a real triumph, an advantage to you, darling." She'd smiled and pressed Cecily's hand and told her: "Your body is stunning; created for love scenes. And what is making love on camera anyway? Especially for the chance you're getting. I would have allowed them to amputate a breast for such fame as will come to you!" And she'd laughed as Cecily had winced.

Eight people. Not too bad, if only two of them hadn't been Freddy and Pandaro.

If only *they* would leave, she could get through this all right.

But who could make the producers, the Money, leave a set?

She began to feel warm. The stage was heating up because of the lights, which had been adjusted, along with a stationary, above-bed, open mike, before Dennings weeded out the crew. . . .

She had no more time to think of the temperature. And she'd soon be able to take off the thick bathrobe, because Rob Dennings was beckoning to her. Because he was saying: "All right, Cecily, let's do this, do it right, and by tomorrow afternoon, we can forget these sequences and go on to real acting."

For which she was grateful. Which helped her walk

to that bed with something like a smile on her face.

He held out his hand as she reached him. He was breathing hard; his hand trembled and was damp with perspiration; she realized he was as tense, as nervous, as she was.

His being nervous could be a lot more serious than anything she might feel. Because a woman could always fake it, while a man . . .

She saw the cinematographer strapping on the harness for the Aeroflex hand-held camera—which surprised her, as she'd never seen a chief cameraman do his own photographing. That's what operators were for.

She saw the assistant director and one of the camera operators heading for the exit door. She saw Dolores Raimon walking after them, waving at Cecily, calling: "With heart."

And then Rob Dennings turned to the wall where Freddy and Pandaro stood murmuring, waiting expectantly, and said: "Gentlemen, the set is now closed to all except my cinematographer and two of his operators. As you can see, we're not even using a sound board; just a set mike. So if you will leave, we can get on with making our fortunes."

Pandaro looked shocked. "I'm sorry. I intend to oversee every stage of this production."

"Every stage but the three sex scenes. Otherwise, there won't *be* a production." He walked to a chair and sat down.

For a moment Cecily was terrified. Pandaro was striding forward. Pandaro could blow up, maybe blow the whole deal.

But then she realized that while he was angry, while he was walking like a man who wanted to kick something, he was walking to the exit.

Freddy came by her, murmuring: "Guess I'll have to look at my own private film." And he too went to the door that Dolores Raimon was holding open, admitting a slash of blazing sunlight into this closed and darkened world.

Which darkened again when the door shut, except for the incredibly bright square that was the bed.

Dennings went to the door, did something to it, and returned to her. "You can relax, Cecily. There are four doors to this stage. Three are now locked. The fourth, the hangar-type sliding doors behind the drawing-room set, is being watched outside by two men I've hired as personal bodyguards. No one will disturb us." He turned. "I've already introduced you to Peter Krianous. These are two operators who have worked with him, and with me, on many films. Nine, as I remember, Peter."

The heavy-set, balding cinematographer said: "Yes. Evan, my focusing expert, has been on all of them. Clete," he pointed to the man loading the BMC stationary camera on the other side of the bed, "has been on six. So relax, Miss Warren. We know why you and Mr. Dennings are here. Same reason we're here. To make a buck." He smiled.

She nodded and turned to Rob. He also smiled.

His smile wasn't convincing. He'd relaxed her, put her in as much of a mood for what they were going to do as possible. But he hadn't done the same for himself.

She waited for his directions.

He talked to Krianous, giving last-minute instructions. He said: "Evan, you'll be our slate board man, if the union won't mind."

Evan looked at Krianous. The cinematographer said: "The union won't mind."

Dennings turned to her. "The focusing's done. The cameras are ready. Are you?"

She said, "Yes," softly, and without his asking her, dropped the robe to the floor.

Dennings wet his lips and didn't move.

She walked up to him. She untied his robe, slipped

it back over his shoulders and let it drop. She put her arms around his waist, her head on his chest, and whispered: "That night, at Freddy's—I wish I'd been with it. Because even half-out, I loved what you did. Like most women, I've dreamed of having Rob Dennings make love to me. Now I've got my chance. Just do what you did at Freddy's. Just that, honey."

At the word "honey," she felt his penis stir against her thigh. She kissed his chest, and moved her hand down. She touched him lightly, with the tips of her fingers, then looked up into his eyes. He was stiffening rapidly.

He took her to the bed. He positioned her on her stomach, lay down on his back beside her, said: "We have an open mike recording automatically. No sound board. No one listening. If we get proper sound, fine. If not, we'll loop later." He turned his head. "Ready? Roll!"

He turned back to her. Krianous moved in with the hand-held Aeroflex. Evan, the focusing expert, came up with the chalked slate-board, held it open between bed and stationary BMC camera, said: "Scene 2-X, Take 1, *Galt's Island*." He snapped the board shut and stepped back and away.

Dennings said: "Darling, I want you to know you can walk out of here any time."

She'd almost forgotten she had lines—very few, true—but lines nonetheless.

"Why would I? I'm where I want to be. Doing what I want to do."

And with that she began kissing his chin, his chest, his belly. With that, the sex scene began.

Dennings had roughed out the "progression of activities" during their private discussion Friday at a studio office, and again yesterday evening at his home. Neither time had he made the slightest move in her direction.

And so she finally believed that he *had* needed one

sex session with her, to overcome a degree of insecurity.

And so now, working her way down toward his penis, she forgave him for accepting Freddy's setup, whether or not he'd known how she'd been stoned . . . but not Freddy for drugging and using her!

Dennings was rigid. Dennings was gasping her name—her character name—over and over. "Amelia, Amelia."

She closed her mouth over his cock. And knew the cameras were getting it all. And murmured and moaned and *loved* what she was doing! Loved this man for how he had handled things today. Respected him and felt lucky to be associated with him.

And later, as he raised her and caressed her and they writhed, she tried to keep the pattern of their love-making in mind—though he'd ended both their "rehearsal" sessions with, "Never worry about breaking the plan. Never hesitate if either of us goes in a different direction. As long as we end the way we have to, with me pulling out and ejaculating over your breasts."

He was on her now and that was a change in the plan, that was a different direction.

She was supposed to be on top for the first part of their coital action, so the hand-held camera could photograph from the rear, from where his organ could be seen most clearly moving in and out of her, and also be made to appear larger.

Only then was he to put her on her back and go for as long as he could before coming onto her body.

But he was already on and in her, gasping, shaking. He was closing his eyes and biting his lip, and while it all looked fine, looked like passion, she could feel that he was actually too far along, wasn't holding out properly.

He suddenly pulled out, raised himself, and masturbated onto her belly and breasts.

Then he fell off her, onto his side, saying, "Damn!" and "Cut!"

They'd planned on between ten and fifteen minutes of pure sex, so as to allow for cutting and editing. Cecily didn't think they'd gotten five minutes, if that. Much too short. Her own body knew he hadn't been in her even a minute.

"How long?" Dennings finally asked, getting off the bed and moving to his bathrobe.

Krianous said: "Maybe two minutes, not all usable."

"And I was worried about getting it up!" But he wasn't joking; not from his grim expression. And he certainly wasn't bragging.

Krianous brought Cecily one of the damp towels Dolores Raimon had piled on a table.

She cleaned herself, and went to her robe. She felt guilty.

But guilty of what?

"Premature ejaculation," Dennings murmured to her. "Can you imagine? Not since I was fifteen!"

He raised his voice. "There're Cokes and sandwiches in my dressing room behind the sitting-room set." He gestured and went to Krianous and they began talking.

Cecily walked slowly across the stage. Evan, a tall fortyish man walked up behind her and past her with a brief nod.

Clete, a younger, smaller man, was already in the portable dressing room. When she entered, he handed her an open Coke and said: "Got ham and cheese, and what looks like chicken or turkey."

"Just the Coke, thanks."

She heard them begin talking, voices low, the moment she left.

She didn't hear them laughing, because they were Dennings's close crew, but that would come later.

And God! they'd have to shoot the whole thing over again tomorrow! Because no way could Dennings have enough left to come *copiously*, which was the requirement he himself had made.

But as soon as she returned to the bed, he said: "We're going to do another take. Not the end, but everything that should have come before. Then we'll edit it in before the come-scene, giving it continuity and climax." He smiled a little. "Climax without the climax."

When the cinematographer turned away for his hand-held camera, she murmured: "Do you feel up to it? I mean . . ."

"I know what you mean." He stepped close. Fastening his eyes on hers, he slipped a hand inside her robe and stroked her breasts. "I believe your considerable talent will carry us through."

They were both laughing when they got back into bed. She felt it was going to be all right.

And it was. It was more than all right.

Riding him, with that camera just inches from her ass, humping that beautiful-looking man, that famous man, that man who had starred in the sexual fantasies of a million women including Cecily Warren's, that nice guy who had emerged these last few hours, she began to feel it, began to gasp uncontrollably, began to claw his shoulders. And saw the stationary camera taking it all in, and saw the hand-held moving around to fix briefly on her face before swinging down to their genitals, and said, "Rob!" and knew instantly she should have said, "Galt" and couldn't be bothered because she was coming.

"Cut," Rob said.

She didn't move off him. "Did I ruin it with your name?"

He didn't go soft. "Not at all. Just a loop."

She finally looked up. The three cameramen were no longer casually professional and at ease. Nor did she think they would do any laughing later. They were wandering around, not talking to each other.

Rob was also watching them. He murmured: "There was a baby boom after World War Two. There'll be another after *Galt's Island*. He raised his voice. "Pete, what do you think?"

"Jesus, don't ask me that now!"

Rob laughed, and called, "Ready?" and the cameramen returned to their positions. "Roll!"

And man, did they ever!

When it was over, she'd come twice more and said: "Did I use your name again? I can't remember much of anything."

He rolled off her. "No. But you did say a few fuck-me's."

"You can edit it out, can't you?" Because they hadn't talked of obscenity, hadn't included it in their plans.

"Easily, but I won't. If our producers think it'll hurt the socially redeeming qualities of the film, they can do it. I loved it. I think the audience will too. One more, in fact, and I'd have blown *tomorrow's* action." He pulled her close. "I envy your writer. I swear I do. I could go a long time with a woman like you."

They kissed. They got up. And strangely, she felt she could face Donny now.

No way of making him understand how well this had gone, how clean it had been. No way at all. Because she herself had felt exactly the opposite, had felt whorish and filthy, before this day's action.

Now she could see Don without feeling guilty.

Not that she would. Not until the second sex scene was finished. Maybe not until a week after that. But soon.

Because she needed him. And would need him even more in the coming months, the coming years, after the film was released.

Dennings was saying: "That's a wrap. See you all tomorrow. Same time, same stage, different set, if our line-producer does his job."

She went home. She told Johnny to put on his yachting outfit and took him to the Lobster Barrel where he met Alan Hale, the captain from "Gilligan's Island," and got an autographed menu. Afterward, they went to a Beverly Hills toy store where she bought him the set of walkie-talkies he'd been wanting. Finally, she took him to a movie. Because she loved him. And because she felt she might be losing him.

The moment Dr. Goodsand saw him, waiting outside the closed door to the offices of Chaselle, Leiman & Goodsand, a Medical Corporation, he said, "My God, man, what have you done to yourself?"

Don was leaning against the wall, gasping for breath as the irregular heartbeat drove his energies, his life force, lower by the moment. Yet he smiled. "Big-time movie, baby. You ought to consider it as a tax shelter."

Goodsand unlocked the door, got him into one of the six examining rooms, and ran the ECG test himself. By the time it was completed, the two nurses employed by the medical corporation were there. They took over for blood tests, X rays, and a scheduled ECG with treadmill, this last canceled when the nurse realized Don was ready to fall down as he got on the movable rubber walk.

Goodsand received him in his red leather office with pictures of wife and children and marble-based pen set and heavy silver letter-opener and first-dollar-sealed-in-plastic, and all the other desk paraphernalia of what was now the most lucrative profession in the world . . . barring that of big-time porno film producer, actor, or writer-with-percentage.

Goodsand showed he knew about *Galt's Island*. "They had an article in the Calendar section of the Sunday *Times* a few weeks ago. Your name among others, and rumors about X-ratings, violence, and

jinxes. Working with a sexpot like Cecily Warren
should be stimulating, not debilitating."

Don leaned over, suddenly nauseated. When he
straightened, he was prepared to start a string of doctor jokes, to irritate the good Goodsand, to begin that
campaign to get himself readmitted to Cedars–Sinai.

It wasn't necessary.

Goodsand said: "You're well into heart failure—
blood pressure down, water forming in the lungs,
heavy irregularity . . ."

Don said: "Cecily Warren is the girl you met at the
hospital ten months ago."

"The one . . . your fiancée . . . ?"

Don smiled. Or hoped it was a smile. "Doctor, I'm
not sure I can keep breathing much longer." And he
toppled sideways, half falling out of the chair.

Goodsand was beside him, and a nurse was beside
him, and he was being given oxygen, and then a double dose of Quinidine and Inderal. The heartbeat
steadied, but just a little. He was lying in an examining room and Goodsand was speaking.

"You should have come to me a week ago."

"Two," he gasped.

"Yes, just like the last time. So it's back to Intensive
Care and electro-cardiac-conversion."

"The hospital's fine. But can't we continue the double medication?"

Goodsand was shaking his head. "Too late to work
it out with chemotherapy. You're in trouble, until we
jolt the heart back into rhythm."

"It scares the shit out of me," Don whispered.

"With some reason. But not one in a thousand . . ."

"Quote me no odds, medical corporation. What if it
was you getting that jolt through the heart?"

Goodsand was turning to the door. Two white-clad
men brought in an ambulance stretcher. "I'll see you
in about an hour," the doctor said, and left.

The orderlies lifted him onto the low, tablelike stretcher and he was wheeled out through the waiting room. People stared and he closed his eyes, smiling a little, embarrassed, because here he was again, a non-man again, perhaps dying, perhaps not, but out of it again. Just like ten months ago. Back where he'd started from. Except this time there would be no Cecily with him, helping, rooting, caring. This time there'd be no children. There'd be no one.

Because he would allow no one to find out.

His car would remain in the subbasement parking lot until he was ready to use it again, or to have it added to his estate.

But that last was dramatics. He didn't feel he would die. Those odds of a thousand to one were excellent. Until, of course, the big pad was placed over his heart.

He would instruct Goodsand to call no one, tell no one.

He would lick his wounds alone, and to hell with anyone worrying about where he was.

He liked the dramatics this time.

He had needed aloneness since the inception of that vile movie project.

And yet, being prepped in his frighteningly modern room in Intensive Care—the futuristic equipment bracketed to walls and more being wheeled in for Goodsand to do his medical-corporation best—he wondered what time it was, wondered if Cecily was in the throes of sexual ecstasy, prayed she had finished so that if those odds didn't work out he wouldn't die while she was fucking.

Then even that became unimportant.

Because Goodsand was there, in those green coveralls the surgeons wore which were, somehow, so much more *butcher-like* than the old whites of his youth, when a tonsillectomy had constituted his greatest danger.

The pad was being placed on his chest.

Goodsand said: "Hold it! Where's the release?"

The surgical nurse had forgotten. The look she received from Goodsand and the specialist on the reviving machinery was withering. She rushed out and was back in a moment, and he tried to jest from his flat-on-back, his thing-on-the-bed position: "Don't hurry on my account."

No one laughed. No one laughs if a sheep baas a jest in the slaughterhouse.

He was handed a pen by the guilty nurse, who transferred her guilt to him by saying, sharply; "Not there, Mr. Baylis. Here."

So he signed a second time, giving his consent to a procedure which might kill him, freeing the doctor and hospital of legal responsibility.

Then the pad was on his chest and Goodsand's reassuring and false smile was turned on him and Goodsand's hand moved to the portable machine's control panel.

He choked on terror. He wanted to say: "No, fuck it, let me alone!" And his heart exploded as electric current hit it, stopping, then starting the beat; exploded but not in pain and so briefly that he was settling back down almost before he'd become aware of leaping upward.

He took a deep breath. It was smooth, steady, as was his heartbeat.

Just like last time. And like last time, he was being injected and told to sleep.

Goodsand was smiling a real smile. "You'll be out of Intensive tomorrow morning." He headed for the door. "With luck, you'll be back home in a week."

"Three days," Don muttered drowsily, already thinking of Cecily and the script and his answering machine. "Got work to do, medical corporation."

"Five days, at best," Goodsand said. "So forget your business, porno corporation."

Which would have gotten a laugh out of Don, if he hadn't been asleep.

Andro and Giselle were flying to New York Friday afternoon for that wedding of Andro's relative, and they would stay until the following Wednesday, six full days. Bub had made a duplicate set of keys to the house and the burglar alarm system. He also had Giselle's passport and a suitcase of her clothing so she could split the country right after they met for the payoff.

Barring floods or earthquakes, he would blow the safe Friday night. Andro would scream, but was second-rate Mafia now and without heavy help would never find Giselle. And never learn who had done the actual job.

Because Bub would put his money in no bank, no deposit box, no place where it could be traced. He would do what his daddy had done when the illegal bread became heavy: "Bury it in the ground, Burleigh, someplace only you know where."

The old man was probably still digging up dollars.

Bub had his hole in the ground ready—actually a hole under the floorboards of the shed behind the tennis courts; the shed he'd used as a film developing room as well as storage area for court maintenance equipment.

His three hundred twenty-five thousand would rest there. Until he decided it was time to leave Freddy, or until Freddy got himself in so much trouble that the household fell apart.

But that wasn't what was worrying him.

Not robbing Andro either.

It was the nitro.

A month old, which wasn't ancient, but which could have changed its nature, made it unstable.

Bub hadn't moved it since September 3rd, when he

first put it in the garage fridge. He would have to move it Friday night.

It was Tuesday morning and he was cleaning up the kitchen. Freddy had breakfasted at the crack of dawn—six-thirty—and then split to do whatever it was he did on that movie. "Change of sets," he'd said as Bub had helped him choose his clothing. "Interior of a power cruiser. Got it into place late yesterday afternoon, but have to make sure."

When Bub had asked how Cecily and Dennings looked in their fuck scene, Freddy had muttered, "Didn't bother hanging around," and Bub knew someone had forced him off the set.

At another time in his life, he'd have been curious enough to dig the truth out of his boss.

Not now. Now the robbery was all that mattered.

And Giselle, though here he'd begun pulling back, drying up the feelings which had grown steadily over the past month.

They'd met three more times. They'd made love, better and better love, and talked better and better talk. This despite her continuing heavy drinking.

But it was all over now. He wouldn't be seeing her again, except to hand her the split. Then she'd be gone.

He started the dishwasher, shrugging.

He'd said good-bye to a dozen cunts in the past few years. He'd said good-bye to at least a hundred in his life. None had hurt; not for more than a day or two. This one might take a week.

He began to think of her sad mouth, her trusting eyes, and reached under the sink for the dope box. He smoked a joint lying on his bed.

The nitro and Giselle. Had to keep from thinking of those two subjects.

It was eight-fifteen. Freddy wouldn't be back for dinner. Bub was free to do whatever he wanted.

He quickly got up from the bed.

He was waiting around too much. Thinking about shit too much.

Jason . . .

The name had popped into his mind; caught him by surprise, or so he insisted.

Wasn't true, though.

Along with the nitro and Giselle, he'd been fighting thoughts of Albert's son.

But why not think of Jason? No problem there. He'd already made up his mind to put a hunk of bread in trust for the kid, enough to give him a start in life when the time came for him to split his slum home.

"Old Lizabeth," Jason had called his stepmother. And indicated she didn't give much of a damn about him.

Eight-thirty.

Too early for any Strip action, any street action. That wouldn't come alive for a good ten, twelve hours.

Drive somewhere.

Beautiful day. Drive out of L.A. and have lunch in a good restaurant on the road. Look around and clear the mind. Come back late enough to hit the clubs: the Good Time in Santa Monica, the Montezuma Massage on the Strip, maybe Gorilla's, where there was always a game of poker.

He went to his Caddy and drove the block to Sunset and west toward the shore. And when he came to the San Diego Freeway, took the ramp for the south entry. By chance, for no special reason, he told himself.

But once past L.A. International Airport, he knew where he was going.

They finished shooting the second hardcore scene at nine-five. It hadn't been quite as easy this time for Cecily, sodomy being what it was, but she'd enjoyed every thing that preceded it. And there was no doubt at all that Rob Dennings had had himself a ball.

Not only that, he was delighted with his *professional* performance as well, having held out for more than half an hour, no easy task with what she'd been doing with her mouth and every other part of her body. He'd finally pulled out of her rectum, groaning, and come all over her buttocks, that hand-held camera just inches from the action.

She'd groaned, too, but only after it was over. Groaned and accepted the robe Dennings handed her and walked slowly to the john to cry a little as the rectal cramp subsided. Then she'd gone to the small dressing room and put on her clothes.

She came back onto the set, and Dennings was telling the three cameramen they had a half-hour break, after which Fanny Batcher and Grant Vasper would arrive and Dennings would run them and the camera crew through rehearsal of the big rape scene, set to be shot tomorrow morning.

Two of the men headed for the door. The third, cinematographer Peter Krianous, continued talking to Rob. She heard him say: "You'll find it tough to trim to the fifteen minutes total you want for yourself. Counting yesterday, we've got almost an hour of usable hot-stuff. Clete and I will do the processing ourselves, probably early this afternoon, so you'll have two days' rushes tomorrow. You're lucky I came up through the ranks, through the old Technicolor film labs."

"I appreciate it, Pete. No problems about using the studio lab?"

"None at all. Pandaro cleared it on your say-so."

Dennings smiled sourly. "He and Freddy want to see me in action as soon as possible."

"Name of the game, Rob. The whole world is going to want to see you."

"Yes, but . . ." He glanced at Cecily; then continued anyway. "But *how* will they see me? That part of me, I mean?"

"Large and clear. The lens work was super. The angles are mainly flattering. And as I said, you have almost an hour's footage to work with, to get the perfect minutes you want."

Rob nodded, and muttered: "Can't believe it's actually ready for editing. Can't believe I've actually committed myself." He turned to Cecily, "I admire your guts, baby. With a son, a mother . . ."

She said: "Yes, well, if you don't need me." Her mouth was dry.

He said, "In a minute," and turned back to Krianous. "Anything else you need, Pete?"

"Yeah. Me and the boys would like to go home to our wives for a few hours, or the nearest cold showers."

Dennings laughed, slapped Krianous on the shoulder, and spoke to Cecily as the cinematographer walked off. "Work on your lines—the opening scene between Amelia and Galt at her father's estate. We'll try to shoot it early tomorrow afternoon, if the rape scene goes off well in the morning."

"I've got everything down pat. And I'm having that drama coach you assigned me over later in the evening. He's a good man, Rob."

"Should be. Coached half a dozen great actresses in his day. A fruit, of course, but who else would understand the feminine approach as well?"

"I'd have thought a woman."

"Got anyone in mind?" He put his arm around her waist and began walking her to the exit. "Because anything that helps the picture is okay with me."

"No, just making talk."

They were at the door. He squeezed her ass and said: "Be here at noon." Then he jerked his hand away. "See what I just did?"

She wasn't sure what he meant.

"The bit with your bottom."

"Oh well. After what we've been through . . ." She shrugged.

"That's just the point. We're going to have to forget the sex scenes. Amelia and Galt don't get around to their first kiss for a third of the film. She's a chilly number during their early meetings, and he's antagonistic because she stands between him and her father."

"Then I'll have to slap you the next time you get familiar."

"Right. Though after we finish this job . . ."

"After we finish, I'm going to talk a writer into marrying me."

He looked at her, and nodded. "I'll remember that."

Again, she liked him for his ways, and couldn't help giving *him* a little squeeze on the rump. "Of course, *you're* not planning marriage." She left him laughing.

And who should be walking toward the door to the set but Miss Fanny Batcher. And about a hundred feet behind and hurrying to catch up, the massive figure of Granite Mountain Vasper.

Fanny's face hardened. But, Cecily thought sweetly, it was naturally as hard as a streetwalker's.

"Hello!" Cecily said, while they were still some distance apart. "Rob was saying he thought your scene tomorrow should go extremely well, if you can just get into the character. Just remember that some women *do* resist a few opportunities for sexual intercourse. Say with lepers, those suffering from gonorrhea and syphillis—you know, all the men you adore. Liberal is the word for Fanny, we were saying."

"You stinking whore!" Fanny had stopped about five feet away. "You come-freak! Once Donny learns just how *low* . . ."

"Ah," Cecily said, smiling and waving past the furious blond. "Grant Vasper. We did a TV show together about a year ago. I doubt you'd remember, because I was on about one-third of a second, and you starred."

The huge man was nervously adjusting the little

plaid cap perched atop his shaved head, and glancing at Fanny.

"I remember you very well, Cecily. You did a damned fine job with very little."

"You mean the hot pants I had to wear?"

He laughed. "That, too." He cleared his throat, glancing again at Fanny. "Everything go, uh, well with you and Rob?"

"Marvelously," Cecily said, bubbling over with goodwill, and hidden venom. "All the fears, the embarrassment, disappeared once we began to work together. I'm sure the same will happen with you two."

Vasper nodded, murmuring, "I think so. We just have to give it our best."

"Oh, Fanny's a real pro," Cecily said, then covered her mouth. "Oops! Meant a real actress." She'd also heard that Vasper was enormous down there—more than twelve inches, if you could believe it—and added, "She can handle anything."

Fanny tried to smile, but didn't quite make it. Neither did she look at Vasper, who was still trying to catch her eye.

"Have to rush," Cecily said, backing off, ready now for her getaway. "Bye, you two! Have fun!"

Fanny walked toward the door without a word. Vasper looked at Cecily, and spread his hands. Cecily was suddenly sorry for the huge man with the pockmarked face and sensitive nature.

"Don't worry," she said. "It'll go great, because *you're* great."

He smiled a little. "Maybe I should do the scene with you.

"I've had my time at the front . . . *and* the back, thank you."

He laughed. She was great at making men laugh. Just about every man, except Donny.

Whom she called as soon as she got home.

That damned machine answered, and she said: "It's

finished, bunny. Call me back, please? Tell me you still care?"

Then she ran a hot tub and soaked her aching ass.

At one o'clock, lying in bed, studying the script, she again called Don. Again the machine, and again she left a message.

At three-fifteen, Johnny came home from school.

She jumped up and said: "I feel like Mexican food. Okay with you?"

He shrugged listlessly. "You mean those dinners in the freezer?"

She ran over and hugged him and kissed him up. "I mean six courses at Casa Cugat on Restaurant Row, Boy Wonder!"

"Wow!" He turned to his room, then stopped. "Better tell you. I got a note from Miss Lowgren, the fool."

"Don't call your teacher names."

"Well, she sends notes for no damn reason! I didn't *try* to get a bad mark in English!"

"The note."

He came back and took it out of his workbook. It read:

Dear Mrs. Warren:

Johnny has failed three quizzes, indicating he isn't doing his homework. His reading, especially, is falling far below acceptable levels. If you could drop in some day at three P.M., we could discuss a remedial program.

Sincerely, Miss M. Lowgren

"What does the M stand for?" she muttered, to avoid the real questions that she didn't want to ask.

"Monster, what else?"

She laughed before she could control it, then began to grow angry.

"Mary or Margaret, how the f . . ." He stopped himself short. "How should I know?"

She wanted to shout at him for skipping his reading assignments. She wanted to shout at him for knowing words like "fuck." She wanted to scream and hit and change him into something better.

And she had no right to scream and hit. She herself had been no better.

"Get dressed. I'm hungry. We'll have an early dinner at Cugat's."

He smiled. "Okay, big momma!" He ran across the hall and into his room. But in a moment he was back in the doorway, looking at her. "How come? I mean, what's going on?"

She knew what he meant, and told herself she couldn't possibly. He was speaking kid gibberish.

"Are you going to change or not?"

"But all this going out and presents . . ." He stared at her. "Are you and dad talking about me living at the farm?" His face was growing frightened, his eyes blinking rapidly. "C'mon, you'd better tell me what it is because I got legal rights."

She ran to him, and he flinched and covered his head. She held him and began to cry. "Oh God," she said, and forced herself to laugh. "What a nut! I just made some extra money and what do I need it for anyway because Don's loaded and he'll soon be taking care of us so just get dressed, will you?"

He drew back, still frightened, still suspicious.

Her heart was breaking. Because he had a right to his fear, his suspicion. Things were going to change, even if not the way he thought. They might very well lose each other.

She called Donny. He'd make it better.

She said, "Donny, damn it!" as his machine answered and his voice rattled on.

She left a short message and hung up.

He'd call back later. He always came through, eventually.

Bub had been parked across the street from Jason's house for half an hour when he saw the kid coming from the corner. Not Jason, but the younger one, Dexter, much smaller, very light-skinned, and with near-white features. Recognized him instantly from Albert's photograph.

Kid looked happy as a clam.

Kid ran across the scraggly lawn and into the house, lugging an armful of books, yelling, "Hey, mom!"

Maybe ten minutes later, Jason came from the corner.

No books. Smoking a cigarette. Swaggering. He kicked at things and moved like a street-fighter. Bub wanted to boot his ass! Because he had personal knowledge of that kind of attitude. Because he knew exactly where it led: to the slammer, with a detour or two for jive-turkey rip-offs.

Before he could control himself, he was out of the car, calling, "Jason!"

The boy stopped, looked up, and grinned one hell of a grin.

"Uncle Bub! Where you been?" He ran across the street.

Bub looked at the cigarette in his hand.

"Oh, man, you like a granddaddy." He flipped the butt away, and his voice hushed. "You hear about old Albert?"

Bub nodded. "Just the other day. That's why I came down here. To say I'm sorry." He put his hand on the boy's shoulder. He wanted to do something more, say something more.

"Real bummer, right, Uncle Bub? While we were having fun, he was getting himself killed." He paused. "Did you know he was pulling that job?"

"Me? I'd've stopped him dead." He wanted to light a cigarette of his own. "Bad business. Just you remember that." He cleared his throat, and felt that it was time to leave. He'd seen the boy. He would help the boy. Period.

He turned back to the car.

"Hey, man, you're not leaving? I got things in the house. A present, man, I made in shop class. Because you took me to Magic Mountain and Disneyland and the beach at night."

"Bring it out here."

"I got other things to show you! I'm no turkey like you think!"

"I never said . . ."

"Yeah, but I can tell it's in your head! Putting me down for school and smoking and all that shit! I got *stuff* to show, man, good as Dexter's!"

"Your mother . . ." He didn't want the woman asking what Jason had been doing with him while his father was pulling a robbery.

"*Stepmother*, man! Maybe she'll be in the john . . . she's got a kidney 'fection. Anyway, we just say hello fast and go to my room—my half. I share with Dexter. Dexter's cool, man. *C'mon!*" He was yanking Bub's hand.

There was no denying him, and Bub let himself be drawn across the street and into the house. Where he was met by a mixture of odors—must, dust, and some sort of oniony cooking.

"Who's that you got?" the sharp voice asked from the gloom of a shabby living room. When Bub's eyes adjusted, he saw the woman seated on a couch to his left; a couch that had springs and stuffing showing.

"Friend of old Albert's who didn't know he was dead."

"Yes. Sorry about Albert, Mrs. Dunster."

She rose. "Goodness! Bringing in company when I'm not even dressed." She drew a print wrapper around her chunky body. Her hair was a frizzled mess; her face round and plain. "Excuse me, Mr. . . . ?"

"Kane."

"I'll get dressed, Mr. Kane. We can have a cup of coffee and talk about Albert. How'd you know him?"

"We once had a drink together, and he said if I was ever in San Diego . . ." He spread his hands.

"I'm gonna show him my room," Jason said, and tugged Bub toward a hallway.

"Don't bother Mr. Kane with your junk!" she snapped. "I got stew on the stove. Dexter's already eating. Have some and get out and play or something."

She shook her head, softened her voice as she addressed Bub. "That boy—just like his father. Rest his soul and all that, Mr. Kane, but Albert lived like he died, looking for the pot o' gold. Dexter now, he's something else." Her voice sharpened again. "Introduce Mr. Kane to your brother while I get dressed."

"Yeah," Jason said. As she hurried out of the room, slippers flapping, he muttered, "Ugly bitch. We was gonna split on her, Albert and Dexter and me, when Albert got the bread."

Bub had a need to get out of this dump. "Let's see that present."

"You'd better meet Dexter. She'll bust my ass if you don't." He led the way through an open door into a kitchen with appliances that could have qualified as genuine antiques, including a Frigidaire with coil on top.

Dexter was eating at the table, and smiled up at them. He was whiter than Freddy. He had bright eyes and the look of a kid who's put it all together.

"This a friend of pop's, Dexter, Mr. Kane."

"Hey," Dexter said, and chewed and swallowed. "You serve time together?"

Jason laughed. Bub said: "No." Dexter said: "He was always looking for the pot o' gold. Looking for it in other people's pockets. That's what mom says."

"*Mom* ain't been around for years."

"I mean Elizabeth. She's our mom now."

"Not mine, man! And you and me and old Albert was gonna split on her!"

"Not me. I'm gonna go to technical high and then college. I'll become an engineer, see if I don't."

"Yeah," Jason said, and glanced at Bub. "I could, too, if I wanted."

Dexter smiled a sly smile. "Mom says you're just like Albert. All talk."

"You want your teeth bent, nigger!"

"Mom's gonna hear you," Dexter said calmly, and continued eating.

Jason glared a moment, then led Bub out of the kitchen to a back bedroom. It was divided into two sections, a cot and dresser on each of its opposing walls. One side was heaped with clothes and papers and assorted junk; the other was clean.

"Guess which is your side," Bub cracked, but the kid didn't smile.

"Forgot to clean up yesterday." And then, "Who the fuck cares anyway! I don't blame Dexter playing up to her. But he's him and I'm me and we're different, man, just like our skins're different! Maybe I *am* like old Albert! So what! So what's wrong with a son being like his daddy anyway?"

"Nothing," Bub said, and wanted out because it was hopeless. He'd been fucked from birth and that's all there was to it. The Dexters were the survivors. The Jasons ended up like Albert, bleeding in someone else's home. Or, at best, sweeping out a garage. And Bub didn't think it would have helped much even if Albert had remained alive.

The only thing that might help was the big hunk of bread he planned to leave the kid. Which gave added importance to the robbery Friday night.

"That present," he reminded.

"Yeah. Got it in the closet. See?" He was pulling

down what looked like a big blue doughnut from a top shelf. "Was gonna write a card. But anyway, for you, Uncle Bub."

When he handed it over, it turned out to be a glazed, ceramic ashtray, not too misshapen.

"Hey, nice, Jason." Bub turned to the door. "Got to split."

"So soon? I got a model plane to show you, almost finished."

"Sorry, next time."

"Well, then, I thought maybe we'd go in your car someplace and have something to eat and rap, you know, like we did at your apartment?"

"I'd like to." And he would have. Except he was pained; he couldn't seem to take Jason's company. "But I don't have the time. My job . . ."

"Not even half an hour? Not even *fifteen minutes,* man?"

Why not fifteen minutes for this kid?

But he said: "I'm late now, Jason. C'mon, walk me to my car."

Elizabeth was calling from somewhere up the corridor leading to the living room: "Dex, honey, get momma's blouse off the line like a sweet thing."

Bub and Jason went out and across the street. Bub got in his car. Jason watched and said nothing.

"I'll come some Sunday," Bub said, starting the engine. "We'll have time then."

"Yeah," Jason said, voice flat.

"I mean it. We'll go to a nice restaurant and talk."

Jason turned and went back across the street and into the house.

No good-bye, Uncle Bub. No wave. Nothing.

He'd gotten the message, old Jason had.

Bub drove away. A mistake coming here in the first place.

He lit a cigarette. Which reminded him of the ashtray. It lay on the seat beside him. Worst looking piece of crap he'd ever seen!

At home, he put it on the nighttable beside his bed.

She figured it must have been her drinking that set it off. Sal had been irritated with her boozing for months now, and Giselle had been careful not to get bombed in front of him, saving her heavy drinking for after he was asleep when she could get downstairs and hit her supply of brandy pints hidden in the garage.

But she'd run out of pints last night, and drunk from his cut-glass decanters, expensive stuff, and he'd hit the roof when he saw how much was gone this morning.

Still, no real sweat—he was always yelling about something or other—until the phone rang about three in the afternoon. He was at the table, finishing lunch, having his favorite dessert, zabaglione. She'd been sipping red wine, which he allowed because it was what his family had "drunk with meals for generations."

He looked from his dish as she went to the phone. Some woman said: "Kate, please."

Giselle said, "You have the wrong number," and the woman said, "Sorry," and hung up.

Before Giselle could also hang up, Sal was lunging across the room. He ripped the phone from her hand and shouted into it: "Who the hell is this!" Then he slammed it down.

She stared at him. "Just a wrong number, Sal."

"Sure! Like all those wrong numbers you get when I'm around! And all the hangups with no voices when I answer!"

"Don't be silly," she said, and turned to leave the room, to let him cool off.

He grabbed her arm. "'Whore! Running away because you can't answer!"

She kept her voice cool and steady, "I just want to give you time to settle down, honey. You know I haven't anyone but you." She forced a laugh. "I don't have time for anyone but you."

He continued to grip her arm. She looked at his hand. "It hurts, Sal."

"If you think *that* hurts!" But then he let her go. Then he went out of the dining room and into the den. "C'mere," he called.

She followed and heard the soft hum.

She couldn't believe it!

But there he was, lying back in his recliner chair, the vibrator seat on, which he used when he wanted her to blow him.

"C'mon, you bitch!" He was pulling his pants and drawers down. "C'mon, suck my dick like you suck whoever keeps calling!"

"Sal, please don't." She swallowed, her stomach churning, tears burning her eyes. "Please don't keep talking to me like that. We used to talk different, normal."

"Normal? A piece of shit like you, normal? I'm the first normal thing you ever had in your life. You were fucking Jews at Xtra. Now it's probably chinks and spics."

"Sal." She was crying.

"Or with your taste, it's probably nigger cock by now. Big black dicks, right? Come change your luck with this."

He grabbed himself with one hand and waved her peremptorily to him with the other.

She wanted to run away, but knew what could happen, knew how bad the beatings could get. She walked slowly, dragging her feet, as if to her own execution.

"Just make believe I've got a big black rod." He grabbed her arm as she reached the chair. He dragged her down to her knees, and put her hand on his short, thick penis. "Say it! Say: 'I'm gonna suck your dick, nigger-baby.' *Say it!*"

"I . . . I think of *you* when I make love . . ."

"Liar!" He slammed his open hand into her face, knocking her back on her haunches. He was coming off the recliner, and he was raging.

She scrambled backward and turned and was running before she came fully erect. She ran out to the foyer and up the stairs to the second floor and her room. She locked the door and heard him coming up after her, shouting filth.

Then he was banging at the door and she was backing away, terrified.

"Please, honey," she called. "We're going to the wedding Friday and we'll be together and we'll be happy."

"You'll be in a motel," he said, voice suddenly calm; more than calm, cold, which was the way he got when he was still full of rage, but tired. "You'll be there to fuck, no other reason. Shit like you don't go to my family's weddings." And he was gone.

She lay down.

She wished she had a pint to drown the hate, the fear, the pain.

She kept forgetting she had something better than brandy.

"Just think of Friday," she murmured into her pillow. "Bub getting the money. And the week after—collecting your half and leaving that pig! Think of how he'll burn!"

She turned on her side, eyes closed, thinking of Spain and her friend Riso who lived in Malaga, whom she'd called by cable from the downtown phone company office, paying in cash so Sal wouldn't find out. And who'd said yes, he'd love to see her and have her stay with him. And the weather was beautiful on the Costa del Sol and, "God, I'm hungry to see those cute dimples and talk American with a girlfriend."

Riso was a painter who barely made a living. But he was kind, he was gentle, he was lover enough for most women, though perhaps not for Giselle, not after experiencing Bub.

No use thinking of Bub. He was lost to her.

But she did think of him, smiling a little, sure she would always smile, even years from now, at the memory . . .

She must have fallen asleep, because the next thing she knew it was shadowy in the room. Someone was knocking on the door.

"Hey, c'mon, let's make up!" It was Sal, and his words were slurred, and she figured he'd been drinking that red wine his family had drunk for generations.

He was sometimes decent when drunk.

She got up, groggy. She went to the door, but didn't unlock it.

"You okay?" he called, knocking again. Knocking, not banging. And talking, not shouting.

"Yes. What time is it?"

"Almost seven. C'mon down. I'm sorry I lost my temper. Let's play gin."

"All right. I'll freshen up first."

She washed and saw the pale bruise on her right cheek, where he'd slapped her. But nothing much; it would be gone by morning; she'd had some bruises for weeks.

She used makeup and changed into the little black sheath Sal liked because she wanted things to go easy, until she split a week from tomorrow, the evening of the day they would return from New Jersey. She and Bub had decided she wouldn't stay even long enough for Sal to discover the robbery. Too dangerous. She'd arranged to meet Bub that Wednesday night. He already had her passport and a suitcase with clothing she'd bought in the past few weeks.

She'd lose Sal at L.A. Airport when they flew in. She'd go to the ladies room, and then to the Quality Inn, where she'd meet Bub for the payoff. And two hours later, she'd be back at LAX, this time at the

International Center, to catch her booked flight to London. Where she would find where to buy a new passport with a new name. Then Malaga and Riso.

Sal was at the round, green-topped table, finishing a hand of solitaire. A bottle and bucket of ice stood on the rolling cart to his right. He scooped up the cards and shuffled and dealt two hands of rummy. He was drinking Jack Daniels, and he was mellow enough to offer her a glass.

"Yes, thank you," she said, arranging her cards.

He chuckled.

She looked up at him as he poured.

"Ice, please," she said.

He chuckled again. "No ice when you belt from those pints. But whatever the lady wants."

She smiled uncertainly. He dropped in two cubes, handed her the glass, and raised his own. "To our trip east. May you like New Jersey."

They drank, and he said: "May you like it a lot, because you're never going to leave it."

"Pardon?"

He raised his glass again. "*Salud,* Giselle, once like in the ballet. Soon like in Madame Fiori's cathouse."

Her heart began banging away. "Very funny. Let's play gin."

"You think I'm joking?" He shrugged. "So did Violet, the one in San Francisco. And—I forget her name—in St. Louis. Both now in Vegas cathouses. You, I'm afraid, drink a little too much for Vegas. Madame Fiori knows how to handle lushes. She's a dyke, you know. She'll train you good. I don't know if you can get nigger cock, but you might get nigger cunt." He roared laughter.

She stood up. She moved around her chair and backed away, staring at him "I won't go with you," she whispered, "even if you're joking."

"I swear on my mother's grave, I'm not joking."

She believed him, because he took that oath seriously. "I won't go," she repeated, horror rising. "I'll die first."

He nodded. "You got that choice." He rose and went to the phone table and opened the little drawer. He took out a gun, one of those he called revolvers. "You're going to get what's coming to you. What's been coming for a long time, you nympho lush. Either in the cathouse or from this."

He was moving toward her, and she feared death. "All right, I'll go to New Jersey with you."

"Well, you've made me doubt that now, Giselle." He was pursing his lips, frowning. And she suddenly felt he was play-acting, mocking her. "You think you'll throw a scene on the plane—call for help or something. You think you'll get away from me there, or at Kennedy."

"No, Sal. I promise."

He was shaking his head. "I can't take the chance, Giselle. I made a mistake telling you what I was going to do. I wasn't going to, until we visited the cat house and I left you there. But you got me so mad with those phone calls, your lies, your goddamn drinking." He sighed. "Lost my temper, Giselle. Guess I'll have to blow up that dingbat head and lose that workable ass."

He was only a few feet away now, and that black barrel was steady on her forehead.

She opened her mouth, gasping, in mortal fear of her life . . . and at the same time didn't really believe it. Something wrong here. He *hadn't* lost his temper. Not since they'd sat down at the card table. Not during the time he'd supposedly made his "mistake" and told her what he had planned for New Jersey.

So it was one of his horrible games, one of his cruel tricks.

At the same time, she couldn't be sure he wouldn't blow her head apart.

Except, he didn't do killings himself anymore—had

said so a hundred times in the years she'd known him.

"Please," she begged. "Put the gun down, Sal. Whatever you say, but put the gun down."

"What's the point? Even if I do, I can't trust you anymore. You know you're either going into a cat house, or die. So there's just no way . . ."

He suddenly stopped. "Got it!" He lowered the gun. "Simple, too." He turned. "Losing your temper clouds the brain. Don't ever do it, Giselle."

He was at the phone table. He put the gun back in the drawer and closed it. He raised the phone. "I can place you in a house right here in L.A. I'll just call a friend and have him drop over. An hour, and you'll be on your way."

He dialed, and kept talking. "First, they'll give you a few weeks of something soothing. Heroin, mainlined. Then, when you're happy, and hooked, you'll do what you're told for your fixes." He finished dialing. "And for some nice money, too, Giselle. You won't have to beg for clothes, or cigarettes. Maybe for a night off to rest your cunt . . ." He interrupted himself with, "Damn, the line is busy."

He hung up. "Gotta go to the john. Just thank your lucky stars we found a way." And he strolled out, through the dining room, toward the foyer and guest bathroom.

He'd left her with the gun!

He'd been drinking . . .

He never drank *that* much. And he'd seemed more sober down here than when he'd talked to her through her door.

He was playing some sort of game.

Still, she ran to the table and tried the drawer. It opened and she was looking at the revolver.

She heard the toilet flush.

Telling her she was going to be turned into a junkie whore was so wrong for sharp Sal Andro. It was *all* wrong, especially leaving her with the gun.

He was coming back through the dining room.

She grabbed the gun, thinking, "It's empty! Or got blanks! He's going to laugh when I pull the trigger."

He was in the doorway. She leveled the gun at him. It was heavy and she steadied it with her left hand and tightened her finger on the trigger.

"Hey," he said, eyes going wide. "Hey, I didn't mean it." He backed up a step. "I was just fooling around, honey, I swear. It isn't even loaded."

But now she knew it *was!*

He'd made the biggest mistake of his life. Because whether or not she could get the money in his safe, whether or not she could get to Malaga, whether or not she could stay alive was relatively unimportant now. Because he'd made shit out of her and she was going to pull that trigger, over and over, and if there were bullets inside he was dead.

He backed even further.

She said, "Pig!" surprised at how strong her voice was.

He said, "No," voice shaking . . . but she didn't believe the shaking voice, and it stopped her as she was about to pull the trigger.

"No, don't, Christ!" he said, and backed around the dining-room table. He didn't duck and didn't run and it was wrong.

She remembered something then. Something he'd shown the visiting thugs from New York the night he'd forced her to go under the table and suck them off. Something she wasn't supposed to understand down there with old whiskey in her gut and old cock in her mouth and not able to see what he was handing around.

"Grenade-gun," he'd called it. "Old idea, almost forgotten, but handy to have around. You got a friend you don't trust, a friend who's an enemy, someone maybe wants to kill you with your own weapon so as to walk away clear, you leave this for him to find."

There'd been sounds of something heavy sliding across the table. One of the old crooks had said; "Look, Brollo. Lead poured down the barrel about half way, so it still has a hole at the end, so it still looks okay."

Brollo had simply groaned, his being the cock Giselle had reached in her rounds. The others had laughed, slapping the table.

Now she looked across the same table at Andro.

That could be why he'd backed away. And why he'd stopped when he felt there was enough space between them, between himself and a gun that would explode when fired. That wouldn't kill the man she was aiming at, but her.

That could be his trick, his game, his act. She lowered the gun.

And immediately saw his act change.

He began to laugh, to sneer. "No guts! I can turn you into a mainline junkie, farm you out for a lifetime of whoring, and you'll take it because you can't pull a trigger! God, what low shit you are!"

She began to walk toward him. "When the gun touches your belly, Sal, then I'll shoot."

His face changed again, but no act this time. *Fear.* He turned to run.

She shrieked laughter. If she fired close enough to Sal, he would die.

Of course, she, too.

But the game had gone too far and there was no longer any hope of getting the money, of getting away.

She ran after him. She had strong legs, fast legs, when she wasn't drinking. And he was thirty-five years older than she and heavy and slow.

She chased him into the foyer and he glanced desperately at the front door. She knew he'd have no time to open it. He knew it, too, and turned to the stairs.

It was like the games of tag she had played as a kid, and she yelled: *"You're it!"*

Sal ran up the stairs and stumbled and she was almost on him, the gun extended. He looked back and scrambled madly toward the landing on his hands and knees, screaming, "Mother of God, don't, it'll explode!"

She caught him at the closed door to the master bedroom, where he'd inflicted so much humiliation on her, and yelled: *"Tag! You're out!"*

He turned on her then, wild, flailing, and she was

But she couldn't be absolutely sure even as she would finish.

But she couldn't be absolutely sure evey as she jammed the gun into his side, even as he twisted, grabbing for her hand, screaming, "Don't! Don't!" even as she pulled the trigger. It could still be part of his trick, his game of tormenting her.

Then she felt the earth move.

Then she felt herself coming apart in bits and pieces.

And was finally sure as pain began and ended in the same microsecond.

Sal Andro wasn't as lucky.

A neighbor heard the blast, which was considerable, since the revolver held a full load of six .38 caliber bullets and all exploded along with the one under the hammer.

Sal was still alive when rushed to Brentwood General, though most of his right side, including the organs residing there, had been blown away.

As the attending surgeon remarked, "He's a goddamn miracle. Too bad we won't be able to keep him alive long enough for it to mean anything."

What it was for Fanny was complete confusion.

Not sex, not acting, but mix-up, mish-mash, hurlyburly, a bonkers brawl between two naked people, one of whom happened to be her.

At first there was Rob Dennings directing and the

three cameramen, two working and one handling len-
ses and slate-board. At first it was comforting that
there were only four people watching. At first she was
aware of camera angles and lines and making an im-
pact on the audience represented by those cameras.

Then it began to change. Then even as she repeated
lines drilled into her brain and showed emotions rehearsed until they were second nature, she began to
lose control of the situation.

It was Grant Vasper, of course. She'd known he'd
get to her, upset her, disgust her. Known it before
she'd seen him without so much as his shirt.

Now they'd passed the scene where he ripped off her
blouse, skirt, and underthings. Now they were finishing the scene where he forced her to undress him,
twisting her wrist, her arm, her entire body so that she
had to reach in unnatural, anguished poses to remove
his shirt, his trousers.

Now she'd broken free and run across the room of
the hunting lodge toward the door and freedom, and
he caught her and threw her down on the wood floor.
Now he stripped off his shorts and rose and stood over
her, naked except for shoes and socks. And now she
really saw him.

He was a monstrous hulk. He was terribly white because he was almost entirely hairless. As she looked up
from the floor, his legs were like tree trunks stripped
of bark. And his penis . . .

She screamed again, not certain it was in the script.
He was a freak! The damned thing stood out as long
and thick as her arm!

Or so it seemed and she didn't know how she was
going to stand making love to him and she looked at
the cameraman and began to crawl there, for help.

Vasper grabbed her ankle. He rolled her over and
kneeled, shoving that huge organ at her mouth.
"You're not gonna deny Rorke his Candy, are you?"
he said.

She didn't know what came next, because it was confusion, mish-mash, hurly-burly, and she twisted, fighting him.

Dennings called: "Cut, damn it!"

She sat on the floor, shaking her head, clearing it, ready to try and defend herself for forgetting the rehearsed sequence. But it was Vasper whom Dennings talked to.

"What's wrong, Grant?"

Then she saw what was wrong. The hulk had gone soft. The foot-long organ drooped. *Thank God!*

Vasper walked off the set to a chair and his robe. He put it on and sat down. Dennings followed. "Want to break for five minutes?"

Vasper said: "It's no good. It won't work."

Dennings lowered his voice so Fanny couldn't hear.

She got up and hurried over—because her robe was on a nearby chair—and heard Dennings say: "You should have gotten to know each other."

Vasper said: "It wasn't possible."

She walked to them, fastening the robe. "Maybe the scene could be changed."

Dennings looked at her. Not a friendly look. "How would you change it?"

She was afraid to say what was on her mind. Vasper said it for her: "Couldn't we perhaps fudge the rape? Fake it? Forget the hardcore?"

"No way," Dennings said flatly. "I did my two scenes with Cecily. You'll do your one with Fanny."

Vasper shook his big, shaven head. "It's not going to work. I can't deal with someone who is so repelled, so turned-off."

Fanny was stunned, hearing it stated so bluntly. "I wouldn't say *repelled*."

"I thought so," Dennings said, turning to her. "You were supposed to start fellatio, and you didn't."

"It wasn't me walked off that set. I'd've stayed . . ."

"You changed the scene," Dennings interrupted.

"You fought much too long. And you looked like you were not only trying to get out of Rorke's lodge, but out of the studio."

She laughed, not knowing what else to do. It was a mistake. Dennings's face and voice hardened.

"Not funny, miss. If you can't do it, say so and leave. I'll have a replacement in an hour and we'll shoot tomorrow."

"I *can* do it!" she almost shouted, tears pushing at her eyes.

"Tell that to Grant. Right now."

She looked at the big man, and couldn't find words. She knew then that the confusion, the hurly-burly, had been in her mind. Knew that her professionalism had slipped away and left her living the rape—the revulsion and unwillingness to comply.

She had to change those fellings, or lose the part. Because no way could she compete with Vasper and his credits and his being so right, physically, for Rorke. While almost any willing blond would do for Candy.

"I'm sorry, Grant," she whispered, wiping at her eyes, drawing his attention to her tears. She needed time to fight her feelings. He could help her get it from Dennings.

"So am I," Vasper said. "Look, Rob, would you consider letting me out?"

"No chance. *She* goes!"

"Neither of us has to go!" Fanny said. "Please! Let's try it again!"

Vasper was looking straight at her face, her eyes. She managed a small smile. "I . . . I'm terribly nervous."

Vasper looked away. She hadn't fooled him.

But Dennings was saying: "All right. We'll break for half an hour. By the clock. You two talk—use my trailer. I've got some Chivas. One drink won't hurt your concentration."

Vasper looked at her again. She pleaded silently. He

shrugged. "If you say so."

Dennings raised his voice. "Pete, get the cards." Then to Fanny: "I want to get past this scene as much as you do. I want all three sex scenes locked away before there can be any leaks, any news breaks. I want to get on with the acting, the directing. So half an hour, Fanny. After that, I'll do whatever is necessary to get rolling." He walked off.

She stood near Vasper. He murmured: "I know you can't help it. Some women react that way."

She tried not to feel his hugeness, his brutal pock-marked looks, his terrible strength.

"If it's of any interest," he said, still murmuring, "I find you extremely attractive. I mean, far more so than . . ." He stood up. "I could do with that drink." He walked toward the back of the set and Dennings's trailer dressing room.

She hurried after him.

She didn't know what she would do.

She didn't know if she could do anything as far as changing her feelings was concerned. She rarely turned off this way. The few times she had, she'd never allowed the men within yelling distance.

This time, however, was different.

This time, she *had* to let him make love to her. Brutal, total, coital, oral, anal love to her. For considerable money and a chance to make a mark in this town which resisted talent but loved publicity.

And notoriety was the best kind of publicity.

She ran a little, and came alongside him. She said: "Grant." He said, "Yes?" without slowing. She touched his hand. Big and hard, it lay still as she curled all her fingers around two of his.

"I gather that this part is important to you," he said.

She knew he was being cynical, but answered straight. "Very."

"It's not that important to me. Maybe Rob will

change his mind about letting me quit. Which I'd really do, you know. I have three other strong offers."

She felt something for him then. Gratitude. Maybe a little liking, but only in the strictest mental sense. "Wouldn't make any difference. He'll bounce me if we don't get into it."

They were at the trailer. He opened the door to let her in. She sat on the couch-bed, and he poured two stiff Scotches over ice. He gave her a glass and began to turn to a chair. She said, "Grant," and patted the couch. "We've got to talk."

He belted down his drink and moved back to the bottle. He seemed to crowd the trailer all by himself!

She said: "Don't. It's not even eight o'clock."

He nodded and came over and sat down beside her. The couch creaked beneath his weight.

She sipped her drink and shuddered. "I've never had booze this early. And on one cup of coffee."

He pulled his robe over a knee that had begun to show.

She gulped the rest of her drink, gasping, and placed the glass on the floor. And in straightening, took the flap of his robe and pulled it aside. "Let's see that great knee again. Like the Rock of Gibraltar."

He laughed, unconvincingly.

The drink was beginning to hit her.

She put her hand on his knee. "Look, a gnat on a bowling ball."

Again he laughed, but more naturally. "You're trying hard, aren't you?"

"Well, changing chemistry doesn't come easy." She parted his robe a bit more. "What does the Bible say about thy rod and thy staff?"

"They comfort me," he murmured, as her hand moved along those tree-trunk thighs to brush those co-conuts he carried for testicles.

He gasped, then moved her hand back down and

closed his robe. And she'd seen no movement along the length of his limp hose.

His voice rumbled: "I don't think people should do things with their bodies they don't want to do."

"Well, I have to Grant. We both know it."

He shook his head, not looking at her.

He was so upset, so nervous, so certain she couldn't want him, that he was now as turned-off as she was.

She put her hand back on his thigh. He wasn't happy about it. She leaned close and raised her face and kissed his chin. "Can't we be friends, Grant? I treated you lousy and I'm sorry, but we've only got half an hour."

"Twenty minutes."

"If you really want to help me, help me be your friend."

He obviously liked that. He turned his face down to hers, and their lips touched.

She opened her mouth. His kiss intensified, but still remained soft.

A gentle man, this ugly hulk.

People had told her so, but she hadn't been able to see past that pitted, brutal-looking face, that shaved head, that oxlike body.

Now she looked at his eyes, avoiding the rest of him. And his eyes were wide and warm and brown.

"You couldn't have been too tough as a wrestler."

"I didn't have to be. It was acting. I've always been a competent actor."

His voice changed toward the end, thinned and shook, because her hand was again brushing those coconuts. And now *she* was beginning to feel something.

And also to see something she should have seen right away.

The man was okay. The man had turned off because she had turned off. It said something for him; for his humanity.

She kissed him harder. His hand went to her face,

covering one side completely, caressing without moving.

It took a while but his other hand finally went to her robe, and inside it. He touched her breasts.

Her nipples stiffened. He felt them with his fingers. She smiled at him, and as she did his penis began to rise.

His cock was definitely connected to his head, to his heart.

She liked that.

She grasped that stiffening yard.

He said: "Lord, baby, I've dreamed of this from the night poor Coleman pointed you out at his party. I knew then I'd enjoy the hell out of you, if you'd only allow me to."

"I'll allow you to," she murmured, and opened his robe all the way to look at him.

Exciting, really, that big hairless body.

"I promise you won't have a bruise, a scratch, after our scene," he said.

"Don't promise that, Granite Mountain. I want it to work. I'm gonna leave a few marks on you."

"You're a hell of an actress, but I don't care. I'm going to believe you, at least for the length of the scene."

"Believe it for the length of this," she said, really perking now, and went down on him.

He groaned deeply, stroking her head; then said: "Better stop."

"All right, *dahling*. But I don't want to."

He didn't answer, not believing her, and they went back to the set.

Forty minutes later, with a perfect take in the can, with not a bruise on her despite what appeared to be a brutal rape, he *did* believe her. And she was thinking she wouldn't have to bother with Amos Brandon and his leather outfits and whips. Or with Don Baylis and his moods and sickness.

Because she and Granite Mountain were going to brunch. Because he was looking at her in a way Fanny-Girl knew very well, a way that spelled "hooked." Because he had plenty of bread, and more important a hot career and an agent who, he said, "could do great things for you. And will, if I ask him to."

Couldn't beat that, now could you, at least for the short haul.

Certainly not with the freaks she'd been balling!

They were free until tomorrow, so at two-thirty they went to his not-so-little house in Encino and skinny-dipped in his pool and that rod-and-staff wanted to comfort her again. She didn't mind, and even began to get used to his face.

At four-thirty, eating the great Spanish omelette he'd made, she said: *"Dahling,* have you got any Milo . . . I mean, Ovaltine?"

When he said he did, and hurried to heat the milk, she knew she'd struck a home, as her father used to say in his saner moments.

Thinking of her father and his madness, and of all the other creeps who could pop up after that rape scene hit the screen, she decided she might even want a hulk like Granite Mountain around for the long haul, if only for protection.

As for other men, a turn-on once in a while, that could always be managed.

She began to feel decidedly happy.

While he was loading the dishwasher, singing some weird foreign song—opera, she was afraid—she went through the house again, looking into drawers and closets. She decided she could do wonders with jazzy drapes, some life in the carpeting, a few changes of furniture . . . and a few changes in Mr. Granite Mountain himself.

She returned to the kitchen. He had everything cleaned up nicely. She pushed him into a chair and hopped on his lap. "Now what shall we do?" she asked.

And damned if he didn't have an answer, again.

By Wednesday afternoon, Don was ready to go home. But Goodsand and the Cedars–Sinai cardiac staff weren't about to let him.

He was on the third floor, where all the rooms were private and fitted with cardiac assistance equipment, including heartbeat monitoring screens, oxygen masks with patient-adjustable flow, cardiac arrest alarm units, and that most important of all electrical recuperative devices, wall-bracketed color TV to contain thought and vegetate the ability to imagine, i.e., to worry.

He'd watched the tube almost all day yesterday. He was watching again today—a better narcotic than the fruit of the poppy, and he was desperate not to think. He'd already had three walks by five P.M., and planned two more before bedtime. They were his basic training, his preparation for the combat a return to the world outside represented.

Dinner came on a tray delivered by a plump Chicano woman.

He'd been eating well, finishing everything, and did so again. He lay back, digesting, eyes growing heavy, brain clouding over, smiling because more time would pass without thought.

He was awake at six, the tray gone, the TV still flickering. He watched the local news and learned that Sal Andro had finally died of "the massive injuries sustained in an apparent gun accident."

He'd heard about it on yesterday's news, and felt sorry for the little blond girl he'd met briefly at his birthday party. The interesting part was the discovery of "a closet full of money." Andro's family claimed it was legitimate earnings, but because of his Mafia background the Feds had been able to obtain a search and seize warrant "pending further investigation." It was unlikely the IRS would ever release that money.

Don was about to go for another walk when a show-biz commentator came on and used Andro for a lead-in to a reprise of speculation on "the mysterious *Galt's Island* film which actor-director Rob Dennings has been shooting on a tightly closed set at Tajunga Studios. Andro was acquainted with several principals of the reputed X-rated biggie . . ." And so on, with stills of Andro, Rob Dennings, Coleman Berry, two thieves Berry had killed some months back, the sheriff's deputy who had killed Berry, and finally two bikini cheesecake shots, one of which made his mouth go dry. "Leading lady Cecily Warren and supporting sexpot Fanny Batcher are involved, some say, in acting which has never before been presented to the general American public via major theater distribution. And *still* might not be, if the jinx that has so far claimed the lives of half a dozen people associated with those in the film continues."

He tried not to think of her. He walked out into the out of bed, and pulled the thin hospital bathrobe over the white, open-backed hospital gown. He missed the pajamas and terrycloth robe which Cecily had brought him during his other incarcerations. He missed Cecily.

He tried not to think of her. He walked out into the hall, and nodded as the black nurse at the podium-like wall desk said: "You'll be jogging tomorrow." He increased his pace, backless hospital slippers flapping. He walked by doors, most open, and heard sighs, groans, once heavy weeping. He came to his own room, and kept walking.

Twice around, heart beating strongly, breath coming quickly.

Twice around, perspiration beginning to dampen his body.

Alive and kicking, by God!

Yet he was glad to get into bed and sink back and watch television.

No more show-biz comments, so no more thinking.

Except that Cecily should be finished shooting the porn now. Probably been calling him. Freddy, too, because of day-by-day script changes.

And what would Freddy do if he learned Don was safely locked away here? Would his need for a writer be overruled by his need for Cecily's ass? Would he figure it was another opportunity to comfort the lonely beauty? And would she be receptive?

His heart was beating too quickly, too heavily. There was just no escaping what waited out there in the world . . . including things he had forgotten (well, almost) since those first grim months after his M.I.

Street toughs. Criminal attack. Insults requiring manly response. Approaches to and assaults on his woman. Anything leading to a physical confrontation, which he again feared.

He promised himself that the automatic would go back in the Mercedes's glove compartment. He would once again be prepared—no, *willing*—to use it.

He took another walk, three times around the floor.

He slept and awakened and it was eleven-thirty. A cute Asian nurse was handing him two pills and a glass of grapefruit juice. "We all right?" she asked.

He nodded.

She fussed around the bed, bending close, smelling good. He thought of kissing her small mouth and grabbing her big ass. And he had an erection.

His strength had returned far more quickly than it had fled. Except in one area. The mental.

He was still very much the invalid there. He was back to Square One there.

He slept again. He dreamt of Freddy. Freddy slouching around the pool. Naked. His prick sticking straight out. Looking at a girl sunning in a lounge. Cecily.

Don hated him. And awakened still hating him.

He totaled all the evidence of Freddy and Cecily being intimate. And added his hunches, his intuitions, of Freddy's having used her, and him.

He lay there in bed, and for the very first time went over it in detail, again and again, nailing home the abuse of friendship, and of love.

He knew the jinx was reaching out.

Knew he wouldn't be able to escape it this time.

Knew he would do something soon. Something foolish. And fell asleep.

He awoke to an Anglo nurse saying, "Breakfast, Mr. Baylis." As he was finishing the meal, Dr. Goodsand arrived, tall and hale, and went through the stethescope bit and checked his blood pressure and built himself a hospital-visit bill.

"We should discuss a bypass operation, Don. That scar tissue might be too much for you."

Don said nothing.

"Not that it's certain you'll need one, but we should at least consider it. Too many of these arrhythmatic seizures."

Don smiled a little. "Consider opening my chest and cutting away dead flesh and taking arteries from my thigh and stitching them onto my heart?"

"It's a reasonably safe surgical procedure."

"As they said to Rod Serling and others who are no longer with us. Let's try a few years of whole-grain rice, shall we?"

Which sent Goodsand out of the room, chuckling, and allowed Don to get back to his combat training, walking the halls, preparing for Cecily. And Freddy.

Eleven

Friday, October 7,
and Saturday, October 8

It was four A.M. when Bub left his room and walked quietly to the garage. He pressed the automatic door-lift button, and tensed as the engine whined and the hinges rasped. The damned thing had never seemed so loud before!

But then again, it had never been important to him before that it operate silently, without waking Freddy.

He waited a few minutes, standing in the open play-room doorway, listening for any possible reaction from upstairs. When none developed, he went out to the driveway and moved his Caddy to within a foot of the open garage, to within five feet of the storage refrigerator.

No use stalling any longer with the nitro. No use planning any more quick ways to heavy bread. It just wasn't going to happen.

He'd heard about Giselle on the radio Wednesday morning, and that the FBI had found the metal-lined closet and cut into it with acetylene torches. He'd gotten good and stoned that night, playing cards with Freddy, who'd been into a tense and nervous thing of his own, complaining that Baylis wasn't returning his calls and he "needed the bastard for day-to-day script revisions."

Baylis still hadn't returned Fred's calls. The boss-man had driven over to the cliffside house no less than three times in the past three days, and still no contact.

Might be a good thing, Bub thought. Might mean Baylis had left town for a while, getting away from what his girl was doing on that set and what he knew she'd done with Freddy. Might just save someone's neck, because Baylis wouldn't play patsy forever.

But he'd had no heart for Fred's or anyone else's problems Wednesday night. And he had no time for them now. He'd mourned his little blond loser with pot and booze all day Thursday, glad Freddy was out most of the time, shrugging when the boss-man noted he was "partying" rather heavily. He'd mourned her last night at the Good Time club with another little blond, a new dancer in from the boondocks who dug snort and Q and black-on-white. He'd made it back here at three-thirty and dressed in Levi's and sweatshirt and now he was opening the door of the fridge.

He removed the six-packs of beer and cola. He cleared the way for removal of the little wooden box, not quite eight inches high, perhaps two inches on each of its four sides. The box that held the tiny tube of pale yellow liquid wrapped in heavy wool batting. The box that could blow this house sky high.

He reached into the fridge, and cursed himself for having partied so much, so long, last night. Because his hands were sweaty, unsteady. Because he had to withdraw them and dry them on his Levi's and breathe deeply.

Giselle had taken a lot of wiping out, a lot of forgetting. Now he had to forget mourning and big rip-offs and get this old nitro the hell out of here and down to the beach where he could pour it—or *try* to—into the sand.

He reached in and took the box between both hands

and drew it out and straightened and turned and walked through the predawn darkness to his Caddy.

And said, "Bub, you asshole," very quietly so as not to jar the box.

He'd forgotten to open the front passenger's door.

So he had to set the box down on the blacktop—slowly, gently, extra moves creating extra danger—and open the door. And pick the box up; more extra moves.

He put it into the car, on the floor. Then, really sweating, turned it slowly-slowly onto its side. After that he paused to wipe hands and face and say, "Jesus!" and meant it as a prayer.

He now had to jam that box under the passenger's seat. Voodoo said it was the only reasonably safe way to drive with nitro, which was why the box was the size and shape it was.

Voodoo himself had put the box into Bub's car that way, but it had been "fresh" then and as stable as nitro could be.

He slid it under the seat, bending, straining, trying to do it in a single rhythmic motion.

And finished and leaned against the car, relieved.

Relief passed in a moment. Now all he had to do was drive to Santa Monica. And once again fuck with that box.

He lit a cigarette, inhaled a few times, then ground it out beneath his foot. No smoking while driving. No taking either hand off the wheel. No sudden turns or stops.

He backed out to Bedford, slowing to a crawl when he reached the break between driveway and street. Then he was on his way.

An hour later—this for what he normally drove in twenty-five minutes—he was in the parking lot at almost the exact same spot he'd been in with Jason.

He smoked briefly, looking around, and saw no one. It was getting grayish-light at five-ten A.M., but the usual morning mist hung over the beach areas, limiting visibility, for which he was grateful.

He went to the passenger's side and opened the door and bent and carefully slid the box out from under the seat, sweating again.

Quite suddenly, he was sick of sweating; couldn't think what he valued so much in this life of his!

He picked up the box—smoothly enough, but no longer praying and dying with each move—and walked to the blacktop path and down to the beach. Where he knelt in the sand and pried the lid off with his fingers, pulling loose the few tiny nails.

The wool batting was next. A tightly compressed handful exposed a red plastic red stopper, all that showed of a glass vial nestling in the remaining batting. He reached in and drew out a small test tube, much like the ones found in kids' chemistry sets, except that this one was three-quarters full of nitroglycerin.

It was almost over now. All he had to do was remove the stopper and pour the liquid into the sand.

He tugged at the bit of red plastic . . . and it resisted him.

He held the tube in his left hand and pulled at the stopper with thumb and index finger of his right. And the mother wouldn't budge!

His hands were wet again and he would have to put it down and wipe them and start all over.

And suddenly thought: Why not cover it with sand and leave it?

But someone might find it. Someone might step on it. Someone might blow himself to hell.

What was that to Bub Kane? Who looked out for *him?* Certainly not the big pimp in the sky who let someone like Bud's father live forever scoring off broads; who watched while Giselle died and Jason went down the toilet.

Without really thinking, he threw the tube at the crashing sea.

There was another crash, *enormous*, and fire flashed before his eyes not thirty feet away. He was knocked backward, onto his ass, so hard he almost somersaulted. As he straightened into a sitting position, he was hit by a ton of sand, some of it wet and heavy, and covered his head with his arms against the stinging barrage.

When it finally ended, he rose, ears ringing, brushing at his hair and face. And saw the crater between where he stood and the sea. Big enough to bury his car!

He began to shake. He'd *thrown* that fucking tube, and if it had gone off in his hand . . .

The ringing in his ears decreased; he heard seagulls screaming.

He looked around, beginning to think, and hurried to the parking lot.

Turning onto the Pacific Coast Highway, he saw that traffic was increasing. A car going north, as he was, came up behind and sped by in the left lane. Two trucks passed him going south. Then a string of cars in both directions.

No one looked toward the misty beach. No one had noticed the explosion.

It was a quarter to six when he entered the house. He went to his room and undressed and got into the shower. There was sand in his hair, his ears, between his toes, even in the crack of his ass! His face and arms stung from the sandblasting they'd taken.

He was dressing when Freddy called from the kitchen. He finished quickly and went to see what was happening. The boss-man was having another of his long days on the movie, really working his butt off as line producer.

They had a heavy breakfast of eggs, sausage, hot cereal, toast, and coffee. Because Freddy planned on working right through lunch. And because Bud felt he'd burned a week's energy since four A.M.

"Hope I can reach that prick Baylis," Freddy muttered, rising from the table.

Bub said nothing.

"Don't forget tomorrow," Freddy said, heading for the garage.

"What about tomorrow?"

Freddy stopped. "I told you Wednesday to prepare for an afternoon pool party."

Bub did remember something said while he'd been getting stoned, mourning Giselle.

"You mean you haven't shopped or anything?"

"C'mon, boss-man, how long does it take to prepare a buffet for one or two dozen people?"

"Half a dozen. I've asked Pandaro and a date, Dennings and his chink, Cecily Warren and, if I can ever reach him, Don Baylis. Seven with me."

"Small," Bub commented. "Intimate. Not your style."

"It's meant to be a working session. We have problems with a few lines between Dennings and Cecily. A few more between Grant Vasper and Fanny Batcher, but Dennings can present their case. Anyway, I'm going to combine a little work, a little lunch, a little swim." He paused. "A little fence-mending with Baylis, which should make you happy."

Bub nodded, but if he had answered, would have said; "Too late, baby."

"Maybe I'll suggest Cecily bring her son along. She'll be reassured by his presence." And then Bub saw the little grin start, the twinkle of the eyes, and knew the old chicken hawk couldn't resist. "If I can't fuck Cecily's ass anymore, maybe her son's will become available."

"Don't dream it, Freddy."

"Hell, it was a joke." But his eyes avoided Bub's.

Bub turned away, thinking of that closet full of

money and how he'd need it when he was out on the
street. And the closet was gone, along with Giselle.
And Jason's trust fund was also gone.

And he had to go shopping and set up a buffet and
chill champagne and forget bullshit. When the time
came, he'd go back to tending bar. Because he was all
out of big deals.

It was going to be a sweet old age.

Umberto Pandaro was in his office at Tajunga Studios at seven A.M. for a little uninterrupted work, a
little quiet thinking.

He'd screened the three porno scenes with Freddy
yesterday, and they'd satisfied him, despite his being
aware of a weakness in one area. But that weakness
gave him considerable personal satisfaction.

Rob Dennings's organ wasn't small, but for such a
big man, such a proud man, such a super-star, it wasn't
nearly large enough. Pandaro had smiled in the darkness of the projection room as those sequences of Warren riding Dennings, the hand-held camera shooting
from the rear, had filled the screen. Cecily Warren was
very full in the bottom. Rob Dennings didn't come off
nearly as well as he might have with a smaller-
bottomed woman, despite really excellent lens and angle work. The contrast of any but the largest penis to
those swelling buttocks, those full thighs, was bound
to reduce the male ego.

Grant Vasper, on the other hand, was enormous, a
true bull, and looked even larger by contrast with the
boyish bottom of his partner, Fanny Batcher.

From a sexual-visual standpoint, it would have been
better to match Dennings and Batcher, Warren and
Vasper.

But the scenes were successful enough. If the rest of
the film went as well, those three exciting sequences
would make him, Umberto Pandaro, a *fortune!*

The studio owned forty percent of the film, Dennings ten, Gower and Baylis three and one-half each, scriptwriter Otis Daimler one percent. Which had left the two main partners with forty-two percent, or twenty-one each. With Coleman Berry gone, he, Pandaro, owned that full forty-two percent! And it was not to be forgotten that he had a third ownership in Tajunga Studios, which stood to earn tens of millions from its percentage.

If *Galt's Island* did the three-hundred-million business Coleman had predicted for it, Pandaro would get in excess of a hundred fifty million! A foundation on which to build in the manner of a Howard Hughes, a Paul Getty! Even if he should want to play cautious and bank it, he wouldn't be able to. Taxes would rip it to shreds. It necessarily had to be put into new ventures, tax-sheltered investments, profit-producing corporations.

He lit a long cigar and paced the office. First he would buy out the remaining stockholders of Tajunga, making the studio his private domain. Then he would accelerate the production of features and television series. At the same time, he would go in with that independent southwestern theater owner.

But for Davis Lance, he needed heavy cash. He might not have enough to buy the studio *and* a half-interest in the theater chain.

He paced and smoked. He totaled possible profits from *Galt's Island*, subtracted necessary taxes, expenses, new investment capital . . . and found himself coming up short.

He went back to the percentages owned in the movie and considered what each point would be worth. And felt, as he had all along, that Coleman had given in to an unreasonable demand when he'd handed over seven percent to Gower and Baylis. Especially to Baylis, who had also received a percentage of budget.

Whoever heard of a writer getting significant portions of a film's profits? As for Gower, he hadn't invested a dime! If Coleman were around, he'd tell him to his face . . .

He stopped pacing. He forced a smile. He told himself not to be greedy. Baylis had done a fine job on both book and revision of script. Gower had discovered the project, and was handling line production well.

And still he felt he should own at least four of that wayward seven percent.

The only percentage he didn't begrudge was Rob Dennings's, because Dennings was the key to the entire project.

He was surprised when he heard footsteps in the outer office. Who would come here at seven-thirty in the morning?

"Mr. Pandaro?" It was a small balding man of about thirty, dressed in a baggy brown suit and scuffed brown shoes, holding a black zipper case under his arm. "You're Mr. Pandaro, producer of *Galt's Island*, aren't you?"

Umberto didn't respond. He was certain he didn't know this shabby person.

"I'm from the Temple of the Sceptered Crown."

"Soliciting is not allowed in the studio. However . . ." He reached for his wallet, thinking it would be worth a few dollars to rid himself of this pest.

"I'm not soliciting. That's handled by others in the temple."

Umberto stifled impatience. "Temple? You are a Hebrew or Buddhist order?"

The little man smiled, revealing blackened teeth. One saw teeth like that in poor countries, but rarely in America. Then he added discourtesy to his other failings.

"Only a foreigner would think such a thing. We're Basic Book Christians. We symbolize the sceptered crown of Jesus—the crown of thorns, more precious than jewels." He pointed a finger at Umberto. "We live by the very word of Holy Scripture and protect it against defilement by all, no matter how powerful, no matter how wealthy."

"Yes," Umberto said, returning to his desk and sitting down. "You must excuse me now, signore. I am busy."

"Too busy to save yourself from eternal hell fire?"

Umberto sighed. *One of those.* "I am Catholic. My damnation or salvation will be determined by my own."

"Damnation for sure. Because you're a peddler of filth." He smiled again, mildly, but his eyes were mad.

Umberto wondered if he could reach Security this early. "If you'd like, you can leave your name and number for Mr. Pandaro."

"You're the Papist," the man said, voice beginning to rise, to sing-song. "Your picture was in the newspapers when the other filth peddler, Berry, was struck down for his sins." He rocked a little. "You are he who defiles the sceptered crown, the pure Christian heart of America. I've read how you think to bring Sodom and Gomorrah to every theater in the nation. I've seen reports on television, itself a mass of filth . . ."

Umberto got to his feet. "I ask you to leave," he said, and came around the desk. "I ask you politely."

"The devil always asks politely," the little man said, and quickly unzipped his case.

Umberto stopped. Did the Protestant fanatic have a weapon? "Why don't you go to the gate and ask the guard for Mr. Pandaro?"

The little man's hand flashed out, holding a book. "Begone, Satan!"

Umberto released pent-up breath, then rushed forward. He grabbed the man's wrist, pushed him back through the outer office, slammed him against the wall. He shouted: "Someone come here! Call Security!"

The little man's face was pale and oily. His breath, panting in Umberto's face, stank. He said: "I wanted to help, to drive out your devil, but you're damned."

Umberto shouted over and over, not knowing what else to do.

No one came. No one answered.

The little man said: "If you'll let me go, I'll get my things."

"And leave?"

"Why would I stay? You've already lost your soul."

Umberto released him and moved back. The little man picked up his case and walked toward him. Umberto clenched both fists. The little man pointed at the floor. "Don't make the fires hotter."

Umberto moved to the left, away from what he now saw was a New Testament. The little man picked it up and put it in his case. "As the other pornographer was struck down, you will be, too."

The man left. Umberto went to the phone and called the gate.

The guard said no one of that description had come through this morning. "But if he's on foot, he might've made it through the back delivery entrance. Two kids sneaked in last week, looking for autographs. Should I find someone to come to your office?"

Umberto said no, the crisis was over. "Just make certain he does not remain in the studio."

The guard said he'd have Security alerted.

Umberto hung up. A studio wasn't a fortress. Such things occasionally happened. No real harm done anyway.

But his train of thought was broken. His peaceful morning ruined. He was forced to recognize that he could expect many more such incidents after the film was released.

Still, every fortune had its price.

He relit his cigar and headed for Stage 8, where Dennings was directing himself, Grant Vasper, and several extras in one of the opening scenes. Later in the day would come the introduction of Galt's group, which included Fanny Batcher and Ben Bright.

So would end their first week of shooting. A week which, he was certain, all concerned would discuss the rest of their lives. A history-making week. A week that would begin the building of the Pandaro financial empire. From a reasonably wealthy man, he would become a tycoon, perhaps a billionaire!

It was that last thought that finally drove the disgusting little fanatic from his mind.

Don was released from the hospital at ten Friday morning, took a cab to Dr. Goodsand's office—or rather to the parking lot under his office—and drove up to his home at eleven-ten.

The first thing he did was to put the .32 automatic back into the Mercedes's glove compartment.

The second was to sit down at his answering machine and run off his calls.

Among them were no less than nine from Cecily, the last five a terse, "Call Cecily." Also five from Freddy.

Freddy's first call was an invitation to a pool party ". . . this coming Saturday, noonish. But before then, we've got to talk some dialogue changes." His next call was a wheedling, "C'mon now, Donny. We've got work to do. Call me right away, at home." After that, he got progressively more irritated. His last call was a snapped, "Damn it, if you've left town just when I need you most, you haven't any ethics!" Which gave Don his first good laugh of the week.

He called Cecily. Her service answered. He said: "Don Baylis is at home."

He called Freddy, spoke to Bub, was told Freddy would either speak to him later, or wait until the pool party tomorrow.

"You are coming, aren't you, Mr. Baylis?"

Don said he'd see.

There were the usual calls from actors and actresses, most of whom he didn't know, looking for parts. There was a call from his ex-wife, chiding him for being late with his alimony "for maybe the second time in all these years." He wrote out the check and addressed an envelope on the spot.

There was an obscene message from what sounded like a couple of pre-teen girls.

There were also half-a-dozen hangups without messages.

He was leaving the room when the phone rang. He answered it, rather eagerly after four days' isolation.

It was Cecily. "Where the hell were you!"

"Nowhere. Just busy."

"That's not so! I came over four times, once at three in the morning, just to see. Your car was gone. Your house was dark. And how come you didn't put the lights and stereo on the way you always do when you leave town? And why would you leave without telling me?"

"Who can ever reach you?"

"That's no answer! You could leave word on my service! I thought you'd died!" She stopped speaking for what seemed a long time.

"Cecily?"

"Yes," she said, voice unsteady. "Were you sick?"

"No. In Palm Springs."

"I'm coming over."

He desperately wanted to see her. But there was also something cold and unforgiving within him. "You going to Freddy's pool party tomorrow?"

"Yes. Johnny, too."

"We'll see each other then. No reason to rush over."

"I'm leaving now." She hung up.

She made it in record time—not quite twenty minutes.

After kissing him in the hallway, she said: "You weren't in Palm Springs. You're pale. I should've called the hospital. That's where you were, weren't you?"

He shrugged. "For tests. Everything's okay."

"You sure? Because we're going to run another kind of test now."

He smiled.

She took his hand and led him to the bedroom and made love to him. She was wild and hungry, and after a while so was he.

Then she did something she hadn't done since his heart attack—lit up a joint in bed. "Sorry, I need it."

"It's all right." He sat beside her, propped up on pillows, not bothered by the sweet, light haze as he was by tobacco smoke. In the past, he had joined her in blowing weed both before and after lovemaking. It had heightened their pleasure in each other's bodies, though he wasn't convinced that marijuana was, as popular mythology had it, absolutely harmless.

She began to get high, began to get talkative.

First she talked about the straight acting coming up next week: "Five major scenes, more than I've ever done before."

Then, singeing her fingers for a few final drags, she told him about the sex scenes with Dennings. "Some pleasure, I admit, but the greatest pleasure for both of us was when it ended. I tried to call you that afternoon."

She reached into her purse and drew out a plastic bag and from it a good-sized roach. She lit up and sucked deeply.

He said: "You've been smoking a bit this week, haven't you?"

She nodded, letting smoke out slowly. "Uptight about not knowing where you were." Another deep suck. "About other things. Johnny, you know, because of the porn. And Teresa and Resordo." Smoke drifted from her mouth along with words. "Got too much for me."

But when she turned her head to him, she was smiling—the happy smile of the stoned. "Feel so much better now that you're home, bunny. So much better that I'm with you." She kissed his cheek.

"So much better that you're high."

She giggled. "Can't you take just a little drag?" She held out the joint.

"Not according to Goodsand. It could change my heartbeat."

"Too bad." She sucked and held her breath, then let smoke out in little wisps. Her voice, changed by this, thinned by this, nevertheless said something that gripped his attention as fiercely as if it had come through a bullhorn. "That night Fanny spied on me . . . saw me go up to the bedrooms with Freddy and stay and then Rob Dennings went up and later Bub took me home . . . that orgy, she said . . . you said . . ."

"You admitted," he interrupted. "At least to having Freddy and Dennings."

"Fred Gower fed me something—Lude.Quaalude. Drugged me. *Gave* me to Dennings. Maybe that part worked out 'cause . . . 'cause . . ." She dragged on the diminishing roach. She was stoned out of her mind, and he had to bring her back to the subject.

"The sex with Dennings worked out because?"

"He was 'fraid on the set . . . but we'd done it once . . . we were closer . . . it worked out."

"And with Freddy?"

She was burning her fingers on a tiny roach. He took it from her hand and dropped it into the ashtray.

"Best part," she complained. "Most kick."

"You don't need any more kick. What about Freddy? How did it work with him?"

She leaned against his shoulder. She reached under the covers and stroked his belly, his genitals.

The four days' rest had done him good. He began to respond. She pulled back the covers and bent to his stiffening penis. "Little kiss for my baby," she muttered.

He stopped her. "First, how did it work out with Freddy, after he drugged you with Quaalude?"

"In wine, the bastard!" Her face twisted. "In my ass, forcing it, hurting me! Ugly, ugly, and later I found my hair . . . he came, or wiped . . . in my *hair!*" She turned onto her stomach, put her face in the pillow. "Hurt me! Made me feel—when I wanted to be different for my Donny—made me feel dirty!"

She was crying.

He turned her to him and held her and soothed her. He told her she wasn't to feel dirty any more. She wasn't to blame.

"Other things," she wept. "Whole life of other things."

"They don't count. I have a whole life of other things, too. Between us, nothing counts until we become committed to each other."

"Didn't that happen already? When we met?"

"No. And not a year ago. And not now."

"When, Donny?"

"When we make the commitment. Which isn't yet."

"After the movie?"

"Maybe," he said, but didn't think so. Didn't think he'd be around that long. Because Freddy had to pay. He just couldn't see beyond that. Freddy drugging her and giving her to Dennings and shoving his nine inches up her ass and coming in her hair and degrading her.

And inviting them to a pool party, *together!* And wanting script changes, wanting to work with him!

An animal. A sick animal. Who had to be put away like any other sick animal.

"Wha's matter?" Cecily asked, trying to revive his flaccid penis with her hand.

"Not now. Sleep a while."

She sank back, tear-reddened, bleary eyes closing. She breathed regularly.

He guessed she hadn't had much sleep the past week. He guessed he was responsible.

She worried about him, looked out for him, had for a long time now.

He worried about her, but hadn't looked out for her very well.

He went to the car and got the automatic from the glove compartment and brought it into the house. He went down to the second level and his work area and his copy of the script. He put the script in his attaché case; placed the small automatic in a Manila envelope; opened the cover flap of the case.

He hesitated a while, holding the bulging envelope; then put it in the flap and closed the case . . .

It was eleven P.M. Bub was downstairs, working in the kitchen, preparing tomorrow's buffet. Fred was in his bedroom, fresh from a long, relaxing tub, setting up the projector and choosing a reel of film from his private collection.

Only one choice, really, after having screened those three sex scenes with Pandaro yesterday.

He'd enjoyed that huge stud, Grant Vasper, brutalizing the tight-assed blond, Fanny. Enjoyed it enough to call her last night, figuring to make her a few career promises and get some of that tight, boyish ass for himself. She'd informed him she was moving in with Vasper. Then, voice dropping. "He's here right now, helping me pack my things. Give me a few weeks and we'll see."

Good enough. But it wasn't Batcher who had set him afire in that screening room. It was Cecily Warren, whose big tits and ass had made Rob Dennings's genitals look like boy's equipment in a man's game. Cecily Warren who had made if difficult for him to discuss the scenes in professional fashion with Pandaro—how much sex footage they could convince Dennings to run, and so on—because he'd been dying to do something he hadn't done in a hell of a long time. Relieve himself with his hand.

Now he settled into his armchair as the images flashed on the white-painted door that served as a screen: Cecily last May during their second go-round, her back to the camera, her skirt up as he caressed her thighs and waited for the tap on the wall that would signal Bub was filming.

Then drawing her pants down. Then filling both hands with her big solid ass. Then bed and ecstasy.

Watching himself spread those round pillars of flesh to kiss and lick, he knew he was going to try and get her again. Maybe he'd have her over for a "script consultation," make her believe Dennings would be here, dope her fast—Q in a soft drink—"while waiting for Rob." She wouldn't yell about it. She couldn't, just like the last time. Not until the movie she'd waited for all her life was completed. And by then she wouldn't want to yell, because he'd be the first to hand her another starring role, a straight role.

He had opened his robe and pajamas and drawn out his rigid organ. He was stroking it, looking at Cecily. He reached for the hand towel he had ready and put it over his penis and groaned and came.

He shut off the projector in mid-scene. He stumbled to the bathroom, bone tired, and washed and returned to the bedroom. He didn't bother putting away the projector, but dropped his robe on the floor and fell into bed.

He thought of Cecily, and planned how to get her over here Sunday.

He thought of her son, and wondered if he was as good-looking a child as she was a woman. Johnny Warren, he'd heard, was twelve. A boy that age could be a sexual feast.

Thoughts of Cecily and her son—serving him *to-*

gether—were filling his mind; his organ was tumescent and throbbing. He grasped it in a frenzy of desire and said: "God, when will I get what I want!"

It was one of those nights, and he needed something stronger than a Valium. He got up and took a Quaalude from the supply he kept in his medicine chest.

It did the trick; knocked him out.

And kept him out, until Bub shook him awake Saturday morning, saying he had only half an hour to wash, dress, and greet his guests.

It was a hell of a rush, and even so he didn't get downstairs until twelve-twenty, by which time Dennings and his chink had arrived. As Fred was greeting them, Pandaro showed, alone.

Fred suggested champagne with the fresh fruit salad Bub had just put out on the buffet. Bub said he'd get a few bottles from the fridge, and the doorbell rang.

Fred caught Bub, murmuring, "I'll get the door. Keep serving. We're a little behind schedule, both of us."

"Don't worry. I'll catch up on everything. Including straightening your room."

"Forget it. I'm not planning to use it today."

Bub turned to the kitchen. "Thank the Lord."

Fred didn't appreciate that, but that's the way Bub had been going lately.

He opened the front door. "Hey! Author and friend! Or star and friend, to give reverse billing its due. C'mon in."

They responded like dead fish, barely nodding.

So he concentrated on the boy, who walked in behind them. "This must be Johnny! How are you, son?"

He stuck out his hand, and the kid shook it, smiling, saying, "Fine, and you?"

"Better, now that someone's talking to me."

He laughed it up big; laughed and held to the boy's warm hand, pressing it, trying to see if, like Sergio, he'd had gay experience.

But this was a much younger boy, who tugged free to hurry after his mother.

"Hope you brought your swim suit," Fred called. "The pool's heated to eighty-six."

Johnny Warren turned. "My mom said a pool party doesn't mean swimming, but I put it in the car anyway."

"Well, have some lunch, then get your suit and I'll show you where to undress."

"Okay."

Fred's pulse accelerated. He told himself to concentrate on Don and Cecily and getting things to move smoothly. And thought of the boy undressing. And thought of tomorrow and getting Cecily to come here. And thought of the changes Don had to make in the script.

"You just might be a little insane," he told himself, and followed Johnny out to the pool, where Cecily and Dennings were greeting each other cautiously—which was funny after their wild sex scenes, but which was necessary with Don there.

Also funny was Don's face. Deathly pale. He had to be loosened up a little.

Fred went over to him. "Let me take this," he said, reaching for the attaché case.

Don jerked the case away. "No."

"Take it easy, Donny. Have a glass of champagne. Have some food. Relax."

"I'd like to do whatever work is necessary, and leave." They stood near the living room's glass doors. The others were clustered around the buffet table, which was midway between the doors and pool. "Help me to do it quickly, Fred, for both our sakes."

His eyes were underscored by shadows. He looked altogether different from the last time Fred had seen him; different, and *worse*.

"You feeling all right, Donny?"

"Yes, except for having to be here with you."

Fred laughed, not knowing how else to react, and began to turn away.

"You're scum."

Fred felt his face burning. "What the devil is wrong with you?"

Baylis didn't answer, but Freddy knew anyway. Cecily had talked.

Baylis kept looking at him with those sick eyes. Freddy finally said: "You're going to make some dialogue changes. Then I'd *like* you to leave."

"Let's get to it," Baylis said, turning back toward the living room.

"In my own good time," Freddy said, and went to the buffet table. Scum was he? The kike sonofabitch! He strolled over to Cecily and put his arm around her waist, saying, "What a week's work, right, hon?" And laughed as she stiffened and looked past him. He turned his head slightly to look, too. Baylis was staring at them. "C'mon, Donny, a little champagne will make you look more like a man and less like a corpse." And he slid his hand up to touch her breast.

Cecily jerked away from him.

"Sensitive, sensitive," Freddy said. "Everyone knows I'm a boor, so why take umbrage?"

Dennings chuckled, not reading the undercurrents. His girl asked him what he wanted on his plate. Cecily's son said: "Mom, I'm not hungry yet. Can't I swim first?"

She said something about his "fighting swimming on the team," but he was already running back into the house.

Fred talked to Pandaro, who was nibbling on roast beef and sipping champagne. Pandaro said: "Let's consult with the writer. And I don't think you should joke about the way he looks. He doesn't seem well, and he doesn't seem pleased with you."

"He's fine. We'll all sit down together in a while.

First I'm going to change into trunks and have a swim and a soak in the jacuzzi. Join me?"

"I've got a three-thirty appointment. I'm interviewing a promising Italian actress my friend Armando discovered at Cinecitta."

That friend was the Roman who pimped for Pandaro.

Fred Gower didn't need pimps. Fred Gower had his action for today in sight, if he could only manage the delicate timing.

He hurried after Johnny Warren. He went to the front door, which was open, and saw the boy bending into Cecily's Jaguar. A full ass, inherited, no doubt, from his mother. The boy backed out, holding a plastic shopping bag with I. Magnin on the side.

He met the kid at the door. "Seems like you and I are the only ones who're athletic today, Johnny. We're doing the swimming, and they're doing the eating."

He put his arm around the boy's shoulders, Uncle-Freddy-style.

He led him to the staircase and said: "Right up to the locker room."

He walked with him, surreptitiously checking him out. "Guest room's right here, Johnny." He moved the boy inside. "I'll go change. See you in a while."

The kid closed the door.

Fred sprinted to his room, pulling off his shirt as he went. He stripped in record time, grabbing his skimpy red bikini trunks from the drawer, and ran barefoot back to the guest room. He called, "Let's go, tiger!" and opened the door and stepped inside and closed the door.

The kid was sitting on the bed, naked except for his shoes and socks, frozen in the act of pulling off one shoe.

Fred strolled casually past him to the dresser. "Your mother said you're on a swimming team. Where's that, champ?" He began straightening his hair in the mirror, while watching the boy's reflection.

"At the Y." Johnny hurried to remove the shoe and sock, and crossed his left leg to get at the left shoe and sock.

Fred's trunks distended in front as he saw the boy's genitals. Now if Johnny would just hold still for the opening gambit.

Johnny was bending for the plastic bag lying on the floor at his feet. Fred said, without turning, "What's that on your back?"

The boy looked up. "Huh?"

"Stand up a minute."

"Well . . ." He was shy.

"C'mon, John."

The boy rose reluctantly, one hand shielding his genitals.

Fred turned and stepped swiftly over beside him, putting his hands on his shoulders, hoping Johnny hadn't had time to see the bulging bikini shorts. He turned the boy around, back to him, and said, "Here," and dropped his right hand down over the smooth flank to the swelling backside. "Right here." And moved his other hand around front to, to the rounded stomach, pulling him back and into his erection.

"What're you . . . ?" the boy began, and Fred dropped his hand lower and murmured: "You're a hell of a man, you know? All grown up and ready for girls, I'll bet, and for this, too." He pushed Johnny's hand aside and cupped penis and testicles and pressed his lips to the still-childish neck.

"Don't," the boy said, his voice a shocked and shaken whisper. "We gotta go swimming."

He struggled, but Fred had him literally by the balls, and laughed and said: "Hey, you think we're not going swimming? I was on the Olympic tryout team in college." His fingers rubbed that good-sized penis, and felt it stirring. "We used to fool around in the locker room all the time. You ever fool around like this?" He began to slip his penis out the bottom of his shorts and rub the head between the boy's buttocks.

This was a true innocent; what he'd hungered for from the time he'd had his first boy. He could come just by pushing his cock into that virgin crack . . .

The door flew open and a hand spun him around. Bub said: "Hey, Mr. Gower, they're waiting downstairs." And to the boy: "C'mon, Johnny, get your trunks on. Your mother's asking for you and Mr. Baylis is, too."

As Fred tried to speak, tried to get just another minute to rub between those marvelous cheeks, Bub got behind him and actually *threw* him out of the room. And shut the door and said: "Put your cock back in."

"You go too far, Bub!" But he pulled his trunks over the hard-on.

"Not as far as you, Freddy." And still behind him, and still pushing, Bub got him down the stairs, both of them almost falling.

"Go soak it in cold water," Bub whispered, shoving him toward the front door and the john off the foyer.

"I should've done it upstairs," Fred said, glancing toward the glass doors, beginning to worry now.

"Sure, but who could trust you up there?"

Fred ran to the bathroom. He didn't have to soak his penis. It was down by the time he closed the door. Because he realized what a terribly dangerous thing he'd done.

He looked at himself in the mirror and said: "Not just a *little* crazy, man."

Then he wanted to cry.

For what he'd risked.

And for what he'd missed.

He went back through the living room, pulling himself together, preparing to greet the boy and shove him into the pool and swim with him and make him doubt that anything had happened.

Baylis was sitting at one of the two glass-topped tables. Cecily was sitting with him, and they were both sipping champagne. Maybe that would take the edge off their nerves.

But when he walked by, smiling and shrugging a little, apologetically, trying to make peace, Cecily looked away and Baylis shook his head, staring as if at some sort of strange animal.

He felt himself redden, and walked the few steps to where Dennings and Joy-Joy sat. He asked how they liked the food, and saw Pandaro bring a fresh plate from the buffet and stand beside Don and Cecily.

Dennings said: "Excellent, as always. Your man's a gem. If he were prettier, I'd steal him away."

Fred chuckled, and saw Pandaro sit down and begin talking to Don. The Italian looked at Fred, and jerked his head a little, asking him to join them. He was probably discussing the script.

But Fred just couldn't make himself walk over there.

He was sure Cecily had told Don about his using magic to tame her so she'd ball Dennings, and him. Told him flat out, the bitch, ruining a friendship and a useful working arrangement and gaining nothing.

He'd punish her for that! If she'd yelled the last time, wait until tomorrow! He'd really hurt her ass! He'd draw blood!

And he'd get her kid, too! The seduction had been working—he'd felt a stirring, an awakening, in the boy's penis. Johnny Warren, like most pubescent boys, could be had by any smart and reasonably attractive adult, woman *or* man. Because it felt good. Fred simply had to find the right time to once again hold those sweet genitals . . .

But he was turning on, and had to run to the pool and dive in before it showed.

He swam, and Bub came over and asked if he wanted anything from the buffet.

"Trying to make up?" Fred joked. "Too late, man, you're out of the will."

Bub smiled. "I can fix you a plate."

"Not yet. I'm going into the jacuzzi and unwind a little. Serve me there. And a Pilsner glass of champagne."

Bub walked away.

Fred swam the length of the pool and shook water out of his eyes and looked around. His guests were eating, drinking, talking. But he didn't see the kid.

He climbed out and trotted over to the jacuzzi hot tub. He checked the thermometer: Hundred and five, on the dot.

He got into the surging, bubbling water and lowered himself onto the concrete seat and called out: "Isn't anyone going to join me in a quick boil?"

Pandaro said something and Dennings and the chink said something and Cecily and Baylis said nothing.

Bub brought over his plate and champagne.

"Where's Johnny Warren?" Fred asked.

"Don't let's push him. If he's upset, give him time."

But Fred would have liked the boy to appear, to swim, to talk, to be friendly, to erase the nagging worry.

Where the hell *was* he?

Johnny had to go to the bathroom. He felt funny; kind of sick.

He pulled on his bathing shorts and looked around and saw the other door. Bathroom, all right. But after sitting on the toilet a while, he decided he didn't have to make after all.

Still felt funny. Stomach hurt.

That Mr. Gower. Creepy guy! Johnny would tell mom!

But what would he tell her, and how? Embarrassing. And maybe she'd get mad at *him?*

Nothing had happened anyway.

Still, he didn't feel like going downstairs and seeing Gower again. Not right away. He'd look around, rip something off, show the creep.

He opened the medicine chest; found nothing.

He went back to the bedroom, opened drawers and closet. Nothing there either.

He opened the hall door cautiously, in case creepy Gower was around. Then came out onto the landing. A room to his left and, nearer, one to his right. He went to the nearest one.

The door was open. He leaned inside, and it was a mess, like *his* room sometimes. Creepy Gower's, maybe. His house, right?

He saw the projector set up facing him. And film in it. But no screen.

Well, he had to go downstairs anyway.

But creepy Gower would be there, talking to mom, maybe saying something about Johnny.

He went inside and looked behind the door, trying to find the screen. Then he saw how white it was, and closed it all the way.

He went to the projector and examined it. Not too different from the one at home. Same kind of On-Off switch. Self-threading, and the film already started anyway.

He threw the On switch. Figures sprang into life on the door. Color and good focus, but there was too much light in the room. He began to turn away, then turned back, thinking he saw mom. He stared, but it was creepy Gower he saw. Naked. Then something—a stiffie going into a cunt.

Porno!

His heart was banging away so that he could hardly breathe. Because he'd thought he'd seen mom.

He turned from the door, telling himself he had to close the drapes, but really afraid to look at those people, that woman with creepy Gower.

He went to the window and found the cord and pulled. The room darkened.

When he turned back to the door, he saw her clearly. Mom. Doing things with creepy Gower.

Doing everything.

And she'd done it with Horgey. And with Don. And now he knew she'd done it with her other boyfriends; that she was what Klaus had called her and dad had called her: *Whore.*

He sat down in the chair beside the projector. He watched. He began to cry. He was sick.

He turned off the projector when Gower began doing it to her moonie. He got up and went out of the room and over to the stairs. Then he had to run back into the room where he'd undressed and into the bathroom. He vomited until there was nothing but bitter brown water. And strained and gagged and kept vomiting.

When he stopped, he felt dizzy.

He went downstairs and outside and over to the table with food on it. Mom said not to eat right before he went swimming.

He couldn't look at her. He looked for creepy Gower.

He finally saw him, his head and shoulders, past the pool, near the gate to the tennis court, sitting in the jacuzzi.

The sun was hot. He felt terrible.

Creepy Gower!

He began to cry again. He saw the spoons and forks. He saw the knives. He saw the bigger knife to cut the roast beef.

He picked it up and ran across the warm concrete decking. He heard mom calling.

He hated her!

But most of all, he hated creepy Gower.

Who had his back to Johnny. Who was drinking from one of those pretty beer glasses that were small at the bottom and large at the top. Who tilted back his head to finish drinking.

Johnny knelt behind him and stuck the knife into his neck, hard as he could. Like that killer on TV. "Kojak"? Maybe "Hawaii Five-O." Who did it three times before he tried to kill the girl and was caught.

Now creepy Gower would choke and fall over and die.

And he did choke and did fall over, but not right away. The knife went in one side and came out the other and came out the front a bit also, where it was too thick for Gower's throat. Johnny was hit in the face with a stream of hot blood and a terrible scream. And scrambled backward, screaming, too. Because everything was turning red and Gower was standing and twisting around like a dancer on "Donny and Marie" and his hands tore at the knife and his mouth screamed and his eyes bugged out. *And it was too much!*

Too much and all wrong because he'd seen it on "Kojak" and "Baretta" and in the movies!

He turned to his mother, wailing, "But dying's not like this!"

Fred Gower danced in agony. First quickly, around and around, the blood pulsing from his neck, staining him bright red to his waist, staining the water too so that by the time the others had risen to start toward him, he stood in a bubbling, rose-pink bath.

He slowed, hands clutching at the knife—at the handle, the blade—pulling in both directions, shredding the fingers of his left hand; then fluttering pathetically, helplessly, as he stopped his dance. As he toppled onto his knees on the concrete seat, head sinking to the decking. As he croaked: "Bub."

Bub was almost there. Fred Gower could no longer see, but his hand rose and again he spoke—a gurgling, gargling kind of speech—and again he tried to say: "Bub."

Then Bub had reached him, grabbed that raised hand, began to pull him out.

Again the mouth moved. But this time it vomited blood. And belched air. And sagged, as did the body that had been Fred Gower.

Bub released the hand. Bub turned to where the boy was being held by his mother and by Baylis. Bub heard the boy shrieking, ". . . with you in the porno movie!"

The others were there. Pandaro was saying he'd called for an ambulance. The Chinese girl was covering her face, crying. Dennings looked and walked her away.

The red torso lay in the pink pool under the yellow sun against the backdrop of green potted plants near the tennis court fence, and it was so very bright, all of it, it was almost pretty.

Twelve

Monday, October 24

The two weeks since Freddy's death had been strange
ones for Bub Kane. But today was the strangest of all,
and he nodded numbly as he saw the elderly Franklin
Pierce Collins to the door and shook his hand and
thanked him and closed the door. And stood there,
trying to make sense out of his life.

"Franklin Pierce Collins," Bub said aloud, as if
Freddy could hear from his grave at Forest Lawn.
"With a name like that, baby, you know he's got to be
a honky lawyer."

He waited for a laugh, and heard nothing, of course,
because the big house was empty.

Bub Kane had been empty, too, for fifteen days, the
time since the ambulance had taken away the body
and the police had taken the boy.

Not that he hadn't been busy.

He'd sat around a while after everyone had left that
crazy Saturday, then gone into frantic action. He'd
drained the jacuzzi and gotten into it and worked with
pool cleanser and rags and removed every last trace of
Freddy's blood. And done the same on the concrete
decking. He'd cleared away the buffet and folded the

tables and stored them in the shed. Finally, he'd gone to Freddy's room, put away the projector, made the bed, and taken all of Freddy's personal pornography, starting with the reel that had been in the projector, and burned it in the fireplace.

The phone had been ringing and he'd finally answered. The story was out and reporters wanted details. He'd said, over and over: "No one is here. I don't know. Good-bye."

His own phone hadn't rung. Few people left alive to call him. No more Freddy, from a late evening, saying to forget dinner. No more Giselle, saying she could meet him. The people left he didn't trust with his number—the hookers, dealers, pushers, gay pimps.

Those few fun evenings with boys, those frequent evenings with chicks and the camera, had finally cost Freddy.

"Told you to cool it," he said into the empty house. He looked up the staircase leading to the fun rooms. "Told you the dues would be too high."

They'd been too high for Johnny Warren, too.

That had been another strange part of the strange week. He'd called Baylis on Sunday, and finally gotten him to return the call. He'd asked if Johnny had talked about the scene with Freddy in the guest room, figuring the kid would be ashamed and maybe blow a good part of his defense.

The boy hadn't said Word One. Didn't even want to tell the cops about the porno film of his mother and Freddy. Was going to have to be forced to explain his actions by the only person he would listen to, his mother.

Cecily Warren had paid dues almost as high as Freddy's.

Bub had testified in a juvenile court hearing last Wednesday. He'd told about walking in on Fred's play for the kid—"the homosexual seduction attempt" as the lawyer Baylis hired put it. He'd told about the porno film Freddy had left in the projector, "Which someone seems to have stolen."

He'd lied a little more, figuring Cecily Warren, sitting in court with head down and people staring at her, holding onto Baylis's hand like someone going under for the third time, had been hurt enough and poor Freddy couldn't be hurt at all and he himself had to take a chance.

He'd changed the date of the magic act, the drugging of Cecily Warren, to the night those films had been taken. Which wasn't much of a lie, since Freddy had tried to Q her that night; *thought* he'd Q'd her. He'd explained that he knew nothing about the drugging, and looked into the D.A.'s cold blue eyes, and figured he was going to pay some heavy dues himself.

He'd found out that filming porno in one's own home for one's own use wasn't much of a crime in L.A., and with Baylis and Warren keeping the D.A. from filing conspiracy charges on the drugging, he'd walked out clear.

Would have been a laugh, right, if something he didn't do put him in that god-awful downtown slammer? Something that got a woman out of the hole with her kid . . . though she still remained a circus act for the great American public.

Johnny had been placed in the psychiatric ward of L.A. County Hospital for testing.

He would be there a few months. Then, according to the news media, would be returned to the custody of his mother—who'd been drugged, right? And who hadn't had her cover blown on the *Galt's Island* porn.

But custody depended on her following the state psychiatrists' recommendations and putting her son in a school they approved. And living "a moral life," which led to something Bub didn't think she and Baylis were ready for.

So maybe Johnny Warren would be able to stay afloat, though for a while it hadn't looked that way. For a while, with his father raising all sorts of hell about custody, it looked like he'd be a football for a lot of people in a lot of ways. But the father had dropped out when the cost of the kid's freedom had become clear—the school would be damned expensive, and every school afterward, and the state would monitor Johnny and whoever had custody of him for a long time. And maybe daddy swung a little on his own, right?

So he'd pulled a noble disappearing act, telling the cameras, "Whatever's best for my son." So with the court looking over their shoulders, Cecily Warren and Don Baylis had been married last Saturday, and begun living "a moral life."

Talk about shotgun weddings! With the D.A. holding the shotgun!

But now, maybe, Johnny Warren wouldn't go down the toilet.

Bub was climbing the stairs to the second floor. "And neither will Jason, boss-man."

Jason would have his trust fund. Jason would have his chance.

But Jason didn't have a Cecily Warren, a Don Baylis, to look after him.

Bub didn't want to think of the years Jason would have to live with "old Lizabeth," who preferred "old Dexter," who was cool and had his act together and would leave Jason far behind and feeling like garbage. Years of reduction, of training for failure, before he came into thirty or forty grand, if he didn't split and disappear.

And what would another Albert—which was what he'd be by then—be able to do with big bread but blow it?

Bub walked into Freddy's room.

His room now.

With the film destroyed, the projector stored away,

he had removed all traces of what had cost Freddy his life.

He suddenly remembered the dope box under the kitchen sink. And was terrified!

Freddy had given him everything and he didn't want to risk losing it and what was in that box could blow years. Especially with the cold suspicion already in the D.A.'s pale blue eyes.

He ran down the stairs, taking them headlong, two at a time. He knew he was being a clown, that a few more minutes, even a few more days, was hardly a risk. Knew it and couldn't stop and bent to the sink and pulled out the box. Opened it and dumped Q's and R's and a few capsules of speed and a beautiful snowy ounce of cocaine Freddy had scored only a week before his death. Dumped them into the sink and turned on the water and switched on the garbage disposal and shredded it and washed it down the drain.

And looked at a lid of prime Acapulco Gold, an ounce and a third of marijuana, so helpful in making the world less bitter. More helpful than booze and only a little less legal.

But that "little less" was something he wasn't ready to risk; at least not yet. "You understand," he said, speaking to Freddy. "You gave me what I couldn't get with rip-offs, what I'd never have gotten any other way. So I'm scared to muddy the waters, to risk even a small bust."

He dropped it into the disposal.

He went to the living room—his living room. He looked through the glass doors at the pool and tennis court—his pool and his tennis court—and said: "Can you believe it?"

He poured a brandy and sat down. "Why'd you do it, Freddy? Why, man?"

And wondered if it had been the other way around, would he have done it for Freddy?

Franklin Pierce Collins had arrived two hours ago, half an hour late at nine-thirty. He'd apologized, saying he'd miscalculated the traffic.

Bub had shrugged, figuring what difference did it make? Whatever the man had to say wouldn't take five minutes: That Bub's houseboy job was finished. That he had to move out because some relative of Fred's was moving in: some secret son or daughter; some never-mentioned brother or sister.

It turned out Fred had no one. "A second cousin, Mr. Kane, but the will is iron-clad, unbreakable, even if I, as author, do say so myself." He smiled his gray-mustached, satisfied smile. "Mr. Gower said he didn't want anyone to have the slightest chance of taking the estate away from you."

"From *me?*" That was the first he'd heard of it. And remembered Fred's joke a few minutes before his death about, "Too late, man, you're out of the will." And learned he'd inherited everything Freddy had owned.

"There's the house," the stocky Franklin Collins had said, looking at a sheet of paper. "Current value, about seven hundred fifty thousand. Inflated, and we'll submit a lower figure, something closer to Mr. Gower's original purchase price, at tax time." He'd looked up with his calm gray eyes. "Or do I presume too much when I think you'll retain us as lawyers and accountants?"

Bub had muttered: "At least until I sell it."

"Better let me finish before you make such a decision. This house is not only a fine place for you to live, it's an even finer investment. Nothing you can find will match the growth potential of a Beverly Hills home."

Bub had nodded, numb and unbelieving.

"There's a half-million-dollar life insurance policy, payable directly to you as beneficiary rather than to the estate. Payment was designated by Mr. Gower to be made over a period of ten years."

He'd held up a check. Bub had looked at it.

"Cashier's, to the amount of fifty thousand dollars. Deliverable to you after signing the proper forms. The house and other property will, I fear, take a little longer to become yours—formally, that is. Though you will continue to live in the house as probate runs its nefarious course. We'll simply keep you on as caretaker." He'd chuckled. "Wonder what salary you'll pay yourself."

Bub hadn't recognized the hysterical giggle as his own.

"I'll summarize the rest of the estate briefly. There are four savings accounts totaling three hundred and twenty-eight thousand dollars." He'd looked up. "In case you're wondering, Mr. Gower did rather poorly in the market, especially with his inheritance some eight years ago. That's why he decided on such large cash holdings. But they're in four-year certificates, so the earnings are considerable."

"If I'd known he was so loaded," Bub had muttered, "I'd've hit him for a ten-buck raise."

"Perhaps why most of the well-to-do keep their true worth under cover. Now for real property other than the house: There's the San Clemente holdings. Twenty acres of beachview, which can be subdivided into one-third acre lots for single-family dwellings. And six acres zoned for commercial development . . ."

Bub hadn't been able to take any more. He'd jumped up. "It's too much! It just doesn't seem right!"

"It's very right, Mr. Kane, because it's what the deceased wanted. Shall we continue? The San Clemente land will, if sold at the proper time, bring you in excess of a million dollars. Minus various commissions, of course."

"Of course." He'd sunk back into the chair. "You're saying I'm a millionaire?"

"Two and half times over. This house has no mortgage to speak of—thirty thousand—and everything else is owned outright: car, furnishings . . . Are you aware of the Picassos behind you?"

Bub had turned. "You mean the feet?"

"Indeed. Reminiscent of detail from *Guernica*. We list those two at about fifty thousand each, but that assessment was made before Picasso's death. You're probably holding a hundred fifty to two hundred thousand . . ."

"Not me, Mr. Collins! Not for feet on the wall! Can you sell them?"

"Easily."

Then had come the signing of papers. Then he'd been handed the insurance check, which he'd put down on the coffeetable.

"I'd bank that immediately," Collins had said, rising. "Fifty thousand draws considerable interest even in so limited a time as one day."

"What's that between us millionaires?" Bub had said, trying to find reality, a laugh, *himself*.

"But I'm not a millionaire, Mr. Kane."

And so the millionaire houseboy had shown his honky flunky to the door.

Bub had wandered around the house.

Bub had spoken to Freddy.

And now, sitting with his brandy, looking at the fifty-thousand-dollar check, he again spoke. "Thanks."

It didn't seem nearly enough, and yet what else could he do? Freddy was dead.

He drank.

Jason wasn't dead.

He told himself he didn't know what the hell that meant.

He picked up the check and went out to the garage and looked at Freddy's spanking new Caddy, his Caddy. But that would take time to accept.

The whole thing would take time to accept.

He went to the driveway and his old Caddy and drove to his bank on Sunset and added the fifty G's to the nine hundred he'd had. And how the respectful shit did fly! He took out a grand in hundreds, and the manager and guard and everyone else smiled him out the door.

Well, Freddy had given it to him and he'd enjoy it. He'd go out and buy himself some threads and later hit the Good Time Club and show that new blond how to paint a town.

But he went home.

He was nervous.

He wandered around and wondered what the hell was wrong.

It was so fucking *empty* here!

Then why hadn't he done what he'd planned to do? Buy the clothes and paint the town?

Because it was fucking empty out there, too.

Bub Kane was suddenly frightened. He had what he'd always wanted. And he didn't know what to do with it.

"*Sheeit,* nigger," he said, mocking himself. "You take your time and learn what to do with it. Collins'll help and the bread will roll in steady and you'll live forever."

His voice seemed to echo in the big house.

He wanted Freddy. He wanted Giselle. He wanted *someone.*

Plenty cunt out there . . .

He wanted Jason.

It hit him as he was reaching for the brandy.

He shook his head and said: "Crazy!"

And went out to his car and headed for the San Diego Freeway.

He arrived at misnamed Gold Drive and the Dunster home at four. They were all there—Jason and Dexter and old Lizabeth.

He asked Jason to walk with him. The kid was sullen, but shrugged and bopped along.

By the time they came back, he was no longer sullen, and he took Dexter outside so Bub could talk to
old Lizabeth.

She was shocked, she declared, that he would even
consider she'd give up her son.

"Stepson. And he'll leave you soon, you know that.
And what'll happen to him then?"

She acted outraged, but when he suggested compen-
sation for her loss, she grew quiet . . . and greedy.

He gave her five of the hundred-dollar bills in his
wallet. She would get another five when she signed the
papers Collins would draw up for him.

Jason packed some of his things. Dexter looked on,
and finally said to Bub, "What good will he be to
you?" His mother turned quickly from where she was
stuffing clothes into paper bags, and said, "Hush up!"
and smiled anxiously at Bub. "That's just his way of
saying he don't want Jason to go."

On the freeway to Los Angeles, Bub told him where
they'd be living.

"What? Two niggers in Beverly Hills?"

Bub laughed. "There are quite a few of us around.
Don't sweat it."

"If you say."

They were quiet a while.

"Uncle Bub, why you doin' this?"

It was a quiet question. It was a deadly serious question. It was the one question that had to be answered
to Jason's satisfaction.

"I want a son," Bub said, "and you're about the
cheapest I can find."

For a moment he thought he'd blown it, buried that
true first part of his answer with that gag second part.
Because Jason's face remained blank. Then the kid
put back his head and laughed. "Yeah! You got it!
Biggest bargain since Kunte Kintel"

After that he relaxed and talked too much and played rock music too loud.

Bub sighed, thinking of all the shit, all the problems, that were coming his way.

But at the house, showing him around, trying to keep his bellows of delight down— "Man, you mean this *ours?*"—he knew one thing for sure:

It wasn't going to be empty anymore. Inside or out.

Umberto sat in the living room, looking through the glass walls at the incredible view, made even more dramatic by dark clouds beginning to move in from the distant ocean. "I must compliment you on your home," he said to Don Baylis, then remembered to include Cecily Warren in his glance. Difficult to believe they were married, when he had in his possession the film of her and Dennings.

But that was why he was here. To use that film as leverage to make the writer's percentage more equitable, more reasonable. A percent and a half was standard, and even that was generous considering that the writer had already received two hundred and thirty-five thousand dollars.

"Thank you," Baylis said, sitting at the left end of the couch on which Umberto sat. Cecily sat on a decorative black cloth chair across from them. Neither she nor Baylis fit the picture of happy newlyweds, married just two days ago. They were both quiet, grim, with Cecily sicker-looking than the cardiac-afflicted writer.

"I must also congratulate you on your marriage. I would have liked to have been there, but I understand why you could not make an affair of it."

"It was affair enough," Baylis said, smiling thinly. "We had quite a guest list. Juvenile authorities, judge, district attorney, no less than three psychiatrists."

"And Johnny," Cecily murmured.

Baylis nodded. "Yes, Johnny."

"He was very happy. He smiled for the first time since . . ."

"Yes," Baylis said.

"I'm glad," Umberto said, "that you were able to work things out to help the boy. I still can't believe what I saw." He shook his head. "Forgive me. It is too much of a tragedy to be discussed."

They nodded.

But it hadn't been that much of a tragedy for Umberto. Because he'd gotten another three and one-half percent of the film, Freddy's share. He was at the point where, projecting profits, he might be able to buy half of that southwestern movie theater chain from the Texan, Davis Lance, outright.

With another two percent, he would be assured the theater chain.

He took the contract from his pocket and laid it on the coffee table. "I was hoping you wouldn't be here, Cecily, when I discussed this with . . . your husband."

"I was there when Rob and I did the scenes," she said flatly. "Remember? You were there, too, for a while."

Umberto wasn't going to be sensitive. He was going to be firm.

"That is your signed contract, Cecily, in which you agreed to do the role of Amelia in *Galt's Island*. Including two fully realized sexual sequences. Now you've informed Dennings that you can't continue in the role. He has been shooting around you for two weeks, but we have reached the point where you must return to the studio."

"You know I can't."

He knew it very well, but it was not to his advantage to admit it. "We are talking about what is currently a four-million-dollar investment, which will probably grow to six million." He avoided saying anything about possible hundreds of millions in profits, because he wanted Baylis to give up most of his percentage of those profits. "We're talking about the loss of those two scenes you already filmed, and the need to find someone to take your place at this late date. Rob Dennings is terribly distraught . . ."

"What will it cost me," Baylis interrupted quietly, "for destruction of the film?" He didn't mention her contract, because they both knew it was unimportant.

Umberto didn't hesitate. "Two percent."

Cecily gasped. "That's insane! What if I just failed to show and let you sue? It would take forever and all you'd get would be my advances."

"And we'd invoke the illness clause," Baylis said. But he was examining the floor, and Umberto knew he understood who held the pistol and who was looking down the barrel, as his father used to say.

"That's right!" Cecily said heatedly. "I *am* ill over everything that's happened. And you're asking us to give up what could be worth two million dollars!"

"Or six million," Baylis said, still quietly, still examining the floor, "if we place that two percent against three hundred million, a figure much used by Freddy and your late partner, Berry."

Umberto picked up the contract. "I am sorry you feel that way. We protected Mrs. Baylis while the court hearings were in progress. But now I must salvage what I can from the scenes she already completed."

"But how can you use them if I'm not around for the rest of the movie?"

Naïve, Umberto thought. Could she not see that he did not have to use them? Had only to threaten to use them?

He allowed her a few seconds for thought, then met her look, a mixture of puzzlement and fright. She was beginning to see the pistol.

"As flashbacks into Rob's, or rather Galt's, Lothario

past. It will add spice, and create additional public interest."

She turned to Baylis. "Donny! They'll take my son from me! And what will it do to his mind if he ever finds out?"

Umberto tried to look upset. "Business often requires harsh . . ."

"It's a deal," Baylis interrupted, still calm. An amazing display of self-control, Umberto thought, and he was grateful for it.

Baylis said: "You'll burn the master in front of me, and any prints."

"There are no prints this early." He felt sure Baylis knew this and was simply playing safe.

Cecily said: "It's blackmail!" She was glaring.

Umberto rose, annoyed by her lack of restraint. "I could have asked for the entire three and a half percent." He looked at Baylis.

The writer nodded.

Still incensed, she also rose. "Then why didn't you? Why not ask for the two hundred thousand back? And the thirty-five for the revision? And my ten thousand in advances? And this house? And our cars?"

"Because I am moderate in all things! The three and a half percent was an outrageous overpayment . . ."

"Easy," Baylis said, still sitting relaxed. "I'm glad to be getting out."

Cecily turned to him, staring. Umberto couldn't help doing the same.

"You mean the jinx, Donny?"

Umberto said: "That is superstitious nonsense, media sensationalism."

The writer smiled. "My sentiments exactly. Last week. Or maybe last month. But Mr. Pandaro, there are more corpses and ruined lives scattered around this movie than in the last act of *Hamlet*."

Umberto matched the smile. "Then perhaps you would like to sell your remaining ownership?"

"Yes, I would."

"Donny, wait a minute!"

"I've always hated the project," Baylis said. "I've never believed it would get made as planned, or if so, would be distributed as made, or if so, would make the money everyone thinks it will."

"Donny, it's *going* to! As long as Rob Dennings is willing . . ."

"How much do you want for your percent and a half?" Umberto quickly asked.

"Five hundred thousand."

"That's not enough!" Cecily said.

"She's right," Baylis said, "and you know it."

"Perhaps," Umberto said, knowing more than that; knowing he had this man in several ways. And the most important, at the moment, was the emotional. "But I'm the only financier left on the film. And I'm desperately short of cash."

Cecily sat down, shaking her head. "Don't," she muttered. "It's our future."

Baylis said: "Exactly why we're getting out. My name removed as completely as yours."

Umberto said: "I can manage to remove your name, but can only pay half that sum."

Baylis smiled at him. And his smile had changed; was mocking, insulting.

Umberto turned toward the door. He'd been prepared to come up to three hundred thousand, perhaps three hundred fifty. But no longer. "A quarter of a million is what I will pay."

"Then we won't sell, right, Donny?" She was smiling, glad the deal had fallen through. As she should have been.

But Umberto knew his man. Umberto walked to the door and waited to be stopped.

"Pandaro."

The *mister* was missing, but Umberto could afford to forgive such slights. He was squeezing this emotional fool like a grape in the press, leaving nothing but an empty skin.

"I'll take it."

It was Umberto's turn to be insulting. "I knew you would."

Baylis nodded, still smiling, and strangely the mockery, the insult, had left his smile.

"If you and Mrs. Baylis will join me and my lawyer tomorrow . . ."

"It'll have to wait," Baylis interrupted. "We're finally getting away for a week. Our honeymoon. Not the happiest time, perhaps, but I want it very badly."

Umberto also wanted something very badly—to have this deal concluded before Baylis could change his mind. "I'll have a simple letter of agreement ready by eight A.M. Is that satisfactory?"

"Afraid not. We were supposed to leave this morning." He looked at his wife. "I put it off because I guessed what you had in mind and wanted to get it out of the way. Now we'll leave within the hour. Can't put off a honeymoon twice on the same day, can we?"

He kept looking at Cecily as he spoke to Umberto. And she looked back at him, emptying of her previous anger, beginning to smile a little.

The emotional writer and the harlot actress had obviously convinced themselves they had something more important than six million dollars.

How ridiculous!

Umberto actually chuckled. "Ah, well, what can a mere businessman do against Cupid?"

Baylis said: "What indeed?" But then he rose and showed Umberto to the door graciously enough. Where they arranged to meet at the studio one week from today.

Driving his Ferrari down the winding canyon road, seeing the first spatterings of rain hit the windshield, Umberto reached for a cigar, feeling good, but not as good as he would feel next Monday at this hour.

And thought he recognized the driver of the shabby Pinto that came around a bend toward him, and past him.

That fat scriptwriter, Daimler, wasn't it?

Perhaps the writers had become friends.

Perhaps the harlot's honeymoon consisted of *two* writers and herself.

He chuckled. He would have liked to have sampled her himself.

Well, someday. Harlots never changed. A woman was either virtuous, or she was not. There were no in-betweens.

He had screened those sex scenes between Warren and Dennings no less than four times since Fred Gower's murder; had used them to stimulate himself for encounters with other harlots.

It would be a shame to burn them.

For a moment he considered making a print.

But only for a moment.

It was beneath him. After all, he was Eugenio Pandaro's son. And his sense of ethics was impeccable.

"How can we go away?" Cecily asked, after Pandaro had left. "There are those sessions with Johnny and the psychiatrist."

"We can't go away."

"Then why did you tell him that?"

"We *can* have a honeymoon. The reporters have stopped bugging us. Pandaro will think we're out of town. We won't answer the phone."

He bent over her chair, kissed her cheek. "And I want him to wait a little, sweat a little."

She smiled, nodded. She knew she had no right to, but she almost felt happy.

"We'll go to restaurants every night," she said.

"We'll go to the beach and walk," he said.

She put her arms up around his neck. "We'll go to

the Getty Museum in Malibu and you'll lecture me on art."

"We'll go to your house in North Hollywood and make love in your bed."

Her arms dropped. "My tenants will be in next week," she said, voice changing, happiness slipping away.

"I know. But we're honeymooning *this* week."

"Donny, please." She stood up and walked to the glass wall. Rain drifted in from the sea like a gray curtain. It was beautiful, seen from here, and it was sad. Resordo had died on a rainy night. Teresa had died on a rainy night. "Too many memories. Too fresh." The rain increased; the city grew dim.

"Yes, I should have realized." He came up behind her. He put his arms around her and caressed her breasts, pressed into her rear.

She didn't move away, but she wanted to. They'd made love twice since that terrible Saturday at Freddy's—last night and two nights before that. Neither time had she achieved orgasm. Because she couldn't forget that it was what she did with her body that had led to Johnny's committing murder.

Still, she wanted to give her Donny—her *husband*, if you could believe!—pleasure. Wanted to make him happy because of his love, his support, his help, everything he'd done for her and her son.

She turned. She stroked his sides, pressed herself to him. She did all the things she'd done when in passion, in heat. Only now she did them by rote.

They went to the bedroom. She undressed slowly, the way he liked. She turned in front of the mirrored closet doors, the way he liked. He lay on the bed, watching, smiling. Then he said something that made her pause.

"I know it's not working for you. I know you're doing it for me. I'd stop you, if I didn't need you so much. I'm glad we had to marry. And I promise I'll do everything to make Johnny's life strong, meaningful, stable. Now come here and suck this!"

She did. He said some other things. He said she would enjoy him again, soon.

She had news for him. She was enjoying him now!

He felt it. He went down on her. He went on and on. And got her off.

They did a missionary. He came, and so did she.

Then a dam broke inside her, and she cried and laughed and slept in his arms. She awoke with rain pounding on the roof, rattling on the glass walls. His finger was tracing the line of her cheek, her chin. She moved her head and kissed him.

"Listen to that," he said, as the rain became a downpour. "Three years of drought. Now months with heavy rain. From cracked earth to flash floods. This whole damned city's going to slide into the sea one day. If the San Andreas Fault doesn't get it first."

"Want to move?" she asked.

"What, and give up show biz?"

She laughed, and ran her hand down his body.

He said: "Hey, no more for the old man."

She got up and looked out the glass wall. "We'll have to skip the restaurant tonight."

She went to the kitchen to prepare dinner. And felt, for the first time, like Mrs. Donald Baylis.

Thirteen

Thursday, October 27,
to Monday, November 7

It was six-thirty in the evening and raining again.

And Cecily was getting ready to go out again.

Don sat at his typewriter and tried to feel excited about having actually started a new novel. It was finally happening—the words flowing, the pages building. Three days, or mainly nights, of work, and he'd finished a thirty-four-page chapter. And knew where he was going.

It had done more to strengthen him than all of Goodsand's medication and treatment. He could almost feel that scar tissue growing more flexible, that pumping chamber pumping harder. He'd even decided he would soon be able to call his children and break the news of his marriage, no small task for the once suburban husband and father.

And it was all due to Cecily.

He stopped working and stood up, forcing a chuckle.

It had been raining, sometimes storming, since Monday. On Tuesday, she'd encouraged him to try writing. "Just to relax, Donny. Just to experiment."

So he had. And it had flowed without tension, without stress.

He'd worked four hours during the day, and

thought to spend the evening with her—Canasta or Monopoly or reading or even television. But she'd been unable to sit still; had paced about and finally said she wanted to "look through the stores on Wilshire and in Beverly Hills. It's my hobby, Donny. The way I relax."

"Fine," he'd said, turning to the bedroom to get his raincoat.

She'd said it would be a waste of time for him. "You're working, and you know how important that is."

He would have persisted, but he could feel she wanted to be alone.

Understandable. The marriage had been forced on her, as it had on him. It would take getting used to. They were both accustomed to freedom. They'd both been single for many years.

So she'd left and he'd worked, and worked well. And been grateful to her. But toward midnight, he'd begun to grow tense. He hadn't wanted to notice the time; had told himself it was just more hours for him to continue along this miraculous road to *Arbeit*. He'd stuck to the typewriter in order not to grow fearful, or suspicious.

At one-thirty, she'd returned.

He hadn't asked any questions. She'd said she'd shopped and gone to see a late movie. "Wanted you to have all the time in the world, bun." But her eyes hadn't met his.

It had rained last night, also. Again, she had said he should write—"Don't stop now that it's beginning to come, bun"—and driven off into the storm. *Quite* a storm last night, and he'd worried and fought it with work.

At midnight he'd found he was sweating, with rage. Then used the rage to fire his writing, as he had in the past, as he'd never thought to do again.

So when she'd returned, a little earlier at a few minutes to one, the ambivalence of his feelings had helped him maintain a calm exterior.

Again she'd given a quick explanation—shopping and a long drive along the Pacific Coast Highway "to think things out"—and failed to meet his eyes.

And again he'd refused to play inquisitor and dig for the truth.

She was in the bedroom right now, derssing for still another night out.

She'd made love to him both Tuesday and Wednesday nights, preoccupied, he had felt, with other things. Made love without the pleasure she'd obviously felt on Monday night, when he'd thought they'd finally begun to jell. She'd given him a payoff.

For what?

Could a woman who'd had him and the old Mexican and who knew how many others, at the same time, could such a woman change just because a judge said marriage was one of the conditions for her retaining guardianship of her son?

He was pacing. He was back to Square One. He was thinking of her with a man, someone she'd known for a long time, had been having sex with for a long time, had begun having sex with again.

But would she be so obvious?

She was in the study doorway. "Back to the typewriter, bun." She smiled, and it was a failure. She looked worn, his wife of two and a half weeks. She looked worse than she'd looked in court. She was *driven;* he sensed it.

He nodded, and sat down again. "Don't be quite as late," he murmured, and picked up a typed page.

"All right. But don't worry. And Donny . . ."

He didn't look up. He was afraid he'd play inquisitor after all.

"Give me a little more time." She came up behind him and touched his face. An incredibly gentle, endearing touch.

But she was an expert at handling men. It was her profession. Marriage wouldn't change that, even if she felt some guilt.

He still couldn't understand the boldness of her actions, the stupidity of her timing.

Could someone be blackmailing her? But with Pandaro ready to burn the porn . . .

Dennings? Hardly his style. More like a cameraman, one of the few who'd been present during the filmings. Someone who was pressuring her with threats to go to one of the toilet-paper publications.

She was terrified of losing her son, and even more terrified that he find out anything that would further damage his image of her, and his mind.

He was guessing, yes, but there had to be an explanation for these nights out!

She was walking down the hallway to the front door.

He stood up. *He had to know*. He went quietly to the bedroom and got into his raincoat. And there in the closet, where he had placed it Saturday night, was his attaché case.

He had taken out the script.

He hadn't taken out the gun.

He heard Cecily in the kitchen, running the water, perhaps swallowing one of the tranquilizers her doctor had prescribed. Dangerous, he felt, to tranquilize and drive, but she did it anyway.

Or maybe it was her birth-control pill. Maybe she preferred to take it before leaving for her liaison.

He opened the attaché case, the flap, and the Manila envelope. He removed the small .32 automatic and put it in his pocket. As he did, his mouth twisted in contempt—*self*-contempt.

He had carried that gun in his car for months and never gotten close to using it.

He had thought to protect Cecily, himself, his manhood, and had allowed every possible horror to happen.

Cecily drugged, after he'd suspected she'd been with Freddy.

Johnny homosexually handled while he, Don, sat downstairs with that gun in his case and made up excuses why not to use it.

So that the child had been the one to strike. So that the child, and Cecily, had paid the price.

He heard her sliding open the front door. "Work hard, bunny," she called.

He didn't answer, because she might wonder why he'd gone to the bedroom.

She hesitated a moment, then left.

He came out of the bedroom. He went to the carport door and heard the Jaguar start and the gate lifting. He watched through the frosted glass as her headlights swung around to the left and moved up the hill.

So she wasn't going to the Basin, the city, Wilshire Boulevard, Beverly Hills, the stores.

Lie One.

He ran out and got into the Mercedes as her automatic control lowered the gate. She was already around the first bend as he reversed the gate and started up and backed out, spinning his wheels on the wet road.

Two bends later, her taillights—or one, since the left was out—came into view, and he slowed, keeping pace with her. He was safe behind his headlights as long as he didn't get too close, or off to the side, where she might pick up characteristics of the SL coupe.

They drove up the canyon road, into an increasing rain, and with each turn he felt the weight of the gun in his pocket, pressing his hip. And instead of being comforted was tormented.

One of the lessons every good writer learned came under the heading of "The Gun in the Drawer."

If you introduced a gun anywhere in your story, you

couldn't forget it afterward. You had to use it. Otherwise, you cheated the reader, the viewer, the listener.

He had introduced a gun and had failed to use it.

Maybe tonight.

He peered through the downpour after that single taillight as it led him down Appian Way, then turned sharply left onto Lookout Mountain. And doubted he could use the gun tonight or any night.

No matter what the provocation.

As he hadn't been able to use it facing Freddy Saturday, hating his guts, inciting the man to strike him, doubting he could use it even if Freddy had attacked.

Cecily turned onto Laurel Canyon, heading for the Valley.

Heading for North Hollywood!

"She's going to her house!" he said. "She's been sitting there the last two nights, thinking, mourning, going through her child's things, counting her sins, reliving the past. A very private thing and she couldn't discuss it with me, admit it to me, not yet. *That's it!*"

They reached the crest, Mulholland, the road dividing city from Valley. And she turned right.

She wasn't going home. That *wasn't* it. He was back to Square One.

Back to that gun in his pocket. Back to the image of Cecily in the arms of another man, and he coming up to them. And doing nothing.

Because he wouldn't kill for that. After seeing Freddy's end, how could he kill for that?

"Goddamn *talker!*" he snarled, despising himself. *"Writer!"*

And it wasn't his pride, it was his shame. *"Bullshit artist! Coward!"*

Mulholland wound almost as badly as Sunset Plaza. Coming around a bend into a straight section, he realized that the Jaguar was no longer in front of him. And almost immediately saw headlights on his left, swinging into position in a parking spot. Saw it was the Jaguar jockeying to face the Valley.

He accelerated, leaving Cecily far behind, hidden by bends. He began to come up with new words, new bullshit, to justify his going home without passing her again.

He feared seeing another car there, catching her with a man there.

At the same time, the talker, writer, bullshit artist felt it was something else entirely. That parking place she'd chosen was either the exact one from which her sister Teresa's car had gone over the cliff, or very close to it.

She was reliving things, thinking things through, where her sister had last drawn breath. And perhaps in downtown Wilshire, where they'd put her old friend Resordo. And at her house, where her son's life was all around her, where everything came together.

So he could go home without spying on her any further. And without turning and passing the Mulholland parking area. He could take Nichols Canyon to Hollywood Boulevard and return to Sunset Plaza.

But that was far out of his way.

Why go out of his way on such a dismal night? Why be so afraid?

He slowed. He fought it out. Then he U-turned and headed back, telling himself he was right about Cecily, his wife, who wouldn't do anything so stupid.

He came around a bend and saw the cars, two of them. One was the Jaguar. The other, parked on a slant behind it, was a compact.

His heart tried to kill him with wild, heavy beating.

He drove slowly around the following bend, and pulled onto the shoulder. He cut his lights because they could give him away, but didn't think of the ignition; just got out and began walking.

The rain soaked his head in a few seconds. Water

ran into his eyes. He could cry if he wanted to and no one would know.

He walked in mud. He wore thin-soled loafers with low sides and felt water and soil reach his socks, his feet.

He came up behind the compact—Toyota, he thought—and heard her before he saw her.

A cry. Of passion, obviously.

It stabbed that scarred heart. It tried to murder him as he came along the left side, the driver's side, and drew the gun and jacked a shell into the chamber.

He pulled open the door. The light went on. He saw them. He knew one thing, she hadn't come to this willingly, and put his gun against the back of the man's head.

The man who crouched like a big animal; who with the dampness and genitalia and sweat in that sealed car *smelled* like a big animal. The man kneeling on the seat, shoving his penis into Cecily's mouth as she lay with her head against the opposite door. The man with one hand on her throat—big, meaty hand, thick fingers crushing viselike—and the other moving between her legs. And her clothes torn and her breasts hanging free and the quiet animal voice just now ending: ". . . fuck you dead."

Otis Daimler.

The shock of that recognition robbed Don of his instant of fury, and instead of pulling the trigger and blowing away the animal, he talked. "Don't move. Except to let her go. Slowly."

The animal's hands (it *was* Daimler, and yet that crouching, that growling, that panting) left her. First her throat. Then her crotch, reluctantly. The animal's head turned just a little, and Don jabbed its temple with the gun. *"Don't!"* And hoped it was convincing, because all he wanted was Cecily out of the car. Couldn't think beyond that.

She was sobbing. She was scrambling out the door,

falling on her knees in the mud. "Donny, he came into my car! He said he did it to Teresa and he was going . . ."

She was running around the front of the Toyota, arms outstretched, coming at him wild and babbling, and if she grabbed him the animal could attack.

". . . to do it to me and dragged me into his car so he could take me to his place later and play . . ."

He swung his left fist at her chin, and hit the side of her head instead. She went down anyway.

The gun had moved as he had moved. The animal jumped away, still on its knees, toward the open passenger's door.

Don said: "I'll kill you."

The animal that was Daimler stopped with one foot out the door. He turned his face fully toward Don and croaked: "Went crazy."

Cecily was sitting in the mud, crying and talking again. "Said he followed me and killed Teresa and killed people, all his life, killed people."

"That's not so," Daimler said, clearing his throat. "Just to frighten her."

But Don noticed that his penis was still rigid. And as Cecily stood up, his eyes went to her. And such eyes! Such wild, *alive* eyes, like a cat's in the dark.

Don said: "Cecily, go to your car."

"I can't drive! He said he killed a girl in a lot! He said he killed a boy on a street! He said he broke Teresa's neck!"

"Go to your car," Don repeated, keeping his voice quiet, beginning to know something without wanting to admit it.

"Let me go with *you*. I can't drive!"

"You'll have to," Don said, and his finger was tight on the trigger and the animal's eyes flickered from the gun to Cecily and the penis stuck straight up, quivering. And the big hands clenched and unclenched, one on top of the seat, not too far from the gun.

Don took a small step back. He brushed water from his eyes, feeling he was in danger. Because he couldn't take this man—animal—to the police. Because he couldn't hold him long enough for Cecily to bring the police. Because the animal wasn't going to wait.

Daimler moved, just a little, but it was a coiling, a drawing together of muscle under the fat, of springs that would power those big hands to strike and crush.

"Drive home!" Don shouted. "Don't do anything or call anyone! *Go!*"

She went, stumbling, to her car. Don saw the *alive* eyes following her.

She started her car. The lights went on. Daimler made a sound—a low groan. The Jaguar moved onto the road, back toward Laurel. Daimler turned his head, following her, groaning. Until she was gone.

Then he turned back to Don.

The penis drooped. The body sagged, seemed to collapse. The hands unclenched. The mouth sighed and closed.

"I'm sorry." Otis Daimler was himself, and began stuffing his penis back into his fly. "Went crazy," he said, as he had before, but now it was something Don could believe.

Something the police, the courts, the psychiatrists could believe.

"She said you killed her sister. Others."

"No. I wanted to frighten her into compliance."

"You're lying."

Daimler held out his hands. "Do you want to tie them, or what?"

Don had sent Cecily home alone, a dangerous thing in her condition. Don had told her not to do anything, not to tell anyone. He had known something then, and knew something now.

He'd known Daimler had to die. He hadn't known if he could do it.

Now he felt he could. Because Otis Daimler was smart; could defend himself in court.

Because too many Richard Specks, Son of Sams, mass murderers, remained alive in the United States.

Because when they killed and killed, they were judged insane.

And even if they weren't, there was no workable death penalty law today in California.

Otis Daimler would survive the law.

Daimler said: "Listen, I know what I must seem to you, but you have to understand. I go out of control. It's not me. I call it the beast. I'm really sorry."

Beast. Animal. It would save this monster's life.

"I'm sorry, too," Don said, but he wasn't. He brushed rain from his eyes and extended the gun. Daimler began to cry out and twist away. Don fired and Daimler sprang out the open door. Don ran around the front, certain he'd missed.

Then he saw him, lying with his face in the mud, one leg still inside the car. The bullet had blown away his left ear.

Headlights flashed by, and Don wondered how many other cars had passed and if anyone had witnessed the shooting.

He knelt, and saw Daimler's right hand twitching. He put the gun to the nape of the thick neck and fired up into the brain. Then he hurried back to his car.

He was home in twenty minutes, and said, "Thanks," a prayer, when he saw Cecily's Jag in the carport.

She was sitting on the couch, wearing her robe, hands clenched tightly in her lap. She had a bruise on her cheek and her eyes were wide and unblinking.

She began to talk, steadily, in a monotone, looking at nothing. She said that Daimler had told her he'd been following her for many weeks; that he had killed her sister because she happened to come out of the North Hollywood house while he was watching; that he had killed several times before; that he planned to take her to his home—her *body*, that is—and "play" with it for at least a day or two.

"He would have killed me Tuesday night," she said, finally looking at him, "when I went to my house, but a neighbor came over to ask if I'd rented. He followed me to Mulholland, but I kept the engine running and the lights on and didn't stay long."

Don tried to stop her, to tell her she should rest. She drew a deep breath, and continued.

"He saw me park there again last night, but police kept passing because of a mud slide further along. And tonight, you know, he didn't even follow me. He decided to check Mulholland and my house and take me wherever I was." She reached out and touched his hand; hers was like ice. "It was a miracle your coming along, wasn't it?"

She was in shock. No use telling her how shabby a "miracle" his being there was. She'd reason it out for herself, when she was able to reason.

He made her drink hot milk and take another tranquilizer.

He put her to bed.

Then he sat down and wrote out a will, leaving her and Johnny half of his estate. He sealed it in an envelope, which he labeled *Last Will and Testament*, and put the envelope with his bank books, which he'd shown her.

Just in case he didn't get a chance to visit his lawyer.

Just in case that hammering heart quit on him tonight.

Or the police came crashing in and killed him one way or the other.

Then he slept like a baby.

The next day they bought the papers and read

about the "apparently unmotivated murder," and about the "jinx" that afflicted *Galt's Island.*

That night they watched the news on television and heard a L.A.P.D. lieutenant say: "There are no definite leads at this time, but Mulholland has considerable traffic and we expect that a witness will come forward."

"A jury will understand," Cecily whispered. "I'll testify."

He nodded, but didn't take the gun from its hiding place under the house. He knew it was dangerous not to dispose of it, but felt that eyes were watching; felt it was more dangerous to go near it.

They waited all day Saturday, and again Sunday. On Monday he called Pandaro and said he was still out of town. "Nothing to worry about. We'll be back next Monday for sure."

"You understand I might not be able to maintain secrecy about your wife's scenes with Dennings," Pandaro said.

"Then you'd lose the entire three and a half percent, wouldn't you?" And he hung up.

They went to their sessions with Johnny and the psychiatrists, and ate in restaurants, and walked along the beach, and visited museums. And made love.

Good love again.

On Thursday, November 3rd, a week from the night he'd executed the animal, she put aside the *Times, Examiner,* and *Valley News.* "With that rain and in the dark, I don't think anyone would have been able to see him rape and kill me, and I don't think anyone saw you shoot him."

"You might be right. On the other hand, cases are often solved months after the fact."

By Monday, November 7th, on their way to see Pandaro, they were beginning to understand something Otis Daimler and the beast had known for years: It was as easy to get away with murder as with passing a traffic light, if no one was around.

And no one had been.

"The jinx, the jinx," Umberto Pandaro chuckled, driving out of the studio behind Baylis's Mercedes. The emotional writer and his harlot wife were on their way to the bank to deposit their pittance. Two hundred fifty thousand dollars for three and a half percent of the film! Cash, yes, and making Baylis's total a respectable four hundred eighty-five thousand. But he could have had *millions!*

The jinx had come up again in the news media because of Otis Daimler. Much was made of his having been the scriptwriter on *Galt's Island.*

Umberto had checked the contracts, gotten Daimler's address and phone number, and made a call to express condolences to his widow.

Classic widow! Marvelous widow! Just out of the hospital. Crippled with arthritis. Had only the heavily mortgaged house and Daimler's Writers Guild insurance. Perhaps a little Guild pension money. What could be better?

Umberto would have visited her, except he didn't want to appear too anxious. He had, however, mentioned that he might be able to help if the "corporation" was willing to buy her husband's percentage.

He was sure she would check with Daimler's agent. Still, no one could tell what a point in this picture was worth. Umberto figured three million, but that was at least two, probably three years in the future. And if he were to die, there would be no picture and no value to the percentages. Because his estate would go to his children, and his wife and her family would see to it they weren't connected with anything so low.

So the percentage point was worth whatever he said it was worth. If the agent had grandiose ideas, Umberto would wait out the frightened widow.

At most, he'd pay a hundred thousand.

"The jinx," he said, smiling, and reached into his breast pocket for a cigar. He lit up and inhaled fragrant smoke and enjoyed the clear bright day. Much rain lately. Nice to see Los Angeles sunny again.

He was approaching Sunset Boulevard. Soon, Beverly Hills and the quiet street called Chevy Chase and later a visit from one of his beauty contest girls. First place or last place, they were all winners, in his bed.

He laughed until tears came to his eyes.

Which was perhaps why he failed to notice the old brown Pontiac behind him. It had been there since the studio, sometimes a car or two back. Now it was right on his bumper.

What he did notice was the young slut, a *prostituta* from the way she licked her lips suggestively at him, stepping out into the crosswalk. Umberto brought his car to a stop, as that was the law here. In Rome she'd have been run down by a dozen cars for daring challenge them without an officer or light!

He smiled, enjoying the roll of her lean hips in very tight, tailored jeans.

She kept her face to him as she came by his windshield, tongue promising oral delights.

He was taken with her, and leaned out his window.

Adolph Wallace of the Temple of the Sceptered Crown had been praying all the way from the studio where Sodom and Gomorrah were being reborn. The Papist pornographer had not responded. Had not gotten out of his car and fallen to his knees and been publicly cleansed.

Adolph had prayed even more intensely, asking for a different solution this time. He'd reminded Jesus and the assembled hosts that Pandaro had thrown the Book to the ground. That he had assaulted Adolph, the right arm of the Sceptered Crown. That he had shown no remorse and responded to no offers of salvation. Obviously, he was possessed beyond help, damned beyond redemption.

"Destroy him, Lord," Adolph pleaded, following Pandaro onto Sunset Boulevard, street of naked flesh and infamy. "Rend him, burn him."

But the red car, as foreign as the pornographer himself, failed to swerve, to crash, to burn.

Which could mean God wanted to act through *him*.

"Help me!" Adolph cried out, stopping behind the Ferrari as a pedestrian used the crosswalk. *"Give me a sign!"*

He was ready to do whatever God wanted, but first he had to know what that was. He was ready to trade his life for removal of the abomination, and had been ready since he had purchased his weapon.

It lay on the seat beside him—a stiletto from the surplus Army and Navy store. He had wandered among bayonets and Bowie knives and machetes and switchblades. And decided on the stiletto because it reminded him of an illustration in a children's Bible he'd once owned—Father Abraham raising such a knife, ready to kill his beloved son if God gave the sign.

Now Adolph waited for such a sign.

He saw that the pedestrian had stopped just past the pornographer's car, and that the pornographer was leaning out the window, talking.

The pedestrian was a woman. A girl. A child, really, perhaps still in her teens. The pornographer pulled to the curb, and the child turned and came over to him.

A blast of horn made Adolph drive on, until he too could pull to the curb. He looked back. The child was leaning in the window. The pornographer was giving her something . . . a card . . . touching her hand . . .

He was perverting an innocent!

Adolph wiped sweat from his brow. He watched the

red Ferrari swing back into traffic, and waited, and swung in after it.

And saw the innocent on the curb, waving . . after whom?

Signs and portents! The wave was for him! A signal!

She was the Wrath of the Lamb; he could see that now! She had pointed the way.

Adolph would do as she had done: Lean in that window the next time the pornographer stopped. Lean in with his stiletto.

He followed close behind. He swung left as the Ferrari swung left to avoid a right-lane tie-up. He saw the traffic light ahead, and it was red.

He stopped, murmuring, "Thy righteous wrath, Lord," and got out and ran to the Ferrari. He tried to lean in with the knife, but the window had been partly raised and he was blocked.

The pornographer jerked his head around, staring at him. Adolph managed to get his hand and knife inside. But by then Pandaro had slid across the seat and was lunging out the other side, into the right lane, from where he could run to the sidewalk.

Adolph groaned in frustration . . . and heard the scream of braked rubber, and higher human scream. And saw Judgment.

The light had changed to green and the right lane was moving and a speeding van with blue metal-flake paint and silver space-ship mural, switching lanes to avoid the tie-up now in the left, hit the pornographer. Hit him so hard he flipped up and landed atop the van, breaking in the middle and in the skull, sending blood and brains in a wide spray.

"Thank you, Lord," Adolph said, and returned to his car. Where he was still waiting, blocked by traffic, when the police came to question him.

After witnessing the burning of the film, and depositing Pandaro's payment in the bank, Don and Cecily drove to the Santa Monica pier. They walked around and drank pop and he dropped the gun off the deep end while she talked to an old man about fishing.

Then they went down to the beach and stood side by side, looking out at the sea. "Do you feel anything about my having killed a man?" he asked. "I mean, I shot him in cold blood. Now that some time has passed, I've had thoughts . . ."

She changed sides, to take his right hand: "The one that used the gun," she said. She raised it and kissed it.

And kissed him.

And hugged him, moving so energetically that they had to cancel their planned lunch and return home, immediately.